FEMME FATALE

Dominic Piper

Books by Dominic Piper

Kiss Me When I'm Dead

Death is the New Black

Femme Fatale

Bitter Almonds & Jasmine

1

A TAP ON THE SHOULDER

We're in the limbo land between the end of the date and the 'your-place-or-mine'.

This phase of the evening has to be handled like a hothouse flower. Too much heat and it'll wilt, not enough and there's a risk of it dying of frost damage. Lame botanical metaphors are a weakness of mine and I'm glad I could share one with you.

Her name is Annalise St Clair. It's a name straight out of Knightsbridge, but she's a black Mill Hill girl who's made a good fist of eradicating her north London accent and now sounds like she's from nowhere-in-particular. She has a low-pitched, carefully modulated voice and when she speaks it's like listening to warm honey pouring out of a jar.

She's tall and sinuous with spectacular curves and a tiny waist which I'm dying to get my hands around. To make things worse, she's tightly wrapped up in a blue/black cleavage-enhancing Agent Provocateur Brandi dress with matching five-inch heels that bring her almost up to my height.

Beautiful too, with a sexy, contemptuous downturn to her mouth and striking hooded eyes made even more exotic by the burgundy eye shadow she's wearing. She's also a senior cardiologist at the Chelsea and Westminster

Hospital, in case you thought it was all about looks.

I met her two nights ago. I'd just finished a tedious insurance fraud case and was winding down with a double vodka and soda in a quiet bar when the quiet bar became a noisy bar. A group of around fifteen people came in. A pharmaceutical company conference had just finished around the corner and a bunch of the attendees had decided to treat themselves to post conference cocktails.

I saw her immediately. I let our eyes meet once and then looked away, keeping her in my peripheral vision while she was serially hit on by the entire male population of Nerd City. After a decent interval, she peeled herself away from her crowd and we started talking. I can't remember who spoke first. I can't remember what we talked about. I was too busy inhaling her perfume and watching her mouth as her words subtly told me she was available and interested.

And now, two days later, we're walking down Wardour Street after a great meal at The Spice Market accompanied by one too many of their spectacular cocktails. She's linked her arm around mine and I can feel her hip brush against my thigh with each step she takes. She's a little unsteady but nothing too serious. I take a look at my watch. Eleven-fifteen and it's been dark for a couple of hours. It's a warm evening with a cooling breeze so we're in no rush. She staggers slightly.

'Shit!' she says, laughing. 'Those B-54 shooters have one hell of a kick. They don't seem that alcoholic when you're knocking them back. I feel quite light-headed.'

'I had a word with the barman.'

'I knew it. You seem the type.'

'Do you need to get a cab?'

'Not yet. I quite like walking like this.'

'Where do you live?'

'Battersea. You?'

'Covent Garden.'

'You're kidding. Really? Whereabouts?'

'Exeter Street.'

'Isn't that just around the corner from Joe Allen's restaurant?'

'That's the one.'

'That's *so* cool. So you've got a flat there, yeah?'

'That's right.'

'And you live there on your own?'

'Last time I checked. You're not fishing, are you?'

'Now why would I be doing *that*, Mr Beckett?'

We keep walking as Wardour Street morphs into Whitcomb Street, one side of which has been taken over by building works. I can smell coffee roasting and a strong aroma of rosemary and oregano, presumably emanating from a nearby Italian restaurant. The frequent roadworks and sections of roads closed to traffic are so disorientating that for a moment I don't recognise where we are.

'We'll turn right at the end here into Orange Street,' I say. 'We can head towards Piccadilly Circus from the other side.'

Orange Street is all road works, hotels, grey concrete, dirty-looking office entrances, joyless pubs and multi-storey car parks. It's fairly busy with people using it to get from one area of the West End to another, just like we are. I can hear two contrasting bass thumps from a couple of nightclubs. Two drunken teenagers walk past and ogle Annalise. Someone is playing opera with the window open five floors up.

'So what's it like being a private detective, Daniel? I've

never met a real one before.'

'It's all dames and guns.'

'I had a feeling it might be. Is your middle name *Danger*, by any chance?'

I look surprised. 'Have you had me checked out?'

She laughs. Great laugh.

And then it happens.

It's as if my subconscious just tapped me on the shoulder and said, 'Did you hear that?'

I stop walking and place a hand on Annalise's shoulder. I let my mind slip back about sixty seconds. I sift through the street noise, the music, the footsteps, the chatter of passers-by, the car horns and the taxi engines, trying to pick out the something my subconscious reacted to but I somehow missed.

And then it comes back.

It was a girl's voice.

Just one word.

'*No!*'

A young voice. Not someone joking with friends. Not someone arguing with a boyfriend. No petulance. No bad temper. Genuine alarm. Genuine fear. Genuine terror.

I close my eyes and try to work out where I was when I heard it. About two hundred yards back. It came from my right-hand side. What was there? I open my eyes and turn to Annalise.

'Listen. I've just got to do something. Wait here.'

'Are you OK? What is it?'

She looks understandably baffled as I run back the way we came. I can hear the click of her heels as she follows me. Oh well. When it feels right I stop and listen, attempting to get my breath back. These things always happen when you've been drinking.

I can hear a male voice, no, *two* male voices coming from inside a small car park across the road from where I'm standing. There's humourless laughter and there are scuffling noises. That's it. That's where the noise came from. That's what my brain heard. Annalise catches up with me.

'What is it? What's happening?'

'I don't know yet.' I nod towards the car park. 'I have to go in there. Can you wait for me?'

She's nonplussed. She thinks I'm eccentric. 'Sure.'

The car park is closed and the entrance is dark. It's one of those small ones that shut down at six or seven o' clock. Maybe it belongs to a business or something. I don't know. I walk into the interior, ducking under the barrier. It's dark inside, too, but not that dark. I take in the scene in a millisecond. Three guys. Mid-twenties. Big. Sweaty. Angry. Aggressive. The type you'd cross the road to avoid late at night, particularly if you were a lone female. All wear smart suits: Canali, Thom Brown, Lanvin. In amongst the typical car park odour of piss and petrol is the sour reek of sweat and alcohol.

One of them is busy ripping the clothes off a young Chinese girl who's lying on the floor, struggling wildly and trying to kick him in the head. She has a scram mark down her face, a bruised lower lip and a look of terror in her eyes. Her turquoise blouse looks like it's already had an arm torn right off. All the buttons have popped out and you can see her bra. It's difficult to tell her age in this light. Fourteen? Sixteen? Eighteen?

The other two guys stand and watch. They're agitated. Drugs as well as booze? Doesn't matter. One of them is rugby-player huge. He takes his jacket off and looks for somewhere to hang it. There isn't anywhere, so he drops it on the floor. I can see huge sweat circles under his armpits. The third guy stubs out his cigarette, runs a hand across his mouth and starts to undo his trousers. They haven't seen me yet: too pissed, too busy. I put as much *ki* into my voice as I can.

'*Hey!*'

Huge Guy turns around to look at me. He has an expression of stupid surprise on his face. 'Who the *fuck* are you? Fuck off, mate. This is nothing to do with you. Fuck off.'

I'm surprised to hear a rather plummy, posh voice.

Crouching Boy glances at me, sniggers, then, unconcerned, continues with the girl.

'It's *everything* to do with me,' I say, heading towards him.

'We're going to sort you out, matey,' says Cigarette Man, laughing and fiddling with his belt. 'Go on, Derek: fuck him up.'

Huge Guy laughs and strides over to meet me half way, his palms outstretched, as if he's going to try and push me over. He's easily over two hundred pounds and looks like he can take a punch or two before his brain computes what's happened. I'm going to have to get him out of the picture quickly so I can deal with Crouching Boy and Cigarette Man.

He looks downwards, pursing his lips, shaking his head and avoiding eye contact as he warns me for the very last time. 'Just go, friend. This doesn't concern you. Just leave it. This is private business, OK? Just go to the pub or something. Best you leave it be, got it?'

He's approaching rapidly, his face serious, his eyes dead. He takes a sudden lunge at me, but he's way, way too slow. When his hands are about a foot away from my chest, I grab both sets of fingers in mine and flick outwards and upwards, breaking both of his wrists. He screams. While he's considering that, I bring my right knee up to my chest and kick him hard, at close range, in the solar plexus. He rockets backwards into Cigarette Man, knocking him down.

Now Crouching Boy realises things are getting out of hand. He punches the girl in the face to keep her down and gets up to sort me out. He takes a swing at my head, which I block and give him a swift knuckle strike just below his nose, knocking a couple of incisors out. I grab the lapels of his suit, pull him towards me and head-butt him while kneeing him in the balls as hard as I can. Twice. Three times. And one for luck. It's not his lucky day.

He bends double with the pain, so I grab the back of his head with both hands, pull it down hard and knee him in the face, just to be on the safe side. Safety is an important factor in matters like these. When he's on the floor, I kick him in the head, just because.

Cigarette Man gets up from under Huge Guy and charges at me. He's furious, but there's fear in his eyes now. Just before he makes contact, I turn away from him, grab the back of his collar and pull him down while whacking him full in the throat with the side of my hand. Amazingly, he gets up for another go, so I give him a three-finger jab beneath the chin and slam his head into a concrete pillar. Tilt.

All three are down and won't be getting up any time soon. I turn around to see Annalise attending to the girl. In all the excitement I'd forgotten she was a doctor. She gently rubs the girl's cheek with the back of her hand and turns to look at me.

'She's OK,' she says. 'Bloodied mouth, but no damage to the teeth that I can see. Bit of a scratch on her face and one on her shoulder but they'll be gone in a few days. I think she's in shock. You got here just in time. Another few minutes…well, it isn't worth thinking about.'

She stares hard at me as I run a hand through my hair and do a quick visual inventory on my new unconscious pals. It wasn't fast enough and I was a little sloppy, but I had been drinking and the light was bad. Those are my excuses, anyway.

'Are you *OK*, Daniel?' she says.

'Me? Yes. Why?'

'Uh – I don't know. I just thought you might have been punched, or were traumatised a little. Or is this what all private investigators get up to on their nights off?'

'They were just punks.'

'Hey! Wait!' she cries.

The girl has pushed herself up onto her feet and made a run for it. In two seconds she's disappeared. Annalise is plainly in two minds whether to go after her or not. She stands up and I place a hand on her shoulder.

'Let her go. If she can move that fast there can't have been anything major wrong with her.'

'Who's the doctor here?'

'Good comeback. Can I steal that?'

She punches me in the chest.

*

We head down the Haymarket towards Piccadilly Circus, her arm linked around mine again, but now she's pressing close. We haven't spoken for about five minutes and I wonder if she's OK. Maybe that little display was disturbing for her. Out of the corner of my eye I can see that she keeps glancing at me.

'That was pretty impressive back there,' she says, still staring straight ahead.

'What – me playing the Good Samaritan with that girl? It was nothing. Had to be done.'

She looks up at me. Her eyes are shiny and her pupils are dilated.

'Well, that, yes. But the – what you did. You know? I saw most of it.'

I take a gamble. 'You mean the violence?'

She looks down at her feet. 'Yes.'

'You liked it?'

She doesn't look up. She licks her lips. 'Yes.'

I move the conversation away from where we're headed, just to give her a brief break. 'It could have been done faster,' I say. 'I couldn't really see very well in there.'

'It made me feel weird.'

'In a good way or a bad way?'

'In a good way.'

'That's OK,' I say, gently, rubbing the small of her back. 'It can affect some people like that. You mustn't worry about it.'

She swallows and licks her lips. 'So what was that you did to those guys? Was that some sort of martial art?'

'I guess it was a mix. A cocktail.'

'Of how many different styles?'

'Four or five.'

'And where did you learn four or five different styles of martial art?'

Time for a subject change.

'D'you want to go for a drink? There's a bar in St James's Market that'll still be open.'

She pulls me around to face her and her mouth is on mine straight away. Her kisses are soft to begin with then swiftly get passionate. I hold her waist firmly, keeping her a little further away than she'd like to be, controlling her hunger, teasing her. She pushes her crotch against my thigh. She's panting.

'I'm so fucking turned on.' she whispers.

'I know you are.'

'Bastard.'

Exeter Street is ten minutes' walk from here. It's going to be a hell of a long ten minutes.

2

THE BLUE LANTERN

I wake up the next morning with a mild hangover, probably due to the unintentional mixing of drinks that can happen when you're with someone who wants to try out lots of different cocktails. I need a glass of water: it feels as if my teeth are superglued together in my mouth. I try to recall a few names, just to see if my brain has been impaired: B-54s, Sazerac, Caipirinha, Dark & Stormy, Chili Apple Martini – the list goes on and on. I start to feel mildly nauseous thinking about the sugariness of some of them.

I reach down and pick up my alarm clock. Ten past eight. I turn over and put a hand around Annalise's waist. She's still wearing her bra and her suspender belt, but managed to get her stockings off at some point during the night. She hums contentedly and pushes her ass against me. Forget the water: I must have coffee.

I get up and head towards the kitchen. I load up the Siemens coffee maker with El Salvador La Joya beans and hit the switch. I think we'll both need a couple of strong Americanos after last night.

When I get back in the bedroom, she's sitting up in bed and the bra has gone. She rubs her breasts and the sides of her body. I can see the marks that the strap and cups have left on her skin.

'That was really uncomfortable,' she says, grinning. 'Let me give you some advice, Daniel – never fall asleep wearing a bra.'

'I'll make a note of it. Can I give you a hand with that?'

She turns around and lets me massage the marks that the closure and straps have made on her back.

'This isn't too much for you is it?' she says, with a smile in her voice. 'I wouldn't want you to get uncomfortable.'

'It's a regular and important part of my morning routine.'

'What – massaging the back of a deliciously naked woman?'

'Can't start the day without it. Anyway, you're not naked. You're wearing a dark red suspender belt.'

I notice for the first time that her lingerie matches the colour of her eye shadow. Classy and unusual: I wonder what was going through her mind when she thought of it.

'True,' she says. 'Would you mind?'

I undo the back of the belt and let it fall over her hips. She arches her back and stretches her arms out to the sides. I'm only glad I'm not sitting in front of her.

'Wow. Is that coffee? It smells good. I really need some right now.'

'I'll get you a cup.'

'Don't knock anything over in the kitchen!'

'Witty as well as smart. I've hit the jackpot.'

I pour two large cups out, put them on a tray and head back into the bedroom.

'This is from a bean-to-cup coffee maker,' I say. 'Your tongue will thank me.'

'I thought it had done that already.'

She takes a few rapid sips of coffee and closes her

eyes. I use the opportunity to allow myself a quick salacious appraisal of her naked body. The words voluptuous and indecent come to mind. She opens her eyes and I look away, but not rapidly enough. She smiles and wrinkles her nose at me.

'This is fabulous. Have you got any food? I'm starving.'

I check in the kitchen. Nothing. Then I remember a thing that came through the door last week. London Town Breakfast Delivery. I find their laminated menu and take it into the bedroom. Annalise chooses three stacks of buttermilk pancakes with raspberry and pecan topping while I have two halloumi, bacon and mushroom English muffins. I give them a call. Twenty minutes or you get it for free and the next order you make is free as well. That's what I like to hear.

'What are we going to do for twenty minutes, Daniel?'

'Do you play chess? Wait. Let me get my wallet.'

'I don't charge. Unless it's a turn-on for you, that is.'

'You could tell?'

She grins. 'Maybe it's a turn-on for me, too.'

I find my jacket and check the pockets. My wallet isn't there. I check all the pockets again. Still nothing. I find the black jeans I was wearing last night and it isn't in there, either. Did I take it out when we got back last night? No. No time. I try to remember the last time I used it. That would have been in The Spice Market. I try to think. I can remember the guy giving me back my credit card. I remember putting it in my wallet. I remember putting the wallet in an inside jacket pocket, no doubt about it.

I check the pocket one more time then take a look around the flat.

'I hope you don't think I'm weird after last night, Daniel. I've never been like that before.' She walks up behind me and presses her body against mine. 'It was as if someone had turned on a light, do you know what I mean? My whole body was tingling. I was ready for anything.'

She sighs. I can smell her sweat and her sex.

'I can't find my wallet anywhere. Have you got a credit card? Sorry about this. Very impolite, getting you to pay.'

'Did you lose it last night? When you were, you know…'

She digs her fingernails into my shoulders and moves in closer. I feel her grind herself against me. I can feel her smoothness and her heat.

'It was just seeing what you did to those guys. It didn't have an impact at first. It took a few minutes. Then…mmmmm. My God. I thought I was going insane. I felt faint with it.'

I can feel her nipples hardening against my back. She's trembling. I try to think what's in the wallet. Two credit cards and a few of my business cards. Maybe sixty pounds in cash. That's it, really. There's a number I can ring to stop the credit cards. It's on my mobile. At least that didn't get mislaid. I turn to face her. Her arms are around my neck immediately. She writhes against me, grinding her hips, biting my neck. She still smells of the perfume she was wearing yesterday: Plum Japonais by Tom Ford. It's sensual and heady. I'm having difficulty concentrating.

'Just thinking about it right now is driving me crazy,' she says, her voice low and husky. 'My mouth is dry. I can feel my heart thumping in my chest. I feel so ashamed. Can we cancel the food order? I'm on fire.'

14

'I think it'll be a little too late. They're probably on their way. Listen – get your credit card out. I have to make a phone call. When we've eaten we can talk about it again.'

'Do you promise?'

'I promise.'

'God. I feel so bad. Am I a bad person? I try to help people…'

I cancel the cards and persuade Annalise to get a robe on just before the breakfast guy arrives, seeing as how she'll have to pay him. The robe is black silk. Someone left it here a while ago, but I forget her name. The way it hangs on Annalise's body makes your head spin. The guy leaves. We take the food into the kitchen and I make some more coffee.

'Maybe someone will hand it in,' she says, cutting a slice off her pile of pancakes with a fork. They look delicious. I wish I'd ordered them instead of my muffins.

'Maybe,' I say. 'It isn't too important. The wallet wasn't expensive. The cards are cancelled.'

'Is there any ID in there?'

'Business cards. Name and mobile number. Nothing else. If someone wants to call, they'll call.'

'Are you going to check that car park out? Just in case?'

'I may do. When are you in work?'

'Eleven. The squeaky floor out there. Is that a nightingale floor?'

'Yes it is. How did you know that? Most people think it's something that needs to be fixed.'

A nightingale floor is a seventeenth-century Japanese invention. A primitive security measure, really. There are strategically placed nails beneath the floorboards which squeak loudly when walked on. It's a noise you can't sleep through.

'I read about it,' she says. 'There's a book called *Across the Nightingale Floor* by Lian Hearn. Was it expensive to have made?'

'Three thousand.'

'Wow. What d'you think happened to that girl last night?'

'I don't know. How old do you think she was?'

'Hard to say. A teenager, definitely.'

She places her fork on the side of her plate and sips her coffee.

'She was out pretty late,' I say.

'Maybe. Depends on her age.'

She undoes the belt on the robe and lets it fall off her shoulders onto the floor. The swell of her heavy breasts is making my brain fry.

'Can we talk about last night again now?' she purrs.

'Where would you like to start?'

'Right at the beginning.'

*

An hour and a half later we're in a cab heading for Orange Street. I get dropped off at the top of Whitcomb Street and Annalise continues on to Fulham. I retrace my steps from the moment I realised something was wrong until I'm at the entrance to the car park. It's open now and the interior is brightly lit.

I take a walk inside. There's no indication of what went on here last night. The floor is clean and there's a strong smell of disinfectant. They probably have people come in at the crack of dawn and give it the once over before it opens, in which case someone must have found my wallet by now and either kept it or handed it in. There are no staff around to ask.

After two or three minutes I realise I'm wasting my time, so decide to get back to the flat, pick up my gym stuff and go down to Soho Gyms in Macklin Street to try and sweat some of the alcohol out of my system.

I decide to walk. Just as I'm turning into Charing Cross Road, my mobile goes off.

'Hello. Daniel Beckett,' I say.

There's a crackling on the other end. I can hear muffled talking, as if someone's got their hand over the phone.

'Mr Daniel Beckett?'

The voice is male, precise, old-sounding and with a trace of an Oriental accent I can't immediately place. Chinese?

'Yes. This is Daniel Beckett. How can I help you?'

He laughs as if I've just made some incredibly funny joke. It sounds so mad that I find I'm laughing myself.

'I think perhaps that I can help *you*, Mr Beckett. My name is Mr Sheng. I have your wallet.'

'My wallet. Really.'

'Yes. I thought we might make some arrangement for you to collect it. If, of course, it is convenient for you.'

'Of course it is. Well that's fantastic. Thank you. Where are you?'

'Do you know Newport Place, Mr Beckett?'

'Yes. It's, er, off Lisle Street.'

'That is correct. You will see the gay bar on the left corner. Walk past that and keep on that side of the road. Stroll along for a short while, then you will see a restaurant called The Blue Lantern. The restaurant will not be open for business, but the front door will be open. Just come in. I will be inside, ready to welcome you. With your wallet!' He laughs again. Cheery guy.

'I'm in Charing Cross Road now. I'll be there in five minutes.'

'Excellent. I will see you soon, then. Goodbye, Mr Beckett.'

He clicks off, but he hasn't done it properly. I can hear a bit of chatter and recognise the long vowel sounds of Cantonese and then the line finally goes dead.

Interesting. I'm assuming he's connected to the girl in some way. I can't think of any other explanation. I don't have any memory of dropping my wallet during that little altercation, but I must have done. Did she pick it up and keep it? Perhaps she thought it belonged to one of her attackers and might prove useful. Could she have been that sharp? I can't really see when she'd have had the opportunity. She was on the floor when I got there and then ran out when I'd finished. I'm sure I'd have noticed if she'd bent down and picked something up.

I walk past Leicester Square tube station and turn left into Little Newport Street. You immediately know you're in Chinatown by the Hanzi characters on the street signs, the smell of Chinese cooking and the orange paper lanterns slung from building to building, celebrating who knows what.

I dodge past the piles of bin bags and avoid the constant scaffolding as I walk along. There are Chinese restaurants, estate agents, herbal medicine centres and hairdressers on my side of the road and The Hippodrome Theatre on the other. I can see the gay bar that Mr Sheng mentioned about fifteen yards ahead, just at the point where the road becomes pedestrianised. There's a telephone kiosk and some bollards, and five seconds later I'm turning right into Newport Place.

I walk past five more Chinese restaurants, a betting shop (of course) and a bureau de change before I spot The Blue Lantern. The scents around here are beginning to make me feel quite hungry. Then something odd happens. There's a young, tough-looking Chinese guy leaning against a street sign across the road from The Blue Lantern. He's smoking an untipped cigarette and looking like he's at a loose end, but he clocks me immediately and doesn't take his eyes off me.

When I'm about six feet from the restaurant entrance, he points to the door and says, 'In that way, mate.'

I look at him, smile and say 'Thanks.' He smiles and nods in reply.

And then I'm inside The Blue Lantern.

3

AND ALL THAT JAZZ

I've patronised a lot of Chinese restaurants in this area, but I certainly missed this one and I can't imagine why. It looks incredible.

It's much larger inside than you'd suspect from the entrance and whoever designed it was excessively fond of red oak. The floors are made from it and so is the delicate lattice work which adorns the walls and the ceiling.

Behind the unmanned reception desk is a large diptych of a scary-looking, red and yellow Chinese sorcerer's mask and the whole place is bathed in warm yellow light from the low-hanging basket lanterns, giving it an intimacy that belies its size. You could just as easily bring a woman on a date here as use it for someone's birthday celebration.

It smells woody, clean and new, is simultaneously traditional and ultra-modern and was probably built and/or decorated sometime in the last couple of months. There's money here: whoever owns it must be making a packet.

Despite the name of the place, there are no blue lanterns featured in the décor. Maybe that was too vulgar and obvious for whoever designed it. At a rough guess, there are about thirty tables, each one six or seven feet away from its neighbour. It could be packed out and you'd still have privacy, if you wanted it.

I'm looking up at the ceiling, with its impressionistic, swirling bamboo patterns when I hear soft footsteps. I look down and see a slim and smartly-dressed Chinese guy of maybe seventy or even eighty approaching me.

He's smiling and has a hand outstretched, ready for shaking, even though he's still about twenty feet way. He walks with a slight limp and I can see a faded semi-circular scar on his right cheekbone, as if, a long time ago, someone tried to gouge one of his eyes out with a broken bottle and missed by a few lucky inches. A well-lined face and a full head of snow white hair. I walk towards him.

'Mr Beckett! I am so pleased to meet you. Thank you for coming at such short notice. I didn't know where you would be. In London, I mean to say. Shall we sit down? Anywhere will do. They are all the same.'

We shake hands. He looks mildly surprised when I match the slight bow he gives me. We sit down opposite each other at the nearest table. I've got my back to the entrance, which I don't like, but I'll put up with it just this once. He's wearing a black-faced Hublot watch, which is worth about eight thousand. His suit is tweed and well-cut. Looks like a Savile Row job. Silver Givenchy cufflinks, white shirt and a black silk Jacquard tie. Money.

The table is partially made up: no cutlery but a few pieces of crockery. I realise that they're willow pattern, but in black and white rather than the traditional blue and white. Very cool. Mr Sheng follows my glance and points at the design on a small plate.

'The doomed lovers turned into doves by the gods.' He leans forwards. 'But that was a later addition to the story, Mr Beckett. The real meaning of the willow pattern became romanticised. But first things first!'

He reaches into the inside pocket of his suit jacket, produces my wallet and hands it to me. I take it with two hands.

'Thanks very much. You've saved me a lot of trouble.' I stow it away without checking the contents. Mr Sheng looks surprised.

'You did not want to check whether your cash and credit cards were still inside?'

'No. I'm sure everything will be in order.'

He laughs and looks at my face, but he's not making eye contact. I wait for him to say something.

'Do you like jazz, Mr Beckett?'

'Some of it.'

'Ornette Coleman?'

'He's OK.'

I'm out of my depth. Help.

'I'm sure you have a good idea how I came by your wallet, Mr Beckett.'

'Not a good idea, but an idea, Mr Sheng.'

He likes this. He smiles and nods his head. 'Some friends of mine visited the car park in the early hours of this morning. Your wallet was on the floor. It was in shadow. It would not have been hard for you to miss it. In case you were wondering, the girl whom you so effectively defended is my grand-niece. She is fifteen. Her name is Li-Fen.' He shrugs. 'They call her Lily in her school. We still have to have our western names!' He leans forwards. 'When will it end?'

He has a good, long laugh at this, which is distracting enough for me to not notice the teenage girl who has appeared from somewhere and is standing right next to me. Mr Sheng introduces us. It's Li-Fen. I stand up and shake her hand. She looks shyly to the floor as I sit down again, but not before giving Mr Sheng a barely discernible and confirmatory nod of the head. *This is him*, she's saying.

If it wasn't for the swollen lip, the start of a nasty black eye and the scratch down her face, I don't think I'd have recognised her. Part of it was all the excitement and the lack of proper light in the car park, but her clothing is different, too. Last night her dress was conventional and smart, but this morning she looks like a typical London teenager: tight black jeans with the knees out, flowery Andy Warhol Converse trainers and a Jim Morrison t-shirt.

She's holding a medium-sized cardboard gift box. It's green, yellow and red with a stylised drawing of a pagoda on the side and the words 'Thank You' in an Oriental-style font on the folded-over top. It looks like a US Chinese takeaway carton, but bigger and classier.

'I'm sorry to have put you to so much trouble, Mr Beckett,' she says, still looking downwards.

Her voice has the cadences of Cantonese, but there isn't really an accent. Mr Sheng looks at her and smiles. He does a lot of smiling.

'That's quite alright. It was no trouble at all,' I say.

'You yourself were in danger,' she says. 'Thank you. And please give my thanks to your lady friend, also. She was kind. I am sorry I ran away. I was frightened.'

'Quite understandable. Forget it.'

'I have made some traditional Chinese candies for you. I hope you will accept this gift. It is a gesture of my gratitude. There is quite a variety: sesame cake, almond cookie, grass jelly, lime coconut bar and many others. I think you will find them tasty and zestful.'

It sounds like this is a prepared speech. I wonder if it

was Li-Fen who prepared it or someone else.

'There is no need to give me a gift, Li-Fen.'

'But please, Mr Beckett. I'm sure you will find them most delicious.'

I decline three times in all before accepting. She places the box in front of me with both hands, looks at Mr Sheng and they exchange delighted smiles. They're both pleased and surprised that I know their customs. Tempting as it is, I don't open the box to look at what's inside, as I know this will seem rude to both of them.

'Wait until you taste Li-Fen's Milk Candy, Mr Beckett. Your mouth will water. But I am being impolite! Would you like something to drink? Tea? Coffee? Fizzy water? Fanta Orange? Coca Cola?'

'What are you having?'

'I will have a coffee. Coffee perks me up!'

'Then I'll have a coffee, too.'

Mr Sheng looks up at Li-Fen. 'Two coffees, please, my dear.'

Li-Fen glances at me and raises her eyebrows.

'A dash of milk and no sugar. Thank you,' I say. Li-Fen disappears into the back of the restaurant. I watch her leave then turn back to Mr Sheng. During that brief second when my glance was elsewhere, my peripheral vision caught an abrupt change of expression: the smile was gone, replaced by a suspicious, icy stare. The second our eyes meet again he's back to his old grinning self. I'm surprised to feel a tiny surge of fear.

'What about Cannonball Adderley, Mr Beckett? Do you like him?'

'I know the name, but I'm not familiar with his music.'

'You should listen to more jazz, Mr Beckett! I shall make you a compilation! On a compact disc!'

'I'll look forward to it, Mr Sheng. How did you know that the wallet belonged to me and not to one of the attackers?' I say.

Mr Sheng has quite a laugh at this. 'Well, we didn't at first, but when we spoke on the telephone and you agreed to come here, I knew that you had to be Li-Fen's guardian angel.' He slams his hand down hard on the table, making me jump. 'If you were one of the attackers, Mr Beckett, it would have been very unwise to turn up and collect the wallet. Would you not agree?'

'True.' I smile at him. 'But I don't understand…'

This gets another laugh. 'You are curious about the speed with which Li-Fen prepared your gift. We just like to be prepared for all eventualities. That always makes for good fortune. We might have traced you, we might not have. If we did, Li-Fen wanted to show her gratitude. She prepared your gift box earlier this morning.' He sits up in his seat and points at his chest. 'If you had not turned up, or we had not found you, *we* would have eaten the contents ourselves!'

Li-Fen arrives with the coffees and places them in front of us. She smiles at me. 'Goodbye, Mr Beckett, and thank you again.'

'You are most welcome, Li-Fen.'

She blushes and disappears once more into the back of the restaurant. So she's fifteen. Is that too young to be hanging around the West End at eleven-thirty at night? I don't really know any more. What was she doing? Was she on her own? I hadn't thought about it before, but it does seem a little odd. I can hear jazz playing quietly in the background. It's Stan Getz. I hadn't noticed it until now.

Mr Sheng sips his coffee and shakes his head. 'It was a

terrible thing, Mr Beckett. Three men like that and such a young girl. Such bullies! Li-Fen said it was quite dark in that car park. They punched her and then dragged her in there. Did you know? She is only fifteen! A child!'

'I wasn't sure what had happened, to be honest. I just heard her cry out and went in.'

'Into the dark. Without any regard for your own safety. Li-Fen said those men were big and strong. And angry.'

I shrug. 'Had to be done.'

'Indeed.' He frowns and produces a black Bookie pen and a crumpled sheet of paper from his pocket.

'Would you say, Mr Beckett, that those men would be in need of hospital attention after your dustup?'

I've already put most of what happened out of my mind. Those events have been obliterated by the subsequent session with Annalise and the perverse urgency of her needs. I run over the events in my mind and try to work out the injuries they would have sustained: broken wrists, cracked ribs, crushed testicles, broken nose, shattered windpipe, concussion – yeah, I think they'd all need a few hours of TLC in their local A&E department.

Mr Sheng makes me tell him their injuries in detail, accompanied by a rough description of each man. Perhaps he's going to report the matter to the police. The Chinese community in London is peaceful and law-abiding and have a good relationship with the local constabulary. Maybe he has contacts in whichever hospital they'd have gone to. Would it have been St Mary's?

With each detail I give him, he either shakes his head, laughs, looks astonished or makes some remark like 'Ah!', 'Oh my!' or 'Painful!'. He stuffs the pen and paper back in his pocket, grins to himself, and takes a sip of his coffee.

'It must be interesting work being a private investigator, Mr Beckett.'

Now how does he know that? Then I remember. When Annalise was tending to Li-Fen she made some remark about what private investigators do on their nights off. Li-Fen must have reported this.

'Interesting enough, Mr Sheng.'

'Does it pay well? I hope you do not mind my asking that of you.'

'Of course not. It pays well enough. I'm probably top of the range. You can't charge too much though, or you're in danger of pricing yourself out of the market.' Or making yourself too conspicuous.

'Yes. Like in all business; and I expect there are always others waiting to take your place. *Probably top of the range!* That is most excellent. And you are such a young man! I am guessing you are probably in your early thirties. May I ask – how much do you charge for your services?'

'A thousand a day plus non-negotiable expenses.'

'That is a good phrase! *Non-negotiable expenses.* You don't want to quibble over matters like that when you have finished a successful case, I expect. That would be the last thing you would want. Do you have a business card? I always like to see people's business cards.'

As if he didn't know. I take out my wallet and give one of my cards to him (with both hands, of course). He inspects it very carefully. It doesn't have much on it – just my name and mobile number – but despite this, he looks at it like it's the most interesting thing he's ever seen in his life.

'May I keep this, Mr Beckett? It has a very striking look to it. But not much information?'

'All you need is there, I think. I didn't want to go crazy, you know?'

This gets another big laugh. 'True, true. But a metal business card! And such an interesting design.'

It does look unusual, I have to admit. It's made from a thin, silvery metal with miniature micro-grills on the top and bottom. People don't throw something like that away in a hurry.

He inspects the card for about another thirty seconds. Nothing unusual about this: it's Chinese business etiquette. He takes a wallet out of his inside pocket and carefully places the card inside. He stares at me for a while. I can't tell what he's thinking. Then his eyes start twinkling again and a smile spreads across his face.

'Mr Beckett. I shall be honest and frank with you. You may think I am a foolish old man, but I think that things that may *seem* to be bad luck can often be good luck in disguise. Do you agree?'

'I understand.'

'Li-Fen's misfortune, for example, may *seem* like bad luck, but it caused our paths to cross, and I view that as *good* luck.'

From somewhere, he produces an A3 size manila card-backed envelope with 'Please Do Not Bend' on the front in red letters.

'I would like to hire you, Mr Beckett, if you are not otherwise engaged, of course.'

As I was walking down Charing Cross Road it was bright and sunny and I could feel the warmth of the sun on my skin. Now there's a bit of a chill, and as a cloud passes across the sun outside, the interior of the restaurant gets suddenly and noticeably darker. Mr Sheng grins, places the envelope on the table between us and pushes it over to me.

4

THE MISSING FACILITATOR

'Oh, this weather!' says Mr Sheng, getting up. 'One moment sunny, the next moment cloudy.' He walks over to the other side of the restaurant and adjusts a lighting control on the wall. The place is now marginally brighter. He returns, sits down and points to the envelope that's in front of me. 'Would you care to look at the contents of the envelope, Mr Beckett? Then we can have a little tête-à-tête. Then you can let me know if you can help me. I do understand that not all private investigators are the same. There are many specialities.'

I open the envelope and pull out the contents. Two big glossy photographs of a good-looking Chinese guy who could be in his late twenties or early thirties. The first is a head and shoulders shot. Dark blue suit jacket or blazer, white shirt, red tie. Expensive, fashionable haircut and a healthy complexion. He's looking straight at the camera. His face has a confident, self-assured expression: cocky, even. There are marks on the side of his nose which suggest that he wears glasses and took them off just before the photograph was taken. He cut himself shaving that morning.

The other photograph is almost full length and very slightly out of focus. He's posing by some rocks by the sea. I can't tell where it is, but the light and the ocean suggest it isn't the UK. He's grinning in this one and he looks more relaxed. He's only wearing a pair of white chinos held up with an expensive-looking black leather belt. The buckle is silver and there's a big gemstone inlaid into the metal, probably turquoise. He wears two green jade rings on his left forefinger.

He's slim, but has a finely sculpted, muscular torso: big pectorals, weighty biceps, powerful deltoids and an impressive six-pack. This is a guy that hits the gym frequently and I get a feeling it's for vanity purposes, though I could be wrong. Both of these photographs have a slightly arrogant and narcissistic 'look-at-me' quality to them. They're the sort of photographs you can imagine being in the portfolio of a male model.

Apart from the photographs, there's a single sheet of paper with his personal details. Chan 'Rikki' Tuan, aged twenty-eight, five foot nine inches high, shoe size eight and a half, weighs one hundred and fifty-seven pounds, black hair, brown eyes. That's it, apart from his address and a mobile telephone number. I assume he's not answering his mobile.

I look up to see Mr Sheng watching me like a wily old hawk.

'So what's the problem, Mr Sheng? Who is this guy?'

He rests his elbows on the table, links his fingers beneath his chin and narrows his eyes. Something's rattling him. It's as if he's trying to work out how to say something that he most definitely doesn't want to say. Something that I have to be told that is really none of my business. It doesn't bother me either way. He says something and we proceed or he says nothing and I go to lunch. After about thirty seconds, he points at the photographs.

'This young gentleman is a business associate of mine. I suppose you could say he is an employee of sorts.'

I wonder if he could possibly ratchet the vagueness up a little.

'OK. What does he do?'

I'm counting the seconds off in my head. This question gets a full minute before I get a response. I'm hoping we can get through this before I retire or die of old age.

'He is a facilitator. Yes. That is it. Chan Tuan is a facilitator. He brings about outcomes. I think that would be an accurate description of his job.'

OK. So the chances of me finding out what this guy does are nil. I'm starting to get mildly annoyed with this now and want him to get on with it. I'm going to have to push whether he likes it or not.

'So. He's important to your business and he's missing. Would that be correct?'

'My apologies, Mr Beckett. I know that I am prevaricating. I do not mean to be obstructive towards you. Sometimes it can be hard to describe the occupation of another. And you are right – Chan Tuan is missing. He has been missing for three days.'

'Is three days a long time for him?' I take a sip of my coffee and keep my eyes on his face.

'Absolutely. It is part of his job to check in with me every single day. Even the weekends. If he was unwell, he would certainly let me know.'

'I take it you've tried to contact him on that mobile number.'

'Yes. It is dead.'

'And you've been to the address on this sheet of paper? It's a flat, yes?'

'Yes it is. And yes – I sent someone to visit his flat. He is not there.'

'And everything looked normal at this flat?'

'Yes it did.'

'Call the police. You can report him as a missing person. He may have been in an accident. The police would check all the hospitals.'

He smiles again and nods his head, as if this highly foolish suggestion has been made to him thousands of times in the last twenty-four hours alone.

'It is a cliché, isn't it, Mr Beckett. It is like on a television adventure show where the kidnapper says *I don't want the police involved!*'

'Maybe it is. You tell me. Has he been kidnapped? Is that what you're saying? Is it a possibility?'

'No, no, no. Not kidnapped. Not as far as I can tell, anyway. No, I'm sure that would be unlikely and we have received no ransom demand. Just missing, that is all. We are a very tight-knit community here, Mr Beckett. We do not like to bother the authorities with our problems. It is part of the Chinese nature. We keep ourselves to ourselves. If we have any problems, we deal with them within the community. It is our way.'

'And yet you're requesting my services: a *gweilo*.'

Using this word makes him laugh. It's usually pretty derogatory when aimed at a westerner, but rather old-fashioned now, and it depends who's using it, of course, and to whom. It's Cantonese slang. A loose translation would be 'Foreign Devil' or 'Ghost man'. Doesn't bother me; both are pretty accurate in my case. I finish my coffee.

'Rikki Tuan, as he liked to be known, Mr Beckett, is enamoured of western ways, perhaps a little more than he should be. I know that sounds very conservative of me. He has always enjoyed a social life that took him away from his friends, relatives and colleagues here. Away from people who care about him. I have sent out feelers, as you might say, to the Chinese community here in London. Also to more…outlying Chinese communities. I thought someone might have heard something about his sudden absence. They have not.'

'Are those sources usually reliable?'

'Always. One hundred per cent. No margin of error.'

'You don't know what he gets up to in his spare time. You don't know where he goes. You don't know who he hangs out with. He's not particularly secretive about these things; he just doesn't talk about them to anyone. Maybe he thinks it's not important. Maybe he thinks it's none of your business. And now it's made it difficult to trace him. Is that about it?'

He looks serious. He's still dancing around whatever the truth is here. Maybe there isn't a truth. Talking like this and having to think like this is actually starting to give me a headache. Or maybe that was last night's booze.

'Precisely, Mr Beckett. Let us say that he is comfortable moving in circles that we have no access to, or are ignorant of, or would be too conspicuous in. If something untoward has happened to Rikki – and I am not saying it has – the appearance of another Chinese person might attract suspicion. Make it obvious his disappearance is being, um, looked into.'

He starts to say something else, but stops himself.

'Or cause any perpetrators of his possible misfortune to flee,' I say.

He slams a fist down on the table. I wish he wouldn't do that. 'That is it exactly! Exactly! Someone like you could make thorough enquiries, no one would be apprehensive and it would contribute to your good luck and it would contribute to your success. There is a Chinese-run private detective agency not a minute's walk from here. They provide an excellent service, but in this case…'

I didn't hear anyone come in, but I'm suddenly aware of a woman's presence. She's behind me, perhaps ten or fifteen feet away and I can smell her perfume, though I can't immediately identify it. I wonder who she is and why Mr Sheng hasn't acknowledged her or even glanced in her direction.

'So, Mr Beckett – what do you say? Would this case be of interest to you? I would be grateful in more ways than you could imagine. I will not be offended if you turn me down. I am already in your debt for your brave rescue of Li-Fen. I put no pressure on you.'

I have to admit that I'm curious. The whole thing is so ambiguous, mildly creepy, suspicious, vague and difficult-sounding that it's attractive to the puzzle-solving part of my brain, but I need something else.

'The case is of interest to me, Mr Sheng. I am curious as to what you mean when you say that you would be grateful in more ways than I can imagine.'

'I am speaking financially, Mr Beckett.'

And there's the icing on the cake.

'OK. I'll do it.'

I can smell tobacco smoke mixed in with the perfume. Whoever she is, she's just lit up. The aroma is rich, spicy and not unpleasant. I'm not an expert on tobacco, but I can detect notes of whisky, orange and vanilla in whatever it is she's smoking. Once again, Mr Sheng doesn't react to her presence. Without turning my head, I glance to the side, to let him know I'm aware and curious.

He ignores my not-so-subtle hint. 'That is excellent! Excellent! Thank you, Mr Beckett. Thank you so much. Let us shake hands on the deal!'

We shake across the table. I must remember not to forget my box of Chinese candies.

'One thing, Mr Beckett. If, during the course of your investigation, you come across Rikki, be sure to tell him who it is you are working for. It would be the wise thing to do.'

'I'll be sure to.'

He laughs again. 'Better to be safe than sorry!'

I jab my finger against the sheet of paper in front of me. 'Presumably you or someone else had spare keys for Rikki's flat. I'll need those. I know you've already been there, but there's a chance that I may see something that you or your colleagues have missed.'

'Of course. That is only right and reasonable. *Flowers look different in different eyes.*' He reaches in his trouser pocket and produces a Maruse Italian leather key ring. A new-looking Yale and a bronze mortice key hang off it. I take it and put it in my pocket.

'I'll return these keys to you once I've taken a look at the flat. Has he got a car?'

'Oh, yes. Yes, he has a car. It is a Mazda MX-5 Miata in metallic red. It is two years old now.'

'Do you have the key for it? The registration?'

'The registration is LY77 FVC.' He smiles at me. 'I have a good memory for such things. I do not have a duplicate key for this vehicle, unfortunately.'

'Do you know where he parks it? Is there somewhere near his flat that I might find it?'

'I am sorry. I cannot help you. His flat does not have

associated car parking. By that I mean there is no car park attached to the block of flats. He would have made his own arrangements. There is a parking for residents area outside his flat, but I don't know whether he uses it. I would think not. Your guess is as good as mine.'

From somewhere above us, I can hear the very faint sound of people having sex. Whoever it is, the woman is faking it, but it's a good fake, a high quality fake, an *experienced* fake.

'OK. I'll start work on this first thing tomorrow morning. I have to tell you, though, Mr Sheng; I can't guarantee the outcome in a case like this. If I find him and he's OK or if I find him and, well, let's say he's not OK, my fee will stand.'

He nods his head. 'Of course. I would not expect anything less, Mr Beckett. And I thank you for your prompt attention to this matter. I am most grateful. I can also tell that you are a man of honour and will be utterly discreet. Now there is someone I would like to introduce you to, if I may,' he says, still smiling. We both stand. He waves a hand towards the front door and I turn around to face the entrance, not quite sure what to expect.

It's then I see her for the first time.

She stubs her black cigarette out in a willow pattern saucer and stands up, blowing the remaining smoke out of her lungs in a long, thin stream.

My first thought is, *Who the hell dresses like that?*

My second thought is, *Wow!*

She's Chinese: tall, slim and savagely stunning. I would guess she's somewhere around thirty years old with beautiful golden skin, a long, elegant neck and a lithe, sexy, small-breasted figure that makes you wonder if she might have been a fashion model in another life. Maybe she's a fashion model in this life. You never can tell.

Her long, straight, lustrous, jet black hair stops about six inches beneath her collarbone. There's a side part on the left and on the right-hand side it almost covers her face. And it's a beautiful face: symmetrical and striking. Gorgeous dark eyes that are at once mocking and humorous with high, chiselled cheekbones and a yummy, full, kissable mouth that's drilling indecent thoughts into my brain. The word 'foxy' comes to mind.

But her clothing is something else. She's wearing an ultra-tight round-necked black bodysuit which is see-through at the midriff, revealing the vague outline of a six-pack. On *top* of this she wears a long line bra and shorts which are embroidered with – wait for it – real peacock feathers. If that wasn't bad enough, there are black suspender straps running from the body suit, travelling across twelve inches of smooth, bare thigh before clipping onto a pair of black silk stockings. Did I mention the black suede ankle boots with five-inch heels?

The overall effect is a licentious cross between high fashion and the crudest eroticism. My mouth is dry and I can feel my stomach muscles starting to twitch. *What's going on? Why am I here in this restaurant? What day is it? Who were my parents?*

'Mr Beckett, may I introduce you to Miss Fan Mei Chow. Miss Chow is an associate of mine. She may be able to help you with Rikki's social habits where I cannot.'

If I could find a job where you had associates like this, I'd leave private investigating like a shot. There are no jobs with associates like this.

She takes a step towards me, flicking a pale green leather biker jacket over her left shoulder, and we shake hands. She has long, elegant fingers and expertly manicured fingernails. High maintenance and well worth it, I think.

Now I can smell her perfume a little better: bergamot, patchouli and iris. It's Ombre Mercure Extrême – very French and very expensive. She holds onto my hand a little longer than is necessary. Her grip is firm, but I get the feeling it could be firmer if she wanted it to be. She's wearing an Apple watch with a blue butterfly on the face.

'I'm so pleased to meet you, Mr Beckett. I'm Caroline Chow. Mr Sheng has told me a lot about you.'

I'd like to reply, but my tongue is currently stuck to the roof of my mouth. Caroline Chow doesn't have much of a Chinese accent, certainly not a London one and she doesn't have the Cantonese cadences of Li-Fen, either. But she definitely sounds foreign, even if she's trying to disguise it.

Mr Sheng was obviously pretty damn sure I'd turn up and take this job. First the pre-prepared gift from Li-Fen and now this. I'm intrigued: everyone seems to know what's going on here apart from me. Mr Sheng starts laughing once again.

'I am sorry, Miss Chow! I forgot to refer to you by your western name. Please forgive me.'

She laughs and it lights her whole face up, revealing a fragile prettiness that I didn't notice a few seconds ago.

'Do you like it, Mr Beckett?' she says. 'The name Caroline, I mean?'

'It suits you.' Not the smoothest response I could have made, but my brain isn't quite in gear yet. Maybe it never will be.

'Caroline Chow.' She savours the name as she says it and rolls her eyes. 'You think it sounds like a movie star?'

she says, raising an eyebrow. Mr Sheng has a laugh at this.

'All young people want to sound like movie stars nowadays!' he says, chortling away. Then he becomes suddenly serious. 'Miss Chow will be my liaison officer in this matter, Mr Beckett. Anything that you turn up, you can let her know and she will pass the information on to me in a confidential manner. Is that satisfactory?'

'I'm fine with that if you are.' I take another look at her. She flashes me a playful smirk. She doesn't give the impression that she works for Mr Sheng or that he's her boss in any way, despite what he just said. She also doesn't give the impression that she's taking any of this seriously. I'm having a little difficulty getting my head around the dynamic between these two.

I go back to the table that we were sitting at and pick up the envelope and the box of Chinese candies. I can hear Mr Sheng and Miss Chow exchange a few quick sentences in Cantonese. It's not a language I speak, so I've no idea what was said.

By the time I'm on my way out, they're back to English again. 'Do you have a business card you could give to Miss Chow, Mr Beckett? She can call your mobile number and you can save her number on your telephone. That is how it works, is it not?'

I hand her a business card. She takes it and examines it carefully, just like Mr Sheng did. She pulls a very flash, expensive-looking, jewelled iPhone out of her jacket pocket and types my number into it. She keeps looking up at me as she does this and I realise that I'm finding the eye contact exciting. She then calls me and I save her number, identifying her only as 'Caroline'.

'I think there are no more words to say, Mr Beckett,' says Mr Sheng. 'I can only wish you the best of good luck and hope you are successful in your endeavours. I hope to hear from you very soon.'

'I'm sure you will, Mr Sheng. Thanks for the coffee.'

After yet another handshaking session, I walk out of the entrance with Caroline Chow a few feet behind me. I'm aware of her eyes boring into my back. She walks alongside me as we turn out of Newport Place and take a right into Lisle Street. Outside, her perfume is even more noticeable and intoxicating than it was in the restaurant.

I'm trying to make some sense of just what went on in The Blue Lantern, but all I can think about is grabbing a handful of her hair and leaving a bite mark or two on that long neck, just to see her face. I must be losing my mind.

*

Lisle Street is busy. It's a narrow, Chinese restaurant-ridden, pedestrian zone with high buildings on each side. One half is in shadow, so we walk on the sunny side.

'I have a full plate this afternoon, Mr Beckett. Business,' she says. 'D'you want to have dinner tonight? I can give you all you need while we eat.'

'Is this a date?'

This makes her laugh. Good. There's a bit of a shell around her which I'm trying to break down. I don't know why. Force of habit, I guess.

'Sure. If you want. It's a date. I've got nothing else to do tonight and you're a pretty good-looking guy. Sure. Why not?'

I have to laugh. 'You think I'm good-looking? I'm flattered, Miss Chow.'

'What about me? You think I'm a good-looking girl?'

'Yeah. You're a pretty good-looking girl. Great hair.

Lovely neck. Cute figure. Nice thighs from what I can see of them.' I lean back and take a critical look at her rear. 'Hot ass.'

She laughs and punches me good-naturedly in the bicep. It hurts. She looks straight ahead. 'What about my face?'

'Beautiful eyes. Sexy mouth. In fact, I thought you might have been a model when I first saw you.'

'Really? A model? Shit.' She turns to look at me and smiles. 'You have a good tongue on you, don't you?'

'That's what all the girls say.'

She gives me a look of mock outrage, followed by a fake, girly 'Oh!'

'So d'you like to eat Chinese, Mr Beckett?'

I laugh. 'I like all sorts of food.'

'You like spicy? Adventurous?' She's watching me carefully now for my reaction.

'The spicier the better.'

'Oh yeah? Most people can't handle it.'

'Most people aren't me.'

'Most people don't like to try something new.'

'Are we still talking about food, Miss Chow?'

She smiles. 'You're a whimsical guy. There's a great restaurant called The Jade Gate.'

'Nice name.'

'Genuine Chinese food. Nonpareil. Not western stuff. I'll book a table there for eight. There's a bar inside. We can meet at the bar if you like. Have some drinks. Shall we say seven-thirty?'

'Fine by me. Where is it?'

'Macclesfield Street. First floor above the Moon Tiger Restaurant, next to the newsagent and across the road from the De Hems pub.'

'I know where you mean. I'll look forward to it.'

'Me too.'

I suddenly notice something that's been going on for about two or three minutes, but that hadn't fully engaged my attention, as I've been so preoccupied with whatever it is that Miss Chow and I have been talking about.

It's a busy time in this street. There are a lot of local Chinese people walking about: some restaurant workers, some not, some old, some young, some male and some female.

But they all have one thing in common. As soon as they see Caroline walking towards them they cross over to the other side. I'm not imagining this. I take a quick look over my shoulder. A middle-aged Chinese man who almost didn't notice her in time, and who quickly crossed the road when he did, has now returned to the side he was on originally.

I keep an eye on it for a few seconds. Two Chinese women in their thirties who are about ten yards away from us cross over when one of them notices Caroline and taps her friend lightly on the arm. A young, punky Chinese guy with a cigarette hanging out of his mouth takes in her appearance for a half second and immediately swerves out of her way without giving her a further glance.

I have to admit I'm stumped. Is it her clothing? Is she too sexy? We arrive at the junction with Wardour Street and she stops and shakes my hand.

'I have to go this way now,' she says, pointing to the right. 'I'll see you tonight, Mr Beckett. I may have some useful information for you.'

'OK, Caroline. Nice to meet you.'

I think.

Out of politeness, I turn left. I somehow don't think she'd thank me for accompanying to her business appointment or whatever the hell it is. After walking for five seconds, I turn around to see if I can get a view of her from behind, but she's gone.

5

LUNCH WITH DOUG

I walk into a Pret, order a macchiato and go outside while they get it ready. I sit at a table and stare blankly at the ten-storey office building being constructed across the road. There's an appetising aroma of deep fried something coming from somewhere, but I can't work out what or where. There's also a thick powdery smell of pulverised concrete floating across from the construction site. Mixed with the diesel fumes from the black cabs, it's starting to give me a headache. And I already have a headache. That's two simultaneous headaches. Not bad going; now my headaches have headaches.

A pretty barista in maroon overalls and a crisp white shirt places my macchiato in front of me. I take a sip and can see her looking at me as she clears away coffee trash from one of the adjacent tables.

'Hangover cure?' she says, smiling at me. She has an unusual accent which I can't immediately place.

'Do I look like I've got a hangover?'

She laughs. 'Yes. Yes, you *do*.'

She's dark, petite and pretty. Mid-twenties. Long hair tied back in a ponytail, very white teeth and a lovely smile. Then I realise where I've heard that accent before.

'You're from Belarus.'

She looks amazed, which is what I was going for. 'Cool! That's incredible. No one ever can work out where it is I am from. Have you been to there?'

'Yes. Once.'

'Whereabouts?'

'Minsk.'

'Wow! That's amazing. I'm from Zhodzina.'

'I know it. Just up the road from Minsk, really.'

'Yes. Hey.' She gives me a curious look. 'Can I ask you out for a drink or something? I haven't met anyone who's been to my country since I've been here.'

'Of course.'

She produces a pen and scribbles a telephone number on a paper serviette. 'My name's Anastasija. Anastasija Novik.'

I shake her hand. 'Please to meet you, Anastasija. I'm Daniel. Daniel Beckett.'

She rolls her eyes. 'Wow! So English sounding! Cool. You will call, won't you?'

'Of course.'

'Tonight?'

'Not tonight. But soon.'

'OK. Cool.' She walks back towards the entrance to the Pret. Just before she goes inside she turns around to face me. 'Don't forget.'

'I won't.'

I decide to have one of the Chinese candies with my coffee. The top of the cardboard container is harder to open than I'd imagined. It's like one of those origami puzzle boxes that get so frustrating after a while that you want to rip it apart. I don't want to damage this, so I persevere. It takes me about three minutes. There are two layers of delicious looking candies inside. I choose what I assume to be a miniature lime coconut bar and pop in it my mouth. It's both delicious and incredibly sweet. If it was any bigger it would have your teeth begging for mercy.

I take a sip of coffee and watch a big group of French tourists walking towards me from across the road. They stop as two of the kids break away and start pointing at M&M's World. One of them starts crying.

Two Chinese girls, probably in their late teens, walk past and look at me, giggling. As they walk away, one of them looks over her shoulder at me and smiles. Hi, girls. It was quite a nice gesture from Li-Fen to make these candies, I guess, even though it may not have been her idea.

I keep looking at the box. Very elaborate. A little too big for the contents, perhaps. I lift it up in one hand. Too big and slightly too heavy. I catch Anastasija's attention as she sashays by and ask her for a takeaway bag. She's back with it in a couple of seconds and hangs around to watch what I'm doing. I point at the candies.

'Would you like one?'

She glances over her shoulder to see if anyone's watching. 'Oh! Thank you!'

I hold up the box. She takes a circular red and white thing, pops it in her mouth, flutters her eyelids, hums with delight and returns to work. Once I'm sure she's gone, I transfer all of the candies into the Pret bag and start fiddling with the base. It comes away easily. There's a packet underneath: white wax paper with a single strip of pale yellow tape holding it in place. I look quickly from left to right as I unwrap it. Instinct tells me that no one should see this, if it's at all possible.

It's money. Fifty pound notes. I flick through it as

quickly as I can. It's a thousand pounds. I really don't know what to think about this. I'll have to keep it: I know they'll find it insulting if I give it back and say *you really shouldn't have* or something.

It's too bulky to put in my wallet, so I shove it in the inside pocket of my jacket. I start thinking about the meeting with Mr Sheng. The whole thing was a little strange and disorientating. On one level I can understand it: one of their guys goes missing, they're concerned, and they don't like going to the police. But on top of that, this guy is different. He has a life, or at least a social life, which is outside the local Chinese community and this apparently stops members of that community from investigating. Having Chinese private investigators buzzing around might be too conspicuous and frighten the pigeons. So they have to hire someone like me. Well, fair enough. For the first time since the meeting I'm starting to get curious about Rikki Tuan's fate.

Then there's the other level. Mr Sheng was cagey and evasive throughout. He himself admitted as much. He wanted to tell but he could not tell. He was vague about Rikki and he was vague about what Rikki did. What was it he called him? A facilitator? Someone who brings about outcomes? Let's not beat around the bush. Let's just call Rikki a criminal. This means that Mr Sheng, despite all his avuncular bonhomie, smiling and laughing, is probably involved in criminal activities, too. And whatever his sources are, he was pretty damn sure that this wasn't a Chinese community matter. He's had three days to find that out.

And now we come to Caroline Chow. Who the hell is *she*? Mr Sheng referred to her as an associate (which is how he'd referred to Rikki) and then he referred to her as his liaison officer. Meaningless titles: more smoke and mirrors. I'm usually good with accents, but I can't place hers. The way she enunciates certain words make me think that she's had extensive elocution lessons, unlike, say, Annalise, who speaks with an altered, educated version of a recognisable accent.

Another baffling thing was the dynamic between her and Mr Sheng, which seemed to change from second to second. Sometimes he deferred to her and other times she deferred to him. Are they equals? Who are they?

I decide to give Doug Teng a call. Doug runs a company called Marton Confidential, which is actually just him. I've used him in the past for electronic counter surveillance, or 'bug sweeping' as it's known. He's also a skilled computer hacker if you can afford him, but that particular talent isn't advertised on his website. The reason I want to talk to him right now is that he's Chinese, or at least London Chinese. It may be a waste of time, but you never know. I take a look at my watch: it's eleven fifty-one. Maybe I can book him for lunch. I call him. He answers immediately.

'Hi there, Mr Beckett. I have to tell you before we go on that I'm extremely busy this week. Working my bollocks off.'

This is his sales scam. He always makes you think he doesn't have time for you, so you have to bung him an extra few hundred quid for the pleasure of employing him and paying him. It's ridiculous, but I put up with it. I'm sure there are others who get worse, like the big corporations he sometimes works for and tirelessly fleeces.

'Hi, Doug. Listen. I don't require your professional services. I need to talk to you. It won't take long. Where are you now?'

'Cock Lane. Pretty funny name, huh? Near St Bart's Hospital. Big financial analysts. Pretty big job. You know Cock Lane?'

'Yes I do. There's a wine bar that does food in Giltspur Street. You're probably three minutes away from it. It's called The Charles Lamb. They do great food if you're hungry. I thought maybe we could have a drink together. I just want to pick your brains.'

'What – *you* having a drink with *me* like normal guys? What's the angle?'

'There's no angle. I just want to ask you about stuff.'

'So it's just like we're kind of friends or something. Just two guys having a few drinks together and shooting the breeze. Cock Lane. I can't help laughing when I say it. Cock Lane.'

'Yes. Two guys having a drink together. I'm in Wardour Street. I'll get a cab. I'll see you there in about ten minutes if you're free.'

'Ten minutes? Sure, Mr Beckett. I can stop here any time I like. Hey…'

I cut him off and after four failed attempts manage to hail a black cab.

*

I haven't been in the City for some time, but I'm not surprised to see that Giltspur Street is a disaster area of noisy construction and roadworks. The Charles Lamb is an enormous place which used to be a furniture showroom and it's already starting to fill up. It's changed since I was here last and has had a major overhaul. There are solid oak floors, a new bar with big chalkboard menus at the back and a variety of retro-looking chain-hung white lampshades covering the ceiling.

I can't see Doug straight away, but then I hear his voice. He's sitting at the bar wearing a charcoal grey suit, chatting to two women in their twenties or possibly thirties. At a guess, they're local office workers, maybe secretaries, maybe not. He sees me and waves me over. We shake hands. I can see him glancing at my Pret bag and Chinese candy box. I've got to get rid of all this stuff.

'Hey, man. I want to introduce you to these two lovely ladies. But first, what would you like to drink?'

'I'll have a double vodka and soda. Thanks.'

The women, one dark and busty, the other blonde and appealingly plus size, turn their attention to me as Doug orders the drinks.

'Do you work with Doug?' says the dark one. 'Are you MI5 as well?'

'Uh, yeah. In fact, Doug and I are going to have to have a confidential chat in a moment. I hope you don't think we're being rude.'

'Of course not,' says the blonde, looking me up and down. Her eyes are amused, wicked and very sexy.

'He's suffering from stress,' I say. 'Pretty near a total breakdown. I've got to try and sort him out before he has his yearly medical profile. Stress, security – the two don't mix.'

Doug returns from the bar with my drink and whatever the bright red thing is that he's drinking. In the split second that everyone's attention is off me, I slip one of my business cards into the blonde's Love Moschino tote bag. You never know.

'OK!' says Doug, grinning. 'This is my friend Daniel Beckett. Daniel...' he says, waving a hand towards the dark and busty woman, 'This is Grace and this is her colleague Daniella. They both work in The Bank of America. Grace is a reporting analyst and Daniella here is a cryptographic consultant.'

'We'll leave you two to it, then,' says Grace, smiling sympathetically. 'Good luck, Doug.' She and Daniella drift away and start talking to a small group of women who seem to know them. Doug looks baffled.

'Shall we sit down and order something to eat?' I say.

'What happened there?' says Doug. 'That was going really well. Why did she say *good luck*?'

'No idea. Come on. Like the suit, by the way.'

Doug laughs good-naturedly. He knows this is the first time I've seen him in anything other than jeans and t-shirt. 'Yeah, yeah – I know. Well, you have look the part for some jobs. You have to fit in, you know? I hate wearing suits.'

We find a table and sit down. Waitress service is speedy here. I tell Doug to get whatever he likes and that I'll pay. I order Eggs Florentine while Doug goes for chunky salmon fishcakes with shoestring fries.

'I need to talk to you about something that's happened with a job of mine.'

'Okeydoke. One of your cases? Wow. Why me?'

'Because the people who are employing me are Chinese. They're London Chinese, like you. Or at least I think they are. I felt that a lot was being kept from me and I didn't fully understand what was going on. I'd just like to bounce the whole thing off you, as much as I can, anyway. See what your take on it is. Confidential, yeah?'

'Sure, man. You know you can trust me. Go ahead.'

I take a sip of my vodka and soda. 'I was out last night about eleven. There was a Chinese girl, fifteen years old as it turned out. She was being attacked by three drunk pricks. I think it was a rape attempt. No. I don't think. It was certainly a rape attempt.'

Doug nods. 'You fuckin' killed them, yeah?'

'Hospitalised. I was in a good mood. She ran away. In all the excitement, I lost my wallet. This morning I get a call from this old Chinese guy calling himself Mr Sheng. He's got my wallet. Some people he knew went to the scene of the attack in the early hours and found it. Apparently, the girl overheard the woman I was with mention that I was a private investigator. The girl, by the way, turned out to be his grand-niece.'

'So he wanted to hire you.'

'Yes. I met him in this Chinese restaurant in Newport Place. It was called The Blue Lantern.'

Doug's eyes widen at this. He looks like he's about to say something, then signals for me to continue.

'This young guy that works for him – he first described him as a business associate and then as an employee – has been missing for three days. This is very unusual, it would seem. The guy checks in with Mr Sheng every day without fail. They've tried his mobile and checked his flat. Nothing.'

'And there's some reason why they can't look into it themselves?' says Doug. 'Very unusual to hire a *gweilo*. No offence. It just is. There are about half a dozen Chinese-run detective agencies within a stone's throw of where you were.'

'That many? OK. I think this guy hangs out with the *gweilo*. The old guy thought Chinese detectives might get alarm bells ringing where silence would be the better option.'

The food arrives. Doug spoons some Cilantro-lime

cream sauce over his shoestring fries. The thought of what that must taste like makes me feel slightly queasy.

'OK. So what's this guy do?' he says.

'That's where it gets weird. The old guy couldn't or wouldn't tell me. He was quite open about his reluctance to talk about this guy's work; apologetic, even. He called him a facilitator. He said he *brought about outcomes*. I'm assuming his work is illegal. It might even be connected to why he's vanished. I have no idea.'

Doug eats a mouthful of his lime fries. There's an amused expression in his eyes. He takes a sip of his red drink and licks his lips.

'What was the old guy like? Mr Sheng, was it?'

'That's right. A neat, smart dresser: suit, shirt, tie, well-polished leather shoes, expensive wristwatch. Very business-like, but not too formal. Cheery, avuncular, quick to laugh: but I felt like it was an act, you know? I felt like he was scoping me out. He was very grateful for me rescuing the girl. Kept saying I didn't have to do the job if I didn't want to. He said he was already in my debt. Oh – and that's the other thing. He wanted detailed descriptions of the guys that attacked the girl and precisely what their injuries would have been after I'd dealt with them. Who knows – maybe he was going to send them flowers and a bunch of grapes.'

Doug looks serious for a moment. 'I don't think so. Anything else about him? Any gut feelings you may have had?'

'Apart from his distaste from having to involve me at all, I felt he was quite a scary guy underneath it all.'

'Not the cheery old and respected man that he seemed to be,' says Doug. He has a quick laugh to himself. 'He wasn't going to take you out fishing with him.'

'No. But there's more. I then got introduced to the person he referred to as his associate and then as his liaison officer. This was a drop-dead gorgeous Chinese woman of about thirty. Sort of like a cross between Maggie Cheung and Liu Wen. Sexy, provocative, flirtatious, confident, and dressed for the boudoir. Peacock feather bra over a black bodysuit. Black stockings, suspenders, five-inch heels, long black hair, well-groomed, fit, expensive-looking. No accent. I'm guessing she'd had elocution lessons. Had an educated vocabulary. Wore expensive French perfume.'

'She got a name?'

I finish eating a portion of Eggs Florentine. The Hollandaise sauce is delicious. I'll come here again. Maybe I'll bring Anastasija here. She had a hot body, from what I could tell.

'He called her Fan Mei Chow, but her western name was Caroline Chow. She thought it sounded like a movie star. I couldn't tell if she was taking the piss.' I suddenly feel tired. I rub my eyes and yawn. 'Even though he called her his liaison officer, I couldn't quite tell who the boss was, you know? She's meant to be helping me with the missing guy. I'm seeing her for dinner tonight.'

He smiles. 'Any gut feelings about her?'

'Nothing I'm going to share with you, but after we left the restaurant, a really odd thing happened. We were walking down Lisle Street. Every time any of the local Chinese people saw her they crossed over to the other side of the road.'

Doug raises his eyebrows, nods his head and sticks a forkful of chunky salmon fishcake into his mouth. 'D'you want to have another drink, man?'

'Let me get these,' I say. 'What's that drink you've got there?'

'It's an Absolut Royal Fuck,' he laughs. 'It's OK. They know at the bar. They won't throw you out.'

I fetch the drinks and sit back at our table. 'So what do you make of it all?'

'I have to hand it to you, Mr Beckett,' he says, laughing. 'You sure are an exciting guy to be around.'

'What do you mean?'

'Well, I wasn't a hundred per cent totally sure when you were talking about the old guy, you know? He was sounding like a small-time crook of some sort, as was the missing guy. But this woman: she was the thing that clinched it for me. When you said about people crossing over the road to avoid her?'

'So what's going on?'

He takes three rapid sips from his Absolut Royal Fuck, places it on the table and folds his arms across his chest.

'You're working for the Triads, man. You're working for the fuckin' Triads.'

6

LETHAL AND GORGEOUS

It had crossed my mind, of course. From the moment that young guy smoking the cigarette pointed me in the direction of The Blue Lantern, alarms bells started ringing, but the idea had just seemed so unlikely that I'd dismissed it. The Triads? Hiring an outsider? Ridiculous.

Both Rikki and Mr Sheng came across as dodgy characters who were probably involved in illegal activities of one sort or another, but that didn't necessarily mean they were part of an organised criminal fraternity, did it? Maybe it did. Either I wasn't expecting it or I was too dumb to see it.

OK, they knew I was coming, they knew roughly when I'd be there and they probably had a rough description of me from Li-Fen. But that might have been caution on their part, as far as I knew. I was someone who'd been involved in a violent altercation. They might have been concerned friends or colleagues, looking out for Mr Sheng.

Who was he, that young guy? Another 'associate'? A bodyguard? Was he the only one keeping an eye on me? Probably not. But if there were more, they were good. I give myself the excuse of a mild hangover for not being fully switched on, but it's no excuse at all. I must raise my game. I can't afford to slip.

I try to think what I know about this organisation. Criminal, definitely, but at the same time, almost like a myth: something you might read about in a book. This is because historically they don't interact with people outside the Chinese community, wherever that may be: at least not in the UK.

In America it's different, though. I remember reading that the Triads had virtually supplanted the Mafia as the main supplier of heroin in the US. I think it was something like every single gram of heroin sold in New York was supplied by the Chinese in one way or another.

Drugs, prostitution, gambling, contract killing, extortion, loan sharking and vice. Ruthless and merciless. That's the Triad image nowadays. But its history goes back a couple of thousand years and it originated in patriotic secret societies, from what I can remember. There's a lot of mythology surrounding their origins, too: it even involves the monks of the Shao Lin monastery.

'So what's going on, Doug? Any tips?'

He runs a hand through his hair and exhales loudly. 'I was born in Hong Kong, you know? My family came over here after the changeover in '97. I was thirteen. People liked Hong Kong as it was, yeah? Most of the people that ended up over here are just ordinary people. Law-abiding, educated, some not so educated but hard-working – all sorts, yeah? And of course you got a big exodus of Triads, too. They weren't particularly keen on the Communists and that's putting it mildly. They came over here, they went to the States, they went to Australia, they went to Canada. There're lots of different lodges, you know? Sometimes the Hong Kong lodges will have contacts in the UK, sometimes they won't. It's all pretty malleable.'

'I didn't know about Australia.'

'Oh yeah, man. They're everywhere. It's a worldwide thing. Everywhere there's a Chinese community you'll find Triad lodges. Australia, France, Japan, Russia, South Africa – you name it. It's an international business. It's like McDonalds or Coca Cola, except, obviously, it's a secret society. But they don't like that term nowadays. They prefer to call themselves *a society with secrets*. Sounds less sinister.'

'They've been here in the UK for a long time.'

'Oh yeah, yeah. Early nineteenth century. I'm not saying there was a big explosion in Triad activity. Just giving you a bit of a background groove. Wherever there's any sort of Chinese community, like in Soho or wherever, you'll find at least one Triad society making a living from it. They call it *squeeze*. Putting the *squeeze* on.'

'What does that mean? Extortion?'

'Yeah, sure. You know – protection rackets, gambling, service industries, vice – the list goes on. If you're Chinese and you're doing something that makes money, then they want some of it *or else*. In a kind of way – my dad – my dad knew about them and he used to tell me about them. Back in Hong Kong, I mean. He could point them out in the street. Discreetly, though, yeah? He called them parasites. They've got this big mythology and like to think they're Robin fuckin' Hood or something, but he said that was all in the past. They're just crooks now, he said. They shake down hard-working people who can't afford it. It's immoral as well as illegal.

'It's why – I mean – it's why he did what he did and in a way it's why I do what I do. Not what I do, but the way I do it, yeah? My dad used to repair household electronic stuff that had gone wrong. He could fix anything from your kettle to your stereo to your refrigerator. But he never had a shop. It was a way of avoiding attention. It was a way of avoiding *squeeze*. He used to say *No premises – No Triads*. In other words, be a freelance. If you didn't have somewhere where they could come and put the *squeeze* on, they sort of didn't see you. You became invisible. You became too much trouble. I guess it's why I'm a freelance, basically. You keep a low profile here if you're Chinese and in business. I mean – it's why I call myself Marton Confidential instead of Crouching Tiger Anti-Bugging Services or something.'

'Lotus Panda Happy Counter-Surveillance.'

He laughs. 'Hey, that's good! I might use that. That's bigtime inconspicuous.'

'Lucky Wok Bug-Sweeps.'

He thumps the table. 'That's the one! It's a toss-up between that and Red Buddha Temple Computer Hacking Incorporated.' He sips from his red drink. 'I'm not too worried about them, though. And I've made some good contacts here if they ever looked in my direction. I mean, I think if I ever got in trouble, or my dad for that matter, I'd hire you.'

'Thank you for thinking of me.'

'My pleasure. Do I get a discount?'

'No.'

'Thought not.'

'So what d'you make of Mr Sheng?'

'Well, first of all, as a *gweilo*, you'll be fed several metric tons of bullshit. They'll tell you stuff without telling you stuff. As far as you're concerned, he's Mr Sheng, though that may not actually be his real name. He's almost certainly senior in some way, otherwise he wouldn't have been talking to you about stuff like this.'

'Is The Blue Lantern his restaurant? Is that a front for something?'

'Very unlikely. Very unlikely it's his restaurant, I mean, though it could be. He just wanted somewhere to have a meeting and probably told all the staff to take a hike while he did some business. That's another thing: calling the restaurant The Blue Lantern. That's pretty blatant. That's pretty ballsy. That's a Triad thing, so they probably have a finger in it somewhere.'

'What d'you mean *blatant*?'

'Nowadays, Triad initiation is called *Hanging the Blue Lantern*. It used to be a tradition to hang a blue lantern outside the house of someone who'd recently died. When you get initiated into the Triads, it's like your old life has died and your new Triad life is starting. They like that kind of thing, that kind of symbolism. Blue Lanterns is also a term for uninitiated Triad members. Kind of *associates*. The important guys have a number, Blue Lanterns don't.'

A waitress appears, takes our plates and asks us if we'd like a dessert. Their specials today are hot Italian doughnuts with a dark chocolate sauce and *Panino al Gelato Limone*. Neither of us fancy a dessert.

'Can we get some drinks through you?' asks Doug.

'Of course,' she says, and takes Doug's order.

'D'you want to get a bottle of wine, too, Mr Beckett?'

'You've got to stop calling me that, Doug. Daniel will be fine. Sure.' I turn to the waitress and smile. I realise I'm feeling rather pissed: last night's booze is still in my system and I didn't get to the gym. 'Could we have a bottle of anything cold, white, fizzy and French, please? Something that doesn't taste of anything.'

The waitress flashes us both a megawatt grin and

sashays off. I stare absentmindedly at her bottom. I imagine my hands on her hips.

'The other thing was finding your wallet,' continues Doug. 'The moment that girl got back to safety, she'd have told someone what had happened. Sheng or someone like him would have sent a little team out to that car park to see if they could find anything. The guys who attacked her don't know how lucky they were. They must have managed to stagger off to hospital before whoever it was turned up to investigate.'

'So what happens if I fuck up, Doug? Will they try and kill me?'

'*Kill* you? Oh no. They owe you. They won't like it, but they owe you. Very honourable in their own way. That girl. Mr Sheng's grand-niece? Well, maybe. Terms like niece or nephew or uncle or whatever are used a lot more fluidly in Chinese society. Maybe she was the daughter of a relative. Maybe the daughter of an employee or 'associate'. Who knows? She gets badly assaulted or killed, they'll waste time on retribution and it fucks up business. Plus, they don't like women being beaten. I'm saying *they*. Do I mean *we*? I feel a bit drunk. Anyway, as far as *they* know, you put your life at risk. You took on three big tough guys to save the honour of a girl. I mean, *we* know that was probably a walk in the park carrying a candy floss and a fuckin' balloon for you, but *they* don't.'

He starts laughing. The waitress places my double vodka and soda and Doug's Absolut Royal Fuck on the table in front of us. I wish it was the evening. It feels like the evening.

'The girl, Li-Fen, gave me this pack of Chinese candies she'd made,' I say, pushing the Pret bag across the table. 'There was a thousand in cash hidden in the bottom.'

'Really? Wow. You could have thrown the box away by accident! That doesn't surprise me, though. As I said, they won't like it that they owe you, but that will have taken a bit of the pain away for them, giving you that. It was kind of that was the least they could do at short notice, yeah? They still owe you, though. That's a big debt there. That girl. Wow. Can I?'

Doug points to the candies in the Pret bag.

I nod. 'Help yourself. So the guy I've got to find: twenty-eight years old, good-looking, works out. That's it. That's all I've got. He's not answering his phone and no one's in his flat. What would you make of him?'

'What was the word that Sheng used, did you say? A facilitator?'

'That's right. And he brings about outcomes, whatever the hell *that* means. Sheng said this guy checked in with him every day without fail.'

'Ah – I might be going on my own prejudices here, you know, but I reckon this guy is probably some sort of enforcer and a senior one at that. If he'd been a victim of some kind of inter-lodge rivalry, they'd have sorted it out themselves. They'd know about it. It would get to them through the grapevine within a matter of hours, if not sooner. They'd get a message saying *look what we've done to your boy*. They have really good communications and have informers everywhere, but, you know, something like that, the other guys would want to brag about it, rub salt in the wound.

'So this is something else. This fellow would be a real hard fuck, you know? The terms change, but they used to call a guy like this a Red Pole. Maybe they still do. A senior enforcer for the clan. A very dangerous man indeed. Someone gets the better of him and it would worry them bigtime. Also, he'd be an expensive asset to lose. The training just for starters, you know? Plus all the stuff he's got in his head. It could be that he brings in money in some way – collecting payments, stuff like that. Or he goes around doing God knows what to people. Hard to say.'

Our bottle of wine arrives. The waitress shows the label to Doug, who shrugs slightly and waves a hand to indicate that she should open it. I notice she's not wearing a bra. I look at the name tag on her shirt. Her name is Machara.

'So he's gone out of his comfort zone and has somehow got into hot water,' I say.

'Possible. You can only guess, really. It could be a timing thing. There may be something going on where his presence is vital, so they've pulled out all the stops to find out what happened to him. That would include the girl, Miss Chow.'

I pour us out a glass of wine each. 'Seems reasonable. So where does Caroline Chow fit into all of this?'

'You know what her name means? Her Chinese name, I mean? It may not be her real name, but I'll tell you anyway.' He loosens his tie and undoes the top button of his shirt. 'Fan Mei. Fan means lethal. Mei means gorgeous. Lethal and gorgeous. Sound about right?'

'Is she a Red Pole, too?'

'Hm. Could be. Could be. Hard to say.' He tilts his hand from side to side, palm down. 'You said she sounded like she'd had elocution lessons. Would you say she was Chinese? I mean, would you say she was *from* China?'

'I really couldn't tell. You sound like you're from London. She didn't sound like you. I heard her speaking

Cantonese to Mr Sheng. Sounded pretty authentic to me. But she was accentless when she spoke English. I would say her English was pretty good. Some phrases and words she used were a bit unusual, like it was her second or even third language.'

'I'm just guessing here, but I'll take a chance and say she's probably from Hong Kong,' says Doug. 'I'm not an expert on all of this. What I know is common knowledge for someone from my background. I don't know what their position is with women nowadays. I don't know if they hire from outside the clan, but they did it with you, so…'

'OK. Why is she here?'

'Well, there could be a couple of reasons for her presence. They'll sometimes bring in people from Hong Kong to sort out disputes between one lodge and another. Someone who's an objective referee.' He laughs nervously. 'That's a terrible description!'

He takes a big gulp of his wine and coughs. Something's bothering him.

'But we don't think that's what this is, do we?' I say, watching his face carefully. 'A dispute? One lodge against another?'

'No, I guess not. I guess not.' He leans forwards. 'These are very dangerous people, man. Very dangerous. You can't imagine. You mustn't mention me at all. You mustn't tell who gave you all this background stuff.'

'They'll get nothing out of me. You said there could be a couple of reasons for her presence. Sorting out disputes was one. What's the other one?'

'Don't think I'm being dramatic. Sometimes they'll import assassins. Someone who'll come in, do the job and get the next plane out.'

I nod my head. 'OK. You fancy a dessert now?'

'I think I'll have the doughnuts with the chocolate sauce.'

7

CITY OF WILLOWS

When I get back to Exeter Street, I make a coffee, fire up the computer, lie in a hot bath and try to allow the intelligence I obtained from Doug Teng to embed itself in my brain and turn into something useful and case-solving. But it doesn't.

The most interesting thing (to me, anyway), is the fact that Caroline Chow may have been flown in from Hong Kong to deal with whatever happened or didn't happen to Rikki Tuan. Assassin or not (and I'm keeping an open mind about that), the most likely scenario is that someone assumed he'd got involved in some sort of 'dispute' between Mr Sheng's lodge and another. They may have feared that he'd been kidnapped, murdered or who knows what.

There must have been some urgency to this, presumably due to Rikki's importance, because it looks as though Caroline hopped on the next flight over. That is, of course, assuming that Doug's assessment was correct and she actually is from Hong Kong. This is something I can find out this evening.

So Caroline gets here and it turns out there's nothing on the grapevine that suggests Rikki may have got into trouble in the London Chinese sphere, so the best she can do is act as a kind of consultant to me. Well, that'll certainly be useful as I have absolutely no way into this case at all. Not yet, anyway.

I get out of the bath, wrap a towel around my waist, make another coffee and sit in front of the computer. I know I should be looking up something, but I'm really not quite sure what. I take Rikki's photographs out of the envelope and stare at them for a while. After what Doug said, that gym-toned body makes a little more sense. If he beats the crap out of people for a living maybe all the working out isn't vanity after all.

I take a closer look at the head and shoulders shot. I look at his eyes. I remember reading something a long time ago about one eye showing you the person behind the mask. Was it the left or right? I place my hand over his left eye and look at the right one. It seems normal – cocky and slightly humorous. When I move my hand and cover the right eye, however, the picture changes. His left eye is cold and utterly without humour. Is this the real Rikki? Is this all bullshit?

I have a sip of coffee and eat one of Li-Fen's miniature almond cookies. I type in 'female Triad assassins' and look at what comes up. As I suspected, exactly nothing. There are lots of them in movies and computer games, but nothing factual. I didn't really think that there would be a list with names, addresses and recent photographs, but I thought it would be worth a try.

I click on 'images' to see what comes up. Generally, it's long-haired, shapely Oriental women in chunky black leather fetish clothing holding samurai swords and black pistols. Well, that ticks some of the boxes, at least.

I close my eyes and think of Caroline. She certainly

seemed fit enough and I remember the outline of a six-pack through the semi-transparent bodysuit she was wearing. But if she is some sort of enforcer, some sort of *Red Pole*, then I must be seeing her off-duty uniform. She's much too smartly dressed, way too conspicuous, far too well-groomed. Just those fingernails alone…

I can't help myself; I try to imagine what she'd look like naked and the image my brain conjures up is a pleasing one, an exciting one: slim, petite, supple, small-breasted. Somehow I know she'd be a ravenous lover.

She's certainly an exquisite-looking woman and despite her confidence and cockiness has a feminine fragility that I'd like to push to its limits. I wonder if her flirtatiousness is genuine or just an act. I wonder what her real agenda is, if she has one. Hopefully, I'll find out tonight.

*

I get to the De Hems pub in Macclesfield Street at around ten past seven. This is across the road from the Moon Tiger Restaurant and I want to, if at all possible, see Caroline arriving for our seven-thirty date. I have to be a little suspicious of her now, and a little bit careful, and I want to see if she arrives alone. I order a vodka and sit by the window.

I look up at the first floor where we're meant to be meeting. There's no sign that this is a restaurant, but there are a couple of circular stickers on the windows with Hanzi characters which I can't read. They'd be just about visible from the street, but unless you understood what they said you wouldn't assume there was a restaurant up there.

There's a door to the left of the Moon Tiger, which I

assume is the way upstairs. This is a three-storey building, though I can't make out what's going on in the upper floors. Some have curtains, some don't. Maybe they're flats. Actually this would be quite a cool place to live, right on the edge of Chinatown and around the corner from Shaftesbury Avenue. If you liked Chinese food and the theatre you'd be in heaven.

A bunch of three young guys walk by, all laughing at something and talking animatedly. They keep turning and glancing behind them. One of them falls over his own feet. I take a look at my watch: seven twenty-five. I can somehow guess what they're looking at.

She looks fabulous. She's wearing a bright red ruched mini dress with a plunging V neckline that stops about six inches beneath her breasts and tantalisingly reveals their modest swell. I have no doubt that this was the detail that was getting all the attention from those guys.

To complete the look, she has on a pair of gold sandals with four inch-heels, a matching gold bangle on her left wrist and a black clutch bag in her right hand. Ostentatious club wear for sure, but it suits her figure and her style. I take a look from left to right. A lot of people are looking at her, but it doesn't seem as if she has any company, intentional or otherwise.

She approaches the door next to the restaurant on the ground floor and presses a button. I can hear the buzz that lets her in from here. I don't want to keep her waiting, so I finish off my drink and go outside. I stand on the street for about thirty seconds, seeing if anything or anyone catches my attention. Nothing. I cross over the road, walk up to the door and press the button.

Once I'm inside, I take the stairs two at a time until I'm facing another door. There's a discreet sign in the centre, reading: 'City of Willows Authentic Chinese Cuisine. Please ring bell for entry.' I ring and I'm buzzed in. This place is obviously exclusive enough for them not to want clientele wandering in off the street.

I'd somehow expected the décor to be redolent of a Chinese restaurant, but I'm faced with a new-looking, minimalist, modern cocktail bar that looks like most of the upmarket ones in central London, with pinpoint lights aimed at the multitude of bottles at the back. There's a door to the left which presumably leads into the restaurant.

Caroline is sitting at the bar. When she sees me she smiles, gets up, puts her hands on my shoulders and we quickly kiss each other's cheeks as if we're not whatever we both are. As if we're a normal couple on a date or something conventional like that. She's wearing a different perfume from this morning. I don't recognise it, but it's explosively sensual: tangerine, musk, vanilla and that's just for starters. It's simultaneously intoxicating and unsettling. It's one of the many smells you want coming from a woman when you're making love to her.

'You look great, Miss Chow.'

'You don't look so bad yourself, Mr Beckett. Shall we order some drinks?'

We sit at the bar. I take a look at the cocktail menu and decide I'll have a Moscow Mule, just for the hell of it. Caroline orders a Revolver. The barman smiles: he can't take his eyes off her, though he's trying very, very hard. I admire his restraint.

'I've got to ask you – what's that perfume you're wearing?'

'You like it?'

'It's extraordinary.'

'Musc Ravageur. Made by Maurice Roucel.' She grins mischievously. 'You think it makes me sexy and mysterious?'

'Without a doubt.'

In fact, it makes me want to grab her and take her right now, but I'm too civilised for that sort of thing. A portly besuited Chinese guy of about sixty walks over, rubbing his hands together. He says something in Cantonese to Caroline, who fires something back at him in the same language, while pointing at me. I can tell she's turned on the charm and flashes him her prettiest smile. I hear the word 'Sheng'. He looks suddenly serious and replies in hushed tones. He bows at me and shakes my hand.

'I am very pleased to meet you, sir. I hope you will enjoying your evening here with us and will enjoy our food.'

'Thank you. I'm sure I will.'

I wait until he disappears into the restaurant before speaking to Caroline again.

'What was all that about?'

'That was Mr Huang. He owns The City of Willows. He said you will always be welcome in his restaurant and you will never have to pay as long as you live.'

'Because of…'

'Yes.'

She turns around on her seat to face me, crossing her legs. In a mini dress like that the effect is stimulating, to put it mildly. I try to avert my gaze from her well-toned legs but end up staring at her cleavage. She notices, tilts her head downwards and flashes me a coy smile, her eyelashes fluttering slightly.

'So. Have you got a girlfriend, Daniel?'

'Me? No.'

'Why not?'

'Too busy. What about you, Caroline? Boyfriend?'

She actually blushes. 'No. No boyfriend. Too much work. Like you.' She leans forwards so her mouth is about six inches from my ear and whispers. 'As we are on a date, you can put your hand on my leg, if you like.'

I almost laugh, about the same time as I'm wondering which planet she's from. 'Are you sure?'

'Yes. I'm sure.'

I rest my right hand on her thigh, about six inches up from her knee. Her skin is soft, and goose-pimples as soon as I touch it. She wriggles with pleasure and takes a sip from her cocktail.

'This is what I call a proper date,' she says. 'Sipping cocktails while a good-looking guy has his hand on my leg. Say things to me like you would normally say to a girl when you were on a date.'

This time, I can't prevent myself from laughing. 'Let me think.' I look into her eyes with mock sincerity. 'Caroline, you're almost certainly the most beautiful woman in this bar.'

This gets a laugh and as an added extra I get punched in the shoulder. But I notice she's blushing again. I like her. She's a cutie. 'That's no good! We are the only people in this bar!' she says. 'What sort of love-talk is that?'

'Is it always this quiet here?'

'It's very quiet this evening. I made sure of it.'

Just as I'm about to get her to elaborate, Mr Huang appears from somewhere. 'Mr Beckett, Miss Chow. Your table is ready. Please come with me, and I hope you will have a delightful evening, the both of you.'

I finish my drink and we follow him into the dining

area, with me resting my hand on the small of Caroline's back. There's a long zip at the back of her dress which I visualise slowly pulling down. I can't say I'm that surprised to discover that we're the only patrons. The restaurant area is bigger than you might expect. I assume it must have expanded from Macclesfield Street into one of the adjacent buildings on Shaftesbury Avenue.

Like the bar, it's slick and modern, with dark Charles Rennie Mackintosh-inspired furniture and IKB/Ultramarine backlighting on the walls and ceiling. The only concession to Chinese culture is a row of three big red ceramic pots next to one of the walls, each with a different pictogram etched in white. Inside each of the pots is a scattering of tall, dried, black bamboo canes. There's a saltwater aquarium at the back of the room and I can spot Black Longspine sea urchins, a dazzling variety of multi-coloured fish and a couple of blue starfish clamped to the side.

Mr Huang directs us to a half circle booth set for two on the right-hand side of the room. We sit opposite each other. The curved sofa seat is in black leather and smells new. A smiling waiter materialises from somewhere and hands us the wine menu. Caroline takes a quick look and points to a two-hundred-pound bottle of Louis Roederer Cristal Brut.

'Is this nice?'

'OK if you like fizzy and expensive.'

'Two bottles?'

'Sure. What are you having?'

'Oh!' she giggles. 'You are terrible.'

'You have no idea.'

I take a look at the food menu. Despite a long history of eating Chinese cuisine of varying quality, nothing on here is familiar to me. 'I've never eaten Chinese food like this, Caroline. I'll put myself in your hands.'

'You want me to decide for both of us? I am so honoured. I will make sure you have the best.'

She scans the menu and another waiter appears and stands by our table. Caroline speaks to him in rapid Cantonese while pointing at the menu. He nods and rolls his eyes in obvious appreciation of what she's ordering, whatever it is.

'So what are we having?'

'I have ordered two starters which we can share. Pork stuffed snail shells with lemongrass and mushroom and chili corn cakes on one plate and chrysanthemum soup buns stuffed with thick crab soup, sprinkled with Chinese crystal sugar and powdered star anise on the other.'

'And that's just the starter?'

She laughs. 'You just wait. I've ordered two main courses, but we can split them between us, so we can both try a little bit of everything. It is what lovers do on a date.'

'Are we lovers?'

'I think we are already lovers, Daniel. As my grandmother used to say – *it is in the stars.*'

'So what have you ordered?'

'Steamed whole sea bass with *siu haau* sauce and sliced sea cucumber. Also goose with ginger and black fungus with four spice. There will be bowls of rice, three types of noodle and various vegetable dishes. It will be too much for the both of us, but that is part of the fun.'

'I can't wait.'

Our champagne arrives and the waiter pours us a glass each. Now to work.

'So where are you from, Caroline?'

There's a miniscule pause before she answers, but it's enough to tell me that she's just checked herself.

'I'm from Guangdong originally, Qingcheng district, but my family moved around because of my father's work. We lived further north for a few years, in Zhengzhou, but then finally settled in Hong Kong. You like this dress, Daniel?'

'It looks great. I still don't believe you're not a model.'

She laughs and waves both hands at her chest. 'You don't think it's too much as I'm not wearing a bra? This is one of those dresses where a bra would not work. It would look ridiculous, I think. I looked at myself in the mirror for an age before I came out. I wasn't sure if it was too much, too impudent. I wasn't sure if I was showing too much of my breasts. But then I decided it was OK. And anyway, I wanted to look sexy for you as we were going on a date.'

'You do look sexy. You speak excellent English. Almost completely accentless. Most people in this country would find learning any of the Chinese dialects much too difficult.'

'Oh yeah, well we all have lessons in English when we're in school. I was pretty good at it. I was usually top of my class. Can I ask you something? Do you think my breasts are too small?'

So this is how it's going to go. I ask a question, she deflects it with some pre-prepared answer, then changes the subject to her breasts. She's almost as cagey as me.

'Too small? No.'

'I thought all western guys like girls with big boobs.'

'Size isn't important.'

'Mine aren't too big, but they're a good shape. They are a sexy shape. I know they are.'

My mouth is dry, so I sip some champagne.

Thankfully, the starters arrive and we eat in silence for a few minutes. The food is delicious. The chili corn cakes have a lethal spicy bite when they're first in your mouth, but it soon disappears. Now's the time to press her on the information she's meant to be giving me.

'Caroline – I've got to ask you some questions about Rikki Tuan.'

'Sure. Go ahead. That's what Mr Sheng said you should do. I am here to help.'

I wait until she looks up so I can make eye contact with her. 'What's his job? Rikki, I mean.'

She looks away. 'Oh, he does a lot of different things.'

'Yes. I heard that from Mr Sheng. He called him a facilitator: someone who brings about outcomes. He called him an employee and then he called him an associate.'

'Yeah. OK. Those sound about right.' She drinks half a glass of her champagne and scoops out some of the pork/lemongrass/mushroom mix from a snail shell. 'These are delicious, don't you think?'

'They're marvellous. Listen, Caroline. I take it that you want to find Rikki, yes? It's important to Mr Sheng and it's important to you.'

'What makes you think it's important to me?'

'I just know it is. I don't know why and I don't expect you to tell me. Unless you want to, that is. Let's make an assumption. Rikki's in trouble. It's unusual for him to go missing like this. Something may have happened to him. He may be alive or he may be dead.'

At the latter suggestion, she stops chewing and looks up, pushing the long black hair away from her face.

'If I knew what it was he did for a living, it will give

me an idea of the sort of people I might be encountering. If, for example, Rikki was the sort of guy that could look after himself, we might be looking for people who were bigger and tougher than he is. Or was. People who are more dangerous. You've got to be straight with me. All this prevarication isn't helping anyone. It certainly won't be helping Rikki.'

'What do you want to know?'

'Is Rikki a Triad enforcer?'

She raises her eyebrows and smiles, though I can tell it's difficult for her. 'Was it that obvious to you? All of it?'

'Yes it was,' I lie. I'm certainly not going to tell her about my boozy tutorial with Doug Teng. She cuts a slice off one of the soup buns and chews for a while. She takes a few, rapid sips of champagne. I'm assuming that Mr Sheng told her to come clean if I asked.

'My suspicion is,' I continue, 'that Rikki is a Red Pole, or something similar. Tell me what he did.'

'I've never worked with him,' she says, as if we're talking about one of her colleagues in the theatre. 'But I know what he was like. I know how he practised his work, I mean. He worked for Mr Sheng. I'm sure it won't be giving too much away if I tell you that Mr Sheng is a Mountain Master. Do you know that term? Dragon Head is another term. That's like the head of the gang, if you want to call it that. The head of the lodge. A Red Pole oversees other enforcers; at least that's what usually happens. Rikki Tuan was a little different. He could have taken a back seat, but he enjoyed the work. He didn't delegate as much as others do. He was *hands on*, if that's the correct phrase. He loved it.'

'Give me an example. Tell me about one of the jobs that Rikki involved himself in. Change the names and locations if you wish.'

She glances at the pots of bamboo canes, as if she hadn't noticed them before, and licks her lips. 'Is this confidential like a priest or something? A doctor?' she says. She's smiling. For a second she's back to her laughing, flirty self.

'Of course it is. Believe me, there's no one I can tell any of this to.'

'About two years ago a rival lodge got into a dispute with Mr Sheng. They were mainly guys who came over from Hong Kong in the nineties. They were cocky. There's a huge Triad-run counterfeiting industry going on in London. Did you know? Bank notes. Never coins. They were mainly involved with human trafficking at the time, so this was a new thing for them. They were greedy. Their boss had a meeting with Mr Sheng which Mr Sheng found very impolite.'

'So what happened?'

'Rikki paid them a visit with two of his lieutenants. Their boss had nine bodyguards with him in this place up near Barnet. You know Barnet? Rikki was very traditional. He liked to use the meat cleaver, but also carried a thirteen-inch combat hunting knife. Razor sharp. He and his guys broke into this place in the early hours of the morning. They hacked all the bodyguards and seven or eight other people to pieces in about five minutes. Then Rikki got hold of the boss. While the boss was still alive, Rikki used his hunting knife to carve all the skin off this guy's head and stuff it down his throat. He kind of made him eat his own face. I don't think he lasted too long, though. Blood loss. Shock. Whatever.'

'Brings a new meaning to *losing face*.'

She looks at me in astonishment for a second and then

bursts out laughing. 'Oh my God. Oh my God. I must remember that.'

'So this was a kind of message, was it?'

'Oh yeah. A big meaningful message. You didn't used to be a policeman, did you?'

'No. So Rikki wasn't the sort of person you messed with, to put it mildly.'

'Yeah. I guess that's true. Shall I get the waiter to clear our stuff away so we can get onto the main course?'

'Sure.'

She raises a hand and a waiter materialises instantly. I can't work out where they're coming from. I get an image in my head of Rikki carving the Sunday roast. I bet he'd be really good at it.

8

HOT DATE

Well, that's certainly given me a useful bit of background on Chan 'Rikki' Tuan. Perhaps a little more than I'd like to have heard. I think I can say with a fair amount of accuracy that Rikki is a dangerous psychopath. I look at Caroline's face while the waiter clears away our plates and tidies the table. Is *she* involved in that type of violence, I wonder? I'm not going to press her about her position or function in all of this. Not yet, at least.

The waiter places the sea bass and goose dishes in the centre of the table, while his colleague arranges the auxiliary dishes around it. We're given sets of fresh chopsticks and fresh plates. The sea cucumber is cut in such a way that it resembles sliced aubergine. Caroline pours the last of the champagne and it's instantly replaced with a fresh bottle in a fresh ice bucket. We spend about five minutes working out what is what and how much to put on each of our plates. Caroline does most of the work. She keeps looking up at me and smiling as she fills my plate. From what I can tell, she's genuinely enjoying herself.

It was worth the wait. This is certainly one of the most delicious meals I've ever eaten. The main courses are mouth-watering, but the sea cucumber is also surprisingly tasty. I'd seen this in the Chinese supermarkets in Gerard Street, but had no idea what to do with it. It isn't too gelatinous and has been cooked with ginger and some other spices which I don't recognise.

Caroline looks up at me and smiles. 'Good?'

'It's incredible. Really tasty. You made some fantastic choices here.'

'Am I a hot date? Is that the phrase?'

'Yeah. You're a hot date alright.'

She opens her clutch bag and pulls out a key ring. The charm attached to it is a gold pineapple wearing sunglasses. There's a Yale and a mortice key attached, plus a car key and what looks like a safe box key. She places it next to my champagne glass.

'Those are the keys to Rikki's flat.'

'Mr Sheng's already given me some.'

She shakes her head. 'Did he give you the address?'

'Thirty-two Slade Court, Great Titchfield Street. A little north of Oxford Street.'

'That is not the address you want. Have you got a good memory? I'll tell you the address.'

'Go on.'

'Flat twenty-one, Fifth Floor, Frampton House, Ebury Street, London SW1. Got it?'

'Belgravia.'

'Yeah. A little more upmarket than Great Titchfield Street, huh?'

'Why has he got two flats?'

'It's a bit complicated. The W1 address is kind of owned by Mr Sheng. It kind of comes with the job. It's fine for what it is, but maybe a bit workaday. Rikki didn't want to tell Mr Sheng that it was not much to his taste, so he rents the Belgravia flat without anyone knowing.'

'But *you* know.'

She shrugs. 'Well, it's not a complete secret. Just from Mr Sheng and some of the senior people. It's not a big thing. He just doesn't like to offend them. If Rikki's needed urgently he can still get to wherever it is pretty quickly. He just didn't want to hurt Mr Sheng's feelings.'

'OK. Why does he need the place in Belgravia?'

She chews a mouthful of the sea bass and shrugs a couple of times. She keeps glancing at the bamboo canes. I'm just going to take her away from the subject for a moment: give her time to relax. I don't know why, but I sense this is all very stressful for her and I don't want to spoil her evening, ridiculous as that might seem.

'Those pots with the bamboo canes – what do those pictograms say?'

She smiles. 'From left to right? Good fortune, serenity and happiness. What do you think of the sea cucumber?'

'It's great. I've never had it before.'

'Some people don't like the texture.' She takes a sip of champagne. 'I've always liked it. There isn't much taste, you know? On its own, I mean. But a skilled chef can work magic with spices and turn it into something really special. It's very difficult to cook.'

I can't stop ogling her breasts. I wonder what it would be like to stroke those long arms. I can feel my mouth starting to water. I must seek help before it's too late. She can tell where I'm looking and smiles to herself, closing her eyes briefly, as if giving me permission to stare for a little longer. I stare for a little longer, then I bring us back to the topic in hand, if I can remember what it is.

'Mr Sheng told that Rikki was enamoured of western ways. I got the impression that he was nonplussed with this.'

'Rikki has a whole social world going for himself outside the Chinese community and outside his work. He hangs 'round with some crazy people. Not bad crazy people, just outlandish people, fashionable people, artistic people. All *gweilo*. They don't know what he does. They have an idea he's involved in crime, I guess, and I think that makes him interesting to them and a little exciting, but they have no idea what he is and what he gets up to. They just like him. He makes light of it. He can be very funny when he wants to be, very witty. Always makes you laugh if he's in the mood. He can be the life and soul of the party. He's a whimsical guy.'

When he's not busy hacking people to death with a meat cleaver or feeding someone their face. Well, at least I'm building up a picture of him, which is more than I had this morning.

'And this flat in Belgravia is to entertain those people, those friends?'

'Very good. Yeah. He wants to make an impression, I guess. It's a much more expensive place, as I'm sure you've realised. He's had it for about a year now. He didn't talk about it much, but he did tell me that some of his friends found it difficult to park near Great Titchfield Street.'

'Have you ever been there? Ebury Street, I mean?'

'No. It's just for him to hang out with his friends. He's a great cook, you know? He likes to hold dinner parties. He likes cooking Thai and Italian. Indian sometimes. He's good at it all.'

'Why have you got the keys to this place?'

'The keys I gave you are spare keys. He gave them to me about six months ago. He said he trusted me to have them in case he lost his. I put them in a safety deposit box in a bank in the City as I didn't want to have them on me. I picked them up this afternoon after we met in the restaurant.'

'And it hasn't occurred to you to go and look at this flat since Rikki disappeared?'

'No. I just got here. You're the detective. I might mess things up for you. Damage evidence or whatever. Crime scene pollution or whatever it's called.'

'You don't know where he parks his car, do you?'

'No.'

I sit back and drink more champagne while the waiters clear away our plates.

'Do you want to try some desserts?' says Caroline. I get the feeling she's willing me not to have any, but I'm so full I don't think I could manage one anyway.

'I'm fine. Maybe another time.'

'So what's the first thing you're going to do?' She's serious now. It's the first time she's taken an interest in me as a professional, in what I'm intending to do regarding this case. I can't make her out at all. Perhaps this is intentional. I decide that I quite like the edginess, ambiguity and confusion.

'I'm going to look at the Great Titchfield Street flat tomorrow morning. Mr Sheng and his colleagues may have missed something. Then I'll take a look at Ebury Street.'

'And you'll let me know how things are going with you?'

'I'll call you as soon as I find anything interesting. You can report to Mr Sheng whenever you see fit.'

'So can we stop talking business and continue our date, now?'

'Of course.'

'Come on.' She pats the sofa seat. 'Come and sit next to me.'

I slide around the seat until I'm sitting right next to her. She smiles at me. 'As we're on a date, you can maybe put your hand on my leg again. If you want to.'

I comply. She shivers but her skin is warm. A grinning waiter pulls the table out to give us more space and then he clears the meal debris away. Mr Huang reappears and asks us if we would like anything else. Dessert? Coffee? Liqueurs? Caroline thanks him and says that we'd like two Hennessey Paradis Impériel brandies and another bottle of champagne. I do hope she's not trying to get me drunk.

Once the drinks are delivered, she rattles off something in Cantonese to Mr Huang, who bows, scrapes and takes his leave. I'm still not sure precisely who or what she is, but she obviously has the power and influence to get an entire restaurant to herself, which is something I've never been able to do.

'What did you say to him?'

'I told him that we needed to be left alone, that we were on a date. You can rub my leg now that we're alone.'

'Thank you. I've been waiting to do that all evening.'

She places one of her hands behind my neck and for a second I think we're going to kiss, but then she changes her mind and runs a fingernail gently down the side of my face. It's a heady experience being this close to that perfume. She runs a hand down my right bicep and gives it a slight squeeze.

'You are a strong guy, I think. I like it when a guy has muscles like that. Not too big. I hate bodybuilder guys. You're more like some sort of athlete. What is your sport, I wonder?'

Very gently, she runs her fingers around the curve of my chin. 'You have a very nice face, Daniel. Very good-looking. You can tell a lot about a person from their face. Do you know what *Siang Mien* is?'

'No.'

'It's Chinese face reading. A very ancient art. My grandmother had the gift. I have inherited it. You have a Sun Face or King's Face. That is what your face shape is called. It means that you are a natural leader. People follow you. They cannot help themselves. And women are attracted to you. Very attracted. Attracted despite themselves.'

She runs a finger over my lips. 'You have a slight downturn to your mouth. That is the sign of a loner. You have had a complicated thread of fate in your life, but you are adaptable. And your ch'i is strong.'

Her hands move around my face. She looks straight into my eyes. 'Your eyes are grey-blue. In *Siang Mien* they are called mixed eyes. Two colours combined. Men with this eye colour make sure that their lovemaking with a woman takes a long time and they care about the woman's satisfaction.' Her fingers lightly brush my eyebrows. 'You have sword eyebrows. This means you are a good problem solver and a good judge of character.'

She adjusts her position slightly, then places both of her hands on my face, a thumb resting on each of my cheekbones and her fingers spread across my temples. I'm quite enjoying this. It's like the lightest of facial massages. She moves her thumbs slightly beneath my eyes. Then suddenly, she jerks backwards, as if she's just received an electric shock. Her eyes look fearful and her breathing has become rapid.

'What is it? What's the matter?'

'You – your face. I have felt that type of face before. Felt those things. You are not what you seem, Daniel. You are a dangerous man. You seem gentle, but you have done a lot of bad things. You are haunted. You are always looking over your shoulder. I don't understand.'

'I don't know what you mean.'

'I'm sorry. I was just surprised. I…' She exhales slowly and grabs the back of my neck once more. This time her mouth is on mine: small, intense kisses, her tongue flicking softly in and out. My hand is still stroking her thigh. I take a risk and slide it higher up. I don't think it's that much of a risk. She pushes herself towards me, opens her legs wide, closes her eyes and groans. I grab her shoulder and push her back against the seat.

'Where are the staff, Caroline?'

'They are still here, but they will not come in,' she pants. 'Do you not find that exciting? Do you think I am a bad girl now?'

She picks up my brandy and places it against my lips so I can drink. 'I don't think you're a bad girl at all, Caroline.' I can feel my heart thumping in my chest.

'Oh, but I am. Come with me. I will tell you how bad I am. I will show you.'

She takes my hand and we stand up. She guides me over to the far side of the room where the ceramic pots holding the ornamental bamboo canes are. She turns to face me, her arms around my neck, her body pressed against mine. 'I'm like you, Daniel. I've done very bad things. Do you mind?'

'I don't mind.'

'You're a nice guy.'

'I think you know that's not the case.'

'As we're on a date, you might want to take my dress

off. But I must warn you about something.'

'What's that?'

She looks down and blushes. 'I may not be wearing anything underneath it.'

'I'll take my chances.'

'I like to be naked in front of a guy who's fully dressed. It makes me feel powerful and submissive at the same time. Does that make sense?'

'I understand.'

'I'm so bad, Daniel. Sometimes I am ashamed of the things I've done. I wake in the night…' She looks up at me, but can't meet my gaze. 'I may have to be punished. I want to be punished. I *need* to be punished. Do you understand? I know you will do it. I know the sort of man you are now.'

Her eyes are shining. My fingers find the slider at the back of her dress and I unzip it as slowly as I can. She closes her eyes and licks her lips. She shivers as the dress falls to the floor. She turns to face me. I place my hands on her hips and watch as her body responds. She's just as I imagined: smooth and sinuous. She grinds herself rhythmically against me, almost as if I'm not there, panting softly, lost in the sensations she's giving herself.

I start to run a hand over that flat, muscled stomach. She turns away from me and walks over to the ceramic pots by the wall. I listen to the click of her heels. I can see the faint traces of straight-line scars across her back and buttocks. She takes out one of the black bamboo canes, runs her hand down its length, whips it through the air and returns to me.

Her eyes meet mine as she hands me the cane. 'I'm not made from porcelain. And, believe me; I'll make it worth your while afterwards.'

She turns her back on me, flicks her hair over her shoulder and presses her hands flat against the nearest wall. Her body is tense and she's trembling a little.

'Now.'

9

HASSLE

Rikki's flat in Great Titchfield Street is roughly a five-minute walk from Oxford Circus and a great place to live if you desperately crave proximity to the West End shops. It's full of snack bars, pubs, restaurants and cafés, plus various speciality shops and TV companies. The garment industry is still pretty well represented, too. I decided to get here as early as possible so I could scope out both of his flats before lunchtime.

I can see why he didn't want to invite his swish pals here: there are parking restrictions everywhere and big parts of the road have a neglected, dingy feel. Fitzrovia used to be bohemian and cool, but not anymore. Many of the buildings look like they're in need of repair and/or tarting up and there are uncollected bin bags all over the place, some of them spitefully blocking your way on the pavement.

On top of that, there are road works almost every twenty yards and many of the buildings are covered in scaffolding for whatever the hell they are or aren't doing. Even if you had double glazing and lived on the top floor, I imagine that this would be a hellishly noisy pace to live, quite apart from the traffic. There's also a constant smell of washing up. I would have thought that the Triads could have done better for their top boys.

The further north you go, the more residential it gets. Most of the flats are early twentieth century, redbrick and purpose built. I spot Slade Court on my right and cross the road to get a quick look at it before I go inside. Four floors and a big pile of soggy free newspapers on the floor near the entrance. Shabby offices to let across the road. Who reads free newspapers anymore?

There are big chunks of resident-only parking outside, so I keep walking for about two hundred yards to see if I can spot Rikki's metallic red Mazda. Most of the cars here are middle range saloons and a car like that would stick out like a sore thumb and be a target for car thieves (if they had a death wish), so it's unlikely he'd park it here, though it would be nice if I found it.

I cross to the opposite side of the road and check all the cars on the way back, but it isn't here. There is, however, a blue Chevrolet Lacetti parked on Rikki's side. No one in the driver's seat, but an old Chinese man sitting on the passenger side, smoking and pretending not to look at me. I make a note of the registration.

There's a common front entrance to all the flats. I push the door. It's locked. I get out the keys and try the Yale lock. It works. The interior is cold and quiet with no reception and a faint odour of cabbage. There's a lift with a little sign next to it, telling you which flats are on which floor. Rikki's is on the third floor. I don't quite understand how his flat is called number thirty-two. There's no way on earth that there are that many flats in this building. Perhaps there's some entertaining historical reason for this.

I don't need to use the mortice key, as Mr Sheng's people didn't bother to lock up properly. I go inside and close the door behind me. I stand in the pine-floored hallway for a moment, until that momentary dizziness I always get when entering strange premises passes.

There's a narrow glass table to my left which is covered in junk mail. There's more junk mail on the floor. I leave it where it is. There are two strange baroque-looking chairs in transparent plastic either side of the table. The air is stale. It's been a while since anyone opened a window. Rikki might not have actually lived here for some time. I have a quick wander around. Three bedrooms, two reception rooms, big kitchen and bathroom. This is actually not a bad place. Its location would probably put it out of the financial reach of most working Londoners. Rikki is a pretty lucky guy.

I check the biggest reception room first. Pine floor again, a big rug with hummingbirds flying all over it, two big sofas, two coffee tables, each with a large ashtray. There's a big television, Blu-ray player, Xbox One 500 and a load of games stacked in a pile. I take a look at the games. Star Wars, Assassins Creed, Fifa 12, NHL 2K7, Quantum of Solace and Green Lantern – Rise of the Manhunters. There are no Blu-rays or DVDs anywhere to be seen. If he has any, they're probably over in Ebury Street.

Beneath one of the coffee tables, there's a packet of Camels. I pick it up and take a sniff: the tobacco's stale. I run my hand down the back of both sofas and come up with a few coins, a single cashew nut and a betting shop pen. There's a print of *Luxe, Calme et Volupté* by Matisse on the wall.

The other reception room, bathroom, toilet and the bedrooms yield nothing interesting, either. This flat just isn't used. The last place I check is the kitchen. Caroline said that Rikki liked to cook, but there's nothing here to suggest that's the case. It's not a bad kitchen, with its red granite surfaces and pine cupboards, but maybe not a bad kitchen wasn't good enough for Rikki's requirements.

I check all of the drawers and cupboards. There are three drawers in a row near the oven hob. The right and left contain cutlery and other kitchen stuff, the one in the centre is what seems to be a 'man drawer', filled with abandoned mobile phones, various batteries and other crap that he was hoarding for no good reason. I have a rummage around, but don't find anything out of the ordinary. It's only when I close this drawer that I notice that it's very slightly proud to the other two.

I pull it out again and tip it up so I can remove it. There're a few things taped to the back, wrapped up in plastic bags. I place the drawer on the kitchen table and start to unravel everything.

There are two cheap plastic key rings. One of them has a Mazda key attached, which must be a spare for his car. I put that in my pocket. The other two keys match the ones that Caroline gave me, so are presumably more spares for Ebury Street that she was unaware of. There's a big lump of strong-smelling black dope, which has been wrapped up in silver paper inside several layers of Clingfilm. I would think it's about a thousand pounds' worth. There are two slightly squashed packets of Diamorphine Hydrochloride, each containing five 5mg ampoules. No idea of the street value of this, but I'm guessing it's high.

There's another, long item wrapped in bubble wrap. From its shape, it has to be a hunting knife. I give it a bash on the side of the table to make sure. No need to unwrap that. I wouldn't want to tarnish his spare psycho weapon of choice. I put everything back where I found it except for the car key and close the drawer again.

I take another quick look around the place and decide to leave. It's while I'm standing in the hallway, absentmindedly staring at a monochrome print of Bettie Page holding a horsehair whip, that I get a small shiver down my spine and it isn't caused by the sight of Bettie's stockings and suspenders. A second later I hear the tiniest of floorboard creaks. There's someone standing right outside the door.

It's doubtful that it's Rikki. If you lived here, you'd just get your key out and come in. Whoever it is, they're standing still and listening, much like me. It's nice that we've got something in common. I don't want to waste time on devious plans. I'm two steps away from my side of the door. I'll take those two steps, pull the door open and drag whoever it is inside. Then we can have a cosy chat. I visualise what I'm going to do, how quickly I'm going to do it, take a deep breath and act.

A half second after I've turned the latch, the door explodes open, knocking me to the floor. Before I can even think of getting up, an immense Chinese guy charges at me and brings his full weight to bear on my chest, pinning me down with his knees. He grabs my right wrist with one hand and flicks open a nasty-looking Spyderco knife with the other. He brings it down fast towards my left eye.

I catch his wrist just as the blade is two inches away from its intended target. He's strong. He's pushing down with everything he's got. I push against him with everything *I've* got. The pressure on my chest means I can't breathe properly. This has to stop. In a few seconds, his arm will start shaking as the oxygen runs out in his muscles. The moment that starts happening I'll know he's reached the limit of his strength. I really hope this works.

The shaking starts. I relax my grip on his wrist and quickly move my head to the right. The blade comes down hard, buries itself in the pine floor about an inch above my shoulder and stays there. While he's pondering that, I break his grip on my right wrist, slam the ball of my hand into the side of his face and dislocate his jaw.

He produces a terrifying noise that's in the no man's land between scream and gargle. I push him off me and snap the Spyderco blade so the business end is stuck in the floor. A shame: those are good knives.

A few moments ago he looked scary. Now he just looks scared. I grab the front of his shirt, pull him up to his feet and slam him against the wall.

'Who are you, you fuck?'

He says something, but I don't understand him. Dislocated jaws and coherent response to aggressive interrogation don't mix. His mouth hangs open, his eyes are popping out of his head and tears are streaming down his face. I give him a hard slap on the side of his face to get his attention. I can't imagine how that must have felt, but I still enjoyed doing it: I don't like knives, particularly when they're inches away from one of my eyes.

'Are you listening to me? Good boy. Your jaw is dislocated. I'm going to fix it so you can speak. This is going to hurt like you won't believe, but if you struggle, or try any funny business, it'll be a million times worse. Piss me off and you'll be in surgery for the next five years and drinking your meals through a straw for the rest of your life. Open your mouth wider. Do it.'

His eyes dart from left to right and he does what I say. I can tell his pulse is racing. I grab a handful of his hair and push his head against the wall for the support I'll need in a few seconds.

'Stay there. Don't move. I'm going to put my thumbs into your mouth and press down on your lower molar teeth, understand? You won't be able to bite me, so don't even try. Then I'm going to push your jawbone downwards and quickly upwards to get it back in the right place. Try and relax. The more tense you are the worse it will be.'

He nods his head a little, which is about all he'll be able to manage. If they did this in a hospital, they'd give you some muscle relaxant first. He looks frightened, but he'd be even more frightened if he knew that I'd never done this before. I stick my thumbs in his mouth and press down on his lower teeth, holding him firmly beneath the jaw with my fingers.

Then, with one quick, hard movement, I push his jawbone down and ram it upwards into the correct location. I can feel a dull thud as it engages. His eyes roll up. He screams. He faints.

I let him fall to the floor and go into the kitchen to get him some water. When I get back he's still lying on the floor. He's semi-conscious, babbling and drooling. I can do without him getting feverish. I decide to use this water to wake him up. I throw it over his face then go back and fill the mug again.

When I return he's calmed down a little. His eyes are open now, he's breathing rapidly and he's looking straight at me, probably wondering what the hell just happened and who I am. I hold the mug of water out to him.

'Drink this. Don't speak. Try not to open your mouth suddenly. Try to avoid coughing or sneezing.'

He takes the mug and half-heartedly slurps at the water. Most of it falls out of his mouth, down his chin and over his shirt. I drag one of the transparent chairs over so I can sit down a couple of feet away from him. I fish my mobile out of my pocket and call Caroline. She answers immediately.

'My God, baby. I was just thinking about you. You treated me so good. I'm still in bed. I'm naked. Talk to me. Tell me things. Tell me bad things.'

'OK. How about this. I'm in Rikki's flat. The one in Slade Court. Some Chinese guy just broke the door down and tried to kill me. I think he's one of yours.'

'Tell me to do things. Tell me what to do. Instruct me. Be really fucking strict. I want to obey you. I'm such a bad girl.'

'Five foot ten, around two hundred and thirty pounds. Could be in his mid-thirties. What's going on?'

'Shall I tell you what I'm doing, Daniel? Just hearing your voice? What I'm doing right now? Ask me. I'll tell you. Do you like me? Oh, Jesus.'

God Almighty.

'Any idea who he might be, Caroline?'

She sighs. 'You're spoiling things for me, baby. Are you punishing me? You're punishing me. I like it that you're punishing me. It's delectable. Let me talk to him. Jesus. You owe me bigtime for this. You better make this up to me. Fuck.'

'OK. Just to let you know, he's suffered a recent dislocated jaw so you may find it difficult to understand him.'

'What? How did that happen?'

I hand him my mobile. He looks baffled.

'This lady would like to speak with you.'

I can hear Caroline fire off a volley of bad-tempered, rapid Cantonese which lasts for two straight minutes. My new pal listens with a dull look of despair on his face. He's sullen, then he's angry, then he's horrified, then he's terrified, then he's stupefied. I'd love to know what she's saying.

When he replies, his voice is slurred to start with, but he soon adjusts and quickly learns to speak coherently with the minimum of mouth movement. I notice his face is looking a little swollen. Whatever Caroline has asked him about, he's giving a hell of a long reply. He sounds despondent. He gets another icy high-speed blast of invective from Caroline and then hands the mobile back to me. He takes a sip of water from the mug and looks at the floor.

Caroline sighs impatiently. 'OK. Ready? This is so fucking tedious, yeah? This guy is called Lee Ch'iu. He's a 49er.'

'What's that?'

'Lowest rank. He's one of Rikki's boyfriends from the old days.'

'Rikki's gay.'

'Oh yeah. Didn't I tell you? Anyway, he's been worried about Rikki, even though they're no longer an item or whatever you call it. He's had a round-the-clock surveillance on the flat without Mr Sheng's permission. He thinks he's in trouble now, so we can use that if you want to question him. He knows who I am and he knows you're working for Mr Sheng so he's peeing his pants.'

The guy in the Chevy. Of course.

'So who did he think I was?'

'He didn't know and didn't care. He's a bit hot-headed. He assumed that if a *gweilo* was in Rikki's flat then it couldn't be a good thing and that you might have killed Rikki and were going to steal his stuff. He probably thought you were one of Rikki's new crowd. He doesn't like Rikki's new crowd and thinks they mean Rikki harm, even though he's never met any of them. He's a bit fucked-up and jealous. I know it sounds crazy, but that's what guys like this are like. They're OK for blunt instruments, but give them a five-year-old's jigsaw puzzle and they go into a catatonic trance, know what I mean?'

'What would have happened if he'd killed me? Did he think of the possible consequences? I don't mean regarding Mr Sheng. I mean generally.'

'Oh. Getting rid of your body, you mean? No problem. There are ways. When are you seeing the other flat? Can I see you today? You should see my body this morning. I feel *branded*. I want to *show* people. I want to be *photographed*.'

'I want to talk to this guy first, then I'll see the other place. I won't know what I'm doing until later. I'll call you.'

'OK. He'll tell you anything you want to know. He speaks English so don't let him pretend otherwise. Be careful with him, though. He's a hothead. Let me know if anything happens.'

'Like if he kills me.'

She laughs. 'Yeah.'

I end the call and watch Lee take another sip of water. He places a hand against the side of his face. He has more colour now and enough energy to give me a resentful, petulant stare. I make eye contact with him and he looks away.

'OK, Lee Ch'iu. I don't have much time. I'm going to ask you questions and I want quick answers. Bullshit me and the jaw comes off again. Got it?'

He nods his head. I can tell he'd break my neck if he

got the chance.

'Miss Chow told me that you thought I was one of Rikki's new crowd. Tell me about them.'

His voice is London, but with a hint of Cantonese, which I think is an affectation. 'Rich cats.'

'Men and women?'

'Yeah. They have dinner parties,' he sneers.

'What sort of people? What are their jobs?'

He shrugs. His speaking voice is slow and listless. I don't know whether this is his usual voice or the recent jaw damage. 'Rikki, he doesn't always say, but sometimes he told me. One guy worked in the theatre. Something to do with the lights or something. Lighting. A technician. And there's a woman who owns an art gallery. Somewhere near St James's Park or maybe Green Park. I can't remember. One guy writes books on where to go in London for tourists.'

Sounds like a crazy little clique. 'Can you think of anyone else he's told you about?'

He holds his chin in his hand and thinks. This may be a waste of time, but it enables me to build up a picture of Rikki's life. Lee has a deep think about this. I can see the big wooden cogs turning. 'Oh yeah. One guy who makes hats. Big hats. Fancy hats. Hats with feathers for showgirls, you know? Like Las Vegas stuff, I think. And there're a couple of actors maybe. Or maybe a film director. I can't really remember.' He sniffs and looks sullen. 'I don't really pay much attention when Rikki talks about that shit.'

'I take it that you don't know people like this. How did Rikki get to know these people? Did they hear of his wit and charm through some Bohemian dinner party grapevine?'

He frowns. 'I don't know. I don't know how he met them. I think he sold stuff to some of them, if that's any use.'

'Drugs?'

'Yeah.'

'What sort?' I don't tell him about the cannabis and heroin I just discovered.

'Whatever, you know? Coke, smack, dope, bufotenine, ketamine: anything, really. Anything they wanted.'

'But Rikki isn't involved in the drugs side of your business, is he.'

'What? No. No, this was like a sideline.'

'OK. Let's leave that for a moment. When was the last time you saw Rikki?'

'There was a meeting we were both at. I can't tell you...'

'I don't care what the meeting was about. When was this?'

He has a think. He's more than a bit slow, I decide. 'Almost two weeks ago.'

'Can you be more exact?'

He bites the inside of his mouth. He drools a little. 'Thirteen days. The ninth.'

'Did you talk to him?'

'Yeah. We still talk, you know? But he wasn't happy. I only talked to him for about ten minutes. We had a coffee together in this place. I had an apple Danish.'

'Why wasn't he happy?'

He looks down to his left. He takes another sip of water. He rubs the side of his face. 'It was just, uh, he said he's been having hassle from these guys. *Gweilo*. It wasn't anything he couldn't handle, he said. It was just annoying him. He said he was going to take care of it.'

'Were these people connected with the crowd you just told me about?'

'Oh no. Not them. I don't know who this was. We're expanding business, you know? Bigtime. We have dealings with *gweilo* more and more. Business. But this was nothing to do with that. This was something else. He was a bit puzzled. He was a bit angry. It was like an irritation or something, you know?'

'Any names?'

'No names, yeah? He said he'd had hassle from some guy and it bugged him. That was it. He didn't say what the hassle was. But it's no surprise to me he has hassle. He hangs around with the *gweilo*. He's inviting hassle.'

'Can you give me any length of time? When you last saw Rikki about two weeks ago, did he give you any idea about when this hassle started?'

His face goes totally blank and I mean totally blank. He's trying to think. I let him get on with it. He shakes his head slightly from side to side, as if the info isn't forthcoming. After maybe three minutes he speaks again.

'He said he was feeling good about himself, because, uh, Mr Sheng said that he was gonna give Rikki two more guys to be in charge of. I think that might have been last month, but I can't be sure. It might have been the month before that.'

'So it was because he was feeling good about himself that this hassle – whatever it was – had brought him down. So the hassle didn't happen before this meeting with Mr Sheng.'

'I guess not. No. It was after that. It was like he was saying he was feeling good about the Mr Sheng thing and then *this* happens.'

'OK. When your smoking guy in the Chevrolet outside

called you, did you think I was one of the people who'd been giving Rikki hassle?'

He looks surprised that I spotted his man. 'Well, I didn't think it was one of his fancy crowd! No way. They don't know about him and they don't know about this place. I know he has a place somewhere else to entertain them, but I don't know where it is. He never invites me there.'

'So as far as you were concerned, I was possibly one of the people who'd been giving him hassle.' I'm getting tired of this now, but Lee is one of those people who has to be prodded slowly and patiently.

'Sure. You can't have been one of his fancy crowd as they didn't know about this place. He was ashamed of this place. He told me. He was always worried that Mr Sheng would find out that he had a nicer place. The *gweilo* we do business with – that's always done somewhere else, so *they* wouldn't know about this place, either. You never invite them to your home. No business is done in homes.'

'So why was your first instinct to stick a knife in my head?'

'Rikki is my buddy. If someone does hurt to him then they do it to me.'

'So even though you didn't know who I was or what I might have done, you were going to stick the knife in my head and ask questions later.'

'Yeah.'

I crouch down in front of him and grab his jaw in my hand. He grimaces with the pain.

'I'm going to give you two pieces of advice, Lee Ch'iu. First of all, get yourself to a hospital and get that jaw checked out. That's the friendly advice. Now the unfriendly advice. Look into my eyes. If I ever see you again, I'll kill you. If you ever see me, just make damn sure you disappear into thin air. Understand?'

He purses his lips, looks down and nods his head.

As I'm taking the stairs down to the entrance, I hear the bleep which means I've got a text. Unknown number. It's from Daniella, the plus size blonde cryptographic consultant from the wine bar yesterday. She must have found my business card in her bag.

'You are a bad boy. Call me. Please.'

This message is accompanied by a kittenish naked selfie taken in her bathroom. She has amazing breasts. I'll call her when this is over.

I decide to have a quick chat with Caroline. She answers instantly.

'You can't keep away, baby. You have to hear my voice.'

'Is it that obvious?'

'You like it when my voice is soft? You like to hear me gasp?'

'You're killing me, Caroline. Can you find out from Mr Sheng the exact date he told Rikki that he was going to get two more helpers? It might have been last month or the month before.'

'Sure thing. Am I your little girl?'

'Get up and get dressed. It's late.'

'Oh!'

I hail a cab and head to Ebury Street.

10

SHUTDOWN

I sit outside a small patisserie with a coffee and an unidentifiable chocolate item that I liked the look of. Ebury Street is definitely a step up from Great Titchfield. It's quieter, greener, cleaner, considerably more posh and is full of chichi little restaurants, art galleries and elegant shops that most people would find too intimidating to enter.

I try to make sense about what I now know about Rikki's 'other life'. Apart from the fact he did a bit of dealing on the side, not much, really. Caroline said he was a witty guy, so I'm sure that has something to do with him being popular. People can get drugs anywhere. If Rikki was dull and boring, they'd soon get tired of him and he wouldn't have gone to the trouble of buying a flat just to entertain, assuming that's all it's for.

The first thing that occurred to me when Lee told me that Rikki was getting hassle from these other *gweilo*, was that it was something to do with the drug sales, as if, perhaps, he was stepping on someone's toes by selling stuff to these people. But the more I think about it, the more that seems unlikely. As Lee said, this was something else. But what? Rikki was irritated, angry, annoyed, puzzled and bugged. Those were the words Lee used. This was hassle and it was a kind of hassle that Rikki wasn't used to and didn't like. I somehow imagine that Rikki's usual reaction to hassle would be quick and violent, but maybe not this time.

I finish my coffee, cross the road and head towards Rikki's flat, which must be about three hundred yards away. As I walk along, I look out for Rikki's car. I don't think finding his car is that important *per se*, but I'd still like to have a look inside it just the same.

There are a lot of smart-looking, three-storey private townhouses here, and I wonder how much they must cost.

When I find Frampton House, I realise that I'm going to have to change tack. I take a quick look and keep walking. There's no way on earth I can just walk in here and let myself into his flat. Rikki's posh pad is in one of three new seven-storey blocks situated in a leafy and impressively large acreage. Rikki's is on the left, which is something, at least.

Each flat, from what I can tell, has a spacious balcony which is festooned with flowers and other assorted hanging greenery. I can see a woman on a silver extension ladder spraying water over the plants on the second floor of the centre block.

There's a main gate with an electronically-controlled barrier to prevent unauthorised vehicles using the grounds as a free car park. I can see eight cars parked about a hundred yards away from the gate, but none of them is the Mazda.

There are six security cameras aimed at the main gate and four on each entrance to the three blocks. Each block has a reception area. Frampton House reception seems to be unattended at the moment, but the other two aren't. I've come across places like this before. The reception staff are usually sharp-witted creatures who know exactly what all the residents look like and can spot a stranger without looking up, even if that stranger has a set of kosher keys and is acting like they were born and bred there.

There's a right turn into a wide street which runs along the left-hand side of Rikki's block. I walk down it as if I know where I'm going, taking in as many details of the building as I can. In ten yards, there's another vehicle entrance with a barrier like the one in front, more security cameras and another car park, once again lacking that elusive Mazda MX-5 Miata.

There are ordinary houses on the other side of this road and a strip of resident-only car parking. A huge guy with a beard is standing outside one of the houses, talking to an old lady who obviously lives in one of them. With enough bad luck, any wall-scaling in broad daylight here would probably get the police on your tail, even if the security cameras didn't spot you first.

Then I see a way in. Next to the wall of one of the ground floor flats is a tough-looking metal structure with a thick concrete base. There's a big hazard symbol on the side: yellow background and a black lightning bolt. Next to that, a sign reading: 'Electrical Shock Hazard – this equipment is to be serviced by trained personnel only'. I immediately recognise what this is: a service connector block for the electricity supply.

Normally, I wouldn't bother with such an insane, high-risk plan, but I promised myself I'd have both of Rikki's places scoped out by lunchtime. There are security cameras nearby, but they've aimed them at the gate, the car park and the rear entrance. The old lady and the bearded guy haven't even glanced in my direction, so I keep walking to get some time to think before turning back.

I'll give myself two minutes. I have no idea what's in that box – there are so many new types now – but I should be able to sabotage it within a couple of seconds of opening it up. Hopefully, this will cut the electricity to the whole block, particularly the reception area, if I'm lucky. If it doesn't, I'll have to think of something else.

It's possible that the security cameras might go down, too, but if they don't, it doesn't really matter. After all, I'm not really going to commit a crime here. I just want to avoid the scrutiny of the reception staff. I want their eyes and attention elsewhere when I walk in and head for Rikki's flat. As far as the staff and residents will be concerned, it'll just be an inconvenient and inexplicable power failure.

They probably have a backup supply, an emergency generator. How long it will take them to get this in place, and who's going to do it is irrelevant. It may be instantaneous, it may be not; it really doesn't matter. I just want a shutdown that'll throw everybody for a short while, turn off their computers and make them fuss, so I can get inside without anyone noticing.

I turn back and walk towards the barrier. I put my hand in my jacket pocket and pull out my keyring. There're two small burglar's tools attached to it which I'll need in a few seconds. I've also got a small tubular pick that I can use if necessary. I put on a pair of thin latex gloves that I always carry with me, set the countdown feature on my watch to two minutes and press the button. Here we go.

I take a left into the main entrance. There's a paved, shrub-strewn pathway that bypasses the anti-car barrier. I head for the service connector as if I have serious, can't-wait business with it. I crouch down in front of it. I realise that I can't be seen by any passers-by thanks to a badly parked silver Volkswagen Golf. When you're doing something like this, there's always a tendency to keep looking behind you which you have to quash. Waste of time. If there's someone there, there's someone there; no point in letting it slow you down, even by a couple of seconds. Plus, it looks suspicious and unnatural; like you're guilty or something.

Two locks: a big, fuckoff padlock and a camlock. Using the burglar's tools, I deal with the padlock in about ten seconds. Its size makes it easy for me. I put it on the floor by my foot. The camlock is slightly more time consuming. I push the tubular pick into the lock and move it from side to side until I hear the clicks that tell me that the pick has got the measure of it. Then I pull it out, tighten the plastic collar, push it back in again and turn. This is just as good as actually having the key. I put the pick back in my pocket and open the door.

What greets me is a totally unfamiliar collection of coloured plastic, wires and screws. No convenient instructions like 'Pull this out, cut this, turn this off'. Never mind. There's a row of green lights at the top. Logic tells me I have to do something that will make them change colour.

I pull two thick yellow wires out of a piece of circular transparent plastic. Nothing. There's a long piece of black plastic with clips on both sides. I undo the clips and jerk the piece of plastic off. The lights start flashing orange, then they start flashing red, then they stop flashing. I think that's it. I can hear a creaking noise behind me. The barrier has opened on its own, even though there's no car there. That's always a good sign.

I throw the piece of black plastic into the shrubbery, close the door and get the locks back to their original state. I take off the latex gloves and put them in my jacket pocket so I don't look freaky. I walk around the side of the building and in through the main entrance. My watch starts beeping. Two minutes. Not bad.

There are two reception staff; a girl of about twenty and a moustachioed blond guy of about forty. She's called him over to look at her computer screen, which I'm guessing has just failed. A hot-looking middle-aged black woman comes out of a room behind the reception area to complain that all the lights in her office have just stopped working. The blond guy looks up at the ceiling lights, says 'fuck' and gets on the phone, which isn't working either. I can hear two contrasting bleeping noises coming from somewhere. Two well-dressed women stand at the reception desk, looking from left to right and tapping their fingers impatiently on the surface.

While they're baffling themselves into a coma, I walk past them, past the lift (not working) and hit the stairs, taking the steps two at a time until I'm on the fifth floor. I take the keys that Caroline gave me out of my pocket and two seconds later I'm in Rikki's flat.

And what a flat. This is like something you see in the back of whatever Condé Nast magazine you favour. 'Fabulous' is the first adjective that comes to mind, 'hot' is the second. And I don't mean that the furnishing is a weird sexual turn-on. It's as if someone has turned the heating up to see how far it would go and then forgotten about it. I can only hope that my forced power cut will cool things down while I'm taking a look around. I take my jacket off and sling it on a white leather chair a few feet away from the door. I stand still for a few moments and expand my consciousness, to see if I can pick up any signs of life. Nothing.

I decide to take a casual approach as it's so bloody hot. I take a look at the hallway first. It's white, classy and spacious. Put a couple of sofas and a television in here and it would make a decent sitting room. There are around half a dozen pieces of mail on the floor. Some are junk mail and a couple look like proper letters. They're recent; the postmarks tell me they got here yesterday. I pick them up and place them on the dark wood table that's attached to the wall on my right.

There's a crystal vase full of fresh, strong-smelling, white lilies on this table, plus a couple of big blue ceramic bowls with nothing in them. The lilies are giving off a stronger scent than usual due to the heat. Behind the table is a huge mirror, which reflects the print of *Andromeda* by Poynter that's on the other side. I turn and take a look at it for a moment. For some reason, I always think of Andromeda as being covered in chains, but this interpretation of her legend only has her wrists tied behind her back. For some reason I suddenly think of Caroline.

On the left-hand side of the hallway is what seems to be an office, but that's an understatement. This is the sort of office you'd expect a top New York lawyer to have. There's a big desk with a computer (and another vase of odorous lilies) plus shelves filled with books which look like they're never read. I pick one out. It's a hardback of *La Rabouilleuse* by Balzac and it's in the original French. It smells new and there's no sign that it's ever been read.

Behind the desk is another large print. This time, a lascivious-looking satyr is performing cunnilingus on a naked and ecstatic nymph in a forest. I've never seen this before. Looks late nineteenth century. No idea who the artist is. I take a photograph of it with my mobile. I'll check it out later. You can never know enough stuff.

I sit behind the desk and attempt to start up the computer, but of course nothing happens. Despite this, I notice that the hall lights are on. Whatever damage I did outside, the lights must be on a different circuit from the computer. I can hear doors slamming. Probably people going downstairs to complain.

There's an Oscar Wilde quote mug on the desk. "We are all in the gutter…" I'm not saying that Rikki doesn't have a true appreciation of art and literature, but I have a strong feeling that the stuff in here and in the hall was chosen for him, probably by one or other of his new pals. Maybe he asked one of them to make this place look sophisticated. Maybe it was an interior designer who decided what books would look good on the shelves and which art would make him look like a class act. It's impossible to tell. I'm beginning to wonder whether Rikki actually owns this flat, rather than renting it.

The main reception room is vast, which by now is no surprise. All white with a medium-dark wooden floor. Two big Bouguereau prints on the wall with more naked mythological women. Two huge white sofas with a large glass coffee table in between them. The lower level of the coffee table has a small stack of hefty art/photography books: *Sumo* by Helmut Newton, a book on burlesque by Dita Von Teese, *Gilbert and George (Obsessions and Compulsions)*, *Paul Klee: Life and Work* by Boris Friedewald and a book of saucy Bettina Rheims photographs. As you might expect, there's a big golden sculpture of a dragonfly next to the unused fireplace and a side table in the shape of a black pig next to one of the sofas.

There's an enormous curved HD 3D Smart TV on the opposite side of the room with a designated sofa, and more bookshelves showing off Rikki's (or someone's) good taste to the left of it. There's also a glass shelf filled with dozens of Blu-rays and DVDs. I take a quick look. Lots of world cinema and Chopsocky: *Mademoiselle Chambon*, *Le Goût des Autres*, *Successive Slidings of Pleasure*, *Flying Swords of Dragon Gate*, *Hand of Death* and *Death Duel of Kung Fu*. On the shelf below, a Bruce Lee Blu-ray box set. There's also a DVD called *Immodesty Blaize Presents: Burlesque Undressed*, with a photograph of Immodesty herself on the cover, wearing an amazing outfit topped off with a sizeable feathered headdress. You could have one hell of a Saturday night here with the right sort of takeaway.

The dining room is much the same as the rest of the place: classy prints and shelves full of classy books. There are two big glass swans on their own table by the window. A gold leopard sculpture on the floor. Two movie studio style spotlights in each corner of the room. A Jackson Pollock on one wall and a poster for *Riso Amaro* on another. The dining table has black metal wrought iron legs with what looks like a white marble top. It seats twelve.

There are four small crystal vases filled with lily of the valley lined up in the centre. They're looking a bit ratty and there isn't much water left. Must be the heat. *Convallaria majalis.* If you don't have any convenient poisons to hand, lily of the valley will always do the trick. They contain three glycosides which will give you heart failure in ten minutes, and that'll be the least of your body's worries. My hand twitches as I hear a couple of unexpected clicks from somewhere in the flat, but it's only the electricity coming on. About time: I was going to make a formal complaint.

Before I do anything else, I decide I've got to have a look at the kitchen. It's pretty enormous and dwarfs the one in Great Titchfield Street. Once again, you could live in here. It's bright, spacious, expensively decorated in maroon, white and beige, with polished marble floor tiles, a circular dining table and six matching chairs, four bookshelves filled with recipe books and plenty of cupboard and drawer space. I should be an estate agent. There's a print of *The Chocolate Pot* by Liotard on the wall.

There's a red Delonghi coffee maker on one of the surfaces, so I find some coffee and start making myself a cup. It's interesting; if someone asked you what the person who lives here did for a living, the first thing that would come to mind would *not* be that he went apeshit crazy with a meat cleaver or made people eat their own faces.

I go back into the office and wait for the computer to fire up. I'll check the rest of the rooms later. I want to have a look at Rikki's files, if he has any. Perhaps the computer is just for show, too. I sit down at the desk with my coffee and look at the screen. It's black. I switch it on and off again. This time it makes a soft starting-up noise. I wipe some perspiration away from my hairline. If I could be bothered, I'd open a window.

While I'm waiting for the computer, I take a sip of coffee and pull open one of the drawers. It's full of pamphlets for various arty things around London. There's a letter from The Royal Opera House asking for Rikki's support, a flyer for a Mozart evening at The Wigmore

Hall and a reminder about a Pre-Raphaelite exhibition at the Tate.

Underneath this pile are two copies of PictureRama's *Burlesque Map of London*. One is out of date and one is current. These attract my attention, so I open the recent one up. It's full of sexy adverts for fetish outfits, stage wear, women's vintage clothing, and details of assorted cabaret venues.

There's a big map of central London on one side, with a number key showing where all the various clubs are located. On the other side there are details of various gigs under the heading 'Entertainment and Shows'. Four of these events, all in the recent past, have been circled in red pen, presumably by Rikki. All of them are straight burlesque performances, according to the meagre details, but it doesn't say who had been performing.

I remember the print of Betty Page in the Great Titchfield Street flat, the Dita Von Teese book under the coffee table, the Immodesty Blaize DVD and now the *Burlesque Map of London* – is Rikki a big burlesque fan? Lee Ch'iu told me that one of Rikki's new crowd was a guy who made fancy hats with feathers for showgirls. I think of the feathered headdress on the cover of the Immodesty Blaize DVD. Did Lee mean burlesque performers?

Just as I'm trying to work out whether all of this has any significance, or might even be a lead of some sort, the computer screen lights up and what's being used as the wallpaper makes me stop in my tracks. I can actually feel the saliva beginning to flood the inside of my mouth. I just hope I don't drool over Rikki's highly-polished walnut desk.

It's a high-resolution black and white photograph of a

ravishingly beautiful woman. She has a delicate heart-shaped face, dazzlingly pretty dark eyes and a full, sensual mouth. I sit back in the seat as if I've been punched in the chest. She's staring straight at the camera, unsmiling. It looks as if she's wearing lipstick, but no other makeup, apart from maybe a light application of kohl around her eyes. She's also naked. Well, almost naked, but we'll come to that later. Her hair is straight, black, shoulder-length with a dead-straight fringe that stops a millimetre above her eyebrows. It occurs to me that it could be a wig. I take a photograph of this startling image with my mobile.

Despite the blank expression, there's a slight upturn to her mouth that gives her a mocking, knowing demeanour. I feel as if she's reading my mind and knows exactly where my eyes are going next. She has high, plump breasts, tied and pushed upwards and outwards in a complex *shibari* harness with black nylon rope, as if she's a model in some upmarket Japanese bondage instruction manual. Maybe she is. There are wide, diamond-encrusted pasties covering her nipples: another link to the world of burlesque.

I take a quick look around the screen to see if there's any information about her, but there's nothing. Just the photograph. But that's enough to make me momentarily forget where this office is and why I'm sitting here. Am I an executive of some sort?

I take a deep breath and bring up Google Chrome. All of the burlesque events that Rikki had circled took place over the previous two months. Four venues: The Kitten Club, SinTease, *Le Tableau Noir* and *Les Seins de L'Amour*. I just hope that they all have sites which keep details of previous events.

I check The Kitten Club first. There were six acts

performing on the night in question. If all the burlesque evenings were like this, I'm never going to remember everything. I look around for something to write on. I open another drawer. It's full of menus from swish restaurants. Well, I'm sure Rikki won't mind me scrawling over the back of one of them.

After five minutes, I have the names of all the performers from each night at each red-circled club. There are four names which crop up on each of these evenings: Coco Delacroix, Sugar Ramone, Véronique D'Erotique and Crystal Chanel. What does that tell me? Probably nothing. It could be that they all have the same agent or something.

I Google each of them in turn. It's obvious that these are big names in their world. Each woman has page after page of images. I take photographs as I go along. I'm not sure that it's my brain which has instructed me to do this. I realise that most of what I've done since I got here has involved taking photographs of scantily-clad or naked women, real or mythological. Maybe it's time to quit.

It's when I get to Véronique D'Erotique that I stop. This is the woman on the computer wallpaper. I enlarge a spectacularly sexy photograph of her wearing a red and silver boned plunge corset. Her hands are clasped behind her neck. This raises her breasts so they're almost spilling over the top of the corset. She's wearing bright red lipstick and this time she has red hair. She looks amazing.

There's a flippant and provocative smile on her face and an overt, crude eroticism which is only hinted at in the monochrome photograph on the computer, sexy as that is. It's insane, but I can feel my heart racing. God alone knows what it must be like to see her in the flesh. I do a rapid and comprehensive search for more images of

Miss D'Erotique, to see if I can find the one that's on the wallpaper here, but there's no sign of it or anything like it. Is this a special photograph? Something that she only gives to the chosen few? Is Rikki somehow a friend of hers?

It would be useful to be able to look at his emails, but there's no sign of an account on the desktop. If he's on Gmail or something, he could access it through Google. I take a look at the search, but there's nothing. Either Rikki cleans up after himself or he doesn't use the computer very much. Most of the stuff on here is games software of one sort or another. I'm beginning to think that this computer is another one of those things that someone advised him he should get to look cool and sophisticated. I clear the search history I've created and switch it off.

I decide to keep the burlesque maps and go and fetch my jacket from the hall so I've got somewhere to put them. While I'm there, I take Rikki's mail. If he doesn't have much use for email, then perhaps I'll find something useful in his postal mail.

I sit down at the desk again and flick through his letters. There's a flyer inviting Rikki to a burlesque festival in Dallas, two pieces of charity junk, a new menu from Domino's Pizza, a free trial for some Amazon thing and finally a hand-written envelope with something like a birthday card inside it. I rip it open. It isn't a birthday card; it's a single ticket to a burlesque evening at a nightclub called Bordello in Ryder Street, which is a little bit south of Piccadilly. And it's tonight. There are two lipstick kisses on the ticket and it smells of perfume. Was Caroline wrong about Rikki being gay? Are he and Véronique lovers, or is he just her greatest fan?

I type in the name of the club and take a look at who's

on. Véronique D'Erotique is headlining and she's supported by Kitty Bourbon, Strawberry Sapphire and 'special guests'. Doors open at eight pm, show starts at nine-fifteen until late. I'm going to have to go. She'll be expecting Rikki and it's unlikely he'll be turning up. Maybe she'll have some useful information. Maybe I just want to go and see her.

I decide to take a wander around the flat and check out the rooms I've missed. I step out into the hall. It's a relief to get away from the smell of the lilies. I don't usually mind them, but they can get a little overpowering when you're sitting two feet away. There's a corridor that leads to a bathroom. I can see a window in there that's a little open, but when you're on the fifth floor in a place like this, the risk of burglary must be minimal.

Before you get to the bathroom, there are two rooms which must be the bedrooms. I can only imagine the level of luxury I'm going to find in these. The first door I come to is slightly ajar. I'm about to give it a shove when the smell hits me. I didn't notice it before because of the scent from all of the flowers.

There's a dead body in there.

11

THE GIRL IN THE FLAT

I breathe through my mouth so I'm not tempted to throw up. It's a girl. She's lying on the bed. She's naked. Her eyes are open. Her throat has been slit from ear to ear. Her stomach is bloated. She's starting to get discoloration of the skin. There are noticeable areas of green and purple appearing over her death-pale torso and on her face. I bite the bullet and start breathing normally. In two minutes, my brain will stop registering the awful smell. That's the theory, anyway. I can hear my brain objecting to this theory and asking me to go to the bathroom and puke.

There are flies everywhere and maggots crawling around in her eyes and in the open wound in her throat. For a moment, I can't work out how the flies got in, then I remember the open bathroom window. With the help of the central heating and the seasonal warmth, she'd be giving off a stench that a ravenous fly and his pals could smell from four or five miles away. They haven't had a chance to have a real go at her yet, but it won't be long.

Under normal circumstances, I'd say that she's been dead for a week, but these are not normal circumstances. Someone has turned the heating on fully to speed up the process. It occurs to me that this doesn't make sense. I have central heating in my flat. It doesn't stay on all the time. When it gets too hot, the thermostat cuts it out. I'll take a good look at her in a moment, but first I have to do four things.

I put my latex gloves on once more, go to the front door and pull the latch down on the Yale. I don't want anyone coming in, even if they've got a key. I close my eyes and make a mental sweep of the flat, remembering every single thing I've touched from the moment I came in. Luckily, it's not much; it's second nature to me not to touch anything unnecessarily when I'm working and I used the gloves to take the electrics down. I find some clean cotton tea towels and wipe down what needs to be wiped: a book, some DVDs, the office desk, computer and all of the coffee stuff. Takes five minutes to do it all to a level that'll fox forensics, even if my fingerprints could be traced, which they can't.

Still holding one of the tea towels, I open windows in the office, the kitchen and the dining room. This is not to freshen up the flat for important visitors, but to dissipate the smell a little. It isn't actually that pervasive at the moment, apart from in the bedroom, but someone wanted the odour from that corpse to be noticed, if not today, then in a few days' time.

Then I look for the thermostat. It turns out to be in the kitchen to the left of the Liotard print. I'll have to take it apart before I can work out what's happened. I carefully remove the plastic casing. I don't know precisely what they did, but there's a small yellow power interface inside which has a green wire hanging off it. That doesn't look right. Next to that, there's a 'system off' switch, which has just been removed and set down at the base of the casing. I push the green wire back into the power interface and click the 'system off' switch back into place.

Immediately, the barely perceptible hiss of the central heating stops and I can hear the radiators ticking with relief. Well, that's that out of the way. Now for the girl. I'm going to keep the latex gloves on, but I'm not going to touch her. For all I know, she might have been booby-trapped. It has been known.

She could be anywhere between fifteen and twenty-five. She's slim, quite pretty (apart from the insect larvae), maybe five foot six, has longish brown hair and, from what I can make out, blue eyes. There's a tattoo of a single rose surrounded by multi-coloured musical notes on her right forearm.

The upper part of the bed she's lying on is drenched with the brown staining caused by most of her blood leaking/spurting out from her jugular veins and carotid arteries. There's a fair amount of blood on the floor, too. Presumably it didn't leak through into the flat below.

She's lying on her back with her arms by her side, palms facing upwards, as if she'd just decided to have a lie down. The cut in her throat is deep – right down to the vertebrae – and pretty neat; not the sort of precise, effective work you could do if someone was clawing at your face and loudly objecting to the whole process.

As it's certain that her throat was cut in the flat, there seems to have been no struggle, so presumably she was unconscious; possibly drugged. I go over to the wall and turn the lights on with my elbow. I take a good look at her arms, looking for puncture marks. As I'm not going to push her around, I'll have to make do with what I can see.

After a few minutes I'm about to give up, then I spot a tiny hole about an inch away from the curve of her left jaw and a couple of millimetres away from the slash. I can't say for sure that this was the result of some sort of injection to keep her subdued while whoever it was murdered her, but I'm betting that it was; possibly caused by something small like an insulin syringe needle or a dental needle. The whole area around her jaw has suffered such a catastrophic injury that you might be expected to miss a tiny detail like that. Or perhaps it wouldn't really matter if you noticed it. Perhaps you were meant to notice it.

Was she a junkie? If so, that's a pretty dangerous/stupid/difficult place to inject yourself, so I'm betting someone else did it. This is all conjecture, of course. I'm not going to perform a toxicology assay on her any time soon and how she was subdued before she died is hardly the point, though it would be nice to know.

So who did this and why? I'm pretty certain it wasn't Rikki. A number of reasons: first of all, people in his line of business don't usually bring their work home. Secondly, she's not Chinese. I know the Triads have been expanding their business to involve dealing with the *gweilo*, but considering Rikki's position in the firm, it's unlikely that this is someone he'd inflict his many talents on. I could be wrong, of course. It could be that he's also a psychopath outside working hours. A man has to have a hobby.

Thirdly: Rikki has gone to a lot of trouble to make this a great place to live, a little designer palace where he can entertain his new friends. Brutally and messily murdering a young girl in one of his sumptuous bedrooms would absolutely fuck everything up beyond repair and I can't imagine that he'd just leave her there and make himself scarce even if he *had* done it.

Another explanation. Caroline mentioned that the rival lodge who felt the sharp end of Rikki's cleaver were involved in human trafficking. Could this girl somehow be a part of that? Girls on the game (if that's what she was) would just be so much dispensable meat to criminals like that. Perhaps killing one of them in Rikki's pad would be just a light-hearted warning or subtle admonition.

They turn the heating up, break the thermostat, the neighbours eventually complain about the smell, the police arrive and Rikki's in deep shit. Could there be some inter-lodge trouble going on and this is part of it? Could this be why Mr Sheng is so keen to find Rikki?

It's a possibility, but both Mr Sheng and Caroline Chow thought that Rikki's vanishing trick somehow lay with his *gweilo*-loving lifestyle and even after what Lee Ch'iu said about Rikki having 'hassle' with whomever the hell it was, I'm basically at a loss. Anyone could have done this, but my gut feeling is that it wasn't Rikki and it was done to get Rikki in some sort of trouble.

OK. Let's say that the people behind this girl's murder did a bit of meticulous planning first. They'd have to select the girl, decide that it was fine to kill her, get her and themselves into Rikki's flat without anyone noticing, slash her throat open with the minimum fuss and noise and then disappear into the night. Or day.

That is one fucking big thing to do. That's a major, fearless operation. It was a hassle for me to get in here and I had a key and no particular criminal intent. I had to create a harmless and effective diversion and I didn't have a half-cut, protesting girl to drag in with me. And another thing – where are her clothes? I haven't done a comprehensive search of this flat, but I'll bet you anything they're not here. Why would the perpetrator get rid of them? DNA traces? Other identifiers? Anyone's guess, really.

Whatever's going on, this girl has to be removed from here before the smell gets too bad and someone calls the cops. I'm aware that doing this will mess up someone's plans, and if they get wind of it, they'll know someone's been snooping around, but it still has to be done. Not doing it will mess up my investigation and I doubt whether the perpetrators will be coming back. I remember what Caroline said when I asked her what would have happened if Lee Ch'iu had killed me. About getting rid of my body. She said 'no problem' and 'there are ways'. I could do it myself, but I think it's her department. Reluctantly, I decide to give her another call. I wonder if she's still in bed and naked.

'Is she Chinese?'

'No. White Caucasian. I can't tell her age accurately. Teens or twenties. I haven't turned her over, so I can't give her a full physical. There's a minute puncture mark on her neck, pretty close to the wound. I think she'd been drugged before they killed her. Everything's too neat. No signs of a struggle.'

'And she was definitely killed there?'

'No doubt about it. Unless that's someone else's blood all over the bed and the floor. It's rapidly becoming a fly hotel in the bedroom. Someone left a window open, maybe intentionally. Listen, Caroline. Is there any chance at all that Rikki would have done this?'

'No way. First of all, he would never kill a woman or a girl or whatever she is. And even if he did, he assuredly wouldn't bring her back to his flat to do it. That would be insane. That goes against all of the stuff we do. He'd be finished. He'd be an unreliable loose cannon. It would be untidy, dumb and unprofessional. Conspicuous. Inviting trouble. None of it bears his mark. He's slit throats, but he's not an aficionado, and the idea that he'd dope somebody out before killing them – ridiculous. Who the hell would do that?'

'Could this be the work of a rival lodge? I remembered you telling me about Rikki's altercation. Maybe they're getting their own back.'

'Very, very unlikely. We'd have known about any trouble brewing in that respect and there's nothing going on at the moment as far as I know.'

'Whoever did it managed to march her past reception and up here without being seen. It would not have been easy. Then they got out again. Also, there's no sign of a break-in here. It would seem they had a key or were professional burglars. Or were using the services of a professional burglar. A professional burglar who had no objection to being party to a particularly sickening murder. Unless…'

'Unless what?'

'Unless they had help here. It's unlikely, but it's another possibility. It was partially an inside job. Whoever was on reception when they got here turned a blind eye to the girl and whoever was with her. Someone managed to get the right person on the reception desk at the right time. I could check it, but I'd have to know which day the perpetrators got here and that's impossible to tell. That theory might also explain why they didn't have to break in. If they had staff help, then they may have had access to a master key.'

There's silence on the other end of the phone. 'What's the sort of clean-up that would be needed?'

'You'll need to get rid of the body and the bed. The

bedroom will need a major spring clean. Even with that done, there's a possibility that her fingerprints may be all over the place. Try and imagine a scenario where they somehow coerced her into coming up here for a drink or something. Even if she's been removed, she could be reported missing and a person or persons unknown might conveniently lead the police here. I think it's best to be over-cautious. The intent was for the people in neighbouring flats to complain about the smell and get the police in here. That's not going to happen now, but you'll have to act fast.'

'I know what to do. I'll need the keys. Can we meet up in about an hour? I'm staying in The Soho Hotel in Richmond Mews. You know it? I'll see you in the bar. We can have lunch! I've been thinking about you all morning.'

I go back in the bedroom and look at the girl again. I decide that I don't like this. Whatever the motivation, whoever did this, I don't think they should get off lightly and I'm going to make it my business to track them down and ensure they're punished, whatever the outcome of this case.

I sit down in one of the bedroom chairs and try and put myself in the position of whoever brought the girl in here. Could she have been a call girl? Could someone have let themselves into Rikki's flat (how?) and called her up? Would reception have noticed her walking into the reception area, getting in the lift and not said anything, not stopped her? Or was it someone the perpetrator knew and she was just visiting him, thinking it was his flat and not realising it was her last day on earth.

It would be useful to go down and speak to someone, but I'm not in the best position to do that at the moment and don't want to link myself to her in any way. I take a look at her fingers. Call girls are usually pretty well groomed and this girl's fingernails have no signs of an expensive manicure. There are no traces of makeup on her face, either, apart from a little kohl around the eyes. Her mouth is partly open and I can see a small but noticeable chip on her upper left canine. Looks like it's been there for a while. No. She just doesn't give off a call girl vibe.

As she presumably didn't lie on the bed and cut her own throat, there has to be at least one other person involved. That person would have had to come in here unnoticed, either with or without this girl. If you were going to commit a cold-blooded murder of this type, you wouldn't want to risk being spotted by reception under any circumstances. That leaves two options, as far as I can see. Either the person who did this was very stupid and uncommonly lucky, or someone involved with the reception staff is bent.

I go back to the office, sit down in front of the computer and get Google Chrome up again. I type in 'Frampton House Ebury Street'. There's a telephone number for the concierge and a load of flattering stuff about the whole site, which they refer to as a 'village'. Then I find what I'm looking for: the people who own this whole thing. It turns out it's an insurance company called Asset Properties and they're based in Millbank. I look at their site. There's another place they own called Bracklesham House in Tower Hamlets. That'll do. I call the concierge.

'Hello. Frampton House day concierge. How can I help you?'

I recognise the voice. It's the hot-looking middle-aged

black woman I saw come out of the office behind the reception area. I use a bright, appealing vocal tone.

'Hi. My name's Leo Marsh. I'm calling about the vacancy for front reception. Harriet North at Asset Properties said I should call you. They told me that you and Bracklesham House had been looking for people for a couple of weeks.'

'I'm sorry, Mr Marsh. You're speaking to the wrong person. You need to speak to the Day Manager, Mr Gallagher, but I'm afraid he's on his lunch break at the moment.'

'Is there someone above Mr Gallagher I can speak to? Miss North said there was someone there who was in charge of all reception staff. I can't remember his name, I'm afraid.'

'That would be Mr Wade, but he won't be in until two today.'

'OK. I'll try and call later. Thanks very much for your help. Oh – could you give me Mr Marsh and Mr Wade's first names? It'll make a better impression if they think I know who they are.' I allow a slight laugh to enter my voice.

'Of course. It's Mr Oliver Gallagher, and Mr Thomas Wade is the Reception Supervisor. I think it's probably him you'll want to speak to. Good luck!'

'OK. Thanks.'

I click off. Oliver Gallagher. Thomas Wade. This may be of no use whatsoever, but I'll file those names away, anyway. I switch the computer off, take a final look at the flat and the girl, open the door and leave.

12

SOHO HOTEL

As I walk up Dean Street towards The Soho Hotel, I try to mull over the last twenty-four hours. All things considered, it hasn't been too bad. A pleasantly fucked-up morning with Annalise, a box of homemade Chinese candies, a thousand pounds in cash, a hot date on the horizon with Anastasija Novik from Zhodzina, a stimulating evening with Caroline Chow (whoever or whatever she might be), an attempt upon my life by an overweight, knife-wielding 49er, a naked selfie from a cryptographic consultant and a naked, dead, maggot-eaten girl in a luxury flat in Belgravia. Beats having an office job any day.

Technically, of course, I've only been on this job for a single morning, so it's going pretty well. I've ascertained that psycho enforcer Rikki is gay, that he hangs out with an arty, semi-Bohemian crowd, that he supplies a variety of drugs to his pals, he has a knockout flat, he's a burlesque fan and that a *gweilo* unconnected with his new friends has been giving him some sort of undisclosed hassle which he didn't like. Also, that he's rubbed someone up the wrong way enough for them to plant a savagely murdered corpse in his cultivated pad.

I have to keep in mind that there's almost certainly

someone working in his block of flats that was a party to this. It's unlikely to be a disgruntled or cranky neighbour, so I must assume it's an employee. Who that might be or what their motivation might be I have no idea. Not yet, anyway. My only lead at the moment is the delightful Miss Véronique D'Erotique, who I'll be checking out this evening. If that turns out to be a dead end, I'll be well and truly stumped.

I turn into Richmond Buildings and notice there's a Chinese travel agency right on the corner. The Soho Hotel is straight ahead. For such a flash, expensive hotel, the road that leads up to it is pretty shabby, which must please them immensely. I take the latex gloves out of my pocket and dump them in a bin. My hands smell like condoms.

Once inside, I'm directed to the bar and restaurant. The bar is an astonishingly hip, well-decorated place, with big, aggressive, abstract oil paintings hung over ultra-loud floral wallpaper. Everything in it, from the furniture to the lighting, manages to be retro and unmistakeably 'now' at the same time.

I can see Caroline Chow standing at a table next to a big wrought iron cage filled with a display of antique glass bottles. There's a smart-suited Chinese guy in his early thirties sitting across from her on a tall bar stool. At his feet, there's a red Woodworm cricket duffle holdall with the white handle of a cricket bat poking out of the top. For a moment, I think it's Rikki Tuan, but on closer inspection it clearly isn't. Rikki is a little slimmer than this guy, but it was an easy mistake to make as they have similar hairstyles and face shapes. Then it suddenly clicks who this guy might be and why he's here.

Caroline looks stunning in a tight-fitting, sleeveless,

ivory cocktail dress patterned with embroidered red roses. Silver high heels. Red nail varnish on her fingers and toes which matches the flowers on her dress. When she sees me approach, she walks over and we air kiss as if we're ordinary people meeting in a bar. She gives my shoulders a slight squeeze as she holds them.

'I want to introduce to you someone, Daniel.'

She nods at the Chinese guy who stands up and grins at me.

'This is Jiang Weisheng. He will be helping us sort out the business at Ebury Street. He can be trusted with all details and minutiae. Jiang – this is Mr Beckett, of whom we have spoken.'

We shake hands. 'I am very pleased to meet you, sir,' says Jiang, the grin never leaving his face. 'Shall we sit down and have a small chat?'

I sit down next to him. Caroline goes to the bar to order drinks. Jiang's eyes follow her. 'She is a very handsome woman, sir. Do you not think so?'

'She certainly is.'

'She has a firm, aggressive, seductive and carnal manner, yet I suspect beneath that there is an insecure young woman who needs to be loved and cared for.'

'Have you known her long?'

He shrugs. 'Ten minutes?'

We look at each other and laugh.

Caroline returns with a vodka and soda for me, a green concoction for Jiang and what looks like a vodka martini for herself.

'Why don't you sit down, Caroline?' I say, smiling at her.

'Thank you. I'm good. I can stand.'

'We might be here for a while. You'll be more

comfortable if you sit.'

She purses her lips, tilts her head to the side and flashes me a frosty and meaningful stare that Jiang doesn't catch. 'Standing will be fine,' she says, her voice glacial.

'Are you sure?'

'Quite sure.'

'Miss Chow has told me the basics, Mr Beckett,' says Jiang, sipping at what turns out to be a Green Mist. 'The item has been there, you think, for three days.'

'I would guess so. That pans out with Mr Tuan's absence. With the heating turned on as it was, the odour and insect activity was about right.'

'Ah, yes,' says Jiang. 'I have taken precautions for that.' He reaches down into his cricket bag and pulls out an aerosol of Raid fly and wasp killer.

Caroline glares at him with alarm. '*Tsh-tsh!*' she says, as he drops the tin back in his cricket bag. None of us can help laughing at this. Jiang's expression of mild offence is so inscrutable that I can't tell whether this was a joke or not. A couple further down the bar look over at us and they start laughing, too. Caroline puts her hand on my arm.

'You will see that Jiang bears a moderately striking resemblance to Rikki. That is why Mr Sheng has loaned him to us for a while, quite apart from his expertise. Mr Sheng made sure that Jiang was clothed in an approximation of Rikki's manner also, to avoid suspicion and wariness when he goes to Ebury Street,' says Caroline, still standing.

'I would like to be able to walk in and get on with my work, Mr Beckett,' says Jiang, as if he's talking about reading the electricity meter. 'Can you give me an idea of the way I should do this? What I will be seeing when I get there? How I should act?'

'Of course. There's a reception area with one or two people usually present. There are a couple of lifts to the left of this. You can't miss them. When I was there, there were seven people floating round, two of them at the reception desk. Keep in mind this isn't a hotel. Be confident. No one will stop you unless you are plainly someone who doesn't belong.

'Occupy your mind with something unrelated, like your last holiday. Your red cricket bag with the bat poking out is a good idea. It's the last thing any unauthorised person would carry. That will help. Do you have sunglasses?'

He produces a pair of Ray-Bans from inside his jacket. 'These OK?'

'Fine. Wear them as you go in, but then remove them immediately. That may be noticed, but it won't be noticed. Understand? Five steps in, take the keys out of your pocket and hold them in your hand. Look as if you've got intent. Look as if you've got nothing to hide. But don't make eye contact with anyone. Go straight to the lift and press the button. Get the lift to the fifth floor. When you get out of the lift, turn right, Rikki's place is two doors along. Don't hesitate for a second, and if someone is there, glance at them, then ignore them.'

'Rikki is not antisocial, but he doesn't make small talk or chitchat,' says Caroline to Jiang. 'Even if someone on the reception desk said something cordial to him, he would do nothing more than give them a polite, noncommittal smile. He does not like to engage with people who are not his friends.'

'I've double-locked the door to his flat.' I produce the

keys and slide them over the table to Jiang, who picks them up and puts them in his suit jacket pocket. 'Don't forget this, and go for the mortice lock first, not the Yale. Open the door quickly and close it quickly. Don't slam it. Once you're inside, lock it and get gloves on.

'It's not smelling too grim in most of the flat, but you don't want to take risks. I've opened a few windows and they're still open now. When you leave, you can close them again and lock them, too. When you get in the hall, walk straight on, then take a left. You'll see the bathroom right ahead of you. The bedroom you want is the first door you'll come to on the way to the bathroom. The smell in the bedroom is…'

'It's OK. I've got a face mask. What's the damage?'

'A pretty deeply slit throat. That's it. She isn't wearing any clothes and I don't think they're anywhere in the flat, though you might want to confirm that. There's blood on the bed and the floor. The sheets and mattress are fucked. You'll have to make your own mind up about the bed frame. If you think the frame's OK, you'll have to put something on top to make it look as normal as possible.'

'Got you. Weight? Height?'

'Rough estimate? Somewhere around a hundred pounds and maybe five foot six.'

'Got you. Prints?'

'I've cleaned up after myself, so you don't have to worry about that. The girl's prints are another thing altogether. If I was doing this, I'd make sure she could wander around the place and was allowed to touch as many things as possible as part of the stitch-up. It'll have to be a full wipe down, if you have the time. Try and imagine there's an advanced police forensics training session there tomorrow.'

'Okeydoke. One thing. I forgot. Any ideas of the best time to do this?'

'Yes. I'll make the assumption that most people who live there work in some sort of job and finish at around five or six in the evening. If I was you, I would walk in there at about six-thirty. It's pushing it a bit, leaving it as it is for another six hours or so, but I think it'll be the smart thing to do.'

'Yeah. I agree.'

'A reception staff changeover time would be useful, but we don't have that. One more thing: I suspect someone working there allowed this girl to be taken up to Rikki's flat. It could have been a member of reception. If that person is on duty when you go in, you may be stopped if he thinks your appearance is suspicious in some way. Get an excuse ready. Frampton House is the block on the left. The central block is called Berrycloth House and the one on the right is McCracken House. You could maybe say you thought you were in one of the other two. Keep cool.'

Jiang laughs. 'I'll just punch their lights out!'

'Good plan. What's in the cricket bag apart from the cricket bat and the fly spray?'

He gives me a broad smile. 'You don't want to know.'

Caroline and I shake hands with him and he leaves. There's some 'stuff' he has to go and buy. He didn't think we'd want to know what *that* was either, but I have a good idea.

'You want to come up to my room and have lunch room service?' asks Caroline sweetly. 'They have a great menu. We can order drinks and you can tell me what has been going on. Mr Sheng likes to be kept bang up to date whenever possible. No pressure.' She flashes me a cute smile. 'Well, no pressure to tell me what's been going on, anyway.'

'But pressure to go up to your room.'

'Oh yes.'

*

As the lift door closes her mouth is on mine immediately. I grab her ass; she gasps and flinches, ferociously grinding herself into me. I grab her shoulders, turn her around and unzip her dress about twelve inches, so I can run a finger gently down her back and see the results of last night's session.

'Who does this for you when you can't find a nice, sensitive guy like me, Caroline?'

Her breathing is so ragged she can barely reply. 'I pay someone,' she whispers.

'Male or female?'

'Either. It doesn't matter.'

'Should I charge you?'

'If you want. I'm a good tipper.'

She's booked into an enormous flower-filled three-bedroom terrace suite, stuffed with wall-to-wall abstract art, luxury furnishings, leopard statuettes and a panoramic view of lots of West End rooftops and the BT Tower. I don't dare ask how much this place must cost to stay in.

We both order spiced chicken breast with sweet potato and black olive tapenade and Caroline insists on getting a bottle of Armand de Brignac champagne plus some Roberto Cavalli vodka. I don't argue with her.

'So who the hell is Jiang Weisheng, Caroline?'

She looks downwards and blushes. 'You bastard, asking me to sit down all the time.'

'Did you sleep on your front last night, Caroline?'

Her breathing is ragged. 'Stop talking about it. You talk about it; I'll want it again. I'm still feverish from the lift.'

'Tell me about him.'

'He's someone Mr Sheng came up with when I told him what would have to be done. He had to find a clean-up guy who resembled Rikki at very short notice. Took him just over half an hour.'

'Where's he from?'

'I don't know anything about him. Well, one thing.'

'What?'

'He used to be OCTB. You know what that is?'

'Hong Kong police. Organised Crime and Triad Bureau.'

'Yeah. They do the Triad countermeasures etcetera. He worked for them for seven years but he was really our guy, of course. Something happened – some bad luck – and he had to get out fast. He's been over here for a while, I understand. He's older than Rikki but can pass for Rikki's age.'

There's a knock on the door. It's the food and alcohol. That's some quick service. Both the champagne and the vodka are in ice buckets. We allow the waiter to set everything up on the black marble dining table and wait until he leaves before we continue talking.

I tell Caroline about the drugs I found in the Slade Court flat and Lee Ch'iu's story about him supplying drugs to his swish new *gweilo* pals.

'Yeah. I can imagine that. But that's nothing, you know?'

'You don't think that's connected to his disappearance in any way?'

This did cross my mind and I dismissed it, but I want to hear her take on it.

'Pretty unlikely, yeah? He sells them drugs, he gives them drugs. They're not going to make him disappear for it, are they? He's got something they want. What's not to like?' She drinks half a glass of champagne and starts work on her chicken. 'And don't forget, he's a likeable guy. Very funny. What's your instinct on these people he hung out with? The *gweilo* dinner party crowd.'

'Well, there wasn't much information on them from Lee; only what they did for a living and that was pretty vague. They seemed harmless enough to me, but there's a possible link to something else from one of them which I'll tell you about later.'

'What else did you get from Lee?'

'He said that Rikki had been getting unspecified hassle from some unidentified *gweilo*. It was irritating him and making him angry. Any ideas?'

'None at all. As far as I know, Rikki's life was in two camps. His *gweilo* dinner party friends and his Chinese brothers.'

'By brothers, you mean…'

'Yes. There was no third group as far as anyone knows. Basically, he would never have the time. He was on call twenty-four hours a day, seven days a week. He wasn't secretive about stuff, except for the Ebury Street flat and anyone in his position would have kept that to themselves.

'It's not like a big, serious thing. It's more like obliquity. If Mr Sheng had found out, he would have been shaking his head at the follies of youth, you know? He'd have given Rikki a dressing down about wasting his money and being ostentatious. Ostentatious is attention-grabbing and vulgar. It causes imbalance. Oh, by the way, Mr Sheng told Rikki that he'd be getting two new guys on the sixteenth of last month. That's five weeks ago exactly.'

'OK. There were signs in the Ebury Street place that he went to the theatre and visited art galleries.'

'Sure. But things like that and his dinner parties – those things would have taken up what spare time he had. I can't see him or anyone like him maintaining a third life, you know?'

'And he doesn't strike me as the sort of guy that someone could easily push around.'

'No. Shall I tell you what the most exciting part of our date was last night?'

'Sure.'

'It was when I asked you to put your hand on my leg and you did. I felt very excited saying that to you. I didn't know how you would react. It was very exciting. Very exciting.'

I smile at her. 'I'm glad to hear it, Caroline.'

'It was as if I was asking for your attentions. I felt very bad. Brave and bad. I felt bad because my body was on fire and I knew what I would be asking you to do later on. I felt frightened that you might reject me. The anticipation and the threat of humiliation made me tremble. What was the most exciting part for you?'

I drink some champagne to kill the dryness in my mouth. 'It's hard to pick out one event, but I quite liked unzipping your dress knowing that you were naked underneath it.'

'I liked that, too.'

We eat our lunch in silence for a while. She frowns and looks up at me. 'What was the other thing you were talking about? You said there was a possible link from one of his dinner party crowd.'

'Yes. Lee mentioned that one of Rikki's friends made big feathery headdresses for showgirls. He didn't give me the guy's name as I'm sure he didn't know it. When I was in Rikki's flat, I noticed a lot of evidence that he was a fan of burlesque theatre. Books, DVDs, gig guides…'

She pours out the last drops of the champagne into my glass. 'So?'

'There was a picture of a girl on his computer. She's a burlesque artiste called Véronique D'Erotique. He'd circled a number of club dates on this guide he had and she was performing at all of them. Whether he went to all of them or not I have no idea. There were a number of unopened letters on the hall floor when I got inside the flat. One of them was a ticket to a performance she's giving tonight at a club near Piccadilly. There were kisses on the tickets and she'd sprayed it with her perfume. At least I assume it was her that did it.'

'I didn't think to order soda. Will a neat vodka be alright?'

'That'll be fine.'

She pours the vodka into a couple of frosty shot glasses.

'Do you have the ticket? Can I see?'

I take it out of my pocket and hand it to her. She sniffs it.

'Issey Miyake. Are you going to go?'

'Yes.'

'You think it'll be worthwhile?'

'It's all we've got. I don't think she's directly part of his crowd. He may have been introduced to her by someone who was: the hat guy. I may find something out that'll be of use.'

She downs her vodka in one. 'Stand up. Let me show you something.'

I empty my shot glass and do as she says. She takes my hand and leads me into what seems to be the master bedroom. One of the walls is almost completely mirrored. She stands in front of me, looking at our reflections.

'What do you think of that?'

'Makes the room look a lot bigger than it is.'

'I think we make a good-looking couple, don't you?'

She leans back against me. She's wearing the Ombre Mercure Extrême again. She flicks her long black hair away from her face. Our eyes meet in the mirror. She sighs as I pull the zipper of her dress all the way down in one sudden, swift movement. I yank the fabric away from her shoulders and the dress falls to the floor. She steps out of it. She's still wearing the silver heels. I take a handful of her hair in my hand and pull her head back. I can see her body react to this and I can hear her breathing become more rapid. She covers her breasts with her hands and her eyes are half closed.

'Shall we order a dessert, Caroline?'

'I don't know,' she gasps. 'What do you think?'

I tighten my grip on her hair. 'They had some nice things.'

Her voice cracks as she speaks. 'The coffee and Amaretto crème brûlée looked rather tempting.'

'I think I might go for the raspberry fondant.'

'Oh, shut the fuck up.'

13

BORDELLO

I walk out of Green Park tube station and cross over Piccadilly, almost getting clipped by a bike messenger zooming past on the wrong side of the road. It was warm when I came out but now there's a chill in the air. I look at my watch. It's just a little past eight-thirty. I feel a little nauseous from the exhaust fumes.

I took a quick look at the Bordello website before coming out and decided that I'd better put on something relatively smart. I didn't want to follow up my only lead to discover that I wasn't wearing someone else's idea of appropriate.

There was no dress code that I could see, and that usually means you should instinctively know what to do. I opted for my only decent outfit, a black Paul Smith travel suit accompanied by an open-necked white linen shirt. I guess I could have worn a tie, but I don't own one. I'm sure they'll have spares for guests if it's an issue. Anyway, this is burlesque, not an interview for an office job.

It looked like quite a classy place, despite that fact that the interior decorators went a bit mad with the gold and crimson. They're pushing a cosy and intimate vibe, but that's just what the photographs are showing. There are thirty bookable tables so it can't be that small. Red drapes on all the walls, big potted plants and Tiffany lighting.

Despite being a two-minute walk from Piccadilly, Ryder Street is not one of those roads you'd normally visit unless you were a big fan of expensive art or antique books. As I walk down the west section, I pass a coffee bar, two art galleries, several office blocks and an estate agent. Helpfully, there are no street numbers on any of the buildings. Well, if I've walked past Bordello I can always come back and check, or, if the worst comes to the worst, ask someone. I have plenty of time before the show starts.

I cross over Bury Street and into the east section. There's a jewellers, a premises belonging to Christie's, a rare books shop and what must be the entrance to some serviced apartments. It's just as I'm crossing over the road to look in the window of Moretti's that I see the entrance to the club.

It's discreet. You'd assume it was the entrance to a private house. You can't just walk in; you have to press a buzzer. I press the buzzer. I'm buzzed in.

A friendly doorman/bouncer in a black suit gives me a wide smile and shakes my hand. He's wearing a discreet earpiece in his left ear. He gives me a rapid once-over, then a busty girl in a black and white polka dot wiggle dress with a big red hibiscus in her piled-up hair asks to see my ticket. I don't think I've ever seen so much lipstick on a single mouth. When she's satisfied, she gives me a big grin and asks me to follow her.

As I suspected, the club is pretty big and it's already quite full. I take a quick snapshot of the clientele when I'm not looking at her ass and tiny waist and wondering how she doesn't fall over wearing seven-inch pencil heels.

There are gay couples, straight couples, singles of all persuasions and the age range is from twenties to sixties.

The women, whatever their ages, are dressed in basques, corsets, bodies, retro, leather, plastic, Forties, Fifties, Sixties, pin-up, Hollywood and every mash-up in between. The men, apart from a couple of drag queens (both dressed like Dusty Springfield), are generally dressed like me, so I don't feel too conspicuous.

There's pushed up and strapped in female flesh everywhere and my senses are constantly being whipped by seamed stockings and suspender belts. The predominant fragrance here is alcohol and expensive scent. I imagine this is what it would smell like if they had a risqué cocktail party in Selfridge's perfume department. In a moment I'll be pinching myself to see if I'm really awake.

From what I can tell, the staff are primarily female and all dressed like the girl whose tail I'm currently watching. There's an L-shaped cocktail bar to my left with two female bar staff and one barman. Some job.

Behind row after row of lit-up bottles is a large frieze of Modigliani nudes. In front of the bar, Bettie Page and Marilyn Monroe are chatting animatedly and down the other end I'm pleased to spot Lieutenant Uhura from the Enterprise, but she's wearing a PVC uniform.

I like this place.

I'm shown to a two-seater table which is right in front of a moderately-sized circular red stage. In the centre of the table, there's a big 'reserved' card with a topless Vargas girl on the front. So that's it. As far as Véronique is concerned, Rikki is a VIP.

I can spot six hefty-looking Cessaro speakers on both sides of the stage. I can see I'm going to have tinnitus tomorrow morning. For the moment, though, the only music being played in the club is cool, medium-paced jazz. I recognise *Générique* by Miles Davis, but only because it was used in a film I saw recently. All this place needs is some old-fashioned cigarette smoke and it would be perfect.

My hot guide tells me that someone will be along to take my drinks order in a moment. There's a food menu on the candlelit table, so I take a look at that while I'm waiting.

As I shouldn't really be here, I'm expecting people to be staring at me, but I'm getting no attention at all, of course. Well, apart from the woman sitting on her own at the table to my left, whom I'm keeping under close supervision with my peripheral vision. She's dressed entirely in red: a red fluffy top partially unbuttoned to reveal a well-filled red bullet bra, a red micro mini skirt, red suspender straps, red stockings and red patent leather shoes. She's about five foot three, maybe mid-thirties or older with dyed platinum blonde hair. A good, pleasingly pretty face: possibly Scandinavian. I'll keep her in mind.

I decide to order fried king crab with a parmesan dip and rosemary seasoned flatbread. When my drinks waitress arrives, I ask for a couple of double vodka and sodas and give her my food order at the same time.

I can see why Rikki would like this club: whether it's his personal taste or not, a lot of the stuff in his flat fits in with this aesthetic. Also, it kind of transports you to another world, and that's even before the entertainment starts. Perhaps he needs a break from the unrelenting, face-scraping horror of his nine to five.

Now I have to give some thought to how he knows Véronique, or rather, why he gets perfumed front row tickets to her performances in the post.

My first guess is it's the drugs. The more I think about

it, the more unlikely it seems that he *sells* drugs to his collection of cut-price connoisseurs. If these people are genuinely friends of his, he probably just *gives* them the stuff. It's no skin off his nose, it'll make him look like The Man and he can probably afford it.

Maybe the subject came up in conversation once and he said he knew a friend of a friend of a friend who could get hold of some high quality gear. He would keep it to himself that he could get virtually anything with a single phone call. I think Lee just made the assumption that money changed hands, and why wouldn't he? As I think of Lee, I find I'm involuntarily opening my mouth and rubbing my jaw.

So let's say that the link to Miss D'Erotique is the guy who makes the feathery showgirl headpieces. This is only a minor possibility, of course, but I'm going to run with it. They get chatting one day and she asks him if he knows anyone who can get her whatever it is she's into. This guy mentions Rikki. He tells her Rikki doesn't want money, but just loves to be a part of exquisitely cultured lifestyles. So Rikki gets on her personal mailing list. He gets her kisses and he gets her perfume on his tickets. I'm guessing she has a lot of gay fans, so Rikki is just another gay fan, but with useful benefits as far as she's concerned.

A different waitress in a green and black polka dot wiggle dress brings my drinks on a *Valley of the Dolls* tray. I can see my blonde neighbour making a note that I've ordered two vodkas and I guess she's wondering who the other one's for. Or maybe she thinks I'm an alcoholic.

Shortly after that, my food arrives. It looks like they're preparing something on the stage now. Someone has killed the ambient lighting and I can hear low level white noise coming out of the speakers. People in black clothing are dragging things around. There's a whirring noise as a pair of black curtains move across the front of the stage and stop you seeing whatever it is they're doing.

Of course, all my theorising about how Rikki and Véronique may have met has no bearing on where the hell this guy is and why he's gone missing. It's not as if he's drifted out of some nice, safe lifestyle into a sinister and dangerous one: quite the reverse. I'm going to have to speak to Véronique and see if she has any theories. If I hit a dead end with her, I'm going to have to get Doug Teng to hack into Rikki's computer and see what that turns up. Ideally, I'd need his mobile, too, but presumably that's with him, wherever he might be. I'd like to speak to each one of his dinner party amigos, but how difficult that will be I have no idea.

My train of thought, such as it is, is suddenly interrupted. The background jazz stops. A single white spot has just illuminated the centre of the stage and the audience chat has ceased. There's a big burst of applause as a guy in a top hat and tails holding an outsize glass of champagne bounces onto the stage.

'Ladies and gentlemen, welcome to Bordello, the most sizzling, the most scorching and the *hottest* and *stickiest* burlesque club in London! My name's Johnny Fuego, the compère without compare, and I'm going to be gently taking your collective hand and leading you into an evil, *forbidden* place where unthinkably *wicked* and *erotic* things dwell.' He pauses for a second. 'But enough about my underpants.'

The audience go crazy and are lapping it up. They obviously know this guy well and love him.

'Tonight's show is going to leave this stage absolutely *covered* in sex. It's going to be *dripping* off the spotlights and *seeping* down into the dungeon. Just make sure you don't get any of it on your clothes or you'll have a lot of explaining to do when you get home, if any of you *have* homes, *which I doubt very much.*'

He takes a slug from whatever's in that glass while raising his eyebrows in acceptance of the audience's continued loud appreciation. I see him look at me for a millisecond, then he clicks his fingers at the lighting guy who's sitting on the far left of the stage.

'One thing, though, ladies and gentlemen.' He taps both sides of his head with his fingers. 'I think I must be losing my memory. It's true. Because *I* thought it was my birthday three months ago!'

I'm suddenly lit up in the glare of a bright white spotlight. This gets a big laugh from the audience and from me, too. I guess you have to expect this if you're sitting at the front. I'll bet Rikki loved this sort of thing.

'Welcome to Bordello burlesque, sir. I hope you have a fabulous time tonight and leave here without a *shred* of decency left in your body, if there's any there in the first place, and I can tell there isn't!' He takes another drink and turns his attention back to the audience. 'We have a fantastic evening of urbane and cultured entertainment for you this evening. Topping the bill, of course, we have the marvellous, the romantic, the *obscenely sophisticated* Miss' – his voice turns to an awed whisper – '*Véronique D'Erotique!*'

The audience go wild at the mention of her name. He waits until the whooping and whistling has died down.

'We shall also be seeing *quite a bit* of the *delectable*, the *pert*, the *almost-too-voluptuous* Miss *Strawberry Sapphire!*'

Miss Sapphire gets an equally frenzied reaction from the crowd.

'But now, ladies and gentlemen, *mesdames et messieurs, Damen und Herron, signore e signori, damas y caballeros* – would you please give a warm, moist, Bordello-style welcome to the bewitching, the pulchritudinous, the unwholesome, the *atrocious* – Miss *Kitty Bourbon*!'

Our master of ceremonies dashes off the stage to more wild applause. The club lights dim. There's a sudden hush and the black curtains slowly open to reveal the backlit silhouette of woman sitting side-on at a desk in the straight-backed posture of a secretary. She's pretending to type on an old-fashioned typewriter. She glances frostily at the audience as the lights slowly come up and the sleazy, saxophone-heavy jazz strains of *Harlem Nocturne* by Earl Bostic pour out of the sound system.

She finishes typing and stretches like a cat, her back arching, her fingers clasped behind her neck. As the stage gets brighter, I can see she's dressed in a dark blue tailored pinstriped jacket and matching skirt. Black stockings, black four-inch heels. It's hard to see what she's got on underneath the jacket: possibly nothing. Her long red hair is tied back in a ponytail and she's wearing black horn-rimmed glasses.

After she's had a long, sensual stretch that gets the audience moaning for more, she suddenly whips her hairband off, allowing her long, wavy hair to fall over her shoulders. This gets a round of applause. Almost immediately, she takes her glasses off, throws them over her shoulder and swivels round in her chair to face the audience, crossing her legs to give everyone a view of her stocking tops and suspenders.

She's buxom and voluptuous, her breasts wide and firm, her lips full, red, and petulant. She stands up and strolls languidly towards the front of the stage, slowly undoing three of the four buttons at the front of her jacket. She gives a funny, questioning look at the crowd, as if asking permission to take the fourth button off. Should she? Should she not? When she does so, the black lace open cup body she's wearing underneath can be clearly seen, as can the black, heart-shaped nipple tassels. Just as I'm taking this in, the jacket comes off, and after being swung through the air a few times is thrown away towards the desk.

Each movement she makes grinds along with the rhythm of the music. The vocal appreciation from the audience is non-stop. People scream when she twirls the nipple tassels. The skirt comes off, the body comes off, the stockings are pulled off excruciatingly slowly. By the time she's down to G-string, tassels and nothing else, she's got everyone eating out of her hand, me included. I'm so close to the stage I can see the moist glow of perspiration covering her body and I can smell her perfume.

Then she slowly heads back to her desk, wiggling her ass at all of us, looking over her shoulder as if all of this is our fault. Just as she's about to sit down again, she's brightly illuminated by a prop door opening to her left, as if someone has come in unexpectedly and caught her at it. She crosses her hands across her breasts, give a shocked look at the audience and then everything is black.

The whole place explodes, of course. I can see the blonde woman next to me applauding enthusiastically. She catches my eyes and I smile at her. A waitress comes and clears my table. I've finished both vodka and sodas so order another. I ask her to ask the blonde if she wants anything. I can hear her order: she asks for a Royal Blush – a red cocktail to match her red clothes.

She smiles at me, stands up and approaches my table.

'May I join you?'

'Of course. Please take a seat.'

'Thank you for the drink. You are most kind.'

She has a slight European accent, but I can't identify it because of all the chatter and the jazz, which has started up again while the stagehands do their thing. She makes herself comfortable and crosses her legs. She has firm, heavy thighs.

I'm about to ask her if she comes here often. There's no way around it. I try to think of another way of putting it, but nothing comes to mind.

'Do you come here often?'

'Oh yes. Well, recently, anyway. I am a big fan of burlesque. My name's Anouk, by the way. Anouk Heijmans.'

'Daniel Beckett.'

Our drinks arrive. I take a sip of mine and try to stop looking at what the red bullet bra is doing to her eye-catching cleavage. Then I have to stop looking at her red stockings and the tops of those white thighs. This is murder. Her name and the accent click into place in my brain.

'You're Dutch. Where are you from?'

She nods and smiles. 'I'm from Eindhoven originally, but I live in The Hague at present. You know it? I perform at the Paarde van Troje.'

'The Trojan Horse.'

Her eyes brighten. 'You speak Dutch!'

'*Genoeg om rond te komen.*'

'*Erg goed!*'

'So you're a burlesque artiste, Anouk.'

'Yes. I'm called Suzette Rousseau.' She blushes as she

says this, as if it's some embarrassing secret.

I take another quick look at her thighs. She notices and crosses her legs the other way. I'm going to sleep with her. 'So are you checking out the competition?'

She laughs. 'I perform mainly in Europe, though sometimes in the UK. I'm here for a brief break. But you are correct, in a way. I like to see the British girls. They are so *innovatief*, you know?'

'Have you seen Véronique D'Erotique before?'

'Oh, yes. I saw her in the Carrousel de Paris last year and the Paradiso in Amsterdam three months ago, but never here. We are friends, you know? We don't see each other socially that often, but barely six months goes by when we do not see each other in some way or other. Also – we have performed together on the same bill from time to time.'

'Here in London or in Europe?'

'Never in London. But we've done a lot of the big European festivals together: The Helsinki Burlesque Festival, The Polish Burlesque Festival – those were last year – and Antwerp, Munich and Stockholm this year. She's always different, always changing. She's amazing – a real inspiration. There's no one quite like her.' She leans forwards and places a hand on my leg. 'She's very beautiful and has an exquisite figure. But I wish she wouldn't – you know.'

'What?'

'She's always been a little too fond of certain of life's pleasures. Things that could be bad for her. We're meant to be her friends, you know? But we never talk to her about her problems. It is foolish, I suppose.'

So this is turning out to be work after all. 'What sort of problems?'

'I heard whispers that she is drug dependent in some way and has been for a few years now. No details. Just rumour. It may be all nonsense, of course. You know how people are. I hate gossip. If it isn't true, it would be *beschamend* to talk to her about it, you know? Embarrassing. She might be hurt and I would never want to hurt her.'

I feel as if Rikki has just walked in the room. I'd like to talk to her a little more about this, but Johnny Fuego has just reappeared on the stage, bombards us with a little hilariously vulgar stand-up and introduces Miss Strawberry Sapphire, who strides onstage in a pink leather trench coat to the *Peter Gunn Theme*, while being systematically and teasingly stripped by two similar-looking female assistants, who shortly get the same treatment in return. Johnny's description of her as almost-too-voluptuous was accurate: her tassel-twirling is a breathtaking work of art.

This is more choreographed than Kitty Bourbon's act, is enhanced by a spectacular, complex and sophisticated light show and is more blatantly and powerfully sexual. Strawberry has a more knowing, smirking presence than Kitty, and does a lot of winking and lip-licking.

The two assistants (if that's the right word) appear to be constantly running their hands over Strawberry's body and Strawberry reacts with shock, displeasure and reluctant eye-rolling delight: though from this close, I can see that they're not actually touching her at all. Obviously well-rehearsed and all part of the tease, I guess.

Throughout the performance, Anouk keeps her hand on my leg, giving it a barely perceptible squeeze whenever Strawberry has an item of clothing removed or makes a provocative gesture with her body.

Earlier, I was thinking that I liked this place. Now I'm definitely going to move in.

14

CHAQUE BOUTON LÂCHE

By the time Miss Strawberry Sapphire has finished her act, Anouk has moved her chair closer to mine and is rubbing my arm. It's getting hot in here in a way that no air-con can fix. I order some more drinks.

'Did you like her, Daniel?'

'Big girl. Very sexy. Great hair. Lovely mouth.'

She laughs. 'Yes. And she's exciting to watch because of that. She was far more – what do you say – *fetishistic* than Kitty Bourbon. A bit like Mimi Mustang. Do you know her? More aggressive, too: this can be a turn-on for audience members of each sex. There are certain types of clothing that can be sent into orbit by a figure like that. I am the same: extra-large bust, small waist, wide hips.'

As if to demonstrate this (as if my imagination wasn't already doing it for her), she removes her fluffy red top and drapes it over the back of her chair. Thankfully, the bullet bra she's wearing is a longline version and stops just above her navel. It is strapless, though. I visualise unclipping it.

She has great shoulders and back muscles and I can see what she means about her waist. It makes me smile: there aren't many venues where you can sit down in what is virtually your underwear and no one takes a blind bit of notice. She crosses her legs again. I take my jacket off.

She runs a hand through her hair. I think about changing a car tyre.

'So is your act similar to hers?'

'No, no. Well, yes. In some ways. I like to wear corsets to show off my waist and accentuate my bust. Long gloves are a favourite of mine, too. There's an art to taking them off. It can be made to be almost as erotic as removing stockings. But my act is more flirtatious, more *debauched*, I think you could say. I like to show pleasure on my face as I strip. I want the audience to see that I am pleasuring myself as I perform.' She stops and laughs. 'Oh dear! My English is still not perfect. I didn't mean it in that way.'

Sure you didn't. I smile at her. 'I know. Please go on.'

'Véronique always says that I am placing too much emphasis on my bust, but I tell her that it is just part of the fun. It's meant to be fun, burlesque, you know? I like it to be quite funny. In my current act, I crawl towards the audience at the end, as if I am a wild animal. I snarl at them like a beast. I think it looks good for the way the breasts hang, yes? Listen – why don't you come and see me? Let us exchange numbers. I will text you when I am performing next.'

Just as our drinks arrive and I'm thinking about taking holy orders, Johnny Fuego reappears, this time in a green lamé suit and black panda eye makeup. He's also wearing a French beret, which I can find no explanation for.

As he strides onto the stage he glances at Anouk and does a pantomime double-take.

'You and me are going to have *words*, missy!' he hisses, which gets another big laugh from the audience. I don't think I've ever been anywhere which has such a great, friendly atmosphere.

As he rips through another five minutes of bawdy patter, I'm suddenly aware of another presence to the left of the stage, standing next to the lighting guy. This is almost certainly a security heavy of some description: grey sharkskin suit, grey shirt, dark blue tie with a wide knot. No earpiece, so I have to assume he's working independently of the guy at the door and whoever else may be on security detail here.

He's well over six foot tall, chunky build, greased-back brown hair, weighs about two hundred and twenty pounds. His eyes are on Johnny Fuego, but he's not laughing. In fact, I fancy he's looking rather disgusted. Maybe Johnny isn't his cup of comedy tea.

I could be mistaken, but I think this guy is probably Miss D'Erotique's personal heavy. Perhaps she's had trouble in the past of whatever type and has someone who drives her to and from gigs and also acts as a bodyguard. He certainly wasn't present during the last two acts. Perhaps he's taking a look around for potential troublemakers. I keep an eye on him while appearing to watch Mr Fuego. His dead, piggy eyes are everywhere and I wonder what or who he's looking for, apart from obsessive fans with an uncontrollable libidinous nature.

Anouk is laughing and has squeezed even closer to me. She still has her hand on my leg. I take a sip of my drink and place a hand on the inside of her thigh, above her stocking top. She doesn't look at me, but crosses her legs, trapping my hand between them. She leans over and whispers in my ear.

'I am going to get a tattoo done tomorrow while I am here. This country is the best next to France and The Netherlands. Would you like to come and hold my hand?'

'What time?'

'My appointment's at midday.'

'What are you going to get done?'

'Just a small one. Two cherries. It is a fertility symbol. They say it resembles the colour of a woman's lips. Others say it represents a woman's lust, or her ability to inspire lust.'

'Where's it going to be?'

'The inside of my thigh. Where your hand is doing all that squeezing right now. I've never had one before. I just felt the time was right. My sister had one last year. I'm always copying her!'

Mr Security takes a slow walk around the venue. Occasionally a brief, wintry smile spreads across his face when he has to squeeze past someone or get out of someone's way. I get the impression that if someone gave him permission to let rip in here with a machine gun it would be the happiest day of his life.

'Where are you going to get it done?' I ask.

'Soho. It is a good place. Highly recommended. We can meet at the shop, if you like.'

I'm just about to ask her the address, when the stage darkens, with only a single spot lighting up Johnny Fuego's panda face.

'And now, ladies and gentlemen, prepare to be dazzled, prepare to be *possessed*, prepare to be eaten up and *brutally* spat out by the enchanting, the alluring, the bewitching, the ravishing, the edible, the succulent, the *wickedly over-ripe…*'

He pauses, to wind up the audience just a little more.

'…the *indecent*, the very, very beautiful, the one and only *Miss Véronique D'Erotique!*'

The applause and cheering is so loud that I can feel the pressure against my eardrums. Johnny exits stage left.

The venue lights dim. Anouk rubs her leg against mine. I can hear the black curtains opening, but can see nothing at all on the stage, which is still in total darkness. Then small points of white light start twinkling, like a miniature storm of fireflies or snowflakes: spiralling, sparkling, appearing, disappearing. I want to put my hand inside them. How are they doing this? Lasers? I decide not to worry and just sit back and enjoy it.

The music starts: two slow, repeated notes on a double bass. It must be the anticipation, but the blackness of the stage, the swirling luminosity of the spooky lights and the two bass notes are already electrifying by themselves.

The stage lighting gradually increases until we see her, sitting on a black velvet chaise longue, looking straight ahead, both hands clasping her right knee, totally immobile. The audience goes wild. It's immediately obvious to me that she's far more ravishing than any of her photographs come close to suggesting. It's as if God's girlfriend has just materialised on the stage.

Her straight black hair is in a short, layered bob, flattering that heart-stopping, heart-shaped face. Compared to the other two acts, she's barely wearing any makeup at all: just a dark red lipstick on those full lips, a thin layer of kohl around her eyelids and a light dusting of copper eye shadow. It's more than she needs.

Everything she wears is black: an underwired lace camisole with shoulder straps and a separate suspender belt, seamed lace stockings and the thinnest of G-strings. I can't see too clearly but I'm guessing those are seven-inch heels. There is also a slim silver collar around her neck with an O ring at the front for all the fetish fans. She acknowledges the audience reaction with a brief flash of humour in those beautiful, big eyes, and then it's gone.

The music develops into a cool, exotic, lazy jazz groove with choppy synth strings. She slowly stretches her arms out, then brings them in hard to the sides of her body, using the balls of her hands to casually caress herself from her hips to her breasts and then back down again. As she does this, she turns her head to the right, bares her teeth, and looks agonised and aroused at the same time.

'What's this music?' I whisper to Anouk.

'It's *Chaque Bouton Lâche* by Lucie Bertillon. Véronique lip-synchs to it. You'll see.'

Back on the stage, Véronique starts to sway in time with the beat. She runs her hands over her breasts and then clasps her fingers behind her neck, tossing her head back, pushing her chest out, licking her lips, biting them, rolling her eyes, slowly grinding herself into the black velvet. It's all for show and yet intimate at the same time: as if you're spying on a woman who isn't aware she's being watched. The small points of white light are still floating around, but now she's being artfully lit from the side and from beneath, giving a tantalising glimpse of her body through the black lace camisole.

Both of her feet are planted firmly on the floor, the heels giving definition to her calf muscles. She spreads her legs wide apart, grasping her thighs from the inside, her shoulders moving sinuously up and down drawing the eyes to her breasts once again. Then she mimes to the sultry French vocal that has begun.

'*Mon cœur est troublé lorsque vous êtes à proximité / Un frisson sur ma peau rend mon corps en feu.*'

She closes her eyes and brings her thighs together, trapping both hands in between them, her body rocking back and forth, her eyes rolling up into her head with the pleasure this motion is giving her. Then she suddenly jerks her head back, teeth clenched, as if in the throes of climax. People start whistling and cheering. Something changes with the music and I can feel the bass notes hammering my chest.

'*Ma peau blanche a besoin de votre caresse / Je veux votre caresse / Ai besoin de votre caresse.*'

The bows on the camisole shoulder straps are untied, agonisingly slowly, one after another. There are no cute or funny glances; no winking at the audience. This is serious and, as a result, far more encitingly erotic.

'*Déshabillez moi / Spoliation moi / Commencez lentement il me brûle.*'

Anouk leans over and whispers in my ear. 'Undress me. Despoil me. Start slowly so it burns me.'

I don't need the translation, but it was enjoyable just the same. She squeezes my leg hard. I hold the back of her neck. She inhales sharply. I have to admit I'm getting overwhelmed. I look for a waitress so I can order some more drinks. I can't see any, but I can see Mr Security again, back near the lighting guy, looking puzzlingly underwhelmed by the whole thing.

Véronique stands and whips the camisole top off in one quick movement, throwing it across the stage. This bit of drama gets big cheers. Unlike the other performers, she isn't using anything to cover her nipples: no tassels, no pasties, but she has applied a little makeup to darken them.

She clasps her fingers behind her neck again, with predictable results on her upper body. She inhales and exhales torturously slowly, making her breasts rise and fall. I can see her stomach muscles tighten and relax. Her eyes are closed; there's a pained expression on her face.

She bares her teeth and snarls as she slowly makes her way to the front of the stage. I flick the collar of my shirt to cool myself down a little. I see Anouk lick her lips.

'*Une pièce à la fois / Tellement lent / Tellement lent / Mon amour.*'

Once again, she slowly caresses herself, stroking her thighs, her hips, her belly and almost, but not quite, her breasts. She turns away momentarily, to give the audience a glimpse of her bottom, which she taps lightly, then she spins around to face them again.

'*Je me sens à vos yeux / Leur regard sauvage.*'

She's right on the edge of the stage now. She gets down on her haunches and nonchalantly unclips all eight suspender straps, her legs wide apart. This must be killing her thigh muscles. The suspender belt is unclipped, yanked off and gets tossed into the audience. I can hear cheers and look behind to see one of the Dusty Springfields holding it up in the air.

She lies on her back, takes her heels off, raises her legs and starts work on her stockings, her movements getting more and more provocative, her back arching, her head rolling slowly from side to side.

'*Je vais voir des bas noirs drapés sur une chaise.*'

Each stocking is pulled down and stretched from her toe to her hand before she releases it. I think this must be quite a skill to master. The white dancing lights have become multi-coloured. A tiny but constant shower of silver glitter falls down from somewhere above the stage. This is like the Cirque du Soleil of burlesque.

Once both stockings are off, she turns over so she's on all fours, stretching and writhing, pushing her bottom back with a slow, grinding rhythm, perhaps to receive an invisible lover. She pants, rolls her eyes and bites her lower lip. She grimaces and squeezes her eyes shut. The stage lights are in tune with her movements, getting more and more frenetic as she gets more and more salacious.

'*Chaque défaite de la sangle / Chaque bouton lâche.*'

Anouk whispers her translation again. 'Each strap undone. Each button loose.'

Véronique gets to her feet once again. The only item she's wearing now is the G-string. Without the heels, I can tell she's petite: maybe a little over five feet. I can't take my eyes off her body: the full, flushed, high breasts, the firm thighs. I can see now that she's covered in some sort of oil or lotion. The glitter falling from the ceiling is sticking to her and a couple of rotating spotlights cause her whole body to sparkle. She hardly moves. She just stands there like some beautiful alien, eyes tightly shut, her arms straight at her sides, her hands bunched into fists, her body goose pimpled and trembling, as if she's lost in some sort of pre-orgasmic rapture. She continues to lip-synch. It's probably the sexiest thing I've ever seen onstage in a nightclub. It may well be the sexiest thing I've seen anywhere.

'*Jusqu'à ce que je suis tout ce qu'il ya / Nue devant vous une fois de plus.*'

Anouk gently places the back of her hand under my chin and closes my mouth. My teeth click together.

'*Déshabillez moi / Spoliation moi / Commencez lentement il me brûle / Une pièce à la fois / Tellement lent / Tellement lent / Mon amour…*'

She opens her eyes and glances down to where I'm sitting. She briefly frowns and her face registers both surprise and alarm. She was expecting to see Rikki. She recovers and turns her back on the audience, walking slowly to the back of the stage, untying her G-string and carelessly, casually, letting it fall to the floor. She returns to the chaise longue and sits where we found her, looking straight ahead, both hands clasping her right knee, totally immobile. The music stops, the stage goes black, the audience goes berserk.

'Oh wow,' says Anouk, clapping furiously. 'She's so utterly fantastic. I love her.'

The lighting goes back to normal and the background jazz comes on again. I'm exhausted. I order some more drinks.

'I've seen burlesque before,' I say. 'But nothing like that.'

She laughs. 'I could tell! It's as if the whole of her show is aimed at you and you alone, isn't it? As if the lyrics of that song are an obscene invitation to you and no one else.'

'Yes. That's exactly it. It was incredible.'

She places a hand on my knee and whispers. 'It's OK. I fancy her, too. Would you like to meet her?'

'Really? Sure. That would be great.'

This is what I want. If I was alone, and Mr Security is her man, he's just going to think I'm some Stage-Door Johnny trying to get into his charge's pants and there'll be hassle. After that type of sexually charged performance, she must get all types wanting a piece of her. There must have been a time when it was murder for a girl just starting out in this field. Perhaps it still is murder.

If I'm with a friend of hers, however, it should be hassle-free.

'We can go backstage,' says Anouk, grinning. 'She knows I'm here and asked me to pop in when she'd finished. We better give her twenty minutes or so. She has to shower and get all the oil off herself. You saw how the glitter stuck to her?'

'Yes I did.'

'It's a new kind of body glitter. When you aim spotlights with a certain type of filter at her body, you get that sparkling effect. You can't see them, but there're also a couple of laser lights aimed at her that enhance the effect. It looks stunning.'

'Have you ever tried it?'

'Only once. I didn't like the oil over my body. I mean, I don't mind oil all over my body under the right circumstances, but I wear a lot of leather onstage and don't want it damaged.'

'I quite understand.'

'Do you?'

A waitress brings our drinks. Anouk smiles at me.

'I'm glad we were able to enjoy that together. I don't like to do things on my own. Not anything. Do you know what I mean? But sometimes I have to.' She finishes half of her Royal Blush and smiles at me. 'Are we going to sleep together tonight?'

'Do you want to?'

'Yes. Do you have somewhere we can go?'

'Yes, I do.'

'It is far away?'

'No. Not too far.'

'Good. I'm staying in a hotel. I prefer not to make love there. The noise, you know?'

She places a hand over mine, smiles, and looks away. I can tell she's blushing. Out of the corner of my eye I can see Mr Security watching us. I'm pretty sure he's got a story to tell and I want to know what it is and how it ends. I catch the attention of our waitress and order some more drinks. I realise that I can't remember what day it is.

15

SO WHAT'S GOING ON?

The backstage corridor is about twenty feet long. There are three doors to the right and two to the left. Mr Security is standing outside the second one the left and I'll bet you anything that's where Véronique D'Erotique has been de-glittering herself.

It's a little like a well-lit narrow art gallery, with each wall displaying framed photographs of many of the burlesque artistes who have performed here: Coco Framboise, Betsy Rose, Missy Lisa, Charlotte Treuse, Polly Rae, Didi Derriere, Gal Friday, Roxi D'Lite – all of them caught in mid performance in various venues around the world and all of them hot as hell. There's a pleasing smell of female sweat and perfume. I watch Anouk's hips sway from side to side. Perhaps I've died and this is one version of heaven.

Mr Security clocks us and turns menacingly in our direction. He looks straight at me, sneers and cracks the bones in his fists. I hate that sound.

Just before he can get heavy and aggressive, the door behind him opens and a diminutive woman in an acid yellow silk robe appears. It's her. Light brown hair. Still beautiful without makeup. Petite but voluptuous. On her feet, fluffy green mules with five-inch heels. She's about to say something to him, but then she sees Anouk.

'Oh, baby – you made it!'

She runs past Mr Security and embraces Anouk tightly, looking over her shoulder and flashing me a quick, quizzical look. She's a woman in need of an explanation, but she's not going to get it yet.

'That was magnificent, Paige, my darling,' gushes Anouk. 'You had them eating out of your hand. I loved it to bits.'

So her name's really Paige.

'Oh, stop it! You think so?' she says. 'Did you see me wobble when I was undoing my suspenders? For a terrible moment I thought I was going to fall backwards!'

'Didn't notice a thing, my love. It was all superb. Had my heart beating so fast. And you were *naked* at the end. I mean *completely* naked. I couldn't believe it. You're so *bold*.' She turns and flutters her fingers at me. 'This is my friend Daniel. I had to close his mouth with my hand! I was so glad the club was a fly-free zone!'

Paige laughs, steps forward and shakes my hand. She has a feather-light touch. 'I'm pleased to meet you, Daniel. Both of you, come in and have something to drink. Anouk and I will try not to talk shop too much.'

'Doesn't bother me.'

'Oh, it will. You wait 'til we get started,' she says.

'What happened to "Always leave something to the imagination"?' laughs Anouk.

'I did leave something to the imagination!' replies Paige. 'And don't quote Tempest Storm at *me*, sweetie.'

I follow both women into the dressing room. I don't look at him, but I can feel Mr Security's eyes on me and they're not very approving. Just before I step through the doorway, he can contain himself no longer and places a brawny hand on my shoulder. I decide to rile him just because I can.

'Hey. No touching until there's a ring on my finger.'

Both Paige and Anouk hear this, turn around and laugh. Mr Security looks crestfallen and furious. He glances quickly at me. If looks could kill I'd be lying on the floor with an axe in my head. Two axes.

'I thought we said no gentlemen in your changing room, Miss McBride.'

The hurt in his voice is killing me, it really is.

Paige McBride's voice suddenly becomes quite terse. 'No, Declan, we *didn't* say that. We said no *unaccompanied* gentlemen in my changing room. That's different. You've been with me long enough to know the difference. This gentleman is a friend of Anouk so that means he's a friend of mine.'

Anouk sticks her tongue out at him and we go inside. Just on a whim, I turn around quickly to face him. He's staring at Paige's back, his face a dark mask of anger and contempt. When he sees I've clocked this he turns away and has a little snigger to himself. Prick.

Her changing room is bigger than I thought it would be. Mainly gold and crimson like the rest of the venue. Down one end is a table covered with large bouquets of flowers, mainly roses, which remain unwrapped and un-vased. There are also quite a few bottles of champagne and other expensive wines. A bottle of absinthe with a picture of Van Gogh on the box. A bottle of Absolut Mango. Can't see any glasses. Three teddy bears, all funfair size. Are all these gifts from admirers? They have to be. I can't imagine that she brings them with her to each gig.

Next to the booze and flower table is a large, empty

costume case and to my left are two hi-tech makeup stations, both with large dressing room mirrors with lightbulbs screwed into the frame, just like in the movies.

On a separate table, two wig stands, one with a blonde wig and one with the black one Paige was wearing onstage, still covered with glitter. There are makeup and hairspray products on every available surface, including a face highlighter called *Watt's Up!* I was expecting there to be a makeup artist or dresser or assistant of some sort, but perhaps she doesn't need one or doesn't think it's worth it.

There's a big red Smeg refrigerator in the corner and a large, monochrome, framed photograph on the wall of a young Yvonne de Carlo holding a 16mm cine-camera. Next to the makeup stations, a large HD television screen and a chess set with an unfinished game on it. There's also a stack of books. The only title I can read without turning my head to the side is a hardback copy of *Les Fleurs du Mal*. Straight ahead is a door which must lead to a bathroom or shower room or whatever it is. Music is playing, but so quietly that I can't identify it.

'Anyone fancy some champers?' says Paige. 'Take a seat. I'll find some glasses. No champagne flutes, I'm afraid. Broke the last one yesterday.'

Anouk and I sit down next to each other on a leopard-skin sofa. Paige opens a cupboard and produces three clear glass tumblers. I watch her as she pulls a magnum of Perrier Jouët out of the fridge, uncorks it and pours us each a glass. The silk robe she's wearing clings to her body contours and I get a sudden flashback of seeing her naked on the stage half an hour ago. In my mind, the actual eroticism of her performance is only just taking over from the shock and awe and I wonder what sort of lover she'd be. She has an appealing wiggle when she walks that I didn't notice when she was onstage.

She sits down on a cherry red sofa across from us and holds her glass up. 'Cheers. Sorry it's only tumblers. Did you see this, Anouk?' She reaches behind the sofa and produces a silver-plated filigree vase. 'It came with this champagne. Limited edition. God knows how much it must have cost.'

'You must have some wealthy admirers,' I say, stupidly.

She smiles at me. Somewhere in that smile was a brief, questioning 'Who the hell are you and where's Rikki?' frown that I couldn't miss.

'That's the funny thing,' she says. 'Usually there's a card with gifts of this sort, but I've been getting these for ages. Months, I mean. Same magnum of the same champagne. It doesn't always come with a bloody silver vase, obviously, but there's never a card with it and no indication as to where it came from. Only happens when I'm in the UK, though. Never abroad. I shouldn't be surprised, really. It does happen from time to time. Shy suitors, married men; you know how it is, Anouk!'

Anouk rolls her eyes.

I take a sip from my tumbler. 'Pert and creamy,' I say, jokingly.

'What a coincidence!' says Paige, laughing. 'That's the title of my autobiography!'

Anouk laughs. 'So are you doing the Sarzana festival this year, baby?'

'No. I was hoping to but the damned agent has me in the States two days before, so I had to give it a miss. Can't do this jet-lagged. Are you doing Berlin?'

'Are you kidding? After last year? I'm never going to

miss that, my love.'

'That hotel!'

'Oh my God! Do you remember Crystal Chanel and Sugar Ramone at that party? I've never seen anything so outrageous. I wish someone had filmed it.'

'Oh, they did, sweetie. I thought you'd have a copy. I'll send you one. So fucking hot.'

'Oh Jesus,' says Anouk, rolling her eyes.

'Oh well that's great. Maybe we can travel together. We'll have to try and work it out.' She turns her attention to me. 'Can I ask you something, Daniel? What did you think of tonight? Don't hold back!'

She's attempting to make normal conversation for Anouk's benefit.

'I thought it was great. I didn't know that you'd be doing that style of strip. It was more like the sort of thing you'd see in Crazy Horse in Paris.'

'Oh, you think so? That's so flattering. Some say that they're not really burlesque, but I beg to differ. Burlesque should have no limitations on what it is and what it can be. It's always been a mélange of whatever's around. What Crazy Horse do feeds into burlesque and vice versa. Dita Von Teese has performed there, but I haven't. Not yet. You've been to *Le Crazy*?'

'Yes. Well, twice, actually. A few years ago now.'

'Wow. So you're a connoisseur.'

'Well, I wouldn't go that far. But seriously, it was riveting and very, very sexy. With all due respect to the other acts, I could see why you were top of the bill.'

She turns to Anouk and laughs. 'I like him!'

'Do you think Anja would mind me popping in for a quick chat?' says Anouk. She turns to me to explain. 'Anja is Strawberry Sapphire. Anja Stipanov. She's Croatian.

The one whose boobs you were staring at.'

'Of course not,' says Paige. 'She'd be delighted to see you. I don't think I told her you'd be here tonight. Or maybe I did. I can't remember.'

'OK. I won't be long. I haven't seen her for almost a year.'

Anouk places her empty glass on the floor, leans over and kisses me on the cheek and heads out. I can see Declan taking a quick, suspicious glance inside to see that all is well. Paige takes a couple of speedy sips of her champagne and stares at me. Her robe has fallen open slightly and I can see the side of one of her breasts. She smells of Tom Ford Neroli Portofino shower gel and Acqua de Parma shampoo.

'OK, handsome. So what's going on?'

'Which part interests you?'

'Well, first of all, what's going on with Anouk? She's a good friend of mine and she's been messed around by some pretty mean guys in the past. I don't want her to…'

'I met her this evening for the first time. I bought her a drink. She asked to sit next to me. That's it.'

'Hm. You were sitting in a reserved seat for a friend of mine. How did you get the ticket? I sent that ticket personally.'

'My name's Daniel Beckett. I'm a private investigator. I've been hired to find Rikki Tuan. He's been missing for three days and there is concern about him. I went to his flat, I looked through his stuff, I opened his mail. I found the ticket. He was obviously a burlesque fan, but you seemed special. He'd circled several gigs on the Burlesque Map of London and you were common to all of them, as well as some other artistes. There was a photograph of you in a *shibari* breast harness on his computer that I couldn't find anywhere online. When I identified you and then found the ticket it seemed the obvious thing to contact you. I have no other leads. That's why I'm here. We need to have a talk.'

I watch her face as this sinks in. Her expression changes from scornful to frightened and concerned. 'What's happened to him? Is he alright?'

I think of the dead girl in his flat. That still doesn't make sense. 'I have no idea,' I say. 'But I only started on this case this morning and so far it looks as if he's disappeared into thin air.'

'But will you find him?'

'Yes.'

'Who hired you?'

'I can't tell you that. Is there somewhere we can go tonight? When you've finished here, I mean?'

She exhales slowly and refills my tumbler and hers with champagne. 'I can't do this tonight. Obviously I want to help you, but we have a party for everyone involved in our residency here. Well, not a party, precisely: we're just going to a club. It's one of the lighting guys. It's his birthday. It's important that I go. I'm the most famous, I suppose. I can't let everybody down. They're…'

'Don't worry. Tomorrow will be fine. What are you doing for lunch?'

'I can book a table at The Dorchester. I'm a regular. Would one o' clock be alright with you?'

'That'll be fine. I'll meet you in the bar.'

She looks downwards and smiles to herself. 'Are you going to be having sex with Anouk tonight?'

'Yes.'

'Does she know about this?'

'Yes, she does. Why? Are you going to give me some tips?'

This makes her laugh. I realise that I quite like looking at her. It's difficult not to let those big doe eyes and enticing lips overwhelm you.

'Tips? Oh my God! No, it isn't that. I was going to ask her to come with us tonight, but maybe it's better she doesn't know about it if she's going to be with you. I wouldn't want to spoil her fun. Or yours.'

'That's very kind of you.'

'You're welcome. And be nice to her.'

'I'll do my best.'

'She's…'

Anouk comes back in and the abrupt silence tells her everything. She does mock outrage as she points at Paige. 'What has that bitch been telling you?'

'I've told him everything, darling. Unfortunately, it just encouraged him.'

16

THAT TOUCH OF INK

The tattoo parlour is called That Touch of Ink. I'd somehow imagined it would be small and poky. Actually, it's as big as a large shop and just as brightly lit. I hold Anouk's hand as she lies on her side having her cherries done by a very attractive woman in her forties who's covered in them. Tattoos, not cherries. Her name is Brionna and she has a hot cleavage. I don't think Anouk had anticipated that the pain would be this continuous and intense, and tears are running down her face, though she isn't sobbing. I can tell her heart rate is up from the pulse in her hand.

'It's the inside of the thigh,' says Brionna to me in between buzzes. 'It's a very sensitive spot for a tattoo. A very sensitive spot for lots of things.'

I meet her gaze and smile. 'So I've heard.'

I'll be coming back here to hit on her when all this is over.

I decide to do a bit of work while I'm waiting. 'Paige seemed very nice,' I say to Anouk. 'Do all the girls have minders like that guy or is it just her?'

'Oh, lots of them do. It all depends. It depends on the sort of venues you're working and how big a star you are. There are lots of factors. It depends on the countries that you work in. Anja has one when she's in Europe, but it's too much hassle to sort one out when she's over here.

'Dawn – that's Kitty from last night – has a driver who picks her up from gigs, but doesn't have what you'd call a minder. Paige used to have another guy who was kind of dishy. I don't know what happened to him. They move on, you know?'

'She seemed to be OK when I met her last night,' I say. 'Very quick and bright. I remember you said that she'd had some problems…'

She looks puzzled for a moment. 'Oh, *that*. Well, as I said, it's only hearsay. Gossip. Ow!'

'Sorry,' says Brionna. I find I'm looking at her all the time. She's wearing green sawn-off jeans with black fishnet tights, Liberty print trainers and an outsize Lemongrab t-shirt. I'm wondering what sort of lingerie she's wearing. That's definitively a push-up bra she's got on and it's pretty sexy that she likes wearing one. I realise that I'd like to take it off, or under other circumstances, leave it on.

'I feel a little faint. Can I have a glass of water, please?' says Anouk.

'Of course,' says Brionna. 'Have a break.'

I take a look at her thigh. The outline is done and all that's left is the colouring of the cherries themselves. There's blood streaming down her leg, but I don't think things are as bad as they look. It's only now that I notice the music playing quietly in the background; it's *Art Star* by Yeah Yeah Yeahs.

'That was fantastic last night. I had such a good time,' says Anouk, running a hand through her hair.

'I know.'

Her lips purse in a petulant moue. 'Do you want to see me again, Daniel? You don't have to if you don't want to.'

'Are you kidding? I'll give you a call later on today. Maybe we can go somewhere tonight. Or tomorrow night. My work hours are unpredictable, but I'll definitely be in touch. I've got your number. Where are you staying?'

'The Corinthia in Whitehall Place. Room thirty.'

'Got it. Listen. Will you be OK now? I have to go to a business meeting which I can't be late for.'

'Sure. Of course. And thank you for staying with me. You didn't tell me what it was that you did.'

'Didn't I? I'm a private investigator.'

Brionna comes back with a glass of water for Anouk. She overheard. She takes an appreciative look at me. 'A private investigator? Really?'

'Yes.'

'Well if this isn't the fuckin' bomb I don't know what is. I'm working in a tattoo parlour in Soho. I'm tattooing a burlesque dancer and she's here with her lover who's a private detective. It doesn't get much better than this. Shit the fuck!'

Shit the fuck! Never heard that one before. I must see if I can work it into a conversation sometime.

*

When I walk into the bar at The Dorchester I can't see Paige anywhere and I wonder if she's stood me up. There're two businessmen in suits talking about football, a couple in their fifties touching each other like they've just started an affair, two Japanese women both wearing some sort of uniform and a solitary, bespectacled woman in a grey Ponte dress and black trim jacket sitting on a bar stool talking to the barman.

I take a quick look at the seating area and then it hits me. I walk up to the bar and touch her gently on the arm.

'I didn't recognise you. You look…'

'Dull and boring?'

'Like a businesswoman.'

'What did you expect? A lacy corset, glittery platform heels and a couple of pink feather fans?'

'Yes.'

"Sorry to disappoint.'

'The glasses suit you.'

'Stop it.'

'I'm not kidding.'

She's wearing light, rimless, oblong frames which suit her heart-shaped face and the lenses are blue-tinted and just dark enough to obscure her eyes a little. Her light brown hair is tied back and twisted into a bun at the nape of her neck. I'm wondering why the conventional clothing she's wearing has an erotic edge and realise it's because I know exactly what's underneath. Well, almost exactly.

'What's that you're drinking? Would you like another?'

'Yes please. It's a Rosemary Mule.'

I order a Vesper for myself and suggest we sit at one of the tables while the cocktails are being made. I want to get her away from the bar and people. Before she sits, she wipes her chair with a couple of rapid hand strokes, though it looked perfectly clean to me.

She sits up straight, crosses her legs and looks straight at me. I feel like I'm at a job interview. It's a little unnerving. She raises an eyebrow.

'So how did last night go?' she says.

'Had its ups and downs.'

'Very good. Anouk's a lovely girl. Did she tell you she

used to be married?'

I shake my head. 'We didn't get round to personal stuff.'

'The guy was a total thug. You can't see it now, but he broke her nose. Thought it was great to get married to a sexy burlesque dancer, but the idea of other men watching her strip enraged him.'

'There're a lot of dopes about.'

She frowns slightly. I can tell she's hurting but I don't know why. 'Tell me about it,' she says.

'I went with her to get a tattoo done this morning. Her first. Needed someone to hold her hand.'

'What did she get?'

'A couple of cherries.'

'Where?'

'Inside of the thigh.'

'Cherries are a very sexual fruit.'

'So I've heard.'

A waiter places our drinks in front of us. Paige gets a nice smile from him. They like her here. I wonder if they know who she is. I suspect they do. She lifts the glass to her lips.

'So what did you want to ask me?'

I watch her sip from her glass. Her eyes roll with pleasure as the alcohol hits. I don't want to push too hard. She's a little prickly and defensive. I'll pretend I don't know about Rikki's drug sideline and see if she brings it up. It's only a theory, but matched with what Anouk told me it may be something. It may also be nothing. That's part of the fun of detective work; the crippling uncertainty.

'How did you know Rikki Tuan?'

'That's easy. Philip Hopwood is a friend of mine. He's

a costume designer, headgear in particular. He knew Rikki. They're friends. He introduced us. I think Rikki had dinner parties at his flat sometimes. Someone took Philip along to one of them and they hit it off right away, if you get my drift.'

'When was the last time you saw him?'

'Rikki? Last month. The thirtieth. That's a little over three weeks ago. I was performing at The Electric Carousel. Piccadilly. It's a lovely little club with a great atmosphere. Not just burlesque, though that's the main thing. Comedians, magicians, some circus acts. They had a Serbian girl from the Cirque du Soleil on that night. Very attractive. Very serious. A body like an athlete.'

'Did he come backstage? Did you talk to him?'

'Not backstage, no. None of the acts like it. As you saw, I made an exception for Anouk last night. And you. I always make an exception for other artistes and their paramours. But that doesn't happen often. If you let one in you have to let them all in. We have to have our safe space. In places like the Carousel, you can come and hang out at the bar after you've been on. You don't get hassle like you do in some clubs. The artistes can mix with the punters and it's cool, you know? I would never have come out and hung around the bar last night at Bordello. It just isn't that sort of place. Don't ask me why. Everywhere's different. Everywhere has a different vibe.'

Here we go. 'OK, Paige. Why did Philip Hopwood introduce Rikki to you?'

'He – ah – he was just a big fan of burlesque, that's all. Philip thought it would be a buzz for him to be introduced to one of the artistes.'

'And when was this?'

'I can't remember the exact date. Two and half

months ago? Ten to twelve weeks? Something like that.'

'And Rikki came to see you perform a lot of times after that.'

'As I said, he was a big fan of burlesque.'

'But in particular, he was a big fan of you.'

'I guess so, yes. Look – what's all this about? How can any of this help find him if he's gone missing?' She looks over her shoulder as if she's expecting someone. I don't think she's expecting anyone.

'Did you see Rikki socially in any way? Quite apart from hanging out in the bar after gigs, that is.'

'No. Not really. There were a couple of parties he came to with me. Sometimes one of the girls might have had a bash for some reason and I invited Rikki along as I knew he'd like it.'

'OK. So what was it about Rikki you liked so much? From here, it looks like he suddenly became your number one fan and new best pal for no apparent reason.' I take a sip of my Vesper and watch her face carefully.

'He was a funny guy. All my friends liked him. The other girls liked him, too. He really gets on well with Twinkle von Tassel, for example. They have the same sense of humour.'

'When you saw me sitting in his seat last night, you looked alarmed. Not just surprised or baffled – alarmed.'

'I like it when he's in the audience. I was disappointed that he hadn't shown.'

'Take your glasses off.'

She looks perplexed, but I know she's faking. 'Are you going to tell me I'm beautiful without my glasses on?'

'I already know you're beautiful. I want to see your eyes. Take them off.'

She takes a sip of her cocktail, removes her blue-tinted

glasses and places them on the table. Her expression is composed and defiant. Her pupils are like pin-pricks.

'I'm not the police, Paige. But I'm just trying to get a picture of what's been going on. What are you taking? Opium? Diamorphine? Oxycodone?'

She hesitates for a moment, perhaps deciding whether to walk out of here or not. 'I'm not addicted, but I would say I was partially dependent, not that it's any of your business. Yes, it's heroin. I can function and it's not making me sick. Not yet. And it never will.'

I've heard that one before. 'So it's still something that you save for a special occasion; for when you want to treat yourself to a little oblivion.'

'That's about right. I know how to control it. Like everyone else, I have my ups and downs. I mean, for example, I was going through a bit of a bad patch in my personal life three or four months ago, but you get over these things.' She puts her glasses back on, tapping the bridge with her middle finger.

'OK. That's fine. So Rikki was meant to turn up with some stuff for you last night. Are you running low?'

'Not seriously, but Rikki said that he was going to be a bit taken up with business this month – more responsibility or something – so he'd get me a little stock now in case he couldn't manage it later. That's what he was like. He was a caring, nice guy. The reason I was a little alarmed when I saw you was…'

'What?'

'Rikki was an OK guy. He knew I didn't like injecting myself – it's always freaked me out a little and I've never got over it – so if he was available, he would inject me. He said it was an honour. He didn't want anything other than to be a part of my world.'

'So he would have gone to that party last night.'

'Yes. And then we'd have gone back to my place and he'd have injected me and we'd have chilled out together. Maybe watched a movie or turned the sound off and played some music. That's all that would have happened. You know he was gay, don't you?'

'Yes I do. Did he tread on anyone's toes, supplying you? Was there another dealer he took over from? Someone who might have resented it?'

'I'm not some major consumer, Mr Beckett. I have it when I need it. I take very small doses. I like the warmth and well-being. It doesn't affect my performances and I'm always straight when I'm onstage. What you see in my eyes was a hangover from last night. I had a little taste when I got home from the club last night.

'I had contacts with friends and colleagues who could get it for me if I asked. I had no idea where they got it from and sometimes they couldn't get it again. That was fine by me. I didn't get withdrawal and I liked the fact that there was a middleman between me and the supplier.'

She pats her hair lightly and finishes her Rosemary Mule.

'So there was, as far as you knew, no dealer who was aware of you as the end-user.'

'As far as I know, Mr Beckett, no.'

'And Rikki didn't mention anything to you that concerned his ability to get hold of diamorphine: where he got it from and so on.'

'He never mentioned it.'

'And he didn't charge you for it.'

'Not once, no.'

She's getting annoyed now. She's trying to disguise it, but I can feel it in her voice.

185

'OK. I was just wondering if giving it to you for free was maybe undercutting another dealer, that's all. He might have made an enemy. It was a shot in the dark. I'm not judging you.'

'Don't worry, Mr Beckett. If I thought for a second you were judging me, I'd have asked you to leave.'

The waiter who served us our drinks approaches to tell Paige that her table for lunch is ready. I may be wrong, but I feel the atmosphere has got a little chilly.

17

LUNCH AT THE DORCHESTER

She asks the waitress to bring us a bottle of 2015 Jurançon Sec while we take a look at today's menu.

'I'm sorry,' she says, smiling. 'I just ordered that without thinking. It's what I always have when I have lunch here. If you want to…'

'That's fine by me. I've never had it before. Is it good?'

'I've heard that wine people call it *nervy*.'

'I was hoping it would be pert and juicy.'

She smiles. 'Another title for my autobiography.'

'I can't wait to read this autobiography.'

'You'll have a long wait.'

'Will I be in it?'

'I hope not.'

She orders the lobster and asparagus and I have seared duck breast and Swiss chard. Once the waitress leaves, she puts her elbows on the table and crosses her fingers beneath her chin.

'So aren't you going to ask me?' she says, raising her eyebrows and tilting her head to the side.

'I'm not sure. I don't think we know each other well enough yet. Give it a few more months.'

She looks amused and purses her lips. 'Most people who know about my habit – and I'm trusting you to keep it a secret – always ask me why I'm doing it. Why a nice girl like me etc. etc. etc.'

'Everyone's different. I guess if you didn't do it, you wouldn't be you. You look good. It's not affecting you physically or mentally as far as I can make out, and you seem to know what you're doing.'

She doesn't say anything. The waitress arrives with the wine. She pours a small amount into a glass for me to taste, but I indicate she should give it to Paige, who takes a sip and nods her head. I look at Paige's face as our glasses are filled. I decide I'm going to break through all her barriers, however many there are.

'I'm curious,' I say, putting the Class A chat on the back burner. 'Do you work out? I imagine you have to maintain a certain level of fitness to do what you do, like any dancer.'

'I have a personal trainer. I go to the gym four times a week when I can. One of those sessions is an hour-long swim. What about you? I'm sure you must get into situations where you have to be fit from time to time.'

'Yeah. Looking at stuff on the computer, being condescending to the police. Thinking. It all takes it out of you. I have a gym membership and get there whenever. I prefer early mornings. If I can't do early mornings, I tend not to bother.'

'It's the same for me. It can be a bit of a chore. It's as if your body and brain don't realise what's going on if you do it early in the day, so you can get it out of the way relatively painlessly. I don't mind the discomfort, though. I used to…'

The food arrives, so we stop talking for a few minutes. I pour some more wine into her glass. She's a little more relaxed now. I watch her eat: small, neat, controlled, economical movements. There's something about her that's really very appealing, quite apart from being the vamp I saw at Bordello last night.

'Sorry. You were saying? About not minding the discomfort?'

'Oh yes. I trained at The Central School of Ballet. I'm sure you've heard how tough ballet training can be. I did the honours degree in Professional Dance and Performance.'

'Ballet. Yes. I can imagine it.'

She grins. 'Hm. Well. I was a late developer. Got a little too busty when I was nineteen. Always a bit of a hindrance for prima ballerinas and I didn't like being strapped down.'

'That's not what I've heard.'

She tilts her head to the side. 'Ha, ha.'

'I think you've found your niche.'

'I think so, too. I love what I do.' She grins. 'I hate it when people say that, don't you? But, yes. There are so many possibilities. Ballet has room for change and experimentation, but it's innately conservative. It has to be. With burlesque, you can make whatever you happen to think up become reality. Well, a sort of reality, anyway.' She chews for a while. 'What do you think has happened to Rikki? It's only while talking about him with you that I realised that I didn't know that much about him. He kind of blasted you with his wit and charm. I suppose he was quite superficial in a way. It made ordinary questions seem a tad redundant. He was someone I either saw at gigs or someone who I was – well, you know. Is he a drug dealer?'

'No. He isn't a drug dealer.'

'But you know what he was.'

'Yes.'

'And you're not going to tell me.'

I take a deep breath. 'It makes it awkward for me, because if I told you, you'd begin to suspect who my client was.'

'And that would not be a good thing?'

'I think the less you know the better.'

She takes a big gulp of wine and frowns. 'Am I in danger?'

'Not as far as I know. If I thought you were, I'd do something about it.'

'How's your Jurançon Sec?'

'Nervy.'

'Told you. Do you think Rikki's in danger?'

'I don't know. If he is, I'd be interested to meet the perpetrators.'

'Will *you* be in danger?'

'Do you care?'

'I don't know.'

Perhaps it's just wishful thinking. Perhaps I'm hoping that talking to this woman won't be a dead end in this investigation. Despite what she's told me, I get a feeling in the pit of my stomach that she's pivotal to all of this, but I can't work out why.

It may be because I have a thing about thuggish private security staff, but I didn't like her minder; his presence and attitude unsettled me. Why was that? He was overzealous, for one thing. He was obnoxious and aggressive when he should have been friendly and firm. It's not as if he was guarding Beyoncé in the wake of several recent brutal kidnap attempts. He put a hand on my shoulder *after* Paige had invited me into her dressing room: bad manners and very unprofessional. I got the feeling that what *he* wanted to do was more important than anything *she* might have wanted. I also got the impression that he didn't care for her that much.

I realise I'm looking at her. We hold each other's gaze for a few seconds, then she shrugs and pours the remainder of the wine into our glasses.

I was rather hoping that the drug thing might have been the key, but it looks like that's not the case. Even the most hardened drug dealers wouldn't give a toss about someone like Rikki slinging the occasional free bit of gear to someone like Paige. They probably wouldn't ever know about it. If he was a business rival in the drug trade it would be something else, but you're not in any sort of business if you're giving stuff away to friends. And even if these mythological drug dealers did take umbrage, they'd soon realise that they'd bitten off more than they could chew, particularly if it was the skin from their faces.

I can't square Paige's take on Rikki with what Caroline told me about his MO. It's as if he's two different people. Superficial and witty. Narcissistic and violent. He's obviously a multi-faceted guy. I wonder if I'll ever meet him. I wonder if I want to.

There's a voice at the back of my head nagging me about something that Paige said in the bar. Something that my brain is attempting to link to everything else. I close my eyes to let it fall into place.

'Are you alright?'

'Hold on. I'm in The Zone.'

'I should have known.'

I can hear the waitress taking our plates away. I can tell she's looking at me. I open my eyes and catch Paige giving me an appreciative once-over. She looks away quickly, but she knows she's been caught. I innocently raise my eyebrows at her. She laughs.

'Oh, fuck *off*.'

'When we were in the bar, you said you went through a bad patch in your personal life about three or four months ago.'

'That's right. Would you like to order coffee or shall we get another bottle?'

'Another bottle will be fine by me.'

'Oh, sorry. I didn't think. Would you like a dessert? It's just that I never eat dessert. Rarely, anyway. I have had them here, though. They do a lovely vanilla millefeuille and a dizzying chocolate fondant.'

'Wine will be fine.'

She calls back the waitress and gives her the order. She turns to face me again. She's impatient and purses her lips.

'It was nothing. It was just boyfriend trouble. Can we talk about something else, please?'

There's a knot here and I'm going to attempt to untie it.

'Have you ever told anyone about it?'

'I don't like talking about personal things like that. And I can't see…'

Our second bottle of wine arrives. I pour us both a glass. I quite like this stuff. I take a drink and just stare at her. I have to drag this out of her, whatever it is. I don't know why, but I have a hunch about it. Perhaps a third bottle of wine might help.

'OK. I'm sorry. Let's talk about me instead. Far more interesting.'

She smiles at me. I don't say anything. I stare at her with an expression in my eyes which I hope is transmitting sympathy, trustworthiness and understanding, as opposed to cunning, manipulation and cynicism. It works as it always does. She fiddles with the stem of her wine glass.

'It was one of those times when having my, er, habit came in useful, you know?'

'This was before you came across Rikki, yes?'

'Yes, it was. It's just a funny thing. It was a funny thing for me, I mean. I was only with this guy for about a month, but I was absolutely besotted, which is un…' She stops momentarily, purses her lips and takes a deep breath. 'Which is unusual for me.'

'It happens. When was this?'

'The middle of April. The seventeenth. Almost exactly four months ago, give or take a few days. I'm not much good with remembering dates, but I remember this one. I put a little asterisk on my kitchen calendar after our first date. I just had a feeling about it. About this guy, I mean. Something told me it would be special.'

'And was it?'

'Yes it was. At least I thought so, anyway. As I said, we were only together for a month, but when he…'

Tears fill her eyes and she just about manages to curtail a sob. She hurriedly digs around in her brown leather tote bag and pulls out some paper tissues. She takes her glasses off and gently presses the tissues against her eyes until it's all over. She's shaking. She takes a big slug of wine. By the look of things, I can't blame her. She nods her head and manages a bitter laugh.

'Can you see why I don't like talking about it? I'm sorry.'

'Don't worry.'

'I'm OK now. I think it was traumatic because it was so sudden. There was nothing leading up to it, you know? No clues that something was wrong between us. Or maybe there were clues and I was too dumb to spot them. It can happen. I'm sure you've had girls dump you for no apparent reason.'

'Never. I always insisted on a comprehensive letter explaining everything, or an hour-long voicemail at the very least.'

She laughs. Good.

'It used to happen to me when I was a teenager, but as I got older I flattered myself that I could spot the signs,' she says. 'Why am I telling you this?'

'You're trying to ruin my lunch.'

'I knew there was some important reason.'

'What did he do?'

'For a living, you mean? This is bound to sound corny, but he was a boxer. You may have heard of him. Jamie Baldwin?'

I'm not a fight fan but I know the name and vaguely remember him. A light heavyweight. Blond hair. A Geordie. Did the Olympics a few years back.

'Wasn't he in the Beijing Olympics?'

'That's right. He got a silver medal. He retired from professional boxing a few years ago and opened his own club. It's doing really well. He's a talented trainer. A lot of his pupils are going to be pretty big, he reckons.'

'Well how about that. Wasn't he from Newcastle or somewhere like that?'

'Close. He was from Washington.'

'How did you meet?'

'Well. It was a bit convoluted. It's due to my agent, really. Like the other girls, I do charity appearances from time to time. Spreads the word, gets exposure and we get to pick which charity we'd like to do things for. Well, most of the time, anyway. One of the charities was affiliated to a thing called Charity Box Challenge, where they train inexperienced people to box and they put on a boxing match to raise money for various charities. They train them for about two months, I think. Jamie was one of the trainers.'

'A silver Olympic medallist. He must have been quite a catch for them.'

'He was. Anyway, my agent wanted to go and see the final event and she dragged me and April Paquerette along with her as there was a party afterwards for all the charity people and she didn't want to go on her own. That's where I met him.'

'So you were inseparable after that night.'

'Yes.'

'So what happened? You don't have to tell me if you don't want to.'

But I'll be pissed if you don't.

She pours us out the rest of the wine. 'He just rang me up. We were meant to be going out to dinner the next night. It was my birthday. As soon as I heard his voice I assumed something had come up and he wouldn't be able to make it and we'd have to cancel. We were going to Oka. Do you know it?'

'The Japanese place off Regent Street. Yes. It's good. Excellent uramaki.'

Tears fill her eyes again. 'We had a table booked for eight-thirty. He just said he had some bad news. He'd been thinking really long and hard about our relationship and felt it couldn't continue. He said it was because of a previous girlfriend that he couldn't get out of his head. He'd split up with her a few months before he met me but realised he was still in love with her. He said he knew it was fucked up, but every time he was with me he felt as if he was being unfaithful to her.'

More tears. I take her hand over the table and squeeze it. She squeezes back. Now I need a little bit more.

'Had he mentioned this girl before?'

She sniffs. 'That's the funny thing. It was a complete surprise to me. We'd told each other about our respective exes, but this…'

She stops to mop her eyes again. I indicate to the waitress that we'd like two coffees.

'This was news to you,' I say. 'You didn't know about this one.'

'No. I thought perhaps he hadn't mentioned her because it was too painful for him. Something like that. We talked for a little while longer. I tried to get under his skin, to see if we could work it out in some way, but he was adamant. He said it wouldn't be fair to either of us if this continued. He said it was definitely over and I wasn't to get in touch with him again.'

'How did he sound? What was his voice like?'

'He sounded as close to tears as I was.'

I can't think of a good way to put my next question. Oh well.

'Do you think he was making it up?'

'What do you mean?'

'That the story about the girl was fiction? That there was some other reason he had for finishing it? It just seems strange that this was someone you didn't know about. Not impossible, but strange. I know you only knew him for a matter of weeks, but did he strike you as someone who would keep something like this locked away?'

'You can never really know people, can you? But having said that: no. This was totally out of character. Is that what you're looking for?'

'It might be.'

'He never seemed distracted when we were together, you know? I'm not dumb. I can always tell when a guy is two-timing me or thinking about someone else.'

I close my eyes as the coffees arrive. There are a couple of things that immediately come to mind. If Jamie still had mixed feelings about Paige, could he have been behind Rikki's disappearance? Was this some messed-up jealous rage thing?

Rikki was a tough guy, I have no doubt about that, but most people would come off second best in a surprise tussle with a light heavyweight silver medallist boxer, especially if that boxer was emotionally motivated and perhaps a little out of control. Jamie Baldwin did a lot of media when his star was in the ascendant. I have a vague memory of him being a bit of a jack-the-lad when he was younger. Some sort of police trouble. I'll have to look it up when I get a chance.

'How soon after this happened did you meet Rikki?'

'I don't know. Maybe two or three weeks later.'

'Is there any way on earth that Jamie could have known about Rikki?'

'No. I mean; I don't think so. Were you in The Zone again there for a minute?'

'Occupational hazard. You must pop in some time. It's crazy. Did Jamie have a temper?'

'A temper? No. He was a very peaceable type. Apart from when he was in the ring, of course. Even then he was very controlled. I've seen films of him when he was fully professional. He had, I suppose, what you might call a scientific approach. Never any anger. Just sizing up the opponent and doing what had to be done to win.'

I think about Anouk and her green-eyed asshole husband. 'Jealous? Did he get angry when other guys spoke to you? Did he dislike guys ogling you when you performed? I'm assuming he saw some of your gigs.'

'Yes he did and he loved them. He said he felt really lucky when he saw the reaction of the audience to my performances. He was proud of me, he said. He liked it that I was his.'

I watch as she drops two brown sugar lumps into her coffee and stirs. She absentmindedly runs a hand through her bun, allowing the hair to fall to her shoulders. She shakes her head from side to side. I treat myself to a little increase in heart rate.

'Are you coming on to me?' I say.

'Oh yeah. Obvs. I'm really in the bloody mood for that.'

'I can always tell.'

I feel sorry for her. She's obviously had her heart broken by this. What it sounds like, *feels* like, is that Jamie Baldwin had some other reason for dumping her and it had nothing to do with him carrying a torch for some ex. It's probably immaterial, but I'm going to have to speak to him. I attract the attention of the waitress and ask for the bill.

'I'll get this,' I say to her. 'I can get it on expenses.'

I don't tell her who'll ultimately be picking up the tab. She has enough on her plate already. She takes her glasses off and pops them in the top pocket of her jacket.

'It's the first time I've told anyone about this,' she says. 'Needless to say, it caused me to treat myself to a little more oblivion than I usually enjoyed. That's why I felt so lucky to find Rikki. Philip Hopwood, the guy who introduced me to Rikki, he knew all about it. He's a darling. He was worried about me. I think he was afraid I'd get hold of any old junk and something would happen, you know? Rikki had access to really good stuff; really pure. I'd never had anything near as good.'

'How can I get in touch with Jamie Baldwin?'

She looks like she's been slapped. 'No. No please don't talk to him. I…'

'I won't mention a single thing that you have told me. Listen. There may be no connection here at all, but I have to follow it through as it's all I've got.' I take a sip of coffee as I hand the waitress my credit card. 'You have a boyfriend who unexpectedly ends your relationship in a way that you find disquieting. Well, it's had the same effect on me. Then you hook up with Rikki Tuan. Not a boyfriend, but a friend all the same. A friend of sorts, anyway. He disappears into thin air. My client tells me that this is wholly out of character. Now either you're very unlucky with the males in your life or those two events are in some way connected. As I said, it might be nothing, but I've…'

She rummages in her tote bag and produces a small black business card wallet. She takes out half a dozen red and white cards which all look identical. She laughs and sniffs.

'How many would you like?'

'One will be fine.'

I take a look: Olympic Boxing Club, 439 – 443 Goldhawk Road, London W12 4AA. Telephone: 020 8522 2121. I put it in my wallet. That would make the nearest tube station Shepherd's Bush.

We make our way out to the foyer.

'Where are you going now, Paige?'

'After three cocktails and two bottles of wine? I'm

going home for a sleep, darling. I'm working tonight.'

She's close enough so I can smell the alcohol on her breath. Mixed with her perfume it's a deadly combination. I want to grab her and kiss her. Thank God I'm a professional.

'I may have to speak to you again, if that's OK.'

'Of course. Oh. I should have given you this in there.' She hands me her business card. I was expecting something in leopard-skin, but it's monochrome, smart and professional. I hand her mine. She pings it with her fingers to see if it makes a noise. It doesn't.

'I'm sorry I lost it in there,' she says, apologetically. 'Well, a couple of times, really. I've been supressing it all or just getting…well – you know.'

'Forget it.'

'I've been working hard to try and get it all out of my mind, but sometimes…'

She bursts into tears. Proper crying this time. Well, maybe she needs to let it all out. She's a bit pissed as well. I don't try to comfort her or invade her space; I just wait for it to finish. The reception staff are discreet, used to minding their own business. Unfortunately, the same can't be said of the two heavily tanned besuited fuckwits who've just spotted a damsel in distress and a hot one at that.

They give me a quick, disdainful up and down, assuming I'm the cause of her anguish. They are going to sort things out.

'Come on now, pretty lady,' says the porkier of the two. 'What's all this about. Has this idiot been making you cry?'

The less porky one pokes me in the chest. He has one more poke to go. No: two. I'm in a good mood. 'Why don't you pick on someone your own size?' he says to me. I don't respond. I hate things like this. The porky one tries to put his arm around Paige's shoulders to comfort her. Paige recoils and moves closer to me. They've both been drinking: not excessively, just enough to make them think this is *OK behaviour.*

'Are you fucking dumb as well as stupid?' says the less porky one, poking me in the chest a second time. The guy at reception is looking up now. He nods at his assistant. The assistant, who's a little burlier than his boss, comes out from behind the desk and walks over to us.

'Is there a problem, gentlemen?' he says to the less porky one.

'No problem, friend,' says less porky. 'Just trying to find out what *this…*'

He starts to poke me in the chest a third time. A centimetre before he makes contact, I catch his index finger in between my middle and ring fingers and press down hard, just below the second joint. He's on his knees with the pain. I don't think anyone saw what happened.

'Too much to drink,' I say to the receptionist, who nods sagely. I touch Paige's arm and lead her out into the street.

'You're a bastard,' she says, once we're outside.

'Yeah.'

18

THE BOXER

I get out of Shepherd's Bush underground station, cross over Uxbridge Road and walk across the common. It's still lunchtime, it's sunny, and there are a large number of office workers sitting on benches, eating sandwiches and smoking, sometimes simultaneously. A small dog barks at me as I walk by and its owner scolds it.

I had considered giving Jamie Baldwin a call before I got here, but a preliminary call often gives a person that chance to say 'no', so I didn't bother. Experience has told me that people are more likely to talk to you if you just turn up in person. If you give them a warning you invariably get a rejection just because they can.

I've tried to keep my mind free of how I'm going to approach this. It's going to be awkward, that's for sure, as my only viable line of questioning concerns the reason he dumped Paige, and the reason I want the information is because it might help me help someone else. Maybe he genuinely dumped her. Maybe that story about the ex was true, but it doesn't feel right. I can't imagine how this is going to go, or even if it'll be of any use. I seem to be getting further and further away from Rikki Tuan.

This part of Goldhawk Road is trashy, colourful, cool and noisy, smells of takeaway food and is filled with off-licences, betting shops, eating places and a conspicuously large number of textile and fabric merchants. There's a predominant smell of cooking fat mixed in with burning tar from where they're fixing the road. Just like in the West End, there's scaffolding crawling up a lot of the buildings. Perhaps scaffolding is the smart business to be in.

By the time I get to the Olympic Boxing Club I've counted off five pawnbrokers. I stand outside for a moment and take a look at it. Looks new with no signs of being run down. Big, too, and it seems like the main building might once have been a church.

There's an internet café across the road, next door to a smart-looking African cuisine restaurant, so I pop in, order a coffee and sit in front of one of the screens. At the moment, and until some better intelligence appears, I'm considering that Jamie Baldwin is in some way responsible for Rikki Tuan's disappearance. It's all I have. He has to be a tough guy and if what Paige said about his dumping her is true, he may be a little emotionally perturbed.

Maybe this old girlfriend really existed (which I doubt), but he still didn't like the idea of Paige starting a new relationship, a new life. Perhaps he attacked Rikki in a fit of misguided, jealous rage and killed him with that scientific approach of his. That sounds unlikely and paradoxical, but if anyone was capable of taking on Triad Lad, it would be a professional heavyweight pugilist. More messed up things have happened.

I type his name into Google and see what comes up. There's a recent sports magazine article about his charity work, detailing the organisations and establishments that he's helped raise money for. I take a look at an interview with him from seven years ago when he was asked if he felt disappointed about not getting an Olympic gold medal. He joked that 'Geordie Gold' would have made a better-looking headline, but he was quite happy with his silver and thought he'd represented England to the best of his abilities and had plenty of praise for the other fighters he'd been up against.

A guy wearing a Danny Brown hoodie brings my coffee and asks me if I need any help. I tell him I'm fine. He looks over my shoulder and points at a black and white photograph of Jamie. 'He's the fuckin' man,' he says. 'The fuckin' man.'

Jamie Baldwin is featured in a lot of 'British Boxer' articles, but they all concentrate on technical details, basic bio and statistics. He fights with an orthodox stance and has had nine wins by KO. He was trained by his uncle, Terence Baldwin, and then trained by Floyd Brooks, a previous welterweight champion from Halifax. Brooks died two years ago. Baldwin hasn't lost any fights. He has plans to open his own boxing club and wants to retire before it starts to affect his health.

Born in Washington in Tyne and Wear, as were Bryan Ferry, Alex Kapranos and Heather Mills. He got a British Boxing Board of Control award five years ago. Likes salads and classic British motorbikes and his favourite band is The Kaiser Chiefs. Loves cricket: playing and watching. Preferred batting to fielding when he was in school. On two separate sites, I find the front page of an issue of *The Northern Echo* with the headline 'Local Boy Makes Good' and a photograph of Jamie wearing his silver medal.

Then I find an interview with him from *Woman's Weekly*, of all places. In it, he talks about his teenage years. He was a bright student – one of the top in his class – but just couldn't be bothered. He was a bully, he says, and was in trouble with the police several times for fighting and also for nicking cars. Frequently arrested. Had to do community service a couple of times. Lucky to avoid time in a young offenders institution.

His parents had divorced when he was thirteen and his uncle seemed to take over as a sort of surrogate father and took him twice a week to the New Herrington Boxing Club. Boxing, he says, saved him, and he put everything he had into it, but he never thought he'd climb as high as he did and be in the Olympic team. He sees himself as an example to other lads from the same sort of background. He says that boxing can teach you about responsibility, integrity and morals. He feels proud of himself.

And, of course, he got Paige McBride. And then he lost her.

*

I don't really know what I was expecting, but when I walk into the reception area I'm quite surprised. This is like an upmarket gym, complete with pretty uniformed receptionist, air conditioning, classical music and a Stoneglow Japanese Maple and Vetivert diffuser on the desk. There are a couple of framed posters for boxing films on the wall: *Million Dollar Baby* and *Raging Bull*.

'Good afternoon, sir. Can I help you?'

She's Scottish. Sounds like she's from Greenock. Great, delicately pretty features, green eyes and cute cheekbones.

'I'd like to see Jamie Baldwin, please.'

'Is it about membership?'

'No, it's a personal matter.'

'Could I have your name please, sir?'

'Daniel Beckett.'

'One moment please, sir.'

I wait as she leans over an intercom and pages him. I glance at her cleavage and imagine kissing it. I can hear her voice echo with a little delay from inside the gym. Expensively cut black hair, burnt orange eye shadow, freckles, sexy mouth. She's wearing a light, flowery perfume. She looks up and smiles at me. I wonder if I'll get an opportunity to ask her out. Fuck it: I'll do it now.

'I don't think he's with anyone,' she says. 'He should be out in a moment. Would you like to take a seat?'

'I'm OK, thank you. Would you like to go out to dinner next week some time?'

She looks taken aback, then laughs. 'I don't know you!'

'I know. But I still thought it was worth a try. Look.' I fish a business card out of my wallet and hand it to her. 'Think it over and if you decide you'd like to, give me a call. I won't be offended if you decide to say no, though obviously it'll be the biggest mistake of your life.'

I laugh and so does she. She's still looking at the card in amazement when Jamie Baldwin appears. I recognise him straight away; he looks much the same as he did during his heyday. He's wearing a grey Pro-Box sweat top, black jeans and pair of lime green Converse trainers. You can tell immediately he's some sort of athlete: all muscle, no fat, healthy skin. He gives me a blank look and looks to the receptionist for help.

'Oh, er, hi, Jamie. This is Mr Daniel Beckett. He said he'd like to see you about a personal matter.'

I put a hand out for shaking purposes, but he doesn't do the same. For half a second I think 'asshole' then realise there's something wrong with his right hand. No. It's not his hand, it's the whole arm. Probably some boxing injury.

'What can I help you with, Mr Beckett?'

He's affable, but cautious. Still got the Geordie accent. I have to get away from here and into his office. I can't make up some lie because I can tell he'll spot it.

'Hello, Mr Baldwin. I'm a private investigator. I wonder if I could have a few minutes of your time.'

He looks dubious. 'A private investigator.'

'That's right.' I hold his gaze. I want to try and transmit to him that this is serious stuff and that he should talk to me. It works.

'OK. Well. Let's go into my office. Would you like a coffee or something?'

'That would be great. Thank you.'

'Two coffees, please, Kina.'

'How do you…' says Kina to me, now almost in recovery mode.

'Black with a dash of milk. No sugar. Thank you, Kina, and thank you for your help.'

I get a sweet smile in return. Got her.

We proceed through the gym, Jamie walking beside me. He looks at me out of the corner of his eye a couple of times and I pretend not to notice. He's tense, and I pretend not to notice that, either. The gym is airy, spacious and the air conditioning makes it just a little too chilly. OK if you're boxercising, I suppose. I wonder what sort of food Kina likes.

The predominant smells are plastic, rubber and leather, as opposed to sweat. It has two full size boxing rings, row after row of assorted punch bags, lots of wall mirrors and a ton of conventional gym equipment, particularly free weights. From the look of it, the floors are hard maple and brand new. This must have cost a lot of money to set up. He's probably accumulated a lot of sponsorships over the years.

As it's lunchtime on a weekday it isn't too busy. There are two women sparring in one of the rings (one with a bare midriff), one overweight guy skipping and maybe seven or eight people attacking the bags. It's a nice place.

His office is partitioned off from the gym by triple glazed windows. He opens the door and indicates that I should go inside. It's warmer in here. There's a desk, two small yellow sofas and a black coffee table in between the sofas. There are two pairs of brown Evo boxing gloves hanging from a metal hat stand and a framed poster of the Errol Flynn boxing biopic *Gentleman Jim* on the wall. I also notice two framed photographs behind the desk. One is of the Olympic boxing team and the other is of Jamie receiving his silver medal. I point to it.

'I remember this. Beijing, yes? No one thought you'd beat that other guy. Was he French?'

This gets a smile out of him. 'Italian. Celio Udinesi.'

'That's it.'

He makes himself comfortable behind his desk.

'Take a seat, Mr Beckett. We'll wait until Kina brings the coffees in and then we can have a chat. So you're a boxing fan.'

I sit down opposite him and lie. 'Oh yeah. I've followed it since I was a kid.'

'Did you ever try it yourself?'

'No. There wasn't the opportunity, really. Why do you ask?'

'I noticed the way you walked. Low centre of gravity. Something that boxers have in common with martial artists.' He gives me a snidey look. 'And dancers, for that matter.'

I suddenly remember Paige. She walked like that. Kina comes in with two coffees, a plate of biscuits and an exciting two seconds of eye contact which I pretend not to notice.

'Thank you, Kina,' says Jamie as she wiggles out of the room, a little excessively, in my opinion. Jamie gives her a strange look. There's a minute of awkward silence as we sip our respective coffees. I have a Bourbon biscuit. Kina's perfume is Dior J'Adore.

'So, Mr Beckett. What the fuck do they want now?'

'You've lost me.'

'Don't get smart with me. My right may not be up to much anymore, but I can still knock you through that fucking wall with my left. Now. I'm going to be nice about this. I'm going to give you a chance. Give me the message then get the fuck out of here.'

'I have no idea what you're talking about.'

'The people you're working for.'

'How could you possibly know the people I'm working for? No one knows the people I'm working for apart from me. I think we're talking at cross purposes. I'm on a missing persons case. I was hoping you could help me.'

His eyes look angry and doubtful at the same time. I suddenly get a surge of elation. This is it. This is the break I've been waiting for, whatever the hell it is.

'Who are you looking for?' he says.

I decide to play it straight with him, just for the sake of breaking through his protective wall. That's not really true, though. I'm not playing it straight with him; I'm manipulating him. Ah well.

'I've been asked to find a Chinese guy who's been missing for three days.'

'And what the hell's that got to do with me? I don't know any Chinese guys.'

'I went to his flat and looked through his things. I opened his letters. I found a ticket to a burlesque show at a club in St James's. It had been sent to him by one of the artistes performing there. Véronique D'Erotique. I believe you know her.'

I hate using clichés, but there's only one that comes to mind at this point, so here goes.

The colour drains from his face. And while we're at it: *his eyes fill with tears.*

'You. What?'

I almost feel sorry for the poor sap. I watch his face as he blinks rapidly to clear the tears and gulps down his saliva.

'She was an acquaintance of the missing person. I had to speak to her. I had lunch with her today and she mentioned you. I found it – *unsettling* that two people she knew had abruptly disappeared from her life in a matter of months. It was suspicious. I wanted to talk to you about what had happened between the two of you.'

'You – you saw Paige for lunch *today*?'

'About an hour ago.'

'In The Dorchester?'

'Yeah.'

'How is she?'

Well, apart from mainlining heroin and hanging around with guys who feed their enemies their faces, she seems fine. We had a lovely lunch during which she whacked through three vodka cocktails and two bottles of wine.

'She's good.'

'What did she say? About me, I mean.'

'She mentioned your telephone call to her. The one when you dumped her. How you were still carrying a torch for some ex-girlfriend and couldn't go on with the relationship. I have to say, Jamie, that your little story sounded like Grade A bullshit to me.'

He looks startled. 'What are you talking about?'

I've got him on the defensive and now I stick the knife in. I have to get him to cooperate. 'Whether it was bullshit or not, you broke her heart and now she's back on the junk in a big way.'

Did he even know about the junk? Who knows, but it seems to have done the trick. I can see him clenching his teeth inside his mouth. He looks around the surface of his desk as if he thinks he's going to find something interesting on it. His breathing is getting rapid. He sits up straight in his seat. He puts the fingers of both hands against his mouth. His eyes dart from side to side. Now his fingers press against the sides of his nose. Then finally, they cover his eyes. He's sobbing.

'Fuck it, fuck it, fuck it, fuck it, fuck it.'

I finish off my Bourbon biscuit and have a slurp of coffee. The coffee's really good. I think it's Sumatran. I'll have to ask Kira on the way out. Or was it Kina? It was Kina. Her bra was dark green and matched her eye colour. I'm reminded of Annalise's underwear matching her eye shadow. Is this a thing? I let Jamie have a few moments to recover. No point in pushing him when he's breaking down like some muscular Geordie beauty queen.

I feel my mobile vibrate and slowly slide it out of my pocket so he doesn't notice. It's another text from Daniella with another naked selfie, this time a rear view, though you can still see the sides of her breasts. I return it to my pocket. If I had to choose between Daniella and Kina, it would be a difficult one. I think Daniella would be the better bet in bed, but you never know. It's interesting to think of them both, with their contrasting figures and looks. I wonder if…no. That would never happen. They don't know each other. Perhaps I could introduce them.

I think of saying something like 'Still going to knock me through the wall with that left of yours, punk?', but decide to save that for another day.

'What's going on, Jamie? What's been happening?'

He has a big sigh, takes a few gulps of his coffee and meets my gaze for the first time in what seems like a while. His shoulders have dropped. He looks smaller. His face looks like it's starting to melt.

'I don't know what's going on, man,' he says. 'I wish I did. I only know about the bit that concerns me. I'd never encountered anything like this in my life before. I didn't know how to respond to it.' He starts chewing a thumbnail. 'There's not a moment since it happened that I haven't felt like an absolute creep, an absolute coward. I can hardly live with myself. I've even been seeing a psychiatrist over the last few weeks. Doing it privately. Costs a packet. Well, not a psychiatrist, a cognitive psychotherapist, but I can't even tell *him* the whole truth. I don't want to hear it coming out of my mouth. They had me over a barrel.'

Well, this is very interesting, but one thing at a time, I think.

'So what you told Paige was nonsense. Let's clear that up first.'

'Yes it was. I was told, no, *ordered* to keep away from Paige permanently. Listen. Listen to me. I had no choice.

If I thought there was anything I could have done to make it different, I'd have done it.'

'Who told you to keep away from her?'

'I'd have done it. Believe me.'

A tough-looking bastard with a Silver Surfer tattoo down his left arm pops his head around the door. 'Shall I put those mats out today while it's quiet?'

Jamie recovers his composure and grins. 'Yeah. Start with the black ones. It'll start filling up in a couple of hours, but just keep going otherwise we'll never get them down. Get Marie to help you if she's around.'

'OK. Dan called in sick eventually, by the way.'

'Oh yeah. Out on the piss last night?'

'Probably. He told me it was his sister's birthday.'

Jamie waits until the guy has left then looks at me. 'D'you fancy going out to the pub? If I'm going to get through this, I'm going to need a drink. Do you drink?'

'Only with written permission from the Church.'

He grins. 'Good. When you hear what I've got to tell you, you're going to need one. Maybe more than one.'

He opens a filing cabinet, pulls out a big white cardboard folder, sticks it under his arm and we leave.

19

FIRST WARNING

The One Anchor is a slick chain pub trying to look like a tourist's idea of what a British pub looked like in a 1950s UK B-Movie. It's almost surreal. It smells of furniture polish. I run my hand over a large horse brass on the wall. I can't tell what it's made from but it sure isn't metal. There are early twentieth century wrestling posters behind the bar and a chalkboard menu. The wall to my left is covered in framed fox hunting prints, because that's what we all do here in Shepherd's Bush.

'We'll need to sit by a window,' says Jamie, now a little more composed than he was ten minutes ago. 'What would you like?'

'I'll have a double vodka and soda,' I say.

I take a seat by a window as instructed and watch him walk to the bar. People here know who he is and a couple of older guys punch the air with their fists as he goes past. I'm curious about this. He's a big, tough guy and I managed to reduce him to tears in a matter of minutes. I get the feeling that there's more than one thing wrong in his life.

He returns with the drinks on a tray. He's having what looks like a pint of bitter with a double whisky chaser. He takes the big white cardboard folder out from under his arm and leans it against his chair. I wonder what's in it.

'What do you think?' he says, waving his hand at our surroundings.

'It's weird.'

'Yeah. Used to be a normal pub until a year ago. It's the oldsters I feel sorry for. Most of them have gone to other pubs or they just don't bother anymore. The breweries don't give a monkey's, of course.'

'Do you live around here?'

'Me? No. I live in Wandsworth. What about you?'

'Covent Garden.'

'Really? I didn't think people lived there. Do you get a lot of trouble from the street artists?'

'They're a bloody nuisance, especially the ones that pretend to be statues. They're the worst.'

He allows himself a terse chuckle at this. He looks straight at me. 'I'm sorry about earlier, man. I thought you were someone else. I couldn't work out why they wanted to get in touch with me again. It could have been anything. And I was always waiting for another visit in the back of my mind, you know?'

He knocks the double whisky down in one and starts on his beer.

'Start at the beginning,' I say.

'I started seeing Paige…' He stops himself, swallows, recovers and continues. 'I started seeing Paige McBride on the seventeenth of April. It was…' He stops and looks upwards to the right. '…on the twenty-sixth that one of these bastards first approached me.'

'You're sure of that date?'

'Yeah. It was my brother's birthday. I'd just been on the phone to him in the morning. I can remember walking along and laughing at something he'd said when this guy approached.'

'OK. What time and where?'

'I'd been to The Cuban Boxing Academy. I was talking to the guy there about getting a couple of his fighters involved in a charity exhibition match that I was beginning to organise. It's in Freston Road, off The Westway. I was on my way to Latimer Road tube station. Normally I'd have gone there on my bike, my motorbike, but it was in dock for a service. This would have been about three in the afternoon.'

'So you'd been seeing Paige for almost ten days at this point.'

'That's right. Ten days. I was in the first flush, you know? You've seen her, haven't you. She's fuckin' gorgeous. She…'

'What happened?'

'This car pulled up ahead of me. Like twenty feet up the road.'

'Type of car?'

'Dark blue Mercedes S Class. New. Didn't clock the registration. A guy got out of the passenger seat an' started walking towards me. He was grinning. I thought it was like – you know when that happens? It must be someone you know and you just don't recognise them? Or in my case it might have been just a fan?'

'OK. I'm going to stop you there. I'm going to get something from the bar. D'you want another drink?'

'Another pint, please, and another double whisky.'

I grab the tray and head for the bar. While the barman gets the drinks I ask one of the barmaids if she has any sheets of paper she can give me. A4 would be good. She doesn't, but she can give me a couple of yesterday's menu cards. That'll do. I haven't had a description yet, but for some reason I found the image of that guy getting out of the car and grinning inexplicably sinister.

I sit down again. Jamie looks baffled. He takes the whisky and drinks half of it then returns to his beer. I take my tactical pen out of my jacket, place the menu on the table with the blank side up and flatten it with my fingers.

'Tell me what this guy looked like.'

'Well, he had, like, a really friendly face. Like he was your favourite uncle.'

'How old?'

'I would say sixty? Maybe? Certainly no older than sixty-five. I don't know, you know? Might have been older than that. I'm not that clever with folk's ages.'

'Height? Weight?'

'About your height, six two, six three. Two hundred and fifty pounds at a guess.'

'Face shape?'

'Sort of square. Overweight. Jowls. Weak chin. But a big guy, you know? Like I said. Strong. Just running to fat a bit.'

I make an outline on the back of the menu. I can see him watching me.

'Hair?'

'Greying. Salt and pepper. Short. Cut en brosse. Wasn't receding or anything.'

I fill the hair in and turn the sketch around so he can see it. 'Getting there?'

'Yeah. That's about it. You've got the jaw right.'

'Tell me about his eyes and eyebrows.'

'Kind of sympathetic, friendly, round eyes with a crinkle at the edges. Smiling eyes. Big eyes. That's why I said he had a friendly face. They were brown, I think. Eyebrows grey like the hair. Salt and pepper.'

'Shape of the eyebrows?'

'Well like an S-shape, I suppose. Quite wavy.'

I show him the sketch again. 'Like this? I couldn't quite manage to get *sympathetic* into the eyes.'

'Yeah. Yeah. Christ that's really good. Eyebrows a bit thicker maybe. You've got him. You've nailed him, man.'

'Nose and mouth next.'

'A small nose, and a bit beaky, yeah? Mouth was really small. Thin. No lips, really, but he had one of those thin moustaches that's just, like, above the upper lip. Moustache was grey like the hair and eyebrows. A downturn to the mouth, like he was unhappy about something.'

I finish off and turn the sketch around so he can see it. 'OK. I can't spend all day on this, but is that him?'

He picks it up and looks at it. His face becomes serious and his lip curls. 'Yeah. Yeah, that's it. That's him. That's the bastard. That was really quick. Were you an artist or something?'

'Yes. I used to be Picasso.'

'I thought I recognised you.'

I get my mobile out and take a photograph of the sketch and another for luck.

'What about his accent?'

'Well, south of England somewhere. I can't really be more precise about that. Not London, I don't think. Not a cockney accent, you know?'

'OK.' I continue. 'So he was walking towards you and smiling.'

'Yeah. I thought he was maybe someone I'd forgotten about. I meet a lot of people, you know? He called me by my name and stretched his hand out to shake hands. He was all smiles.'

'And then what?'

'He said he was really pleased to meet me. He'd been a big boxing buff and it was a great honour. I thought then that he had to be a fan, right? But then it turned weird. He asked me to get in the car. He said he wanted to have a serious chat with me about something. I said I wasn't getting in the car with him. I started to think he might have been some sort of pervert or something, you know? No one was that smiley and friendly, right? I said that whatever it was he could tell me here, on the pavement. He didn't like this. He gave me this look like I'd really inconvenienced him. Almost like I was stupid for not taking up this wonderful opportunity to get in the car with him.'

I take a mouthful of my vodka and soda and swallow. 'I'm assuming that at no time he said who he was or gave you his name or identified himself in any way.'

'No. But then he started going on about Paige, right? I couldn't believe it. I couldn't believe my ears. I could feel my heart beating, you know? It was really disorientatin'. It was like some fuckin' *stranger* had a window into my personal life, and a creepy stranger at that. I was wondering who the hell he was, you know? His face didn't change. He was still all smiling and friendly. I asked him, like, who he was and how he knew Paige. I was starting to get angry, but I kept it under control. I have to know how to do that, you know? He said that Paige had a great future ahead of her and that it would be for the best if I didn't ever see her again.'

God Almighty. *I'm* getting angry with this guy and I wasn't even there. I feel drunk just watching Jamie plough through his scotch and beer.

'Did he give any reasons for this?'

'Yeah. He said that he knew all about me and that I was a bad lot. Some very important people didn't want Paige's career damaged by her associating with the likes of me. All stuff like that.'

I actually spit some vodka down my shirt from laughing. '*Some very important people*? Did he say *who*?'

'Didn't say who, but he said they were people who could do a lot of damage to my career and to my business. It was all for the best. She was only a girl after all. There were plenty more fish in the sea. I could just walk away from this and her career could get back on track and mine could continue as if nothing had happened. He was still smiling while he said all this, but his eyes were sort of dead now, d'you know what I mean? Cold fish eyes. Intimidating eyes.'

'When he said he knew all about you – what did that mean?'

'I've no idea,' says Jamie, but he doesn't meet my gaze when he says it.

'What did you say to him?'

'I told him that I had no notion who he was or who these *very important people* were, but what I did with my personal life was no one's business except mine and who the fuck did he think he was etc. etc. I can't remember all I said, but it was getting quite heated. I got cocky. I said who the fuck are you to tell me who I can and can't go out with?'

'Did that work? What you said to him?'

'He just smirked. He shook his head and said I was making a big mistake. I told him that *he* was the one who was making the big mistake and that if I ever saw him again, I'd break his fucking jaw for him, no matter what the consequences were for me. He just laughed. He said he'd be in touch and just strolled off and got back in his car as if nothing had happened.'

'Did you see his driver?'

'Smoked glass.'

'So was this it?

'No. Then there was the second encounter.'

'What happened on the second encounter?'

He reaches down and picks up the big white cardboard folder by the side of his seat. He turns it upside down and taps it against his hand. Two X-rays slide out. He hands them to me.

'Don't worry about touching them. They can't really be damaged by the sweat on your fingers or whatever. I've got two of each, anyway.' He grins. 'This is why we're sitting by the window.'

I take the X-rays off him and hold the first one up to the light. It's a forearm. Both bones have horrific-looking fractures about six inches down from the elbow. The radius looks worse and parts of it have been shattered into fragments.

'Holy shit.'

'Now take a look at the other one,' he says. 'It's like before and after.'

It's the same forearm, but now the radius has been repaired with a six-inch-long metal plate which looks like it's being held in place by half a dozen screws which go deep into the bone. The ulna has some sort of metal rod fixing both parts of the fractured bone together. This is about four inches long. Airport security's going to be murder for this guy.

I hand the X-rays back to him and finish off the rest of my drink. I can feel my forearm aching.

'You were asking what happened on the second

encounter, Mr Beckett.' He quickly taps the X-rays with his forefinger three times. '*That's* what happened on the second encounter.'

20

IRON BAR TREATMENT

I get in another round of drinks. Mr Sheng will be paying, after all. Jamie is now on his third pint of bitter and his fifth Scotch. He isn't slurring his speech; not yet, anyway. My theory about him being somehow involved in Rikki Tuan's disappearance is starting to disintegrate. He's agitated, sweating and is shaking a little. It may be that he's drinking on an empty stomach.

I take a closer look at his face. He's a little gaunt: he has a barely noticeable nervous tic under his left eye and both eyes have dark shadows beneath them, as if he hasn't been sleeping properly for quite a while. I've got to keep him on track. I have to get a logical sequence of events out of him. People who've suffered some sort of trauma have a tendency to leap back and forth in time with their story and unintentionally muddy the waters. I take a sip of my drink. They've put tonic in it instead of soda, but I'm not going to complain about it right now. I'll put it writing when I get home.

'When did this second encounter happen?'

'About three weeks after the guy got out of the car.'

'So we're talking about May the sixteenth? Seventeenth? Eighteenth? Try and remember. Do you remember what day it was?'

'It was a Thursday because I'd been teaching at the juniors' club.'

'Hold on.' I take my mobile out and bring up a calendar. 'It must have been the sixteenth. That was a Thursday.'

'Yeah, OK. Whatever.'

'Tell me what happened from the beginning.'

'You've got to remember that apart from anything else, what I'm going to tell you is a bit embarrassing for me. You know – despite what I can do, I'm not switched on as much in real life as I am in the ring. No one could be. You'd be crazy to be like that all of the time.'

'I understand.'

'OK. It was about two-thirty in the afternoon. I'd been on the computer catching up with some admin stuff. Paige had called, so I'd spoken to her for about fifteen minutes. She was working three nights in a row, so I wouldn't be seeing her again until the Sunday, I guess it would have been. Yeah.'

I don't say anything. I just look at him.

'So anyway, I live on the fourth floor of a modern block in Wandsworth. There's a reception desk with usually one guy and one woman on duty.'

'Twenty-four-hour cover?'

'Yeah. So there's a knock on the door. Thursday afternoon. Wasn't expecting anyone and I'd only just spoken to Paige. Usually a caller would be stopped at reception, but I didn't think of that at the time. You know – someone knocks on your door and you answer it.'

'Sure. Do you have a spy hole in your door?'

He looks sheepish. 'Yeah, but you know…'

A couple of attractive middle-aged women sit behind

Jamie. One of them has a knockout figure and I realise that I can check them out at the same time as paying attention to what he's saying.

'So I open the door and there's this really big guy standing outside with a big grin on his face. And I mean a *really* big guy. A real big bastard. Over six foot five. Three hundred pounds at least. I mean, I'm not short or slight or anything. I'm five foot ten. But I got an immediate feeling of physical intimidation from this bloke.

'So he's grinning and he goes "Yeeeaaahhh! Jamie Baldwin The Man!" Very deep voice. And then, like, just punches me. A real sucker punch. A really powerful uppercut. Actually lifted me off my feet. I saw flashing lights, the lot. I mean, you know, it wasn't the *first* time I'd been on the receiving end of a punch like that, but it was the first time I'd copped one outside the ring, you know?

'So I was lying on my back on the floor in my hall and this guy comes over and just drops down onto me with his knees on my chest. I heard all the air come out of my lungs. You can imagine what it was like with someone that heavy.

'It took me a couple of seconds to realise what was happening and then I let out a couple of jabs at his face, as hard as I could. But I was unfocussed. He started holding my arms and slapping my fists down. He took my face in one of his hands and starting squeezing like he was trying to crush my jaw. Then the other guy came in.'

'Friendly Face?'

'Yeah. Friendly as fuckin' usual. He, ah, he just kicked me in the head, like. Just the once. I couldn't – I couldn't seem to think straight. To do anything, I mean. To defend myself. I felt really fuckin' angry, but that kick and the big bastard's punch. I wasn't expecting them. I wasn't prepared. I felt like an idiot. I felt pathetic. It was the surprise. It was…'

'Stop beating yourself up about it. Keep focussed on what happened.'

I make eye contact with the woman with the knockout figure. She has long, light brown hair, freckles, green eyes and is wearing a wedding band. She smiles to herself, looks away and starts talking to her friend. I'd say she was mid- to late forties.

'I'm not sure if I actually passed out for a few moments, but I must have done. Might have even been a few minutes. I remember thinking that I might have been concussed by that kick to the head by the friendly face guy. It sounds crazy but I was worried about getting a blood clot on the brain. Anyway…'

He pauses, takes a long drink from his pint and looks down. He's keeping stuff back. Whatever happens next is difficult for him to articulate for some reason. I decide to distract him for a moment.

'Let's give these people names so we both know who we're talking about. It'll be more convenient. Let's call them Friendly Face and Big Bastard. Sound good?'

'Yeah. Yeah. OK.' He finishes off the rest of his Scotch. 'I looked up and Big Bastard was naked apart from like a *thong* – you know the sort of thing that bodybuilders wear? I don't know whether he'd oiled himself down before he came in or whether he'd done it while I was incapacitated, but now he was glistening with it. Just like in a muscleman competition, you know? And it looked like he might have been one. You know when blokes go too far hitting the gym? When they're covered in big veins everywhere? He was like that.

'Friendly Face was holding me down, still smiling. He let go of me, then Big Bastard stooped down, lifted me so I was sitting up and got me in this really strong grip around my chest. I really, really couldn't move. He grabbed my wrist and pulled my right arm out to the side. I tried, I really tried to resist, but he was much too strong. I couldn't breathe properly. I had ringing in my ears. I thought I was going to pass out from the pressure he was putting on my chest. Then Friendly Face pulled a chair up and sat in front of me. He had a bag with him which I hadn't seen. A smart brown leather holdall. Expensive, it looked. He reached inside and pulled out an iron bar. Maybe this long.'

He holds his fingers apart to show me. Somewhere around eighteen inches. The woman behind him keeps glancing over at me, but I pretend not to notice.

'It had a two-inch diameter. Something like that. A big, heavy, solid fuckin' thing. God knows what it would have been used for. He leaned forward in the seat. He held this bar in one hand and kept smacking it into the palm of the other, trying to intimidate me.

'He said he'd tried to reason with me. About Paige, that is. But I was plainly incapable of obeying orders. He knew that I was still seeing her.'

'How did he know that, do you suppose?'

'No idea. I'd only been seen in public with her once, if you call going to one of her gigs and having a drink afterwards *in public*.'

'Keep going.'

'He said once again that I was a bad lot and that it wasn't fair on Paige's career and her life if I continued to see her. He said that he'd tried to be reasonable with me, but that people like me were evidently unable to listen to reason. He said he understood that I probably wasn't very bright, but this was a clear message that anyone could have understood, even me.'

'Nice guy.'

'Yeah. So we went through the bad lot speech again and that her career could be in danger and so on and so forth. Then he said that he was going to have to teach me a lesson.'

'With the iron bar.'

'Yes. But he said that he was going to give me one last chance. There was one thing I could do that would stop him smashing my arm.'

'What was it?'

He shakes his head in disbelief. 'He said he could get hold of this equipment. Cameras and sound stuff. All state of the art. It would be set up in my flat and in Paige's flat with my help. It was undetectable and discreet. Only him and me would know it was there.'

'And the oiled muscleman thong guy who you were now pretty tight with.'

He laughs nervously. 'Well, yeah. Him, too.' Despite the laughter, I can see he's getting angry recalling this. His left fist keeps clenching, even as he drinks more beer.

'How old was Big Bastard, by the way?'

'Early forties to mid-forties, I would reckon. Could be wrong.'

'OK.'

'He wanted me to set it up so that whenever I was with Paige – like making love, yeah? – it would be filmed. Either filmed or transmitted to somewhere. He wasn't clear, or if he was, I didn't understand.

'At that point I tried to break loose from Big Bastard, but it was no good. He was too strong. It brought a new meaning to the phrase "vice-like grip", you know what I'm sayin'? I could hear him chuckling in that awful deep voice. It was vibrating through me. If I could have got loose, I'd have fuckin' killed both of them. I'd have beaten them both to a fuckin' pulp. Going to prison would have been worth it. If you'd seen Friendly Face's look, his expression, you'd have known why.'

'So you didn't go along with this.'

'No. I mean – *what*? I'd never heard anything so ridiculous in my life. But it didn't end there. He said they'd be giving me instructions. Things they wanted me to do with Paige, things they wanted me to do *to* her, when we were in bed being filmed. Choreographed. That was the word he used. They would *choreograph* what we got up to. He said he was sure it would look good. He said that both Paige and I were a fine pair of physical specimens. I really couldn't believe my ears.'

'So you told him that wasn't going to happen.'

'I don't think I had to tell him, you know? I think he could tell from my expression. But I told him anyway. I told him he had to be fuckin' insane. That that was never going to happen in a million years and if he suggested it again I'd find him and I'd kill him. He shook his head. He kept looking really disappointed with me all of the time, d'you know what I mean? It was as if I'd been offered a million quid as a gift and had turned it down.

'So then he nodded at Big Bastard who held my arm out straight. I was really trying to struggle now, but it was useless. My arm was shaking, you know? Friendly Face stood up, put a hand on my shoulder and started shaking the iron bar up and down. He was pretty angry now. He said this was going to be a warning I'd never forget. It was just a taste of what they could do. I knew he meant it.

And then he said if he even got an inkling that I was in touch with Paige, they'd grab her. He said that they'd grab her and they'd rape her and then they'd disfigure her. And it would be my fault. And I'd have to live with it. It was such a shame. She seemed such a nice girl. So pretty. It was when he was talking about that that he *really* gave me the creeps. It was exciting him, you know? Doing all that to Paige. Talking about it, yeah? His mouth was watering. He kept on licking his lips and wiping saliva away from his lower lip.

'Then he brought the iron bar down on my arm hard. Twice. That was all it needed. He was grinning like a madman when he did it. It was as if doing this was all he lived for. I mean, I've taken some hammerings in the ring, but this was something else entirely. The pain, I mean. It was fuckin' excruciating. I'd never had anything broken before. I didn't scream or anything. I wasn't going to give him the satisfaction. But I was sick all over myself. I could feel that I was losing consciousness. Big Bastard let me go and I was just lying on the floor in my puke. I couldn't do anything. I could hear Friendly Face saying that I was not to worry. It was all going to be OK. He was going to call an ambulance.

'He said if anyone asked what had happened, just tell them that some lunatic had tried to hit me with a baseball bat and I'd put my arm up to defend myself. I didn't get it at first. Best not to tell them the truth in the hospital, he said. It could get me into a lot of trouble. He said not to worry. Just stick to that story and it'll all be OK. They might not believe me, but they can't do anything about it.

'So I just lay there. I could feel my breathing was getting rapid. My mouth kept filling with saliva. I watched Big Bastard getting dressed. This is stupid, but I was worried he'd get oil all over his clothes.'

'Big Bastard's accent.'

'Northern, but it was on its way out, you know? I caught a trace of Lancashire or maybe Manchester. Can't be more specific.'

I catch the woman's eye again. I raise my eyebrows at her. She smiles and continues chatting to her friend.

'Did you hear him call an ambulance?'

'Yeah, I did. I couldn't tell how long it took to arrive. I was pretty delirious. I was sick again, too. They'd gone by the time the paramedics arrived. Before he left, Friendly Face squatted down by my side, patted me on the shoulder and said that he hoped I'd learned my lesson.'

'Was it a private ambulance company?'

'No. NHS. They took me to the Chelsea and Westminster. The ambulance guys gave me a morphine jab as soon as they saw my arm. Here. Look.'

He rolls up the sleeve of his sweat top. There's a seven-inch scar down the thumb side of his forearm. It doesn't look new anymore, but it's still pink. Would the hospital have called the law? Unlikely. It would look like a defensive wound of some type and they only report gunshot or knife wounds to the police.

'What did you tell them?'

'I told them what Friendly Face had told me to say. Lunatic with a baseball bat. The doctor who was treating me raised her eyebrows at that, but she didn't say anything. I don't know if she knew who I was, but made no comment if she did.

'I had two operations. First one two to three hours long and the second was about four hours. They had to do bone reconstruction on the radius. I was in hospital for six days altogether. I'm having check-ups every six weeks. I'm seeing a physio and now I'm seeing a psychotherapist, like I told you. Eating was a real pain in the arse. I can see you're right-handed like me. Ever used a fork with your left hand? Murder.'

'Why the psychotherapist? The trauma from the injury?'

'Partially that. But I can never box again. I'm not even allowed to hit a bag with all that metal in my arm. So all my exhibition matches, all my training and sparring with up-and-coming boxers – it's all gone.'

'When did you call Paige during all of this?'

'That was the next day, before the first op. I decided to do it while I was still thinking properly and wasn't on the really heavy painkillers. I was afraid for her, so it had to be done quick. I called her, told her it was over then switched my phone off. I thought – I don't know what I thought.'

Tears are filling his eyes. I take a deep breath. 'Did you think of calling the police? This is serious assault. Assault with menaces. Grievous bodily harm and God knows what else. The police would go to town on this. You're a relatively famous sportsman. You've got an Olympic silver.'

'After what they said they'd do to Paige? You've got to be fuckin' kidding me. And there was something else, too. I used to be a bit of a tearaway when I was a kid. Had a lot of contact with the police, if you get my drift. I can smell police. And those two were police. And if they weren't police, they were ex-police.'

'Are you sure?'

'You're a private investigator. There're a lot of them about and a lot of them used to be in the police force.

But I can tell that wasn't the case with you. I'm right, aren't I?'

'Yes you are. Even so, after what they did to you, I…'

I catch his eye and hold his gaze. It's only a flicker in his expression, but it contains a lot of information. Something he said earlier comes to mind. Something that Friendly Face said to him the first time they met. About the fact that they knew all about him and he was a bad lot.

'What have they got on you?'

He finishes the last of his pint. 'I don't know what you mean.'

'All that shit happens and you don't go to the police? Come on. Tell me. Quickly. Think. What am *I* going to do? I'm not the police, I'm not associated with your sport and I'm not investigating you. But you've got a couple of things hanging over you that are going to be there for the rest of your life. You come clean with me and I might be able to make them disappear.'

He sighs. 'Do you want to get another drink?'

'Fuck the drink. Tell me. What have they got on you?'

He looks down at his lap. He clasps his hands together. He's gone pale. The nervous tic under his left eye is doing a jig.

'I didn't think there was any harm in it. I…'

'What did you take?'

'Oxymesterone.'

'An anabolic steroid.'

'Yes.'

'And you won your medal while you were on it. And they didn't detect it.'

'No. I'm not proud of it, you know?'

I remember his interview in *Woman's Weekly*. What was

it he said boxing could teach you? Responsibility, integrity and morals, I think. Oh well.

'How did you get away with it? Beijing was really strict. Wasn't their official slogan "Zero tolerance for Doping"?'

'It was a mix-up. Well, more like an intentional cock-up. There was a guy who you could sling some money to who would adjust the records. Adjust the results. Of the blood tests an' all of that. Urine. I don't know how it was done, but done it was. Cost a packet. It wasn't the Chinese officials that were in on it. That would never happen.'

'Who knew about this?'

'Just me and the guy, as far as I know. I got the drug when I was on holiday in Italy. I posted it to myself so it wouldn't get found on me coming back into the UK.'

'How did you know how to get in touch with this guy?'

'I met a boxer a few years ago who told me. Emelyan Muravyov, the Russian welterweight.'

'So it was just the three of you were in on it.'

'Well, just the two of us really. Muravyov would never have known whether I went and did it or not.'

'But Friendly Face and his pal knew.'

'Yeah. Friendly Face mentioned it after he'd said I was a bad lot.'

'Any idea *how* they knew?'

'No. It's like *impossible* they would know, yeah?'

'Who was the guy that fixed it for you at the Olympics?'

'I'd rather not say.'

'Listen to me. I'm not going to pop round his house and give him a dressing down. Tell me. Was he somehow attached to the British teams?'

'Yes. There were a lot of people floating around, you know? His name was Henry Parsons.'

'What was his official job there?'

'He was a manager of some sort. I think his title was Senior Commercial Manager. It's one of those jobs that deals with the budgets of the teams for travelling, paying suppliers – stuff like that.'

I sit back in my seat and press my fingers into my eyeballs. This has suddenly got rather complicated. What an idiot this guy is. This is all very intriguing, but how it relates to the disappearance of Rikki Tuan I cannot imagine. Not yet, anyway.

Before he gets too pissed and maudlin, I get Jamie to help me with a sketch of Big Bastard and take a couple of shots of it with my mobile. These may be of no use, but I want to be able to recognise these two scumbags should I ever encounter them. It would be helpful if I had a couple of names, but you can't have everything.

Jamie goes to the bar. A couple of garrulous Asian teenagers slap him on the back and insist on buying him a drink. I bet he feels really shabby.

21

A FRIENDLY VISIT

I walk him back to the gym. He's staggering, but only very slightly. Once I've dumped him off I'll have to speak to Caroline Chow, but I'm not going to give her all of this stuff; it would be too confusing and possibly not relevant.

'You won't tell Paige about this, will you?' he says. 'It's between you and me, right? I bet you think I'm a right piece of shit.'

I hold both hands up. 'This is nothing to do with anything as far as I'm concerned. I may not even see Paige again. And I don't think you're a right piece of shit.' I just realised I forgot to follow up all that eye contact with the woman in the pub. Working gets in the way of everything.

I hand the right piece of shit one of my business cards. 'If you think of anything else you can tell me, no matter how insignificant, give me a call, OK?'

'Sure will, mate. Oh. There was one thing, but I don't know if it'll be any use to you. Only struck me as maybe a bit weird afterwards. I was still on a lot of medication when it happened.'

'What was it?'

'Well, after I'd had the second op, I was in a side ward on my own in orthopaedics. I had my arm in this orange splint thing to keep it immobile. You know what I mean?

It had Velcro straps over it so you couldn't move your arm.'

'I know.'

'And this consultant came in to check how I was doing, you know? Very posh guy, I remember. A voice like on the radio. A newsreader or something. Maybe in his fifties somewhere? Anyway, he looked at my notes and my X-rays and was just chatting about general stuff. He said I had to take it easy for a few months with fractures like that. He said he'd broken his arm mountaineering when he was a student. He knew how painful it could be. But he had a funny manner, you know? Nice and chummy, but kind of stern at the same time. Not threatening exactly, but kind of dominating. Hard to put into words. He wasn't the sort of person I would normally meet, so I couldn't...'

'Sure. So what was weird about it?'

A couple of office girls walk by and distract me for a moment. One of them looks like Jena Goldsack, the model. Why don't I get clients who are models?

'Well, he asked me how I did it. I repeated the lunatic with a baseball bat story. I wasn't happy tellin' that story, man. It just didn't come natural. I just felt everyone who heard it knew I was lying, you know?'

'What did he think of that? Did he buy it?'

'He seemed...happy. Happy with the explanation. Happy like I'd just given him an expensive gift for his birthday. He smiled. He nodded his head. He patted me on the leg and said "Good". Then we chatted about nothing for a bit longer then he wished me all the best and left.'

I stop walking. Alarm bells are ringing in my head. Apart from the "Good" part, it's the 'nice and chummy but stern and dominating' that doesn't sound right, unless Jamie's impression is incorrect. I turn to face him.

'That's it? You gave a consultant a bullshit explanation which he *must* have known wasn't true and he said "Good"?'

'It's strange. It was as if – and this might be my imagination – it was as if he was *daring* me to say what really happened. Just a feeling, yeah? Nothing I could put my finger on.'

'Would you say it was as if he *knew* what had really happened? I mean *exactly* what had happened. And who was involved?'

He stares into the middle distance for a few moments. He appears to be looking at the traffic. He sways slightly. I think all the Scotch is catching up with him.

'I don't – yeah. Yeah. If that turned out to be the case, I wouldn't be surprised, you know?'

'Have you got a name for this gentleman?'

'Funnily enough, yes. I saw his badge. His name was Footitt. It's an unusual name. I remembered it because of the cricketer, yeah?'

I shake my head.

'Mark Footitt? Surrey? No? Left-arm fast-medium bowler? No?'

'OK. Well, that's something. I'll check him out. Have you got anything else interesting to tell me?'

A millisecond's pause before he answers.

'That's it. Listen, mate. If anything happens like you finding out who these bastards are, will you let me have a go at them?'

'I can't guarantee anything. I may call you again, if that's OK.'

'Sure, mate. Thanks. I think.'

'And one more thing. Is it easy to find out where you live?'

'What d'you mean?'

'They must have got your address from somewhere. I take it the gym doesn't hand it out over the phone.'

He looks a little rattled at this. 'I didn't – I didn't think of that. No. It wouldn't be easy to find out where I lived. Over-eager fans and stuff, you know? The press. I guess I'm a sort of celebrity and you have to keep some things private. I've always kept a lid on that sort of thing.'

'Sure you have.'

Once we're outside the gym I carefully shake his hand and turn back towards Shepherd's Bush.

On a whim, I give the Chelsea and Westminster Hospital a call. I just hope I can hear them over all the traffic noise and drills that they seem to favour around these parts.

'Chelsea and Westminster Hospital. Can I help you?'

'Could you put me through to orthopaedics, please?'

'One moment, please.'

I'm really annoyed about forgetting about that woman in the pub. I think about going back, but it's probably too late.

'Orthopaedics.'

'Oh, hi. My uncle's just had surgery for a broken arm. He's being looked after by Dr Footitt, the consultant. I wonder if…'

'There's no Dr Footitt in orthopaedics. There's a Mr Fincham. Is that the name you want?'

'No. It was definitely Footitt. Would you mind checking, just to be sure? I want to buy him a tie.'

'Hold on, please.'

I'm going to have to get back to my flat at some point

to process all the stuff that Jamie Baldwin told me. There's quite a lot there that doesn't make sense.

'I'm sorry, sir. You must have got the wrong name. There's a consultant in psychiatry called Dr Footitt. If it's orthopaedics, it must be Mr Fincham. He's the only name there that's even remotely similar to Footitt.'

'OK. Thanks very much for your help.'

I click off. Now what would a consultant psychiatrist be doing having a friendly, if rather spooky chat with someone with a badly fractured arm?

Annalise. She works there. Wrong department, but you never know.

'Hey. It's Daniel. Are you busy? I thought we could meet up for a romantic coffee which you can buy as you're a wealthy NHS doctor. I may even request a slice of red velvet cake.'

She sounds nervous and unsure. 'You're still speaking to me after the other night? I was afraid you'd think I was weird. I've read about women like me.'

'Not at all. To be honest, it made you far more interesting.'

'Really? That's hot. Do you want to do something tonight?'

'I've got a lot on today, but we can do something tomorrow, maybe.' I'll have to see if I can squeeze in Anouk tonight, so to speak. 'Look – I'm in Shepherd's Bush. I can get a cab and be with you in about fifteen to twenty minutes.'

'Text me when you get into reception.'

'Will do.'

It takes less than fifteen minutes to get to Fulham Road. I text Annalise a few minutes before I arrive and she's waiting for me near one of the reception desks. She looks very smart in a khaki and navy wrap dress, a big leather belt around her waist and a hospital ID tag on a blue ribbon around her neck. I think about her the other night and get a surge of adrenalin.

'Do you want to get something in here or go outside?' I ask.

'Outside.'

We cross over Fulham Road and find a small Italian café. We sit down at a window table with our coffees. She rubs her foot up the side of my leg.

'I've been thinking about the other night almost without a break. It's been very frustrating.'

'I'm sure. Listen…'

'I'll bet all your other girlfriends are really conventional, aren't they?'

'Usually girl-next-door types.'

'I knew it.'

'Listen, Annalise. Something has come up on a job I'm working on and it concerns this hospital. I just need to run something past you.'

'If it's confidential, I won't be able to…'

'Nothing like that. At least I don't think so. A male patient was admitted here about three months ago. Severe fractures to both bones in the forearm. Brought to A&E, then two operations to insert pins, metal plates and all the rest of it. That would have been Trauma and Orthopaedics, yes?'

'Yes. What happened?'

'He was hit twice on the arm with a heavy iron bar.'

She licks her lips. Her eyes meet mine. 'And this is a case you're working on?'

'This is a side issue. At least it is so far.'

She leans forwards, her foot still against my leg. Her

voice is suddenly husky and excited. 'Wow. Who would do such a thing?'

'Your coffee's getting cold, tiger.'

She wrinkles her nose at me and spoons the froth off her cappuccino into her mouth. 'So what's the problem?'

'This man is in a side ward here, recovering after the second operation. A consultant comes in to have a chat with him. A very friendly chat. Asked him how he was feeling, looked at his notes and his X-rays…'

'Nothing unusual about that. It was probably the orthopaedic surgeon who operated on him.'

'This was a psychiatric consultant.'

'What? Was it someone the patient knew personally?'

'No.'

'Well, that's ridiculous. There's no way on earth that a psychiatric consultant would have any reason to see someone recovering from a couple of operations like that. Was this guy manic or crazed when he came in?'

'Just in a bit of pain. He'd had a morphine jab on the way here in the ambulance. I think that helped with things.'

She shakes her head. 'It would never happen. Consultants don't go around giving pep talks to other doctors' patients, particularly when it's not even their field. You wouldn't even *know* about the case, d'you know what I mean? Besides, we have enough to do without doing things like that. And even if we did, it would be seen as unprofessional and not very polite. Are you sure that the arm was the only thing wrong with him?'

'Absolutely.'

'The only people who might be expected to visit him would be nurses, orthopaedic staff, pain management staff and possibly whoever dealt with him when he came into A&E, but even *that* would be unlikely. They might pop in when they were passing as a friendly gesture to see how things turned out, but…'

'That's what I thought. The only official aftercare was with a physiotherapist. This guy is seeing a cognitive psychotherapist now, but not one connected with your hospital.'

'Well, the physiotherapy would have been sorted out later, just before he was being discharged. Once again, no psychiatric consultant would have been involved. I mean, I'm a cardiologist. It would be rather like me looking in on another doctor's patient who'd just had an op for an ingrowing toenail. Do you know this consultant's name? This psychiatrist?'

'Footitt.'

She rolls her eyes. 'Oh, *him.*'

'You know him?'

'Not personally. I know who he is and I've heard things about him. An arrogant public school shit. No one can understand how he got to be a consultant. His colleagues think he's hopeless. I've heard people say that he's had a lot of cock-ups professionally, various accusations of incompetence that were never proven or followed up and there was the thing about the blood. Just a rumour.'

'What thing?'

'Can I see your hand? Your right hand?'

She takes my hand gently in hers and runs her fingers over it. There's a small cut on the centre knuckle of my middle finger which is just starting to heal. I notice the hairs on my forearm are standing up. I drink some coffee.

'Is this from when you knocked that guy's teeth out?'

'What was the thing about the blood?'

'Oh, it was just a rumour. You know how we have blood in hospitals for transfusions and so on? The blood that's supplied by the public? Donors? People like you and me? It wasn't in this hospital, but apparently Footitt had been selling industrial amounts of this blood to private clinics over, like, years.'

'Isn't that extremely illegal?'

'It's *getting struck off* illegal. It's *going to prison* illegal. But somehow he got away with it. As I say, it's a rumour, but, you know…'

'How long has he been a consultant?'

'Oh, I don't know. Two or three years? I can find out, if you want.'

'Don't worry. Was he made a consultant after these rumours started?'

'Oh, yes. Those rumours go back about ten years at least. There was also some gossip about him assaulting one of the nurses in some other hospital, but I don't know if that's true or not. Lost his temper after a failed groping and hit her in the face. Something like that. If it *was* true, nothing came of it. Rumours like that, you somehow *want* them to be true, you know what I mean? It would be great if they were, but you feel they're just urban myths.'

She lets go of my hand and looks at her watch.

'I've got to get back.'

'Sure. Is there a chart for the staff in each department? D'you know what I mean? With photographs of all the doctors? I want to see what Footitt looks like.'

'You can do that by looking at the hospital website, but there's a thing on the wall by Psychiatric Assessment. Lower ground floor. There are five psychiatrists, a psychiatric nurse, two secretaries and a receptionist. I think that's it.'

'What's Psychiatric Assessment?'

'A pretty small department, really. They have a room up by A&E, as well. If someone comes in acting strangely, they'll be called to that room to assess them. I never deal with them. I can take you down there if you like.'

'Don't worry about that. Come on. Let's go.'

We cross over the road and head back into the hospital. I tell her to go in first as I don't think it's a good idea that she's seen with me. I promise I'll call.

Once she's disappeared, I go into the gift shop and take a look around. Eventually I decide on a vanilla and apple scented candle in a glass jar. I take the lift down to the lower ground, as I can't find the stairs. Some detective.

Luckily, the solitary psychiatric receptionist is busy with an angry couple, so I'm able to get a good look at the staff photographs on a nearby wall. And there he is: Dr Barnaby Footitt, consultant psychiatrist, student mountaineer, namesake of famous cricketer, flogger of donated blood and sinister hospital visitor.

He's smiling in the photograph. Good teeth. He's got male pattern baldness, dyed black hair, dead straight black eyebrows and humourless pale green eyes. I imprint that image on my brain and wait my turn at the reception desk.

The angry couple go off to be angry somewhere else and I'm alone with the receptionist. I don't know what the fuss was about, but I give her a sympathetic roll of my eyes to get her on my side. I don't actually know what I'm going to say. If Footitt suddenly appears I'll have to change my plan and my story. I can only hope he's off visiting someone who's had a recent hip replacement or an appendectomy.

'Can I help you, sir?'

I give her a big smile. 'I hope so, sweetheart. I was wondering if Dr Footitt was around. My old dad came into A&E in a very bad state last week and Dr Footitt was very kind and understanding towards him. I wanted to give him a little something.' I hold up the scented candle. She looks at it and frowns slightly, as if I've made a terrible choice of gift.

'I don't know exactly where he is at the moment, but I know he's got a busy day today,' she says, as if she gives a toss. 'The only thing I can suggest is that you try and catch him after his shift finishes. Or you can give that to me and I'll make sure he gets it.'

'Um – what time does he finish?'

'He's on until nine tonight. He usually checks in here just before he leaves to have a quick look at what he has on the next day. But you better not be late, dear. He always leaves on the dot and not a minute after.'

'OK. Well, look. I'll hang on to this and pop in later. Besides, it'll give me a chance to wrap it. So if I come down here at about ten to nine, I'll probably run into him. See if I can give it to him before he runs out and gets a cab home.'

She laughs. 'Dr Footitt getting a cab? That'll be the day. He's got a flash sports car. Very proud of it. You can always hear the engine if you're walking along and he's on his way to the car park.'

'What's he got?'

'A Ferrari of some sort.'

'Oh, they're great cars. What colour?'

'Red.'

'Lovely. I expect he's got his own personal parking space, has he?'

'Same as all the other doctors. Just a space with his name on the wall in the main car park next door. But I'll tell you one thing: if I had a car like that I wouldn't park it in there. You never know what might happen. People scratching it out of spite, for example. It happened to one of the other doctors.'

'What did he have?'

'A lovely old Bentley. Someone used their keys on it. Big three-foot scratch down the side.'

I shake my head sadly, like I give a fuck. 'It's a crime, isn't it, really. OK, well thanks for your help, love. I'll come back later.'

She gives me a saucy smile. 'My pleasure.'

I get back up to the ground floor, dump the candle in a bin and go outside. The car park is on the right. Unfortunately, it's packed solid with vehicles and it takes me at least ten minutes before I find a staff parking area.

The Ferrari is easy to spot. It's a bright red 458 Italia. These are fast. I can only guess, but I would think it does 0 – 60 in about three seconds. There's not much he can do with that sort of engine power in central London, but it's something I'll have to keep in mind. I take a look inside, memorise the registration and go back out into the real world.

I look at my watch. It's exactly four o' clock. I give Anouk a call. She seems really pleased to hear from me.

'So how's the tatt?'

'Oh my God, I can't walk. It's when my thighs rub together. It feels really awkward. She put Clingfilm over it. It's like a patch. She said to take it off really carefully and wash the whole area in this antibacterial soap she gave me. It's a liquid. I'm going to do that in a few minutes. It feels very tender.'

'I'm going to be working later on tonight. Why don't you get a cab over to my place at about six? I'll make us something to eat. Then you can show me what it looks like.'

'I'd like that. But you'll have to be careful with me.'

I remember those firm, heavy thighs and fabulous breasts. 'I can't guarantee that.'

'You are evil.'

'You don't know the half of it. See you later.'

There's a stationery shop right next door to the café where Annalise and I had coffee. I buy an office wall calendar, which they've knocked seventy-five per cent off because it's August. The girl rolls it up for me and slides an elastic band around it. Our hands touch briefly as she hands it to me.

Then I go and hire a motorbike.

22

MR X

I decide upon a red and black Ducati Multistrada 1200 S. Fast and sleek with powerful acceleration in low and high gears: just what I was looking for. When I get back to Covent Garden, I park it outside a busy restaurant in Tavistock Street. There are enough tables with a street view to discourage any potential thieves; having it pinched would be a real inconvenience.

I was slightly concerned about the colour and design making it a little too conspicuous, but most of the bikes I passed on my way back were just as flash. They didn't charge me for the helmet rental, which was a very cool-looking Shark Evo-One in gloss black.

When I get inside the flat, the first thing I do is to unroll the wall calendar and put it on the kitchen table with a couple of mugs placed on either side to help flatten it out. I find an unused A4 pad of cartridge paper and a pen and place them next to the calendar. I load the Siemens coffee maker with Mocha Djimmah beans, hit 'play' and go and take a shower.

When I come back out, I make myself a coffee and sit at the table with a towel wrapped around my waist. I think I look pretty cool. I pick the pen up and wave it over the cartridge pad. There are a few things I want to get down on paper before they drift out of my brain into the land of forgotten thoughts.

According to Mr Sheng, the last time he saw Rikki would have been on the seventeenth of August. That was the last time anyone saw him, as far as I can tell. He said Rikki had been missing for three whole days when I spoke to him yesterday.

The last time Lee Ch'iu saw Rikki was on the ninth of August. He was quite specific about that. He said that Rikki had mentioned that he'd been getting hassle. This hassle started happening shortly after a meeting with Mr Sheng and stopped him feeling good about the consequences of that meeting.

Caroline Chow told me that Rikki's meeting with Mr Sheng was on the sixteenth of July, but I don't know the exact date that his hassle began or what form it took. Perhaps I never will. But it was probably sooner rather than later, so I draw a line from the sixteenth to the nineteenth of July and write '?Rikki Hassle Begins?'

It occurs to me that the hassle that Rikki was referring to might not have been unrelated to the first warning that Jamie Baldwin got; when Friendly Face popped out of the Mercedes and told him he was pissing off those very important people.

I have to close my eyes to dredge that date up from my subconscious. It was the twenty-sixth of April. At that point, Jamie and Paige had been seeing each other since the seventeenth of April; I clearly remember Paige giving me that date this morning.

Jamie got the iron bar treatment on the sixteenth of May and he dumps Paige the next day, the seventeenth, a month after they started seeing each other.

I copy all of the dates/events that I've got so far onto the wall calendar, which is still stubbornly refusing to stay flat without help from the mugs.

But there's some other information from Paige. She said that the last time she saw Rikki was at The Electric Carousel on the thirtieth of July. That's eleven days before Lee Ch'iu last saw him.

She also said that costume designer Philip Hopwood introduced her to Rikki roughly two and a half months ago. Ten to twelve weeks. That would make it sometime around the beginning of June. I draw a line on the calendar from the first of June to the tenth and write '?Paige/Rikki?' next to it. I just hope I'll remember what that means tomorrow morning.

I think that's all I've got at the moment. I pin the calendar to the noticeboard and take a look at it, hoping that something magical will jump out and help me solve the case. As usual, it doesn't.

The gap between Jamie getting the first warning and getting assaulted was a little under three weeks. I can't be as specific with Rikki, unfortunately.

So Rikki's meeting with Sheng was on the sixteenth of July, but his 'hassle' could have been any time after that, up to the point he mentioned it to Lee on the ninth of August, but probably closer to the meeting with Sheng than to the time that Lee spoke to him. So maybe the gap was a little over three weeks.

This is frustrating. Without more accurate information I can't tell if there's a pattern there, even though I'd like there to be. Something like: *you get a warning about Paige and if you're still seeing her three weeks later, something bad happens to you.*

And now we turn to Friendly Face, Big Bastard and Dr Barnaby Footitt, the Ferrari-driving mountaineering psychiatrist and possible Charles Dickens character.

Friendly Face first. First of all, it's pretty certain that he wasn't threatening Baldwin for his own personal benefit: he was doing someone else's dirty work for them, latterly with the weird assistance of Big Bastard. He was a foot soldier. All that 'very important people' stuff – it may not have been an elite cabal of Véronique D'Erotique admirers, but it would have been at least one person. I'm not going to bother myself with that now, however.

There was a bit of skewed logic going in all of his threats. The pressure and intimidation were all over the place, in fact, but if you were the disorientated victim of it, like Jamie was, you wouldn't notice.

First of all, it was for Paige's benefit that Jamie would have to back off. She had a great future ahead of her. Jamie was a bad lot and Paige's career might be damaged if he continued to be a fixture in her life. The 'bad lot' part was, by implication, his Olympic doping incident, unless he was implying that boxers were a bad lot generally.

This doping incident was, and had to be, a closely guarded secret, which had suddenly and mysteriously come into the public domain, or at least Friendly Face and Big Bastard's version of the public domain, and whoever they were working for, of course. That was a careless piece of information for Friendly Face to drop and is a loose thread that I may have to tug later on.

Then he told Jamie that if he walked, Paige's career could get back on track again. But who said that Paige's career was *off* track in the first place? She seemed to be doing OK to me and didn't mention anything when we spoke. Anouk didn't mention anything, either. Not about Paige's career, anyway. I'll check this with Anouk and

Paige, just to be sure.

So it's likely that he contradicted himself as far as his assessment of Paige's career was concerned. First of all, she had a great career ahead of her, then her career had to get back on track. Lots of interpretations here. This sounds as if he was making it up as he went along. Or perhaps he was just as confused as I am.

Then he gave Jamie a way out. Suddenly Jamie splitting with Paige and the advantage it would give to Paige's career, on or off track, went on the back burner. Now an X-rated spectacular of Jamie and Paige's sexual activities (as dictated by whoever) would suffice instead. This, of course, contradicts the idea that whoever is behind this had some sort of caring, concerned attitude where Paige was concerned. They were obviously fuckers of the highest order.

And Friendly Face, it would seem, has access to state-of-the-art camera and sound equipment. He, or somebody else, had the wherewithal and knowhow to create an undetectable professional surveillance setup in two separate locations. This, as well as the Mercedes S Class and 'chauffeur', points to there being money behind Friendly Face. This money, no doubt, coming from whoever is behind the whole thing, who I'm going to christen Mr X.

But when it became obvious that Jamie Baldwin would never, in a million years, cooperate with the filming idea, we flip back to Jamie just backing off and dumping Paige. It's almost as if Friendly Face (or someone) was thinking 'Oh well. It was worth a try' when the D'Erotique porn film deal fell through.

But this time, things had become a little more menacing and nasty. Not only is Jamie going to get a taste of the iron bar as a 'warning', but now, out of nowhere, comes the threat of Paige's rape and disfigurement, with a view to making Jamie feel guilty (if he wouldn't be feeling bad enough already).

On the one hand, this is something that Friendly Face could have thought up on the spur of the moment, to put the shits up Jamie. Well, on that level, it certainly worked. But if you combine that with the filming of Paige having sex (with choreography advice from, presumably, Mr X), then there is, possibly, an interesting subtext of a none-too-subtle hatred and contempt for Paige, or perhaps women generally. And it's a morbidly sex-fuelled hatred. It also has strong hints of an unhealthy obsession with her. Now where's *that* coming from?

This contradictory, sloppy, logic-free mess of threat, appeasement and punishment could have another rationale, of course. Friendly Face and Big Bastard had to use everything to hand, everything they could possibly think of to scare Jamie Baldwin off. It *had* to work because of who they were doing it for. It could not fail. The *very important people* were much too important to let down, hence the sledgehammer-to-crack-a-nut approach.

Someone, somewhere, has given this whole thing a great deal of thought. There's not only money behind it but there's also good intelligence (the discovery of Jamie's doping) and planning, not to mention willing and able personnel.

There's also the fact that they knew of Jamie's existence in the first place, of course. They found out about him and what he was, hence that particularly ruinous damage to his right arm. Does Paige use social media? Would Jamie have turned up on it in some way? Is she being cyber-stalked?

On top of that was Jamie's instinct that Friendly Face and Big Bastard were either police or ex-police. If they were currently serving, they were putting themselves at incredible risk pulling something like that.

If they were no longer on the force, which seems likely in sixty-something Friendly Face's case, they were still at risk, even if it was just from a powerful right hook from an angered professional light heavyweight boxer.

Unless, of course, they didn't feel they were at risk in the slightest.

Unless, of course, they felt they were invulnerable.

And then there's the matter of the ambulance. They were confident (or stupid) enough to allow Jamie to be taken to hospital in an ordinary NHS ambulance, presumably driven and staffed by people who were not party to the whole affair. If it had been from a private medical company, that would have been something else, but it wasn't. Logical, really; using a private company would have been a liability for everyone concerned. I, for one, would be speaking to them right now. Jamie's case disappearing into the NHS would have been the best bet. Only Footitt wearing his ID badge let the whole thing down. Perhaps he thought it just wouldn't matter.

Jamie lived in Wandsworth, and unless I'm mistaken, the Chelsea and Westminster would have been the closest hospital with an emergency department. So off he and his morphine drip go, he tells them the Big Lie, has his operations and then gets his complimentary visit from Footitt.

But what if Jamie had lived somewhere else? What if he'd lived in Hampstead, for example? He'd have been taken to The Royal Free. Would there have been a Footitt waiting there with a reassuring smile and a mountaineering anecdote? Do they, whoever they are, have a Footitt in every hospital?

By the time Anouk arrives, I've been in The Zone for about ten minutes, staring at the thick metal grilles on my kitchen window. There's something about all of this Friendly Face business that I find disconcerting. It's as if one part of me knows what's going on, but isn't letting the other part of me know out of spite. Occasionally, I get vague and hazy hints of what the answer might be, but they soon disappear into the mist.

'So what do you think?'

After I embrace Anouk and we drift into a long, passionate kiss that almost ends up in the bedroom, she pulls her skirt up and places a high-heeled foot on one of the kitchen chairs. She peels the plastic wrap away so I can see. It looks good and it looks brightly coloured and new. I run my finger gently over it and she flinches.

'You'll have to avoid that area for a while, my love,' she says.

'Don't worry.'

I get her to sit down and I turn the coffee machine on. She's wearing a loose-fitting blue/black skirt and a dark green blouse. The colour of the blouse makes her blonde hair seem lighter. She smiles at me.

'Paige's show was really something, wasn't it?' I say. 'I could tell you were enjoying it.'

'Oh, she's at the top of her profession. I don't steal from her, but I can allow myself to get inspired, you know?'

'It must be a precarious career for some, though.'

'Maybe. Yes. But not for Paige. At least I hope not. She has always gone from strength to strength. I mean, now she's even getting her own clothing line. There is a launch tomorrow night at The Steel Yard. Do you know it? I was going to go, but my sister is over and I'm having dinner with her.' She suddenly looks excited. 'We're going to The Hard Rock Café!'

I look mock-shocked. 'You didn't tell me you had a sister.'

'As I said before, you are evil.'

'But you like it.'

She glances downwards. 'Yes.'

So much for Paige having a career that needed to get back on track, then.

'Are you hungry? Do you want something to eat now?' I ask her. 'I can make…'

'Not yet,' she interrupts. 'Just coffee will do for the moment. You said you were working later on tonight, my darling,' she says, slipping the blouse off and letting it fall to the floor.

'I have to leave here at about eight-twenty.'

'Can I stay here when you are out?'

'Of course. Just don't answer the door to anybody.'

She reaches behind her back and undoes her bra. She slowly pulls each shoulder strap down and then crosses her arms across her chest.

'You must promise to be careful.'

'I don't make promises I can't keep.'

'Good. I am glad.'

*

The tiny chimes of my watch alarm drift into my subconscious. I let go of Anouk, turn over, switch it off and take a look at the display. Eight o' clock. I get up, have a quick shower to revive myself, go into the kitchen and make some coffee. I'll let her sleep.

I find my mobile and send a text to Paige: *'I have to speak to you. Can we make an appt for tomorrow? Daniel.'*

While I'm waiting for her to reply, I find my battered leather messenger bag and dump it on the kitchen table. Then I go into the bathroom. One of the wide stone tiles on the floor of the shower is removable. This is one of the last places in the flat where you would look for a safe, but this is where it is.

I press the top right and bottom left corners of this tile twice and the springs below allow it to pop up and be removed. Beneath it is a Burton Claymore Underfloor safe. I type in the five-digit code and after ten seconds of deliberation, the door finally decides to open.

I pull out a Nikon D610 digital camera and a night vision zoom lens. The lens is big and cumbersome, but just about fits into my messenger bag. Once everything is back in place and locked up, I head back into the kitchen.

Paige has replied to my text. *'Last night at Bordello. Party after. Call me 11am tomorrow. PS – who are you?'*

I text her back: *'Send nude pics bbe.'*

It's still warm and summery, but I put on my leather jacket, grab the crash helmet and sling the messenger bag over my shoulder. As an afterthought, I grab a copy of the London A-Z Street Atlas and stick that in the bag as well. Five minutes later I'm on the Ducati and heading towards the Chelsea and Westminster Hospital.

23

ROUGH TRADE

I turn off Fulham Road into Nightingale Place, park next to another motorcycle so I look relatively inconspicuous and flip up the visor on my crash helmet. This is the road right next to the hospital and the one you have to drive along if you've been in the Chelsea and Westminster car park.

I get the London A-Z out of my bag, open it and pretend to read it, not looking up but listening for approaching cars. I'm going for the 'motorcycle courier who doesn't know where the hell he is' look. Despite sitting on twenty thousand pounds' worth of Italian engineering, I know that in London, at least, I'll be virtually invisible.

The Psychiatric Assessment receptionist said that Footitt didn't stay in work for a moment longer than was necessary, so I'm hoping I won't have to hang around here for too long. I take a look at my watch. It's another six minutes before he finishes. I get a text from Paige. It's a still of her from one of her shows: naked apart from the black G-string. I have to laugh. I text back: *Sorry. You must have a wrong number.* I remember that I haven't had a saucy selfie from Daniella the cryptographic consultant for a while. I wonder what the next one will be like. I kind of hope she doesn't lose interest.

I look up as I hear a car approaching, but it's a grey Lexus NX. I attempt to work out what information I'll need to get from Paige tomorrow, but can't really focus. That minder/chauffeur or whatever he was still irks me. What was his name? Declan? Such a strange, unpleasant attitude. The anger and contempt on his face when Paige had given him a mild bollocking about letting unaccompanied males into her changing room.

Of course, it could be that he was a bit of a simpleton, but that look when her back was turned worried me a little. If I was her manager or whatever and had caught that look, I'd have fired him on the spot. I'd have thought she wasn't in safe hands.

So, relevant or not, I have to keep in mind a tenuous link between Declan's attitude and Friendly Face's more unpleasant threats. I can imagine the two of them getting on really well in the pub.

I'm just wondering whether Nightingale Place is named after Florence Nightingale when I hear the unmistakable growl of the Ferrari. I concentrate on my A-Z but scope out the car with my peripheral vision. It's definitely him. In a second I spot the MPB and the dyed black hair. He's wearing a dark blue suit, a white shirt and a pale yellow tie. With his left hand he rubs the hair on the back of his head and looks from left to right. He doesn't look in my direction at all. When he gets to the end of the road, he indicates and turns right. I count to ten, fire up the bike, flick the visor down and follow him.

I keep a hundred and fifty yards and three cars behind him as we proceed down Fulham Road. He's doing about forty, which I can easily keep up with. A part of me knows that I'm doing this out of a sense of desperation. For all I know he may be just going home and having dinner. But even if I can find out where he lives, it'll be something. It means I'll not only have a name but an address, and I can always give his house a visit later on, if I have to.

It's getting a little darker now, so I turn the lights on. I'd prefer not to, but that would just make me seem conspicuous and open to a pull from the police. The Ford Focus immediately in front of me turns left into Drayton Gardens. I decelerate and drop back about ten yards. I'm probably being a little too careful, but old habits die hard.

I can see the Ferrari signalling left and a moment later he turns into Cranley Gardens. Thirty seconds later I'm behind him again. One of the remaining two cars kept going straight ahead, which was a bit of a pain, but the orange Mini still tags along behind him. In fact, the Mini is tailgating him slightly, which will be useful; it means his attention will be on it and not on me.

This road is relatively narrow, due to the car parking on both sides, so he drops down to thirty. I decelerate again. I can see traffic lights in the distance, and I want at least two cars between me and him. Luckily, the silver BMW behind me gets impatient and overtakes.

I don't think I've ever been down this road before. There are big, four-storey houses on my left and what must be the actual gardens on my right. Looks expensive, but then it is Chelsea.

This road leads into Old Brompton Road, a major thoroughfare. The traffic lights are five seconds away. They're on red, so we all stop. I can hear him impatiently revving the engine. When the lights go amber, he puts his foot down and goes straight ahead into Gloucester Road. There's no one ahead of him now so he's driving a little faster. I get stuck behind the Mini, which can't keep up with him, so I overtake and keep about a hundred yards between Dr Footitt and myself. I wonder where we're going?

At the north end of Gloucester Road things start to slow down a little due to traffic congestion, odd for this time of night. There are a lot of black cabs and I allow three of them to pull out in front of me. There are continual holdups due to parked vehicles and people attempting to cross the road. He hits the horn a couple of times and makes a couple of dangerous manoeuvres. It seems as if he's in a hurry.

By the time Gloucester Road morphs into Palace Gate, I start to get worried that he might be going further than my petrol tank will allow. Perhaps he's going on holiday to the Lake District. Perhaps I've got the wrong car. At the end of Palace Gate, he takes a sharp left and I can hear his tyres screech, even though I'm four cars behind him now. Kensington Church Street is busy and built-up, but he takes it fast, almost running down a couple using a zebra crossing at one point.

For a second, this speed increase makes me wonder if he's spotted me, but it's extremely unlikely. I've taken all the precautions; assuming at all times that he's expecting to be followed, is switched on and sharp and can spot surveillance. I've kept two to five cars between me and him wherever possible and only got close when it was unavoidable, like at traffic lights or junctions. I think he's just an impatient driver.

Five minutes later we're in Queensway, one of the busiest roads in the area. Even though it's late, things are just warming up here. Everything's open: iPad repair specialists, restaurants, souvenir shops, supermarkets, snack bars, bureaux de change, massage parlours, fast food chains, boutiques, camera shops, nightclubs, dentists – you name it.

This is one of those areas where you can get anything you want, at any time of the day or night, and as I watch Footitt make a quick right turn and park, I'm wondering what it is that he's after.

I pull over, flip my visor up and get my A-Z out again, while keeping a discreet eye on him. I've no worries about him seeing me: I'm even more inconspicuous here than I was near the hospital.

He gets out of the car and locks it. He's parked in a restricted zone, but that doesn't seem to concern him, so presumably he has no plans to spend a great deal of time here. Looking out of place in his smart suit, he puts his hands in his trouser pockets and strolls slowly along the pavement, as if he's a tourist, or a local doing a bit of window shopping to kill some time.

I lock the bike and saunter along at about the same speed, but on the other side of the road and ten yards back. There are tons of good-looking girls all over the place and I wonder where they're coming from or going to. Maybe it would be worthwhile checking out some of the pubs and clubs here sometime. Two expensively-dressed Indian girls with amazing big hair and voluptuous bodies giggle and smile at me as they walk by. Jesus.

Footitt stops in front of a Halal restaurant and checks out the menu in the window. Then he backtracks a few yards and looks in the window of a small currency exchange shop. While he's studying the latest exchange rates, he keeps glancing from side to side, as if he's waiting for someone. Now he crosses over to my side of the road. I brazen it out and walk right past him as he feigns intense interest in a closed dental surgery.

Then it hits me. He's *making* himself conspicuous and I suddenly realise why. As if on cue, one of the local rough trade takes the bait. He's a skinny white kid in his late teens or early twenties wearing a tight-fitting camouflage t-shirt, mauve jeans and Ellesse sandals worn over filthy white socks. Two crappy tattoos: a green snake on his left forearm and some writing on his neck that I can't make out. He's got a lit cigarette in his left hand, but he isn't smoking it and it's burning up.

I cross over the road and watch them in the reflection of the Vodafone shop window. Footitt is talking and laughing and whatever it is he's saying, the kid nods in agreement. A moment later, they shake hands and the kid walks away. Footitt stays where he is. I can't work out what's going on.

I walk further down the road until I find another decent reflecting surface, this time in a betting shop window. Footitt is sauntering again, smiling to himself. He checks his watch a couple of times. Then the kid returns. He's with a girl; dressed in what a naïve tourist would think punk rockers wore in the 1970s. She's heavily made up, with too much kohl around her eyes, pale purple blusher on her cheeks and wearing lipstick which is a bizarre combination of dark red on the lower lip and powder blue on the upper.

Even though my view of her is impeded by distance and window reflection, and despite the makeup, she's actually quite pretty with a nice mouth. But she's older than the kid: I would guess mid- to late twenties. Floppy brown biker jacket, naked Kim Kardashian t-shirt, green jeans with the knees out, black Doc Martens with white marbling and an indiscernible tattoo just below her collarbone.

Footitt is very cheery to her, but she's sullen. I wish I could hear what they were saying. Their conversation goes on for a while and at one point the girl storms off. Then the kid shouts something at her and she returns. She seems very argumentative and it's all aimed at Footitt. The kid looks either angry or bored. He places an open hand on Footitt's upper chest, but Footitt calmly brushes it away, while talking amiably to the girl, who can't or won't meet his gaze. It's getting a little overcast now and I wonder if there's going to be a summer storm.

He places a hand inside his jacket and produces a wallet. I can't see what he's taking out, but it's a pretty hefty bunch of notes, perhaps fifties. The girl makes a move to take them, but he's too quick. He puts them in his suit pocket and folds his arms. He's laughing. This is some sort of standoff. The kid looks at the girl and mumbles something at her. Did she hear him? She folds her arms, mirroring Footitt, and after thirty seconds of morose deliberation nods her head.

As they cross over the road, I walk away in the opposite direction, keeping an eye on the three of them in various reflecting surfaces. They're heading back to the Ferrari. I walk back to the bike, put my helmet on and wait. After a few seconds, I hear the roar of the V8 engine and see it being slowly and carefully reversed out into the main road. Then Footitt puts his foot down and it roars right by me.

He turns left at the end of Queensway, then we're speeding down Bayswater Road. I can only assume that the girl must be sitting on the kid's lap in the passenger seat, or vice versa. I keep a bus and three cars between us. After a minute or so I can see him signalling right. He turns into West Carriage Drive, which takes you through the centre of Hyde Park. This is a real pain: no buses and very few cars. I keep well back.

There's a horse riding track on my left and fields to my right. I wish I hadn't worn the leather jacket now as it's getting hot. I can feel my mobile buzz in my pocket with a text. I'm overtaken by a black cab and a green Mercedes sports. In the distance, I can see him park in a deserted car park next to a wooded area. In case he spots me and gets nervous, I keep going until I can find somewhere discreet to stop and assess.

I choose a small area on my side of the road next to a water fountain with one motorbike parked and a couple of cars nearby. I stop there and get the camera out of my messenger bag. A couple of girls jog past. I can see a small group of teenagers smoking dope and listening to music about forty feet away. Footitt and his new pals are about two hundred yards from me and not visible. They're in a pretty deserted area and I've no doubt this is intentional. All the facilities, running/riding paths, members of the public and the way to The Serpentine are on this side. I can see the back of the Ferrari until the lights go off, but I can't see Footitt & Co. This is good. This means they hopefully can't see me. It's a terrible theory but sometimes feasible.

I press a button on the side of the Nikon and turn on the night vision zoom lens. This lens was specially customised for me a few years ago and will have no problem spotting my quarry at this distance. It also has a colour night vision facility, so I don't have to put up with everything being various shades of dismal green.

I look through the viewfinder and quickly locate the car. I pan from left to right until I can see Footitt. The kid walks next to him and the girl trails three or four feet behind. They're heading for a small enclosed square with some sort of statue in the centre and hedges all around. The hedges are about four foot high.

Now the kid is in front. He opens a gate and the three of them troop into the square. Footitt talks to them and waves his hands around a lot. It looks as if he's giving them a lecture on something. Maybe he is. I wonder what he thinks he's playing at. He's in a relatively isolated spot, it's mid to late evening, but there's still a fair amount of people around and the park doesn't close until midnight. Perhaps he gets a buzz from the risk factor.

I can see him undoing his trousers. The kid gets on his knees in front of him. My view of precisely what's going on is impeded by the hedges, but I could give an educated guess if someone insisted upon it or was offering me money. The girl stands in front of Footitt, looking straight at him. She's pretty tall. He's probably only got a couple of inches on her. I take a couple of pictures.

As the kid proceeds with the tool of his chosen trade, Footitt raises his head as if he's decided to have a look at the stars and I can see him rocking gently backwards and forwards. I take a photograph of this pose as it's so weird. The girl is still looking straight ahead. I don't understand this. Does he just want a female witness standing close to him or something?

Then I get my answer. Footitt slowly lowers his head and slaps the girl hard across the face. I can hear the impact from here. She rocks to the side a little, but continues to stay in place. Then he gives her a backhander on the other cheek. This is a harder blow as she staggers a little, but soon gets back into position. I wonder how much he's paying her. He slaps her again and again for maybe a minute. As far as she can, the girl stays where she is throughout. The kid is still on his knees. Then Footitt gives her an almighty punch on the jaw and she disappears. This was so sudden and shocking that I almost drop the camera. I lower it to waist level and look straight ahead, as if this will enable me to see things more clearly, which is plainly ridiculous. Did that really just happen?

I get them in view again. The girl still isn't visible. Once again, Footitt is staring at the heavens. Did he knock her out? My instinct is to run over there, get Footitt's head in both hands and knee him in the face, but I have to supress it. This is a job. Then the girl reappears. From my limited perspective, she looks a little dazed. I can see blood dribbling from the side of her mouth. He hits her again. This time it's a swift and powerful uppercut that would deck a well-built male. She falls backwards and out of sight. I can see that he's smiling now and I can hear him cry out.

Fuck this.

I put the camera back in the bag and sling it over my shoulder. I can't use the bike: he'll hear me coming. I keep his position in my mind and run across the road, heading towards the little square. I know he's paying her, but I've got a red mist in front of my eyes, and whatever that freak has to do with this case, he's going down.

I'm about fifty yards away from him when I see the Ferrari's lights come on and hear the engine rumble into life. Damn it. He does a quick, gravel-spraying reverse turn and then he's coming out of the car park and straight towards me. I guess that was just a quickie for him.

I'm so angry that for a second I can't think what to do. I can't let him see me. I get off the path and press my back against some sort of concrete memorial pillar. A second later he roars by and is back on West Carriage Drive. I can see him turn right and head towards Kensington Road.

That fucker doesn't know how lucky he is.

*

I get back on the bike and speed off after him, almost doing a spectacular wheelie when I misjudge the acceleration for a second. For a moment, I'm afraid I might have lost him, but there seems to be a delay ahead and I can see the blue flashing light of a police car. Have they stopped him?

I'm twenty yards away before I can work out what's going on. It wasn't him they were after, but it's stopped him turning left. The police have pulled over a woman in an orange Peugeot 208. She's arguing with one of the officers and when she rests her hand unsteadily against the roof of her car I realise that she must be drunk.

Footitt is immediately behind the Peugeot and the police lights are illuminating the inside of his car. He's alone. Not too surprising, but you never know. His reversing lights come on and it looks like he's trying to get past this inconvenience by backing away from it, but he's blocked in by a black cab that's going nowhere.

I'm out of his visual range to the left of the rear of the cab. He's isn't signalling, so presumably we'll be going straight on into Exhibition Road. I do hope he's not going to arrange another pickup. It occurs to me that with the photographs I took, I'm got some pretty good blackmail leverage on this guy if I'm ever short of cash. I may even do it just for fun. I'm still trying to get my head around the stuff he was up to. He's a major pervert, certainly.

The police finally realise the holdup they're causing and wave everyone on through a red light. Exhibition Road is a restricted zone with a twenty mile an hour speed limit which everyone is keeping to due to the cop activity. I keep three cars between myself and the Ferrari. After a while, Footitt gets the courage to speed up a little and in five minutes we're heading west on Brompton Road.

For a moment, I wonder if he's heading back to the hospital, then he takes a right into Yeoman's Row. This is a narrow, residential cul-de-sac and useless for a good tailing job. I park outside The Bunch of Grapes pub, turn the engine off and watch what he does and where he's going. I can't imagine that he's going to find any casual pickup down here, unless he's going for a better class of sex fun.

He drives halfway down the road and pulls over into a resident's parking space which has been suspended due to road works. He turns his engine off and kills the lights. He gets out of the car and locks up. In his right hand there's a black leather case. It's three foot long by a foot wide with a depth of roughly six inches. I can only conclude that it's a musical instrument case of some sort. I try to think what you could get in there. A mandolin? A trombone? A violin?

Is it simply that Footitt belongs to some amateur musical ensemble and likes to be fellated in public by a rent boy while slapping a woman around to get himself in the mood for an hour of Vivaldi?

He crosses the road and walks up the steps of a detached four-storey redbrick house. I'll wait until he's gone in before I take a closer look. He takes some keys out of his jacket pocket, unlocks the door and goes inside. It could be that he lives here, but a sixth sense tells me that he doesn't.

I wait for ten minutes. Nothing happens. But then a very smart-suited guy in his seventies walks past me. He's accompanied by a younger man who looks like he's dressed for the golf course. They're talking about tennis. They cross over the road and stop outside the house that Footitt went into. The younger man produces a set of keys and they go up the steps and let themselves in. They too carry cases, but these are more like ordinary attaché cases, if a little bulky. Perhaps it's the conductor and flute player. Whatever they are, it's an odd time for any sort of meeting. I look at my watch; it's just past ten.

I wait for a few more minutes and take a walk along the road on the opposite side from the house. This is a bad road for a nonchalant surveillance stroll. As it's a dead end, you really have to look as if you're going somewhere. Apart from the houses, there's an estate agent, a beauty salon, a clothes shop and a couple of small restaurants. I take a look in the windows as I walk by. Finally, I get to the house itself.

A quick glance at the front door of this place tells me nothing. It's number sixty-one. There's an ordinary Yale lock with a mortice lock beneath it. No brass plaques or nameplates, so it seems to be a private residence rather than a business. Two small security cameras: one aimed at the front door, the other at the steps and pavement. On one side there's a similar house undergoing renovation and on the other a mismatched two-storey house that looks like it was built fairly recently.

I walk to the very end of the road, take an impatient

look at my watch in case anyone's clocking me and then return to the bike on the other side, taking another glance at the house. There's a light on in one of the second floor rooms, but that's it. There's nothing more I can do here at present; he could be here for hours, whatever it is he's doing. I check my mobile to see what the text was. It's another selfie from Daniella, this time taken in her bedroom. Jesus Christ. I get on the bike and head back to Exeter Street.

I park and lock up in Maiden Lane, outside Rules restaurant and across the road from a nightclub which is only just starting to warm up. As I'm walking back towards Southampton Street, I almost collide with a young, ostensibly drunk Chinese guy who puts his hand against the wall of Corpus Christi Catholic Church to avoid falling over. 'Hey, man!' he says. 'You OK?' I smile at him and nod. *Keep at it, my friend; you were almost convincing.*

24

PAIGE'S PLACE

I unwrap myself from Anouk so I can check what the time is. My watch says nine-fifteen. I pull the sheet away so I can look at her body. I run a finger down the outside of her thigh. She smiles and stretches. I want to get up and make a coffee, but I'm going to allow myself a few more minutes inhaling her scent and appreciating her curves with my fingers. I watch her body respond as I gently run a finger across her lips.

I'm hoping that a good night's sleep might have allowed some of yesterday's information to form itself into some sort of logical and enlightening pattern. The first thing I think about is Footitt. Taken in isolation, his evening's entertainment was nothing special, apart from maybe the lateness of that meeting in Yeoman's Row, if a meeting it was. Perhaps it was a gentleman's club or private drinking establishment of some sort. Did Footitt's taste for risk extend to drink-driving in a car that conspicuous?

But his pickup of the kid and the girl was interesting nonetheless. No matter how tenuously, that activity linked him to Friendly Face and Big Bastard in a way that was separate from all the Jamie Baldwin injury/hospital stuff. I don't know what to call it: an interest in relatively unsavoury sexual activities, perhaps?

Now you might not call Big Bastard getting his thong on, oiling himself up and holding Jamie Baldwin like they were engaged while Friendly Face destroyed his arm an unsavoury sexual activity *per se*, but it certainly isn't ordinary behaviour and you could argue that it had deviant overtones.

If you were in a situation where you were beating or torturing someone in their own home, even with a colleague present, it would be unnecessary and time-wasting at best. And, so far, pointless. I just can't imagine why you would do something like that, unless you liked showing off your musclebound physique at every opportunity, no matter what the risk. You'd have to really *need* to do it. In which case, you'd certainly have psychiatric troubles. Could that be a link? Friendly Face and Big Bastard have psychiatric troubles and Footitt is a psychiatrist? Is he *their* psychiatrist?

And now we have Friendly Face's suggestion that Jamie and Paige be filmed having sex for, quite possibly, a third party's pleasure. And then mentioning that if Jamie didn't play ball she could be raped and disfigured. Now thinking up something like that is *definitely* in the unsavoury sexual activity ballpark, particularly when you mix it up with the aggression and threats.

Whatever – all three have a strangeness in common that I've set my subconscious to work on while I think about the other stuff.

Anouk leans over and flings her arm across my chest. 'I'm not going to open my eyes,' she purrs. 'Do something. Anything.'

'Is there something you had in mind?'

'Mm. Perhaps that thing last night, you know?'

'Are you sure?'

'Pretty sure. Yes, I'm sure.'

As if on cue, my mobile starts ringing. I reach down. I pick it up. I answer it. It's Mr Sheng.

'Hello?' he says.

'Hi. Daniel Beckett. How can I help you?'

'Good morning, Mr Beckett. I do hope that this call is not too early for you.'

Anouk climbs on top of me, brushing my chest with her breasts. She runs a hand through her hair, pushing it away from her face. She has a morning after stale perfume smell on her that I like.

'No, it's fine. I was just about to start my regular morning workout.'

'Good, good. Please do not think I am checking up on you, Mr Beckett. Miss Chow has spoken very highly of your investigations so far. She told me that you have made good progress. Exemplary progress.'

'I've been looking into Rikki's personal affairs. I'm building up a picture of his life and who he was in contact with. I've already interviewed several people.'

'Excellent! I had a feeling you would be a fast mover, so to speak. Oh. By the way, Miss Chow told me all about your evening together.'

I certainly hope not.

'I found her very useful, Mr Sheng. She has a lot of knowledge which I put to good use.'

Anouk closes her eyes, smiles, opens her mouth and sighs.

'I'm sure. She is a very professional young woman. It's just that she forgot to tell you that it is not only The City of Willows restaurant where your money will not be accepted from now on. There are forty-seven others. I have made a list of them for you. I have taken the liberty

275

of putting crosses against the ones that I consider to be the best. There are nine.'

Anouk places her hands on my shoulders. As slowly as possible, she rocks her hips to and fro while closing her eyes tightly, as if in pain.

'That's very kind of you, Mr Sheng. You should not have gone to all that trouble.'

'It was no trouble at all. And Li-Fen has made you some more candies.'

'Give her my thanks, but tell her I cannot accept such a gift.'

I can hear the smile in his voice. 'I will pass that on to her, Mr Beckett.'

Anouk bites her lower lip, a look of intense concentration on her face. I can feel her trembling. Even though it's still cool in here, droplets of perspiration are starting to appear on her forehead. She whispers something obscene in Dutch.

'I'm sure you have heard this many times before from many people, Mr Beckett, but it must be such an exciting job being a private detective!'

Anouk continues her slow rocking motion. Now she presses her body tightly against mine. I hope Mr Sheng can't hear her harsh and uneven breathing.

'It has its moments, Mr Sheng.'

'You must do things that ordinary people do not do.'

Anouk pushes herself up suddenly, her eyes heavy-lidded and unfocussed. She moans quietly to herself. That pained look hasn't left her face.

'That's often the case, Mr Sheng. Well, I thank you for your call and the information, but I must leave you now. I have some important matters I have to attend to. I'm sure I shall be meeting you very soon with some good news.'

'Of course. Good luck, Mr Beckett.'

'Thank you, Mr Sheng.'

I click the mobile off, grab Anouk's shoulders and flip her onto her back.

*

Paige McBride lives in a spacious three-bedroom flat in St John's Wood Road, just across from Lord's Cricket Ground. When I phoned her at eleven, she sounded a little odd. But of course there was a party last night for the end of her Bordello residency, so perhaps she was just a little hungover.

She answers the door wearing a pink silk pyjama set, with long trousers and a loose, sexy top that's prevented from falling open by a wide sash belt which accentuates her small waist. Very 1930s and very decadent. All she needs is a foot-long cigarette holder with a black Sobranie poking out of the end to complete the look. I want to tug the belt so the top falls open. I badly want to see what it looks like when she's just wearing the pyjama trousers. She's wearing no makeup, but she has one of those faces where there's no point; it would only spoil things. She sees me smiling at her appearance.

'You like it?'

'Very louche.'

'It's from my own range. Come in and I'll tell you about it.' She looks at the rolled up wall calendar under my arm. 'Have you brought me a poster?'

'Charlie XCX.'

'Lovely.'

'Thanks for the naked pic, by the way.'

'Was that you I sent it to? I do it so often I lose track.

It wasn't one of the very crude ones, was it?'

'I'm afraid so. Who were the other girls?'

She laughs. 'You should be so lucky, darling. Besides, I've deleted all of those.'

Her fourth floor flat is mainly cream, beige and brown. It looks professionally done, rather like Rikki's secret flat. There's a big white marble fireplace with stone cats either side and there's a row of modern gold candle holders on the mantelpiece. Above them is a large abstract print which I don't recognise; wide orange and green semicircles, the paint continuing off the canvas and onto the frame.

'It's Howard Hodgkin,' she says, noticing where I'm looking. 'It's called *Lovers*. Would you like a coffee?'

'Please. Black with a dash of milk. No sugar.'

I follow her into the kitchen. This, like the living room, looks like she's had the interior designers in. White, roomy, loads of tech; there's even a red leather sofa in the corner and a bookshelf filled with cookery books. Big windows and a great view over Maida Vale. I sit down at a large, dark wood kitchen table and watch her as she makes the coffee. Her movements are measured and elegant and I think I might guess she was some sort of performer if I didn't already know.

She places two blue and white Marimekko coffee mugs on the table, then leaves the kitchen briefly, returning a moment later with a large red folder which she places in front of me.

'That's the Mademoiselle Véronique lingerie collection. All of the ideas are mine, but all the hard work was done by Adonay Robel. He's a marvel. All you have to do is describe what's in your head and he's sketching straight away.'

She heads towards the kitchen hob and starts making whatever it is we're going to be eating. I flick through the pages. Paige is the model in all of them. It's lingerie, corsets and loungewear. All have a slightly retro look to them, but that's no surprise; it's been the fashion for quite a few years now and is well-suited to her professional image.

Wearing a variety of different wigs and appropriate makeup, she looks incredible in every shot, particularly the ones featuring the leather corsets. She has a fresh, youthful prettiness in the photographs that offsets any latent sleaziness. These look quality and so does she.

'Anouk mentioned that you had your own clothes line,' I say. 'I didn't realise it was this sort of thing.'

'What did you expect? Big purple feathers and nipple tassels?'

'Yeah.'

She places two plates on the table. Waffles with a dark chocolate sauce. They look delicious. I place the red folder back on the table and start eating.

'Which is your favourite?' she asks.

'The black and red velvet corset that pinches your waist in and makes your hips look really wide.'

She purses her lips and nods her head. 'Was it the design you were appreciating or just that photograph?'

'Not sure. I'll have to get back to you on that when I've discussed it with my sex therapist.'

This makes her smile. 'I think I'm starting to like you, Mr Beckett.'

'That would be a mistake. I'm poison.'

She laughs and shakes her head. We eat in silence for a while. I know she wants to ask me about Jamie Baldwin. I'm not sure how much I should tell her.

'What's that thing you've got rolled up there, then?'

'It's a wall calendar.'

'I've already got one.'

'I need to work out a timeline with you. I've done a bit of it, but I need some more information.'

'Did you speak to Jamie?'

'Yes I did.'

She drinks some coffee and eats a piece of waffle. I'm grateful for this small respite.

'What did he say? Did he say anything about me?'

I take a deep breath. 'I'd be grateful if you didn't tell anyone what I'm about to tell you. I don't really understand what's going on, but there are some very dangerous people involved in all of this, and I don't yet know what their motivation is. Well, that's not strictly true. At present, their motivation seems to be stopping you having a relationship with anyone.'

She goes suddenly pale and her voice quavers. 'What?'

'Jamie Baldwin was coerced into finishing your relationship. He was threatened and seriously assaulted.'

I tell her about the visit of Friendly Face and Big Bastard. I leave out the fact that Big Bastard was covered in oil and only wore pants. I leave out Footitt's involvement as that would just complicate things. Besides, Footitt may have no direct connection to Rikki Tuan, whatever the hell might have happened to him. I leave out the anabolic steroid business for the moment, though I can't see how I can avoid telling her if she presses. I leave out their threat to rape and disfigure her and I leave out the request to film them having sex. I've already left out so much I don't know what we're going to talk about. The weather, perhaps.

'What did they do to him?'

'They broke his arm with an iron bar.'

Her hand flies up to cover her mouth. 'Oh, Jesus. Oh no.'

It takes her a couple of minutes to be able to speak. She's crying. I resist holding her as it would be too sexy and I have no self-control when it comes to women.

'Why didn't he go to the police? Why didn't he tell me what had happened?'

As I start to think how to put this into words, I almost feel admiration for those two bastards. Jamie was completely stitched up from several different directions at the same time. They did a thorough job: he's fucked on every level imaginable. And I wouldn't put it past those two to expose his steroid use just for the hell of it one day. And the iron bar thing was thoroughly gratuitous; just for fun, really. The steroid use and the threat to Paige would have been enough on their own, I suspect. Sledgehammer to crack a nut indeed.

Then it occurs to me: perhaps the iron bar was simply punishment – punishment for sleeping with Paige. God Almighty.

'First of all, they had something on him that he would not have wanted to be in the public domain,' I say.

'They were blackmailing him? Is that what you mean?'

'Pretty much, yes.'

'What – what was it?'

'He'd taken a performance-enhancing drug at the Olympics.'

'When he got his *medal*?'

'Yes. If that had got out, everything he had would have collapsed. His reputation as a sportsman would be in ruins, it would have reflected badly on the entire Olympic team, all his sponsorships would have been cancelled, all his training of younger boxers, all his exhibition matches for charity; it would all have vanished in a puff of smoke. And who knows what would have happened to his club. He wouldn't have been able to call it The Olympic Boxing Club anymore, that's for sure. They hit him where it hurts.'

Tears start to form in her eyes again. 'So he'd lied to me, then. All that stuff about the integrity of sport and all the rest of it. It was all bullshit. God. I mean – I wouldn't have even met him if it hadn't been for that silver medal.'

'It's doubtful.'

'How did these men find out?'

'I don't know. We don't even know their names. But I'll track them down, and then we'll know.'

'How will you track them down?'

'They were a little careless. They gave me a lead without realising it.'

As I say that, an idea occurs to me, but it's exceedingly cynical and unduly exploitative. I'll probably do it.

'So he wasn't the person I thought he was at all,' she says.

'Hard to say. I think he regrets it, if that's any consolation.'

'So he dumped me just to save his reputation and business interests.'

'It's more complex than that.' I'm going to have to give her all of it. She'll be more likely to help me out if she's motivated. At the same time, I don't want to alarm her and make her freeze up. I'll have to choose my words carefully.

'So what else was there?'

'They threatened to harm you if he didn't leave you alone. That, I think, was his main motivation for dumping you. He didn't want to see you hurt.'

She looks understandably alarmed. When I first met her, there was only concern for Rikki and her supply of smack. Now there's all this. She's edgy and starts drumming her fingers on the table surface. Then she collects herself and speaks slowly and calmly.

'What sort of harm?'

'Does it matter?'

'Yes.'

'They threatened to rape you and disfigure you.'

She sits back in her seat and looks out of the window for a few minutes. I don't say anything. I look over at the kitchen surface. I see she owns a red Delonghi Dedica coffee machine.

'What sort of people would do this, Daniel?'

'I've no idea. I suspect that the threat against you was just words. My theory is that they were using any leverage they could on Jamie to get him to leave you and they just threw that into the mix. However, he couldn't take the risk that they were bluffing.'

'Do you think they were bluffing?'

I drink some coffee. It's getting cold. 'I never assume that anyone's bluffing. I take each point as being a genuine statement of intent.'

'Am I in danger?'

'I think you should be vigilant. You have my mobile number. If you see anything out of the ordinary, no matter how small, let me know immediately. An unfamiliar person standing across the road, someone trying to gain access to your changing room, someone speaking to you in a way that strikes you as odd: anything. Let me know straight away, any time of the day or night. I'm never going to be that far away from you. As long as

I'm around, you have nothing to fear. There was something else as well.'

'What?'

I may as well make Jamie look like he's got the smallest shred of integrity. 'They said that Jamie could continue to see you if he filmed the both of you having sex. They told him they could set up discreet cameras in his flat and in here. He refused, so he got the iron bar treatment.'

I give her a few seconds to process all of this. She licks her lips and rubs her left arm. I can see from her expression that she's trying to make sense of it all, but it's impossible, of course. Repeating it like this to another person makes me want to really crush these guys. She stares into space for a few more seconds then recovers.

'And what about Rikki? I keep forgetting. That's what this is all about, isn't it?'

'Rikki is work in progress. All of this will lead to him eventually. I just don't know how or when.'

She tightens the belt around her pyjama top and stands up. 'Would you like some more coffee, Daniel?'

'Yes please.'

'You said you needed to work out a timeline with me.'

'It would be a great help.'

'Let's do it.'

25

CAFÉ ROYAL

I straighten out the wall calendar on Paige's kitchen table. It still has an overwhelming desire to roll itself back up, but we finally manage to pin it down with the help of two mugs, a small burnt orange tagine and a bottle of Bourgogne Rouge 2013.

I watch her as she takes a look at what I've already done. She's not wearing any perfume, but there's a warm, feminine smell coming from her which I'm finding a little too enticing. I really, really have to focus. Then my brain kindly lets me know that she's certainly naked beneath her fashionable silk pyjama set. I take a deep breath. I'm taking a lot of deep breaths.

'OK. I have you starting with Jamie on the seventeenth of April. Who was your boyfriend before that and how did it end?'

'Is it *all* going to be this personal?'

'I haven't even started. Think of me as a priest.'

'Difficult.'

'That's what all my parishioners say.'

'Well, before…hold on.' She gets up and goes over to the kitchen surface, opens a drawer and comes back with a small appointments diary. She flicks through it for a few seconds.

'I remember this date because I was performing at

Kettner's in Romilly Street. I'd rung him and dumped him that afternoon. I didn't want to have it on my mind while I was performing. I have to be focussed. Yes, I can see you looking. I still use a proper diary.'

'What was his name?'

'Gilles Fugère. Here we are. It was March the first.'

I mark it on the calendar. 'Why did you dump him?'

'Lousy in bed. Life's too short, you know? Rather like his performance time.'

This makes me laugh. 'OK. And before we continue, Jamie's abrupt dumping of you was something that you'd never experienced before.'

'You saw the show, Mr PI. What's your guess?'

'Beautiful and modest with it. That's a killer combination.'

'Have you always been this witty?'

'Snappy comebacks, too. Let's get engaged.'

So logically (and hopefully), the antagonism towards Paige's boyfriends or alleged boyfriends must have started sometime after Gilles, otherwise he'd have been approached by Friendly Face and it would have been him who would have dumped Paige and not the other way around. At the moment, I have to assume that's the case. I have to have *something* vaguely factual and logical to hang on to.

'I'd like to talk to you about your minder or whatever he is. Declan?'

'That's right. Declan Sharpe.'

'What's his job?'

'I guess you could call it general security. When I'm performing in the UK, he picks me up and drives me to the venue. When we get to the venue, his job changes from chauffeur to that of bodyguard, basically. When the gig is finished he becomes the chauffeur again and drives me home. Sometimes he might drive one of the other girls home.'

'Why have you got someone like that?'

'It's the level I'm at. I'm well known enough to be hassled by fans and have the money to be able to afford someone like him. If I don't feel like talking to people, it's better for my image that someone else tells them to go away rather than me. Also, once in a blue moon someone in the audience will get carried away and try and make a grab for you, so it's handy to have security. I'm not the only one. Many burlesque performers do it like this, but there's no pattern. Everyone's different. It also depends on what country you're in.'

'Where did he come from?'

'Who hired him, do you mean? My agent hired him. I'm with Kelly Senac. She would have got him from an agency somewhere. I can give her a call and find out which company, if you like.'

'That would be really useful, but not now. Do it when I've gone and text it to me. Anouk mentioned that he replaced another guy who she described as dishy. Who was that?'

'Oh, that was Tom Nyström. He was a darling. Everyone liked Tom.'

'Was he from the same agency?'

'Do you know, I'm not sure? I'll have to check with Kelly again. Really, all this sort of thing is her department. I'll ask her when I talk to her about Declan.'

'Why did Tom leave?'

'He had family trouble, poor dear. He was recently separated from his wife and his father was seriously ill.'

'Who told you that?'

She looks taken aback by my scepticism. 'He did. He was very sorry to leave. I think he rather liked all the razzmatazz of working for me.'

'So you only had his word for it.'

'Yes, but…'

'When did Declan start and how soon after Tom left did he start?'

'That's easy. The first gig that Declan was with me was at Club Noir. Hold on…'

She flicks through her diary again. I don't know where this line of questioning is going, but it feels right.

'That would have been on the twenty-fifth of March. Declan officially started on the twenty-fourth, that was five days after Tom left.'

'So Tom left on the nineteenth of March, would that be about right?'

'I guess so. Yes. We didn't ask him for notice, poor love. You could see he was distressed and I wasn't really *that* busy, so…'

I scribble these details onto the wall calendar. I can see her watching me. I intentionally don't look up as I speak.

'So Tom didn't give any notice. He told you about his problems and the next day he was gone.'

'That's right.'

I tap the pen against the table surface. 'And five days later, Declan turns up.'

'Just in time for my next gig. Lucky, really.' She leans across the table and looks straight into my eyes. 'What is it? What's wrong? Do you think Declan's involved in all of this? In Rikki's disappearance and all the rest of it? God Almighty. I mean, I don't particularly like the guy, but…'

I smile reassuringly at her. I've been practising this

smile and it usually works. 'He's not necessarily involved. I just want to eliminate him from my enquiries, as the police say.'

'Oh, of course. I see.'

Was that convincing? I trust Declan about as far as I could throw him and intuitively dislike him, but don't want to alarm Paige unnecessarily. I could be wrong about him, of course. He may just hate the job and be a bitter, hateful individual for some reason that I can't imagine. Nevertheless, his rotten attitude has linked him in my mind to Friendly Face, so I'll continue to treat him with suspicion.

'What did Declan do before he came to you? Any idea?'

'Previous jobs? I don't know. But he did mention he'd been a policeman. I don't know how long ago that was, though. We don't talk very much. I'm not involved with him at the venues and in the car I'm a bit of a silent passenger. On the way to a gig I'm stressed and on the way back I'm knackered.'

'Was he a policeman in London?'

'He didn't say.'

'Can you give me Tom Nyström's mobile number, please?'

'Are you going to ring him?'

'I don't know. I'd just like to have it in case I have to cross check any facts with him.'

She flicks to the back of her diary, finds his number, writes it down on a piece of paper. She pushes it over to me and I slip it into my pocket. I don't know if I'll call this guy, but I know exactly what to say to him if I do.

'Now this is going to be a real pain for you. Do you have a list of all of your gigs since the first of March?'

'On my computer, yes. Shall I print it out?'

'That would be great.'

'Are you sure you want this? It's close on six months' worth.'

'It could be important.'

She gets up and wiggles her way into one of the other rooms. I can hear the sound of a computer and a printer starting up. I don't know what I'm looking for and looking at her gigs may be a waste of time, but I'm hoping something will leap out: a pattern, a genie, anything. At least I feel I'm closer to Rikki, being here and talking to her. I can hear the printer spewing out sheets and I'm hoping there won't be too many.

'Here we are.'

Each month's gigs are across two A4 sheets. Well that's not too bad. I spread them across the kitchen table in chronological order and look at them. The first thing you notice is how busy she is. It looks as though she has an average of seven to nine days off a month.

'Do you ever go on holiday?'

'Is that an offer?'

'Of course, but I'll insist on separate rooms.'

'Aw.'

I scan a bewildering selection of venue names. It looks as if she hardly ever plays the same place twice. In the UK, many are in London and the Home Counties, with a few further afield in places like Lincoln or Bristol. There are entire weeks spent in European cities like Paris, Helsinki, Prague, Dublin, Belgrade and Amsterdam. I wonder how much money she makes.

'I'm going to have a shower. Can I leave you to it?'

'Of course. Don't forget to rinse your hair properly.'

'Thank you.'

I take in one month at a time, my eyes darting to and fro from the gigs to the notable dates on my calendar. I can see the residency at Bordello that she's just finished. I can see the gig at the Electric Carousel, which was when she saw Rikki for the last time. She's got three nights coming up at the Café de Paris in a week. Maybe I'll go and see her. I start thinking about the performance I saw her give two nights ago. That was really something. I can barely remember the other two acts. Picking up Anouk was a good move, though. Or was it her that picked me up?

There are two framed prints on the wall next to the refrigerator. Both feature monochrome photographs of burlesque artistes and both have an accompanying quote by the subject. The first one is of Lilli St Cyr, posing in an opened silk robe in front of a Chinese lantern, her breasts almost three quarters exposed. The quote says "Sex is currency. What's the use of being beautiful if you can't profit from it?" The second photograph is of Sally Rand, naked and partly concealed behind a pair of white fluffy feather fans. The quote: "Whatever happens, never happens by itself."

That's quite a quote. I try and crowbar it into this case, but it's not playing ball. I look at the date that Tom Nyström left. The nineteenth of March. Paige had gigs outside London on the twentieth and the twenty-first; presumably without a driver or protector of any sort. Then three days later Declan Sharpe starts. She had nothing on that day, but the next day she was performing at the Pompadour Ballroom in the Café Royal, Regent Street, so that would have been Declan's first gig, so to speak.

There was a gig at the Café Royal earlier that month,

too, on the eleventh. In fact, there are four in all, the only time on the list that she's been at the same venue more than once, but not as a residency. So we have gigs there on the eleventh and twenty-fifth of March, the ninth of April and finally on the third of May.

The Café Royal is quite an upper-crust place and a substantial change from the other venues she performs at. I remember reading that The Pompadour is a Grade II listed room, which is quite an achievement for a room. All the other rooms must be burning up with envy.

I don't hear Paige as she comes back and twitch when she gently places a hand on my shoulder.

'Found anything?'

She's wearing perfume now: I can smell black cherry and cardamom. There's also a light odour of coffee and cloves, which must be from the shampoo or shower gel she's been using. I turn around to look at her. She's wearing a short cream dress with a red flower print on the front. Damp hair. Still no makeup. You'd never guess it was the same person who lip-synched to *Chaque Bouton Lâche* in such an arresting way the other night.

'Nothing's jumping out and offering to solve the case quite yet, unfortunately. I was surprised to see you played at the Café Royal a few times. Were those special gigs?'

'In a sense, yes. They were charity events.' She pulls a chair across so it's next to mine and sits down next to me. The scents of her recent shower are even closer now and I have to try and block them out.

'Which charity?'

She doesn't answer, but leans across me and points at my calendar.

'You've missed something out.'

'What?'

'Some private eye you're turning out to be. Don't you remember? When you and Anouk came backstage? The magnum of Perrier Jouët? The anonymous admirer sending the champagne? Ring any bells?' She moves close and whispers in my ear. 'Could be a lead.'

'I'd forgotten about that. When did that start?'

'Here.' She points to the thirteenth of March. 'I was performing at the Century Club. I remember it clearly because we were all a little drunk after that gig and the champagne helped.'

I write 'The Century Club/PJ champagne starts' against the date in question.

'So the magnums of Perrier Jouët started two days after you first played at the Café Royal and it's been a regular fixture since then.'

'That's right. As I think I mentioned, it only happens when I'm in the UK. It isn't every single gig, but enough of them for you to notice. It may be that that particular secret admirer doesn't know about some of the gigs or has run out of money.'

'And there's never a card or any clue where this particular champagne came from.'

'No card. I think FedEx deliver it. I've never bothered to look into it, to be honest. I get lots of stuff sent to gigs: flowers, drink, fluffy toys, lingerie – you name it. I don't bother to investigate them all; it would take forever. But most of them have a card with a name and a message, particularly if it's a posh make of champagne and especially if it's a magnum or Jeroboam. Followers who go to that sort of expense usually want you to know who they are. If something nasty got sent to me, I'd probably report it to the police, but other than that...'

'OK. The next time the Perrier Jouët arrives, let me

know. Keep the packaging and all the paperwork. You didn't have a gig on the twelfth.'

'No. Well, there was going to be one at Cirque du Cabaret, but it was cancelled. They had a big power failure and we need electricity, you know? I was…'

She stops in mid-sentence, as if she's suddenly remembered something important.

'Jesus Christ. How could I possibly have forgotten this? Hold on a minute. I just have to get something from the bedroom.'

She stands and leaves. I turn to watch her walk away. Once again, I note that she has a cute wiggle. I want to slap her ass. She returns a few seconds later holding a beautiful fur jacket.

'It's Russian silver fox,' she says, stroking one of the sleeves.

I stand up and take it from her. It's heavy. I run the back of my hand down the soft fur. Definitely the real thing.

'Where did this come from?'

'It turned up when I was playing the Wam Bam Club at the Bloomsbury Ballroom on the thirtieth of April. It was my birthday. It was in a very smart presentation box.' She looks amused as she remembers. 'I didn't think it was real at first, but one of the other girls confirmed that it was. The terrible thing was that that gig was a benefit for PETA. You know? The ethical treatment of animals people? I could have *died*. I've never worn it anywhere and I never would. I hate the idea of animals being killed for – for *this*, beautiful as it is.'

'Any idea who sent it?'

'No. One of the door guys was handed it by a courier. He didn't have to sign for it and couldn't remember the name of the company when I asked.'

I take a look at the label. Sometimes, fur coats have a serial number which you can use to trace it back to its origin, but not this one. I place it carefully over the back of one of the chairs.

'How much would a jacket like this cost, Paige?'

'One of my friends, Zareen Atta, is a bit of a fur coat fan, I'm afraid. She said it would have been anything between eight and ten thousand pounds.'

'Is this the first time you've received such an expensive gift?'

'Pretty much. Yes.'

We sit down again, both of us looking at the coat, both of us wondering about it.

'Oh!' she says suddenly. 'And there was this. This was a little unusual. Hold on.'

She disappears again and comes back holding a painting. It's oil on canvas in a smart golden frame. The subject is a red-haired girl, naked, draped in a blue sheet with her back to the viewer. She's reclining against some cushions. I can see Weguelin's signature at the bottom right. I take it from her and lightly touch the surface. When I worked as an insurance investigator in Italy I developed quite a nose for fakes and this doesn't seem to be one. It's certainly not a print.

'This turned up at a gig?'

'May the tenth. Privée of Knightsbridge. They hold avant-garde cabaret and burlesque evenings. It's a supper club, really. I was performing there with Kiki LaRoque and, um, Trixie Blue. It arrived while I was on stage. No clue who sent it. No card, no nothing. Why? Do you recognise it?'

'It's called *Rodantha*. It's by an artist called Weguelin.

Rodantha was a nymph who was turned into a rose by the goddess Diana. She did it so Rodantha could avoid unwanted male attention.'

'It's a copy, yes?'

'Yes. A very good one.'

'I keep it behind the sofa. I've got no space to hang it, really. Quite nice, though. I'll probably find a home for it eventually.'

'Sure. It's nice. Look after it.'

It's not a copy.

'You were telling me about the charity gigs at the Café Royal.'

'The charity is called Fly a Kite. It focusses on children with disabilities caused by genetic disorders. They approached my agent. They'd heard that burlesque was an up and coming thing and wanted to try a burlesque evening to raise money. But it had to be classy. They were a little apprehensive, I suspect. They'd done things at the Café Royal before and people liked the venue, so...'

'Did they ask for you specifically?'

'No. Three of us were chosen by Kelly Senac, my agent. This was last year. The gig was four months away when it was fixed. The three of us she chose were free on that date, on the eleventh. She decided upon me, Kara la Fraise and Misty von Tassel.' She laughs. 'I suppose we were the classiest acts she had on her books, though I don't really like that term. If we're *classy*, what does that say for the rest of the girls? I find it a little snobby. It's also a bit insulting. You could take classy as meaning tame, and neither myself, Kara or Misty could be described as *tame*.'

I take a look at the other Café Royal gigs on the calendar. 'So you did the same gig for the same charity at the same venue another three times after that in the space of – what – seven weeks? Were you performing for nothing?'

She smiles and looks down at her lap. 'No. It doesn't work like that. It's a PR thing, really. It looks as if we're caring people, giving our services for free for a good cause. It's good for our image and it's good exposure. Actually, the charity pays us the usual rate to perform and we still get our cut of the ticket money. It's just that these events are for the rather well-heeled, so the tickets are insanely expensive. That's how the charity makes its money, from the ticket price mark-up. The ticket price includes dinner and a certain amount of free alcohol.'

'Did you find it strange that you were asked to do the same thing another three times?'

'I didn't give it any thought, to be honest. It was a nice venue. Lots of yummy champagne afterwards. That's it. It was slightly odd that the subsequent gigs were organised so quickly considering that the first was planned quite a bit in advance, but…'

'Did you change your act?'

'Not at all. I lip-synched to *Chaque Bouton Lâche*, just as you saw the other night. I'd only just introduced it into my act. I felt like a change from big feathery headdresses and sparkling corsets. I'd never water down what I did just because it was a charity. They get what they get.'

'When you were rebooked, did they ask for the same performers?'

'Yes they did. In fact, they were quite emphatic about that, according to Kelly. They said it was because they wanted to create the same atmosphere as the first gig.'

'Have they asked you to do any more for them? Any more gigs, I mean?'

'Not as far as I know. But even if they had, I for one would have been too busy. All you've got to do is look at my gig list here. It always gets hectic from the middle of May onwards, particularly with the European shows.'

'Can I take a look at this charity on your computer?'

'Sure. Come on.'

We go into a small room full of bookshelves. She has a lot of books. I remember I saw *Les Fleurs du Mal* in her changing room and a quick glance confirms that she's into French literature of all types, many of the books in the original French. I spot *Thérèse Raquin* and *Germinal* by Zola, *On Wine and Hashish* by Baudelaire, *Cruel Tales* by de l'Isle-Adam and *L'immoraliste* by André Gide. I recall Rikki having *La Rabouilleuse* in French in his Ebury Street flat. Did he and Paige talk about this type of reading matter when they were together?

Beneath the books is a shelf full of DVDs. Many of them are French and Italian cinema (plus one Icelandic), but there's also a smattering of hardcore porn. Paige McBride gets more interesting all of the time. She sits down in front of a large computer screen and starts typing. I pull a chair over and sit next to her.

The Fly a Kite site is upbeat and colourful. There are photographs of children enjoying various outdoor activities and it's thankfully easy to navigate around. There's a section called 'Events'. Paige clicks on it and a page opens with details of how they raise awareness and raise their money.

They do a lot of stuff: half marathons, clay shoots, golf days, skydiving, high ropes and zip wire challenges. Nothing even remotely like burlesque evenings. There isn't anything particularly suspicious about that, though. Perhaps they're image conscious and don't want casual browsers to see that they use, in effect, *strippers* to help them with their fundraising, although the burlesque evening was a first. Still, there might have been *something* a little showbizzy on here, perhaps comedy nights or musical events.

There's a name to contact if you have any enquiries: The Honourable Cordelia Chudwell. I keep it in mind and memorise the address and telephone number.

'Any use?' asks Paige, smiling. She's an intelligent woman. I'm going to have to share my theories with her.

'I might have a word with them at some point. Can I ask you not to mention to *anybody* that I'm a private investigator? I've got a weird feeling about all of this. I think a lot of people around you are being played, but I've no idea who by, or why they're doing it.'

'Played? What do you mean?'

'It may be nothing to do with this charity. Not directly, anyway. When did the requests for the subsequent Café Royal gigs come in?'

'I can't remember the exact date, but it was pretty soon after the first one. That was on the eleventh of March. It could have been within three or four days.'

'So we might be talking about the fourteenth or fifteenth of March?'

'Possibly. I'd have to check with Kelly.'

'Can you check with her now? Make it sound casual.'

While she's making the casual call, I take another look at the Fly a Kite site. It looks perfectly respectable to me. It's a registered charity, complete with official number. It has a history. There have been celebrities involved with it in the past and many of them have appeared in advertisements for the various fundraising events. There's a group of trustees who look genuine enough: a bunch of doctors, businessmen, retired nurses, retired corporate financiers and a couple of minor aristocrats. Paige clicks off her mobile.

'She said the charity got in touch with her on the fourteenth. Late morning. They said they'd like to do more burlesque evenings and those three dates were all she could do with the same line-up as before. Apparently the girl from the charity said that it was a lovely atmosphere and they'd like the same performers if at all possible.'

'The fourteenth was a Monday,' I say, checking the calendar. 'So the first Café Royal gig was on the Friday before that. That means they got back in touch as soon as they could, which was quick work. I'm assuming that the charity isn't open at weekends.'

'Damn!' she says. 'I could have asked her about the security companies that Tom and Declan came from.'

'Don't worry about that for now. What about social media? If the idea of you having an infatuated affluent fan at the Café Royal comes to nothing...'

'I've got Facebook, Tumblr and Twitter accounts. A girl at my agent's maintains them and posts stuff. I just pop in every now and again to see what's going on. I made a little announcement that I was in a relationship with Jamie, but nothing ostentatious.'

'How many followers. Any idea?'

'Phew. Well over fourteen thousand on Twitter the last time I looked and God knows how many on Facebook. Loads. Is it important?'

'Does anyone contact you directly on any of these?'

'Oh, there are always people trying to have chats. The girl who deals with it all – her name is Sofie – never engages unless it's a straight request for gig information.

There have been loads of attempts over the last five years or so to have a friendly talk. You know how it is. Anything really weird and Sofie dumps them. Let me show you something, though.'

She signs into her Facebook page, clicks on the 'photos' section and then we're in an album entitled 'The Electric Carousel London July 30'. And there he is: Rikki Tuan, Triad enforcer, burlesque aficionado and face-scraper extraordinaire.

There are three photographs. In two of them he has his arm around Paige's shoulders and in the third he's clinking champagne flutes with an extremely, *extremely* well-endowed girl in an amazing black lace hat who almost looks like she belongs in a 1950s Norman Parkinson Vogue shoot.

I wonder if Mr X saw these? I wonder if Mr X is hidden amongst all of Paige's social media followers, almost certainly under an assumed name. There's a chance that a detailed trawl through all her followers might bear fruit, but I suspect it would be a waste of time.

It's quite odd to see Rikki laughing and having fun. It's almost as if he's a mythological creature now. He's wearing a well-cut black velvet waistcoat over a flashy red, blue and yellow shirt which is covered in prints of macaws and palm trees. His hair is different from the photographs that Mr Sheng gave me. It's longer now, but still looks like it's been cut in some expensive salon. He looks more relaxed, too. Probably a little drunk. There is nothing to indicate a relationship of any type with Rikki in these photos, but he and the girl are name-checked on one of them. The girl's name is Giselle Laprise.

'Tell me about the girl.'

Paige rolls her eyes. 'Giselle? I thought she'd catch

your attention. She's a good friend of mine. She's a retro glamour model. One of the best.'

'Do you have her number?'

She turns and looks straight at me. 'Are you serious?'

'Later will do. Let's go back in the kitchen.'

I sit down at the table again. Paige sits by my side. I write 'charity get in touch' on the calendar. I bring my finger down on the first Café Royal gig.

'This is where it started, whatever it is. You play this charity gig at the Café Royal, the regular magnums of Perrier Jouët start turning up, the charity is after you to do more, your security guy leaves, your *new* security guy starts and two weeks later you're at the Café Royal again. A month after that, your boyfriend gets warned off, four days later a ten grand fur jacket turns up at The Wam Bam Club, your boyfriend gets assaulted and now we have the Rikki business. And that's just the short version.'

'What do you think's going on?'

'I think someone saw you at the Café Royal and got obsessed. I don't think we'll find them on your social media. If they're following you, it'll be done anonymously. You said it was a well-heeled crowd. I think whoever it was wanted to see you again, but they were not habitués of the kind of venues you usually played in. Perhaps they felt out of place, or felt uncomfortable, or felt they'd be too conspicuous for one reason or another. I've no idea what it was. They *could*, however, send you bottles of champagne, so at least they were there in spirit. Plus, they found out when your birthday was and thought nothing of blowing all that money on an anonymous gift. I'm assuming it was them, though I could be wrong.'

'My birthday would have been on Facebook.' She taps her front teeth with her finger. 'So if they wanted to see me perform…'

'…it'd have to be a venue that they felt comfortable going to.'

'Like the Café Royal.'

'Exactly. So somehow, they got the charity to arrange further gigs there. But it's more than that. After that first gig, your relationships with any type of male started to turn sour. I know there were only two, and one of them wasn't a real relationship, but they weren't to know that.

'As far as their intelligence was concerned, which was faulty intelligence, Rikki was a boyfriend. I said earlier that their motivation was stopping you having a relationship with anyone. The two guys who assaulted Jamie are unknown quantities and have vanished into thin air. What I have to do now is flush them out of the woodwork.'

'How are you going to do that?'

I turn around, smile and look her straight in the eye. '*We're* going to have a relationship.'

'My prayers have been answered.'

'That's what they all say.'

26

THE CUSP OF A RELATIONSHIP

We decide to find a pub to have some lunch in. The nearest one is The Lord's Tavern, right next to the cricket ground, so Paige gets ready and we go out, me with my wall calendar under my arm and Paige's gig sheets rolled up inside. I'm going to have to prep her up on what to do, what to say and how to act. She doesn't speak as we walk down the road and neither do I. As we left her flat and she closed the door, I noticed a curved scratch by the lock, which I didn't mention as I thought she'd been alarmed enough for one day. It looked like the result of a slip of the hand by a clumsy burglar. The scratch was too thin for it to have been done by a Yale or mortice key.

I'm pretty sure about two things: whoever is behind this, they're getting their information about Paige's social life from somewhere and I strongly suspect it's her chauffeur/minder, Declan Sharpe. I can't think who else it could be at the moment. However, I have no intention of confronting him; I want to keep him in place.

The second thing is that Rikki's disappearance is unquestionably the work of Friendly Face and Big Bastard, unless there's another creepy perv team taking on some of the work. Perhaps Friendly Face and Big Bastard are outsourcing.

Whoever is behind this (and I'm still thinking of

them/him/her/it as Mr X), they have confidence, they have risk-taking, willing personnel and they have money. I think confronting any of them directly would be a mistake; it would just frighten them off and then I'd never discover what was going on.

There's always the option of grabbing one of them, taking them somewhere discreet and torturing the information I need out of them, but if I decided to do that, I'd have to be damn sure I lifted the guy with all the info, and I'm not sure who that might be. Not at the moment, anyway. If I chose the wrong sucker, the others might make themselves scarce while I was busy with the pliers and that would also defeat the object: finding out what the hell happened to Rikki Tuan.

The other thing that's making me reluctantly cautious is an uneasy feeling that there's a network of these people, and I'm not yet sure how far it spreads, how big it is, how influential it is or how dangerous it is. In other words, I can't trust anyone and have to be careful what I say and who I say it to.

Another factor which, amazingly, I keep forgetting about, is the dead girl in Rikki's Belgravia flat. Who she was, where she came from and why she was there is still a mystery. But it gives me a gut feeling about these people: under the right circumstances, other people's lives are of no importance to them whatsoever. They are manipulative, dangerous, sadistic and ruthless.

I try to think about all the little threads in this case and attempt to pull them together. The first thing I think about is Jamie Baldwin's story about his doping. As soon as Mr X decided that Jamie had to be got out of the way, he was able to get quick and easy access to Jamie's biggest and darkest secret.

Just over a week into Jamie and Paige's relationship, Friendly Face's initial threats hinted that he knew about the doping; that Jamie was a bad lot. Now under any circumstances, that was damn quick work. And that makes the blood test fixer Mr Henry Parsons a person of interest.

Friendly Face also said that the people who wanted Jamie out of the way could do a lot of damage to his career and business. Now how could they do that? Do they have people in The British Boxing Board of Control? Do they own the lease to his gym? What?

Now on to the dead girl at Rikki's flat. Someone got her in there without arousing any suspicion at the reception desk and presumably nobody noticed that she didn't come out again, or weren't bothered whether she came out or not. This is where the Day Manager Mr Oliver Gallagher and the Reception Supervisor Mr Thomas Wade come into their own. I have yet to speak to either of them, and it may be that I'll never have to, but those two are also on my naughty list.

I've yet to acquire the security company information from Paige's agent, but wherever he came from I'll bet anything that Tom Nyström was pressured to make up that story about his marriage and ailing parent to give him an excuse to leave Paige ASAP and get replaced with Declan Sharpe, The Spy in the House of Burlesque. Whoever organised that had some clout and, once again, was capable of speedy work. Too bad that Declan had such an obnoxious personality, otherwise it might have taken me longer to make the link.

And another thing: according to Paige, Declan used to be a policeman. If Jamie's gut feeling was correct, and I think it was, Friendly Face and Big Bastard were ex-police, too. It may be nothing, but it's still worth thinking about.

Then of course there are the gigs at the Café Royal. There's a definite feeling of Mr X the puppet master doing some subtle manoeuvring behind the scenes here. So Fly a Kite is under suspicion and so is The Honourable Cordelia Chudwell, despite her charming and aristocratic name.

There's also my feeling about the convenience of Footitt working in exactly the right hospital. What if Jamie Baldwin had lived somewhere else and hadn't been taken to the Chelsea and Westminster? It occurred to me before and it occurs to me again: do they, whoever they are, have a Footitt in every hospital?

I'm starting to feel responsible for Paige's safety.

We go to the bar, get some drinks and order food. I really don't feel that hungry after the waffles, but get something anyway. Paige orders one of the pub beefburgers with a glass of Shiraz and I have tempura prawns with a cheeky little double vodka and soda.

We sit down at a window table with our drinks. I can't stop myself from glancing at her. She really is extraordinarily pretty. I wonder what The Central School of Ballet think of her and her exotic career.

'You don't have to keep looking at me out of the corner of your eye, you know,' she says, laughing to herself. 'After all, we're on the cusp of having a relationship.'

'I was just checking that you were good enough for me.'

'I see. How did I measure up?'

'Not bad. Almost there.'

'Now I'm anxious.'

Two girls who look like office workers come in and go straight to the bar and order. While they're waiting, they turn around, stare at me and start whispering to each other.

'Friends of yours?' asks Paige.

'Never seen them before.'

'They're checking you out. Does this happen to you a lot?'

'All the time. It's a curse.'

'Am I going to have to put up with this when we're married?'

'You'll put up with it and like it, young lady.'

'I love it when you talk to me like that.'

'I know you do.'

Our food arrives, so we busy ourselves with that for a while. There's no ice in my drink and I can't remember whether I asked for it or not. They should have put it in without me having to ask. I'm surprised to see Paige eating a huge burger with fries. I imagined that she'd stay away from the carbs. I also imagined that smack killed your appetite. Just shows how wrong you can be.

'Is there any way of finding out who bought the tickets to the Café Royal gigs?' I ask.

'And checking each of the four nights to see if…'

'I'm calling him Mr X.'

'To see if *Mr X* has gone to all four?'

'That would be a great leap forward.'

'Yeah. I don't think it can be done. The venue sells the tickets to ticket agencies and *they're* not going to let you look at their confidential sales files. It would be a huge breach of trust and possibly even illegal. You could buy the Café Royal tickets on a couple of burlesque sites, but you still had to buy them through those same agencies ultimately. I think there were two of them. For a charity gig like that one, the charity would probably be allocated a certain number for their important people; donors and all the rest of it.'

'But the charity isn't going to be giving those names out to someone like me.'

'Very unlikely. It's just impractical. Just try and imagine asking The Prince of Wales Theatre or somewhere to give you the names of all the people who bought tickets to whatever was playing last night. They're just going to laugh at you. And the Café Royal is posh and reputation-conscious, which would make it even more difficult.'

She takes a huge bite out of her burger and chews for a while.

'Besides, if you went and did something like that, you might run the risk of starting alarm bells ringing somewhere,' she says. 'You might be asking someone who's *involved* in all of this. Anyway, even if you *were* able to look at some fictitious list of who attended those gigs, it might not mean much. When I've done residencies anywhere, there are *always* people who come night after night. It's just a thing that happens.'

She's right of course. It was still worth asking, I think. And if the worst comes to the worst, I can always ask Doug Teng to hack into the ticket agencies' computer files. We finish our food and a waiter appears and asks us if we want anything else. I really feel full now, but Paige orders sticky toffee pudding with vanilla ice cream and I order some more drinks. I get my mobile out. I didn't want to do this earlier as I thought it might upset her, but I think she can handle it now.

'Can I show you something? When I spoke to Jamie, I got him to describe the two men who assaulted him. I made sketches of both of their faces. Now these are not going to be anywhere near as good as a photograph, but could you take a look and tell me if either of them look familiar?'

I get Friendly Face up on the screen and hand the mobile to her. She sips her wine, takes a look and shakes her head.

'Not familiar at all. Sorry. I'd have remembered that moustache, for a start. Not many people wear them like that now. He could well have been in the audience at the Café Royal, but it's one of those places where you don't mingle afterwards.'

'Take a look at the next one.'

She wipes a thumb across the screen. This will be Big Bastard.

'God. He looks like a creepy sonofabitch. Is he the one that used the iron bar on Jamie?'

'No. That was the other one. This one just held Jamie down.'

'He must have been strong.'

'I think he was.'

She holds on to my mobile and flicks back in the other direction. Her eyes widen.

'Oh my *God*! Where did you get this?'

She shows me. It's the photo I took of Rikki's computer wallpaper, featuring Paige in a *shibari* breast harness. I look up at her. She's blushing. Cute.

'It was on Rikki's computer. I didn't know it was you at that point, but I thought it might be someone who was important to him in some way.'

She laughs. 'I'm blushing, aren't I. Why am I so embarrassed? It's crazy. I mean, you've seen me...you know.'

'It was only when I Googled the names of some of the girls who Rikki seemed to have an interest in that I was able to identify you.'

'I did a photo shoot for this photographer. He wanted to use a variety of showbizzy women in different bondage-themed photographs for a book he was doing. You know; a sort of classily erotic coffee table book.'

'That costs a lot of money.'

'Yeah. There was me and another burlesque artiste, a couple of models, some actresses, a ballet dancer; but something happened and the book was never published. I still like that photograph, though. It was a shame. It would have been a cool book. I emailed it to Rikki. He was delighted to have something of me that no one else had seen. I didn't know he'd made it his wallpaper. How could I?'

She gives my mobile screen another flick with her thumb. Her expression becomes incredulous.

'What the *hell*?'

'If we're going to be in a relationship, you're going to have to get used to photographs of satyrs going down on nymphs on my mobile.'

She laughs. 'All my boyfriends have said that. Where did it come from?'

'It's a print on the wall of Rikki's flat. I was curious about who painted it. And it might have significance. You never know. Does that sound lame?'

'The style doesn't look familiar. Good, though. Look at the way she's lifting up her leg.'

She finishes her dessert and starts on her second glass of wine.

'Anouk was telling me that you have a launch tonight at The Steel Yard.'

'For the Mademoiselle Véronique range. Yes. Do you want to come?'

'I have to come. Like I said, the only chance I've got to find out who the guys that worked over Jamie are is to pose as your latest boyfriend. It's a long shot, but I'm hoping it'll work.'

And with Declan present, I suspect, there's a damn good chance that it will.

'What do you want me to do?'

'First thing you can do is to give Declan a call. Tell him he won't have to pick you up tonight. Tell him that I'll be bringing you. He probably won't ask you any questions, but just keep this in your head: we met two nights ago after the gig at Bordello. Anouk introduced you to me.'

'And then you slept with Anouk. Were you playing hard to get?'

'Yeah, well he doesn't have to know about that.'

'You think it's him, don't you.'

'He's on my list of suspects. I don't think he's Mr X, though, if that's what you mean.'

'Go on.'

'When Anouk went off to chat to Anja Stipanov, it was obvious that there was an instant and powerful sexual chemistry between us. We kissed passionately. I had to push you away. You begged me to take you there and then and you didn't care if anyone came in. In fact, you *wanted* someone to come in. You welcomed it. The thought thrilled you.'

This makes her laugh. 'How long have you been thinking about this?'

'Ever since the moment we met. So you give me your number and demand that I call you. When I prevaricate, you start to get hysterical, so I reluctantly agree. We arrange to meet the next day. We go out to dinner. Despite the delicious, exotic desserts on offer, you can't wait to get back to my place and insist that we leave immediately after the main course. You're still chewing a difficult piece of meat as we leave the restaurant. Our first night together was comparable to the frenzied rutting of demented wild beasts. Your cries of ecstasy and foul-mouthed encouragement could be heard in Guernsey.'

She rests her chin on one of her hands. 'This is the most exciting relationship I've ever had. I had no idea I was like that.'

'Obviously you want to see me as much as possible, so you ask me along to your lingerie launch tonight. Now I assume that you'll be busy for a lot of the evening, but whenever you get a chance, find me and act as if all I'd just told you had actually happened. I want people to see us together and I want them to think it's serious. There needs to be a lot of touching and knowing glances. No overacting.'

'And you'll be bringing me back home as well?'

'Of course. You may find you want to leave early, such is your lust. Make it obvious that that's the case.'

'Got it. So Declan will only be there as my general minder throughout the event.'

'Yes. And to make things even sexier, I'll be taking you there and back on a flash Italian motorcycle that I've hired. Don't tell Declan he won't be bringing you home when you call him. Save that for when you're at the venue. I'll get you a helmet later on today. Now, I know that'll be a problem for you with your clothes. Can you get someone to take what you'll be wearing to the venue so you can change when you get there?'

'I'd be changing there anyway.' She takes a hefty slug of wine and delicately wipes the sides of her mouth with her fingers. 'I have to do a little presentation at the beginning and at the end of the show and I'll be wearing a different outfit for each presentation. I'm sharing the changing room with the models.'

'Can I come in and check you're all OK?'

She laughs again. 'What sort of person are you? There's a friend of mine who'll be going tonight, Emma Antonsen aka LouLou DuBonnet. She's lovely. You should see her act. Verges on the pornographic. If I'm going on your bike, I'll pay for her to get a cab over to my place and take my stuff to The Steel Yard. I can go and pick it up tomorrow. Oh, and that's another thing: Emma always hits on everyone else's boyfriends or lovers. It's just the way she is. If she tries it on with you, you'll know we've been convincing.'

'Are you sure you'll be OK with all of this? I know it's asking a lot.'

'I want to do it. Don't forget, these people have screwed me over as well. They've caused me unhappiness. And don't worry about tonight; I'm a very good actress. I'll make everyone there think it's serious. I guess we'd better get used to each other so it's not a shock if we have to kiss.'

'What d'you mean?' I ask, like a total idiot.

She closes her eyes and leans forwards. Her lips are soft. She gently opens and closes her mouth, her tongue lightly flicking against mine. I can hear her breathing and smell her perfume. I notice for the first time that she's wearing Miss Dior. I hold the side of her neck and she gasps. I don't know how long this goes on for. When we finally separate she opens her eyes and smiles at me.

'See?' she says. 'Totally convincing and yet I felt absolutely nothing.'

'I don't even know what it is you're referring to.'

She punches me in the arm and continues work on her sticky toffee pudding, the faint taste of which remains in my mouth. I keep having to remind myself that I'm with an expert in The Tease.

27

MORE SEX

There's a motorcycle supplies shop near Embankment tube station, so I pick up a cab from The Lord's Tavern and get it to drop me off right outside. I buy Paige a green and black HJC helmet, which turns out to be considerably more expensive than I'd imagined, but what the hell.

Taking her to The Steel Yard on the Ducati is a nice touch, even though the bike thing wasn't planned. I want to speed things up and I want Declan Sharpe to hate my guts, and the bike will help. I suspect he's already nonplussed with me after I made a tit out of him at Bordello the other night, so everything's useful. I only hope my hunch about him is correct.

I walk up Villiers Street, cross over The Strand and take a convoluted route back to Exeter Street, heading north up Bedford Street, then west into Henrietta Street where I parked the bike last night outside a branch of Bella Italia. The bike is still there.

The road is clear as I walk towards my flat. If I clock anyone suspicious hanging around, I usually just keep walking and try again later. Probably unnecessary, but I simply can't help myself.

As soon as I let myself into the ground floor entrance I know I've got a visitor, and I know who it is.

By the time I've climbed up the stairs to the third floor, the scent of Musc Ravageur is getting stronger and now I can smell traces of an unusually aromatic tobacco.

I unlock the door and push it open with the ball of my hand. I have to admire her: to get past the two enhanced Yale cylinder locks, you have to open them simultaneously with the correct keys. If the second one isn't opened within three seconds of the first, the first one locks itself again. This would foil even the most accomplished burglar, though with the right sort of skills, equipment and motivation it isn't an impossible task. Miss Chow gets more interesting by the minute.

'Honey, I'm home!'

I find her sitting at the kitchen table with a cup of coffee and one of her black cigarettes on the go. She flicks some ash into my red Murano glass ashtray. There's a big Under Armour sports bag on the floor next to her. She's wearing a black leather jacket, unzipped to reveal a matching push-up bra. This look is completed by a pair of vermilion high waist cigarette trousers and black high heels. She's something else, she really is.

'So,' she says, blowing smoke into the air. 'Imagine if we're married and you come back to *this* after a hard day's work at the office.'

She stubs her cigarette out, stands up, takes off the leather jacket, drapes it over the back of the chair, flicks her hair back, places her hands on her hips and thrusts her breasts out. 'You won't want to mess around with those secretaries at work with *this* girl waiting for you at home, I tell you *that* for nothing. I can cook, too.'

'What's your speciality?'

'Sweet and Sour Fuck.'

'Sounds delicious.'

'You better believe it, honey. Number sixty-nine on the takeaway menu. Very popular. Big helping. You'll want more half an hour later.'

I can't stop myself laughing. 'Those secretaries won't stand a chance, Caroline. Would you like another coffee?'

'Sure. Where've you been? I've been worried sick. I called the police helicopters out.'

I put Paige's bike helmet onto the table and fire up the Siemens after filling it with La Joya beans. Anouk's Samsung Galaxy is next to the sink. She must have forgotten it. I pick it up and pop it in my jacket pocket. 'Working on finding Rikki. What have you been doing?'

'This and that.'

'Oh really?'

'Yeah.'

'Mr Sheng called me this morning. I'll never have to pay for a meal in any restaurant, anywhere, for the rest of time.'

'Oh yeah. I forgot to tell you about the others. Got distracted, I guess. What else did he say?'

'Nothing much. He said you spoke very highly of me.'

She's behind me, massaging my shoulders. This isn't a casual, anyone-can-do-this massage; this is professional and is hitting all the right spots. I feel a mild headache I've had all day vanish immediately. That perfume she's wearing is a bastard. I want to grab her. I can smell her sweat, the tobacco on her breath, the Italian leather of that bra.

'I'm going to have to pick your brains about Rikki in a moment, Caroline. The more I've looked into all of this, the more complex it's become.'

'OK. And stop being so cool about me being here. I know you want to ask me stuff.'

'What do I want to ask you?'

We return to the kitchen table. She sits opposite me and lights up again, placing her silver S.T. Dupont lighter on the table. I wish she'd put her jacket back on.

'You want to ask me how I knew where you lived, for a start.'

'I've had Mr Sheng's people floating around me like a swarm of tiger mosquitos from the moment I left The Blue Lantern three days ago. How many examples d'you want? The two girls walking past the Pret in Wardour Street, the pretend drunk guy leaning against the church in Maiden Lane, the laughing couple in Catherine Street two nights ago. Shall I go on?'

She looks genuinely shocked. Good. I'd forgotten that I promised to call Anastasija from Zhodzina.

She shrugs. 'Mr Sheng likes to know everything about people who are working for him. It's nothing malevolent. He still owes you bigtime for that girl, you know? He'll never repay that. He did say, though, that, uh, you were impossible to – how did he put it? – he wondered if he had *imagined* you.'

'What does that mean?'

She fiddles with her bra straps and gives me a sweet smile. 'Just an expression. We are very old-fashioned in some ways; very traditional. But we are very modern, also. There are ways of finding information about things and people in the blink of an eye.' The smile disappears from her face. 'But not about you.'

She pulls her long hair away from her face and holds it behind her head in an approximation of a ponytail. 'You think I would make a good secretary in an office? You think you would ask me out to dinner and then to have sex?'

319

'It's very probable.'

'So what's going on with you? I'm curious, you know? I like you. You're a good-looking guy. Good body. I liked the sex we had. That was good sex, you know? And the rest. It's rare that someone can give me what I need without me having to pay for it. That's why I'm here now. To get more.'

'I'm charging this time.'

'But this flat: the bars on the windows, the metal grills, the nightingale floor, the tricky locks, the ballistic glass everywhere – it's really crazy. It's like you've got a pathological fear of armed burglars or something. I found your compartment under your shower but the lock was beyond me.'

'Sorry about that, but I'm glad you were so thorough.'

'I mean, it wasn't impossible to get in here, but that was only because you weren't in and I knew what I was doing. It took me ten minutes to work out your front door and I didn't expect your squeaky floor, you know? I froze when I stepped upon it. I was expecting booby traps. I was expecting a crossbow bolt to fire out of the fucking wall.'

I laugh at this. 'That's something I may consider in the future.'

'So what is it? Have you got people after you? Are you being hunted? Mr Sheng told me what you did to those guys in the car park. The damage. That's not just some private detective shit, is it. I've met private detectives, you know?'

'Were they as charming as me?'

'Hah! You're right-handed, but you always hold your drinks in your left hand. And you're switched on all of the time. What's with that? One of the guys sent to find out where you lived said he was following you after the two girls had dropped out and he took their place. He said you just vanished into thin air. He said like he felt you were playing with him. Then he saw you getting a cab. He said you were behind him and that it was impossible.'

'Maybe he's not as good as he thinks he is; just like Lee Ch'iu. Listen, Caroline. I need to talk to you. Can we forget about me for a moment, difficult as that may be for you?'

'I'm going to find out, baby. I'm going to find out. I'm gonna make you my special project. What d'you want to know about Rikki?'

'OK. Here's what's going on. Rikki had a relationship with this woman. She's a burlesque performer. Her name's Paige McBride.'

'Rikki? Impossible.'

'I said he *had* a relationship, not *was in* a relationship. He was a big fan of her as a performer and supplied her with heroin from time to time. OK so far?'

'OK. I get it. Go on.' She keeps glancing at her sports bag. I wonder what's in it.

'Now this same woman used to have a boyfriend. It hadn't been going on for very long; maybe about a month. But this guy was warned off by a pair of really creepy characters.'

'Warned off going out with the girl?' She pulls both of her bra straps off her shoulders. I ignore this, but it's difficult.

'Yes. He didn't do what they said, so they eventually put more pressure on him and seriously assaulted him. So then he backed off and dumped her.'

'How did they seriously assault him?'

'They broke his arm with an iron bar.'

'The fucks.' She slowly rubs her shoulder to get rid of the thin marks the bra straps have left behind.

'Yeah. I spoke to this guy and he told me exactly what happened. Now I'm going to describe a scenario to you and I want you to tell me how Rikki would react under the same circumstances. This may not be what happened at all, but it's a possibility.'

'Why is it so warm in here?'

'It's August.'

'Oh yeah. I forgot. Haven't you got air con?'

'So Rikki is walking along the street minding his own business when a car draws up beside him. A heavy-set white guy in his sixties gets out of the car and addresses Rikki by name. Even though Rikki has never seen this guy before, the guy knows who he is. He's very polite and smiling. He's very friendly and avuncular. It could be that he implies that he's a police officer, although he may not have a warrant card to show. He may just give off a police officer vibe.'

'OK. I get it. Rikki would be cool. If he thought the guy was the police, he'd take it easy. He wouldn't want trouble.'

'But then this guy's attitude changes; perhaps he invites Rikki to get in the car with him, perhaps not. He tells him that he doesn't want him to see Paige McBride anymore. Maybe he has an obnoxious or aggressive attitude when he says this. Rikki looks at the car this guy has got out of. It's a Mercedes S Class. There's a driver in the driver's seat. Maybe a chauffeur, possibly an accomplice.'

'Rikki would be wondering what was going on.'

'Exactly. A lot of things would be going through his head. Does this guy know about the heroin? Is he the police? No, he can't be. The police don't act like this; neither do they go around in chauffeured Mercedes. What's this all about? Is it Paige McBride's boyfriend? No – he's too old. Rikki would feel, rather like the real boyfriend did, that a stranger suddenly had a window into his personal life.'

'He'd be starting to get angry now.' She stubs her cigarette out and raises her eyebrows. 'He has a short fuse, but he's aware he has to control it when he's out in the *gweilo* world, you know? He'd still be cool, I think. He'd disguise what he was feeling.'

'Sure. But now the guy threatens him. He says that he knows all about him and could make life very difficult for him if he doesn't stop seeing Paige. Rikki doesn't know if he's bluffing or not. Rikki doesn't know whether this guy realises he's speaking to someone who would be quite capable of slitting his throat.'

'Or pulling his fingernails out one by one.'

'That as well.'

'Or chaining him to a hot radiator for three days without food or drink.'

'Now you have to remember that this guy thinks Rikki is Paige's boyfriend; a boyfriend who's a nuisance and has to be scared off. I think *this* is what this is all about. I think there's a guy out there and he's obsessed with Paige McBride and if you're her boyfriend or if he *thinks* you're her boyfriend, you better watch out. I'm calling him Mr X.'

'So the old guy in the Mercedes – is he the one? Is he Mr X?'

'No. I think he's a foot soldier. Him and his assistant both.'

'Is the assistant the chauffeur?'

'No. The assistant is a different guy. Forget the chauffeur. So by this time Rikki is royally pissed off. Is there any chance he'd pull a knife on this guy or something?'

'He always carries a flick-knife, but as I said, this would not be an occasion to use it. Not in broad daylight in the street and certainly not with a *gweilo* who wasn't connected to business, especially if there was a chance he might be a policeman. If something like that happened, Rikki would probably get washed, no matter what his value. The last thing that someone like Mr Sheng would want would be hassle from the police. Murder of *gweilo* is bad publicity and would be very, very bad for business, particularly now. Things are very delicate at present.'

'Sorry – *washed*?'

'Killed. Rubbed out. Chopped. But I couldn't say one hundred per cent, you know? Rikki might have been rubbed the wrong way in some way I can't imagine. Maybe he didn't care for this guy's attitude. Then he might use his knife. He can be capricious. I can't really tell without being there, you know?'

'Now Lee Ch'iu told me that Rikki had been getting hassle from some *gweilo* and that it had bugged him. I'm assuming that the scenario I've described actually happened in some way, perhaps more than once, and that's what Lee was referring to.'

'Could be. Hard to say without asking Rikki.'

'Now with the real boyfriend, there was an initial warning and then three weeks later he gets the iron bar treatment. The three-week gap may mean nothing, of course. With Rikki, the warning seems to have taken place around the sixteenth of July, but Rikki was still around a month later. Might not be significant; perhaps they had trouble finding him.

'The genuine boyfriend was a boxer. He was a tough, fit athlete. Two men, including the one from the Mercedes, went around to his flat and worked him over. One held him down while the other did the damage. Could Rikki look after himself in a situation like that?'

'Oh yeah. I mean – shit. He was a crazy Bruce Lee fan. Started Wing Chun when he was eleven and Jeet Kune Do when he was fourteen. I think it was so he could do all the moves in Bruce's films to begin with, but then he got serious about it all. That's sixteen years of training. Two *gweilo*? Two anyone. No problem.'

'They took the other guy by surprise, even though he could probably have killed one of them with a single punch. One of them knocked on his door, he opened it – bam! – a totally unexpected uppercut. Completely out of the blue.'

'OK. So we don't know who these people are at all?'

'There's a third person involved. Directly involved in the boyfriend's assault, I mean. I'm working on him. But the two I mentioned just disappeared into the ether.'

She flashes me a wicked smile. 'I know how you can get them.'

'Yeah. So do I. I'm going to be doing it tonight.'

'You and her. Are you going to…'

'Jealous, Caroline?'

She blushes. 'I meant…'

'There's a fashion show tonight at The Steel Yard. She has this bodyguard or minder or whatever he's called. I think he's supplying Mr X with information about the men in her life. I'm going to give the impression that I'm one of them.'

'Are you going to kiss her?'

'Of course not. This is work.'

'What time does this fashion show start?'

'Nine o' clock.'

'OK. You want to have sex now?'

'Sure.'

'I'll go and take a shower. Take a look in the bag.'

She heads for the bathroom, looking over her shoulder and giving me a coy smile. I pick her sports bag up off the floor, put it on the table and unzip it so I can take a look inside. She's been shopping. Like I said before, she's something else. She really is.

28

THE STEEL YARD

The Steel Yard is basically three converted railway arches in Allhallows Lane, a tiny passage that's literally a stone's throw from the River Thames and right in the middle of the City of London's financial district. Considering that it's been frequently used for raves, this seems an incredibly inappropriate spot for such a venue, but it seems to be doing well and is still obscure enough to be cool.

Paige and I arrive there just as people are starting to mill around outside. They know who she is at the door so we walk straight in like big celebs. I'm wearing the same clothing I wore at Bordello, for the sole reason of making it obvious to Declan who I am, in case it had slipped his mind, if he has one.

I didn't know what to expect, but this place looks amazing. Exposed brick railway arches are spectacularly lit up by orange and purple LED lighting which is constantly changing in tone and brightness. Right above our heads is a hi-tech lighting rig which is firing bright patterned spots at the floor and walls. The floors are brand new and look like pine, but are probably something harder to withstand all the dancing. The predominant smells are fresh paint, alcohol and perfume.

There's a big bar to our left and next to it a DJ is playing about five seconds of a variety of tracks before settling on a bass-heavy ambient thump you can feel in your chest and teeth. As this starts, the lights change to a deep blue which somehow makes this huge space seem smaller and more intimate.

Straight ahead of us is a large stage which has been extended into a catwalk and on the wall behind it is a massive black and white photograph of Paige in a black wig with *Mademoiselle Véronique* underneath in curvy pink neon lighting. It's a head and shoulders shot which makes her look as if she's naked when it was taken. Maybe she was.

Paige points to our left. 'There's a chillout area over there if it gets too much for you.'

'It's already too much for me.'

'Come here.'

She puts her arms around my neck and we kiss.

'Did you feel anything that time?' I ask.

'Less than nothing. In fact, I feel slightly nauseous. Declan is right behind you, about ten feet away. He's watching. Hence the kiss.'

'Let him watch. I don't care who knows about us now. And you don't have to keep on making excuses. I know you want me.'

'Caught out again. You're so brash and devil-may-care. My parents will hate you.'

I grab her shoulders and pull her closer in. I can feel her breathing change. I've got to dump these motorcycle helmets somewhere.

'What's the changing room situation here?'

'There's a proper changing room right behind the stage and a sort of green room to the left of it.'

'Got it.'

I disengage myself from her, turn around and head straight for Declan. He looks alarmed when he sees me coming.

'Hey there. Remember me? It's Damien, isn't it?'

'Declan,' he growls, puffing his chest out in an attempt to become taller. This never works; it just doesn't.

'Oh yeah. Listen.' I hand him both crash helmets. He holds them in his hands as if they were several tons of rotting boiled dog shit. 'Would you mind finding somewhere to put these? Paige and I don't want to carry them around all night. Maybe you could put them by Paige's stuff in the changing room. It's back there. Nice to see you again, Damien.'

I turn my back on him and walk back to Paige, who has been to the bar and got me a non-alcoholic cocktail.

'How did it go?'

'He wants to kill me.' I take a sip of the cocktail. 'What is this?'

'It's called Sham-pagne. Elderflower, fizzy water and lime cordial.'

'Delicious.'

'I'm going to tell you a secret. That was the first time I've ever been on the back of a motorbike.'

'What did you think?'

'Exhilarating. I particularly liked the way you took an insanely long route to get here so you could enjoy having my arms around your waist for a little longer.'

'You see right through me.'

'It's not difficult. I'm going to go and get changed. I don't know what you're going to do. This is what will happen. I'll get changed, then at nine o' clock I'll go onstage with Adonay Robel and do a quick talk about the line. Adonay will then say something. We haven't planned anything.' She stops and yawns. She looks tired. 'Then the models will come on and do the fashion show. Then Adonay and I will go onstage again and thank everyone.'

'You have a tough life.'

'I'm glad someone appreciates it. After the show, there'll be food and then the DJ will start with the dance music for those that want to dance. I never dance, in case you were hoping for a smooch.'

'I wasn't going to ask.'

'Now I'm hurt. Take a look at the seating around the catwalk. All those seats are reserved. Your seat is on the right six down from the front of the stage. I'm next to you on the left and Emma is on your right. Oh, and just so you know; we don't call each other by our professional names in social situations, so Emma Antonsen is Emma and not LouLou.'

'I understand.'

'Oh! Here she is now.'

Emma Antonsen is tall, has very short blonde hair and amazing eyes that are lined with blobs of yellow makeup which look like she daubed them on when she was drunk. Undoubtedly an expensive, professional job. She's wearing tight blue denim jeans and a matching jacket which is unbuttoned to reveal a mouth-watering cleavage. She hugs Paige and almost crushes her.

'Baby,' she says to Paige while looking at me. 'So what's going on? Is this your new man? I put your stuff over the back of your chair. Can I get free samples? I love you.'

'This is Daniel Beckett,' says Paige. 'Daniel. This is Emma.'

'Hi, LouLou,' I say, to get a cheap laugh from Paige

who punches my arm. Emma air kisses me. She smells of soap. It isn't soap; it's Calèche by Hermes.

'You're sitting next to Daniel for the show,' says Paige. 'No touching.'

'As if I would do something like that!' grins Emma, before heading off to the bar and leaving us alone again.

'Listen, Paige,' I say. 'I'm going to visit Fly a Kite tomorrow, just to sound them out, and I'm going to let Declan know I'm doing it. I need a fake occupation to make my reason for going there convincing. Any ideas? He's watching us. Kiss my neck before you answer.'

'This is some job you have, isn't it?' She leans forwards and plants the gentlest of kisses on the side of my neck. I experience a brief adrenalin surge. 'You could be an associate of Kelly Senac, my agent. You might be visiting the charity to discuss the possibility of more charity events featuring Kelly's clients. No. Don't say you're an associate. That would be suspicious because of the other night when I was introduced to you by Anouk. If you were an associate, I'd have known you.'

'So much for that, then. Thanks, anyway.'

'Tell him you're a freelance who connects charities to entertainment agencies for a commission. They do exist. I've met them. They're assholes. I really have to go and get changed. Have fun.'

'I'll try.'

'And if I see you look at another woman I'll kill you.'

She kisses me one more time and wiggles off. I go to the bar and get another Sham-pagne. After the first sip my teeth beg for mercy. I look around for Declan, but I can't see him anywhere. I take a walk around, just to make myself noticeable if he's hiding somewhere and spying on me. There are a lot of great-looking women here. I somehow expected the age range to be lower, but it's more like seventeen to seventy.

I decide to take look in the green room. Before I go in I can feel a presence and I know it's Declan. As I enter the room, he's just slipping his mobile into the jacket of his monkey suit. He looks up at me as if I've just caught him on the toilet.

'Hello, mate,' I say to him in as cheery a way as I can manage. I look at my watch. 'Few more minutes to kill then it all starts happening.'

He grunts and looks away from me. I sit down across from him. 'I guess Paige has told you that we're an item. I'm sure I don't have to tell a guy like you how lucky I am. I guess you've seen more of her than most! And she's so *nice* as well, you know?'

'Congratulations.'

'Thanks. That's very nice of you. It was just one of those…I mean, it hit me like an express train. Her too, I think. Sometimes there's an instant chemistry between two people that's impossible to ignore. How long have you been working for her now? It must be a while.'

'A couple of months.'

Try almost *five* months, Declan.

'I'll bet she feels safe from harm with a big guy like you working for her,' I say. 'Were you in the army?'

'Police.'

'Oh, really? Which branch?'

'Serious Crime Division.'

'Sounds exciting, mate. Were you in the Met?'

'Greater Manchester Police.'

'What made you leave?'

'You ask a lot of questions.'

Busted out, then.

'Just curious. Actually, it's pretty lucky that I've made contact with Paige in this way. Between you and me, it'll help me in my work. Don't tell her, though!'

I look him straight in the eye and flash him a weapons-grade smirk.

'What's your work?' he asks.

'It's a bit complicated. I don't know if you'll be able to grasp it. I'm a kind of freelance enabler. Paige told me she'd done some shows for this charity. Fly in the Sky or something? No. Hang on. Fly a Kite. Anyway, I put people in charities in touch with agencies like Paige's to help them organise and be involved in charity events. I hadn't heard of Fly a Kite, so this is a good contact. In fact, I'm going to see them tomorrow morning about getting in touch with this other agency I work for. I haven't made an appointment. I'm just going to turn up at about eleven. It's the best way. Catch them unawares!'

'Well, good luck with that,' he says with total disinterest and contempt, but I can see the cogs spinning.

'Thanks, mate.'

He stands up, sick of my conversation. 'I've got to go out there. They'll be starting soon.'

'Sure.'

He stands up and goes out. I count to ten and then follow him. For a moment I can't see him, then I spot him strolling around by the entrance. He's on his mobile. I zoom in on his face. It's a serious conversation. As he speaks, his left hand shields his mouth, as if he has a pathological fear of lip readers (like me). Obviously, I have no idea what the person he's speaking to is saying, but whatever it is it seems to please him. He grimaces, nods his head a few times, then puts his mobile away, glancing from left to right to see if anyone has been watching him. He's a cautious guy; I like that about him.

I go to the bar and get a glass of Veuve Clicquot then take my place at the side of the catwalk. Emma is already there. She smiles at me, takes my champagne out of my hand and drinks half of it.

'Do you know Volupté, Daniel?'

'What's that?'

'It's like a supper club, cocktail bar and burlesque venue all in one. It's in EC4. I'm stripping there next Wednesday, if you're interested.'

I smile at her. She knows that I am. She reaches into her clutch bag and produces two sparkly tickets.

'Here we are. Bring a friend if you must. You can pop in backstage afterwards. I'll be waiting for you. Don't tell Paige. Don't think I'm a bitch.'

'I won't.'

'But I can be if that's what you want.'

She grabs one of my hands and squeezes it. That's her fooled, then.

In a few minutes, Paige comes onto the stage to wild applause. She looks amazingly sexy and funky in a sleeveless brown leather mini-dress tied at the waist with a wide cream leather belt. She's wearing the black wig she wore at Bordello, or one very much like it. Heels are seven inches, I'm guessing, and the overall effect is sexy and imposing. The glittery black eyeshadow she's wearing looks as if it's been finger-painted on. There's a bald guy with her wearing a leopard-skin toga over some black briefs. His look is completed by black cowboy boots covered in rhinestones. I assume this is Adonay Robel. I wonder if Mr X is here.

'Thank you all so much for coming this evening and yes – it is me.'

This gets a big laugh, which is lost on me for a second, until I realise she's referring to the fact she's wearing clothes. She talks for maybe three or four minutes and then Adonay praises her inventiveness and his own talent for another five. Then she leaves the stage and the lights dim.

As the music starts and the laser lights flash, Paige appears and sits next to me. 'I just told Declan you were taking me home tonight,' she whispers.

'Are you wearing that dress on the way back?'

'Too racy for motorbike travel?'

'Does nothing for me at all. On the other hand, I'll be going back to Maida Vale via St Albans.'

Whoever booked the models for this show isn't relying on the usual catwalk girls. There's a wide variety of figure and age going past. A girl wearing a fabulous high-legged crimson body reminds me of Anouk; she has the body of a burlesque performer as opposed to a fashion model. She winks at Paige as she struts past us. I start thinking about Anouk having her tattoo done yesterday. I liked the look on her face as the pain got to her.

A couple of girls who look like genuine twins go marching by in matching black basques. None of the emotionless middle-distance staring for them, either. They chat to each other as they get to the end of the catwalk, turn, and head back the way they came. I can see Declan to my left, about twenty feet away, his gaze vacant and bored. I wonder who he was speaking to.

'What do you think?' asks Paige, as a white-haired mature model swaggers by in a see-through floral patterned bra and matching thong. She waves at Emma who shrieks and waves back. It's getting warm in here now, so I take my jacket off.

'They all look great. Classy, crude and sexy all at the same time.'

'That's it! That's exactly what I was going for.'

Thinking about Anouk's tattoo makes me think about the girl in Rikki's flat. The tattoo she had on her arm was a single red rose surrounded by black musical notes. I wonder what it meant. This case is progressing slowly, but I'm pretty sure I'm going to encounter whoever slashed that girl's throat at some point, and things aren't going to go well for them when I do.

My train of thought is interrupted by the sight of a model wearing only suspenders, stockings and heels. She stops right by us and bends down to give Paige a kiss on the mouth. Everyone cheers.

The something I hadn't thought about before clicks into place. The girl that Footitt picked up in Queensway. The one he was using as a punch bag. I couldn't see her very clearly because of the distance and the fact that I was watching her reflection in a shop window, but she had a tattoo as well. I couldn't make out what it was. It was near her collarbone. And the kid that Footitt solicited. He had a couple of cheap-looking tattoos on his neck and forearm.

I'm not suggesting that everyone involved in prostitution has a tattoo, but was Footitt the source of that girl in Rikki's flat? Was she someone that he procured during one of his night-time cruising episodes? He seemed to have no qualms about punching a girl like the one in the park. Would he be that worried about leading one of them to her death?

Of course, it sounds insane. He's a senior hospital consultant. He'd have too much to lose by committing murder. Unless it wasn't him that did it. Maybe someone like Friendly Face knew Footitt's predilections/contacts and just asked for a girl to be delivered to Rikki's place and took it from there.

Whatever, as Footitt is still my only wholly identifiable lead, I'm going to push in that direction. That place in Yeoman's Row, whatever it was; I'm going to have to pay it a visit and I'm going to do it tonight.

After the last scantily clad model leaves the runway, there's a standing ovation. Paige and Adonay take to the stage again, thank everyone, hug each other and start crying. The music and lighting change once more as the dance music starts up. I find Paige talking to a bunch of people over by the bar. When she sees me she kisses me, grabs my arm and introduces me to everyone. Declan is standing by the side of the stage watching. If, as I suspect, he's reporting this activity to someone, he's going to have a lot to tell them. Quite apart from my conversation with him, he's got the evidence of his own eyes thanks to Paige's collusion. She's doing well. I hope this works.

An hour later we're on the Ducati, heading back to Maida Vale. I can't say I'm not getting a buzz from having her arms tight around my waist. Once we're back at St John's Wood Road, I park the bike outside the main entrance to her block.

I take my helmet off and in the same moment have a quick look across the road. It's a no parking zone, but there's a dark green Audi Quattro over there with the engine turned off. Tinted windows, but I can see two people inside, both staring ahead. The guy in the driver's seat, thinking he can't be seen, turns and looks directly at me.

When we get inside, Paige goes into her kitchen to fix us something to drink. She comes out with two double vodkas and ice.

'So. Did it all go as planned, do you think?' she asks.

'Did you see the car across the road?'

'No.'

'Could be nothing, but it's an odd place to park and sit at this time of night. I'll keep an eye on it before I go out.'

'You're going out? Where are you going?'

'I have to break in to this place. The later I get there the better, I think.'

'I think I'd prefer it if you stayed here all night. I'm confused by all of this and I don't feel safe.'

'I'll come back here when I've finished. If the people across the road don't stay there all night, they may be back in the morning. If that's the case, I'll want them to see me leaving here. I'll want them to know that I stayed the night.'

She places her drink on the table, walks over to me and puts her arms around my neck. For a spine-tingling moment I think this is going to turn into a kiss, but it turns into a hug, with her pressing her face against my chest. She looks up at me, her expression fragile and apprehensive.

'Can I ask you something?'

'Sure.'

'It's a lot to ask, particularly as I don't know you very well. It may be something you're not comfortable with or are unable to do. I'll understand, I really will.'

'D'you want me to guess? It could take a while.'

She smiles. 'It's something I told you that Rikki used to do for me. It's just that I…'

'Go and get changed and get the stuff.'

A few minutes later she appears in a diaphanous black see-through gown with a sash belt tied around her waist.

She's naked underneath. The atmosphere is astonishingly and weirdly erotic. Maybe this is her way of thanking me for doing this, who knows? She sits on the sofa and smiles shyly at me as she gets the gear out of a transparent plastic box.

Once she's drawn some of the diamorphine into the syringe, she hands it to me, along with a bottle of alcohol and some cotton wool.

'Where do you take it, Paige?'

'Well, in my armpit would be OK. Please don't worry. It's only a low dose. I won't die on you.'

'Let's hope not.'

'I just – after tonight and combined with everything else.'

She pulls down the robe on her right hand side, exposing her shoulder and breast. She rests her left arm across the front of her body and raises her right arm, looking away as I daub a suitable area with alcohol. I can see her armpit hair is starting to grow back. I hear her gasp as I push the needle into a vein and slowly push the plunger down.

When I've finished, she rubs her armpit and is able to look in my direction again. 'Thank you. I know I'm fucked up. You're kind.' She finishes her vodka, gets up and heads for the kitchen. 'Do you want anything to eat or drink?'

'I better have a strong coffee. I'm going to be up for a while.'

'Biscuit?'

'OK.'

She returns a few moments later with a couple of coffees and a plate with some Belgian chocolate and hazelnut cookies. She finds a DVD of *Populaire* and sticks it in her player. As the film starts, the drug kicks in and she groans with pleasure and stretches, looking up at me and smiling.

We're just like an old married couple.

29

BREAK-IN

I park the bike down the far end of Egerton Garden Mews and dump the helmet out of sight behind a white van. It was quiet when I was here last night and now it's like the grave. The only sounds are coming from Brompton Road: a few cars, the occasional thundering HGV and late-night partygoers shouting and singing. I look at my watch. It's twenty-two minutes before three.

Before I set out, I picked Paige up and put her to bed, helping myself to a Maglite mini torch I found in her kitchen and one of her front door keys. When I left her flat, there was no sign of that dark green Audi Quattro. If they were involved in all of this, I reckon they were just there to check whether I dropped Paige off or went inside.

I try to visualise the house that Footitt went into. Two security cameras by the front door and no way in through the windows without being conspicuous and/or noisy. Any loud burglary sounds you made here would be heard a few streets away and in a posh area like this they'd be more than likely to call the police.

The house to the left of my target was undergoing renovation and there was scaffolding and dark green plastic sheeting all down one side. I'll have to go in that way.

I take a deep breath, turn out of the mews and into Yeoman's Row, keeping a close eye on all the doors and windows and listening out for any anomalous sounds.

There's a slight breeze and I can hear the sheeting flapping against the side of the building from about ten yards away. This is good. It means I can get away with making small noises without attracting undue attention.

I walk down the side of the house with all the confidence of someone who lives there and after I'm twenty feet away from the road I stop and look upwards. I know it's only four storeys high, but it looks a lot higher from down here. I really must try to avoid falling off.

It looks as if they're sandblasting the outside of the house and the sheeting is to stop the resultant mess drifting out into the street. There's a gap in between two of the sheets. I pull them apart and slip through. Now I'm out of sight.

It's dark in here, but I don't want to use the torch, so I wait until my eyes adjust. There's an aluminium ladder to my left and they've carelessly left it leaning against the scaffolding. I make sure it's sturdy enough then slowly and quietly start my ascent.

Unfortunately, the ladder is only big enough to reach the third floor and dragging it up to help me get to the fourth and/or the roof would be time-consuming, cumbersome and make too much noise, but it's better than nothing.

I get off the ladder and walk along the working platform that's been constructed outside the third floor windows. The planks have been tightly lashed together so there's absolutely no creaking and the whole thing feels safe and stable. There are no curtains or blinds on the windows here and the rooms inside look empty. It may be that the whole house is being renovated from top to bottom, inside and out.

Now I have to get up to the fourth floor. This is going to be a little dangerous because of the lack of light and the lack of ladder. I'm going to have to shin up one of the vertical scaffolding tubes. I wipe my hands on my jeans to get the sweat off and make the ascent as quickly as I can, gripping the tube until my knuckles are white. I almost have to stop because of the pain in my deltoids and lower back, but keep going until I can pull myself up onto the fourth floor platform.

I straighten up and give my back and shoulder muscles a quick stretch. Now for the difficult part. No ladder, no scaffolding. I look upwards and can see a couple of old-fashioned chimney pots on the edge of the roof. A car backfires about half a mile away and the sound makes me quickly and instinctively reach under my left armpit for a gun that isn't there. I take a slow deep breath to help dissolve the adrenalin fallout.

Then I spot a shape to my left. I give it a rapid onceover with the Maglite. It's a damaged scaffolding trestle with a fair amount of thick orange nylon rope wrapped around it. I look up at the chimney pots and then down at the rope again. It takes me about five minutes to unravel it, but it's my only chance of getting up onto the roof, short of developing superpowers.

The rope is only fifteen or sixteen foot long, but that should be enough. I tie two fat knots in one end and take another look at the chimney pots. If they're damaged or fragile, this could be a terrible mistake, but I've decided that it's worth a go.

I take three steps to the left, twirl the nylon rope around like a lasso, and throw it up at the pots, with a view to looping it behind them so I can get the knotted end back down here. It takes me five frustrating attempts before it finally succeeds. I work the rest of the rope upwards and the weight of the knots very slowly brings the business end down far enough so I can jump up and grab it. I notice I'm sweating.

I tug at both ends of the rope to see if the chimney pots can take my weight, even if it's only for about thirty seconds. It seems as if they can. If it turns out they can't, I'll know soon enough and so will everyone within a half mile radius.

As slowly and quietly as I can, I make my way up the wall, grabbing both sections of rope hand over hand, my feet pressed against the bricks for balance. I'm almost half way up when I hear a grating noise that sounds like broken pieces of terracotta grinding against each other. Not good. I stop moving and count to ten. Nothing happens, so I continue my ascent.

After what seems like an age, I'm on the roof. I pull the rope up and leave it in a discreet pile a few feet from the edge. I sit down to recover and rub my aching muscles. After a minute, I get up and make my way across the roof tiles, crouching low and occasionally patting one hand on the surface for support and balance. There's a slight slope up here which I didn't expect. I'm glad it hasn't been raining.

I walk to the other end of the roof. I take a look at the gap between this house and the one next door, which is, of course, where I'm headed. The gap is maybe eight or nine feet and I'm going to have to jump it. I just wish the light was better. I get out of my crouch and stand up straight. It's a great view from up here; I just hope it's not the last thing I ever see.

I visualise the jump about half a dozen times, take ten steps back and run at the gap as fast as I can. Things don't quite work out as I'd planned.

Whether it was the dim light or my failing judgement, I'm not sure, but I was about eighteen inches out. I managed to grab the edge of the other roof just before getting slammed against the side of the building. It hurt.

I'm hanging over the edge with my arms flat against the surface, my legs dangling and the wind knocked out of me. I hope no one heard me spit out an exasperated 'Fuck it!'

I manage to pull myself up, my shoulders and stomach muscles hurting like a bastard, not to mention the entire front of my body. It could have been worse: someone could have been watching.

This roof doesn't have any gable windows like its neighbours. There's a large, brick, Victorian chimney stack in the centre, so I walk over and crouch down next to it, just like Cary Grant in *To Catch a Thief*.

To my right, there are two glass skylights, both big enough for me to get through. They're not obviously alarmed, but I can see that they're locked from the inside with sizeable mortice locks. At present, the only way in would seem to be to smash a small area of glass and pick the lock, which is out of the question; too much noise, too much hassle.

Hassle. The word reminds me of Rikki. It seems strange, but I keep forgetting about him. He's the reason I'm up here on this roof in the middle of the night. I hope I'm not on a wild goose chase.

I slip on a pair of latex gloves and run my hands over one of the skylights. In a couple of seconds, I find the solution. Amazingly, there are eight reinforced plastic clips holding the glass in place which are on the *outside*. I'd read somewhere that skylights are a weak point in building security and now I can see why.

I start work on the clips. The burglar's tools I use are only three inches long and extremely slim, but they're made from titanium and carbon steel so they don't snap under high pressure. It takes thirty seconds to get all eight clips off. I place them in a neat row next to the skylight and lift the glass up. Almost immediately, there's the dank, mouldy smell of an unused room. I place the glass next to the clips and take a quick look at what's below using the Maglite. It looks empty apart from some plastic office cartons, stacks of old newspapers and magazines and a dilapidated easy chair.

Now I have to move fast.

I drop down into the room after an unpleasant few moments hanging on to the rim of the skylight by the tips of my fingers. I straighten up and listen for sounds. It's quiet, but then it is a time of day when anyone who lives here would hopefully be fast asleep.

I close my eyes, breathe deeply and allow my consciousness to expand into the whole building. I know this sounds borderline demented, but it's saved my life several times in the past when an apparently empty building wasn't really empty at all.

After a minute, I'm satisfied that I'm the only person here. I switch on the Maglite and take a more comprehensive look around. As I thought earlier, this is a storage room of some type. There are two big wooden filing cabinets against the wall immediately to my left. I try to pull one of the drawers open, but it's locked. It's an old-fashioned type that can't be broken into without causing obvious damage, so I'll leave it alone.

There's a dusty dressing table next to the filing cabinets. The mirror is spectacularly cracked. It looks as if someone threw something small and hard at it with quite a degree of force. Both dressing table drawers are empty. Over by the other wall is a wrought iron garden seat with a deflated basketball on it. There are two old dining table chairs, both with worn-out fake leather seats. I place one of them directly under the skylight. I'll be needing that later.

The only other item in here is a rickety metal work bench, covered with tools which look as if no one's used them in years: two pairs of rusted pliers, a big pair of scissors, some small plastic things I can't identify, an enormous screwdriver, a broken spirit level and a steel club hammer. I pick the hammer up. It's a hefty tool and feels as if it weighs about five or six pounds. I put it back on the bench in exactly the same place I found it.

This can't be the only room on this floor, so I decide to check out the rest of them. The door to this room isn't locked and leads into a small landing. I find a medium-sized bedroom, that looks and smells like it hasn't been used for some time. There are cobwebs all over the only window, but no spiders. The bed isn't made up. There's a book on the bedside table. I pick it up. It's called *Edgar A. Guest Remembered* by Jean Elizabeth Ward. I put it down.

I go back out onto the landing. Across from the bedroom, there's a small bathroom and a separate toilet, plus a small cupboard filled with cleaning gear. There must be a way down to the next floor, but I can't find it. Is this floor sealed off from the rest of the house for some reason? Then, when I hit a small doorknob with my hip, I realise there's a door right next to me. It's just been wallpapered to blend in with the rest of the wall. For a moment I think it's locked, but it's just stuck. I pull it towards me and find that it opens directly onto a narrow, uncarpeted staircase.

I flash the torch ahead of me. I'm guessing that this must have been a family house with servants, and the fourth floor was part of the servants' quarters. It's quite possible that there were originally two staircase systems so that the residents didn't have to bump into the help more than was necessary.

The third floor smells much cleaner and there's also a faint smell of cigarette smoke in the air, but I don't think anyone's been smoking in here for about a week. There are six rooms here: a small sitting room with a couple of sofas and a television, another sitting room which seems to double as an office, a pokey bedroom, a smart-looking kitchen, plus, once again, a small bathroom and separate toilet.

The second sitting room contains an old-fashioned walnut bureau. The writing flap is pulled down and there's a computer resting on it. The bedroom has terrible bright green wallpaper and there's a print of leopard cubs hanging by the bed. The bed isn't made up and the mattress isn't new. This may well be someone's flat or pied-à-terre. I don't really know what I'm looking for here, but I don't think it's on this floor, though I may come back and check the computer if I can't find anything else of interest.

I go back into the office/sitting room. Taking into account that some computers take an age to fire up, I switch this one on. It's a new-looking Mac with a big screen. I find the button round the back, push it, close the curtains and head down to the second floor.

This time, I use what could be called a 'proper' staircase. It's carpeted and the carpet smells new. After three steps it takes a sharp left turn and becomes a little steeper. Flashing the Maglite ahead of me, I think, for a moment, that this heads straight into a wall, but then I see a door. It's becoming rather difficult to work out what's going on in this house, and now I'm not sure in which direction I'm facing.

This door is solid oak. I place a hand against it and give it a quick shove, but it doesn't move an inch. There's an ordinary door knob, but when I try to turn it, nothing happens. I crouch down and shine the Maglite into the door jamb, but there's no sign of a latch bolt: it's a dummy.

Beneath it is an ordinary Yale mortice. This is real and it's been locked. Before starting work on that, I take a good look at every inch of the door with the torch to make sure there's no electronic surprises coming my way. It looks clean, so I get my burglar's tools out again, and with the Maglite in between my teeth, pick the mortice in about five seconds.

I open the door into pitch blackness. The door opens to my left, so I shine my torch on the wall immediately to my right to see if there's a light switch. There isn't. It's cold in here and smells of floor polish, male sweat and wood.

I give the whole place a fast sweep with the Maglite. Unlikely as it seems, it appears to be a small chapel. Or maybe it just looks like one. Does Footitt come here to do penance in the wake of his nefarious nocturnal activities? Does he fling himself onto the floor and beg for forgiveness? Is it an open-all-hours confessional centre for mountaineering psychiatrists with male pattern baldness?

Or perhaps it's a small, private concert hall. I've seen chamber music performed in places that look a little like this in Venice and Naples. That would fit in with my theory of Footitt being an amateur musician and would maybe explain his black leather case. But a theory is just a theory.

There are two big windows to my left, both of which are covered with thick wooden blinds which are tightly closed. I decide I can risk turning the lights on to get a better look. The light switch turns out to be lower down the wall than I'd expected. When I turn it on, I have to pause for thirty seconds to take in what I see in front of me. This is not a chapel and it certainly isn't any sort of music venue. I don't know what it is.

It's incredibly ornate; probably nineteenth century and very well maintained. There's an awful lot of red marble and teak; the marble would explain the cold I felt when I opened the door. It's more like an old-fashioned town hall meeting room than a chapel. To my left and right there are rows of well-polished leather-padded wooden seats: twenty on each side at least. The floors are made from some dark wood and in the centre there's a big rectangle of alternating black and white floor tiles. Looks like a large elongated chess board, but I'm sure it isn't.

Down the far end, there's what looks like a modest wooden throne. This has a couple of smaller seats either side of it, presumably for the lieutenants of whoever gets to sit in The Big One. I walk down to have a closer look and then I see it. Carved in wood and attached to the wall above the throne is a Masonic Square and Compasses.

So Footitt is a Freemason. Hardly surprising: a lot of

people like him are. Important professionals who don't *quite* feel important enough yet: doctors, lawyers, teachers, policemen, estate agents and just about anyone else who fancies belonging to a female-free secret society with all the advantages and perks it's purported to supply.

So now it falls into place. The leather case that Footitt was carrying may well have contained his masonic regalia. The same was probably true of the two men who followed him into this house the other night. A little late for a masonic meeting, I would have thought, but then I have no idea how they organise themselves, so anything is possible. Perhaps there are different types of meeting. Perhaps not everyone in a lodge attends all of the meetings at the same time.

Freemasons are often on the receiving end of a lot of negativity, as befits any male-only clique with alleged power and influence. I've read quite a bit about them over the years, but can't remember most of it. Wasn't Mozart one? Wasn't there a theory that he'd been murdered by them for giving away their secrets in his music? Weren't they somehow involved with the failure to catch Jack the Ripper?

I remember what Doug Teng said about the Triads. They didn't like the term secret society, preferring *a society with secrets*. I smile as I remember that I'd read that exact same phrase in an article about freemasons, the connotations of the phrase 'secret society' being bad for their modern-day glasnost.

I sit down on the wooden throne, stretch my legs out and look around. Charity work is one of their big things, I seem to remember. People say that they help their brother masons whenever they get into trouble of any sort, sometimes in ways that can seem grossly unethical to outsiders. Wasn't there some book written about how ambitious, bent police mixed with known criminals at masonic meetings to both of their advantages?

I stare into space for a moment, trying to clear my mind, but then it all comes rushing in; so much of it that I start to feel a little panicky. I remember wondering what would have happened if Jamie Baldwin had been taken to another hospital after his assault. Would there have been a Footitt waiting there to put the pressure on? Annalise telling me that no one could understand how Footitt had become a consultant. All that stuff about selling off the donated blood and somehow getting away with it, not to mention the assault on the nurse. Then there was Jamie's gut feeling about Friendly Face and Big Bastard; that they were almost certainly police or ex-police.

Suddenly, I get a cold feeling in my stomach. Freemasons and their long-term association with charities. Paige's unexpected rush of charity gigs, all for the same worthy cause, coinciding with the disruption to her private life, partially orchestrated by a couple of probable ex-cops. The inside information about Jamie's steroid use, the hassle-free smuggling of the soon-to-be-dead girl into Rikki's swish flat, Paige's minder, ex-cop Declan Sharpe and his bad attitude.

And let us not forget Mr X.

I get up and leave the chamber or whatever they call it, turning the lights off and carefully locking the door with my burglar's tools. I run upstairs to the third floor, taking the steps two at a time. I sit in front of the computer, which seems to have turned itself off. Then I remember it's a Mac and click the mouse once.

The background is a big colour photograph of the earth as seen from space. I'm slightly surprised; I think I was expecting something more sinister, more *occult*. I look at the dock and click on 'Finder', then on 'Documents'.

There are six folders and a bunch of PDF files, the latter looking like invoices or receipts. The folders are called 'Brethren 2068', 'Complaints', 'Eleemosynary', 'Lodge Payments', 'Catering Expenses', 'Maintenance & Repairs' and 'Social'. Quite reasonably, I wonder what the hell 'Eleemosynary' means.

'Brethren 2068' looks like a logical place to start, so I click on it to open it up. Nothing happens. I try opening the other folders with exactly the same disappointing result. I look a little closer. Each blue folder has a tiny symbol on the bottom right-hand corner; two stylised, bearded faces looking in different directions. Is it the god Janus? I need to have access to whatever's on this computer. It may be the key to finding out what the hell's going on. I decide to give Doug Teng a call. I take a look at my watch; it's five to three. Ah well, I'll make it worth his while.

'Hey, Mr Beckett! So what are you doing in Yeoman's Row at this time of day?'

'Stop showing off. I need your help.'

He pauses for two seconds before replying. I can hear gunfire and helicopters in the background. 'Oh yeah?'

I know exactly what the two second pause was for.

'Yeah. And I'll make it worth your while. Double your usual rate.'

'Okeydoke. Phone consultation three o' clock in the morning. Double the usual rate. One thousand pounds straight up. Special low price as it's you.'

'Done. Are you watching a film?'

'Sure thing. *Under Siege 2.*'

'When do you sleep?'

'When I get tired. What can I do for you?'

I run a hand through my hair and sit up straight. Fatigue is starting to get to me. 'OK. Get ready. I'm in a bit of a hurry.'

30

MARTON COMPUTER SOLUTIONS

I give him the make and model of the computer and describe what I can see on the screen.

'There's some sort of security lock on these files that I've never seen before. It's like two bearded faces looking in different directions. The graphic is yellow with blue edges.'

'Yeah, yeah, yeah. That's Janus Encryptions Inc. That guy with the beards, that's Janus. The original two-faced bastard. He was the Roman god of doorways and gates. Looking backwards and forwards. January is named after him, yeah? But he was also the protector of locks and keys, you know? Quite a clever name, really. Bit too obscure and subtle for me. Some real smartass thought that one up, I'll bet.'

'Are you taking amphetamines?'

'Ha, ha!'

'Can you crack it?'

'I'll be honest with you, Mr Beckett. It's a bit of a mega-challenge to put it mildly. Janus Encryptions won the Computing Security Awards three years in a row. Virtually impossible to get past, I would say.'

'But you can do it.'

'Oh yeah. No problem. Piece of cake. First things first.

I take it that you've burglarised somewhere and that you shouldn't be sitting in front of this computer in the first place.'

'That would be correct.'

'And, er, it's not a Triad computer.'

'Absolutely not.'

'OK. So we don't want to leave any trace whatsoever that this computer has even been *used*, let alone had its expensive, top-of-the-range security system bypassed. I take it you're wearing gloves?'

'Oven mitts.'

'Excellent. OK. Click on Safari, then type in Marton Computer Solutions. You should see my website. Click on the link.'

The website appears on the screen. For some reason, I'm quite surprised to see that it's really slick and professional-looking.

'Done. Hey – this looks really smart, Doug.'

'Thanks, man. Cost a packet, though I had to doctor it a bit. Now click on 'About Us', then click on 'Services'. Do you see where it says 'All emergency incidents catered for'?'

'Got it.'

'Triple click on the word 'incidents', count to five then double click.'

I do what he says. The screen goes black for a couple of seconds, then a whole new menu appears. There are six Chinese words, which mean nothing to me: Dao, Nu, Ji, Yue, Qiang and Gong.

'OK. I've got the screen with the six words in front of me.'

'Pretty clever, huh? All my lethal programmes are named after ancient Chinese weapons.'

'This is beyond sophisticated, Doug. What now?'

'Click on "Yue".'

The screen instantly goes black again. After five seconds, a small white circle, about a centimetre in diameter, appears in the centre of the screen and very slowly starts to expand. I have no idea why, but there's something rather scary and sinister about this.

'What's happening, Doug?'

'The Yue was a big fuckoff axe used for cutting through heavy armour, especially against cavalry. Cut straight through their fuckin' horses, too, if they didn't watch out. This program is cutting its way through the Janus programme. Shouldn't take too long.'

After about a minute, the screen is completely white, then we're back to the Marton Confidential homepage again.

'It's finished, I think.'

'OK, man. Let's have a look at those files again.'

I bring the files up and the small Janus logo has disappeared. I click on 'Brethren 2068' and it opens up straight away, revealing a long list of names. Much as I'd like to stay and read all this stuff, I really have to get out of here.

'It worked. How can I make a copy of all of these files?'

'You got a memory stick on you?'

'Let me check. No.'

'No worries. I take it you have an email address somewhere.'

'I might have.'

'Go into Safari again. Get your email account up and sign into it.'

I call up a Gmail account which I use for nothing in

particular at present. I know what he's going to suggest. 'You want me to send these files to myself, yes?'

'You'll be after my job next, man!'

It takes ten long seconds for all the files to upload. Once they're finished, I click on 'send'.

'OK. So we don't want any record of what's just been done. What do I do?'

'Still got my website up? OK. Go into 'About Us' then 'Services' then the sentence 'All emergency incidents catered for' like before. Quadruple click on the word 'emergency'.

This time, the screen goes white. Four circles appear in a horizontal line across the screen: red, purple, orange and black.

'Got the circles up? Triple click on the orange one, count to five, then triple click again.'

Black screen once more, but then it gradually becomes apparent that this is a big black circle, which is slowly getting smaller.

'What's going on now?'

'It's putting the Janus security coding back on all the files and locking them. Tell me when the black circle's gone.'

This takes about thirty seconds. For a moment, I think I can hear a noise from downstairs, but I think it's just the house creaking.

'Black circle's gone. Coloured circles are back.'

'Okeydoke. According to my stopwatch that took us a little over nine minutes, so we're going to reset the whole computer to eleven minutes before you started the whole process. This'll delete the Safari history, but only the stuff *you* used and there'll be no evidence of any actions by you or me in the background tasks. It'll be as if you were never there. Quadruple click the purple circle, count to five, then single click it.'

'That it?'

'You can leave now. This will take about five minutes and it'll turn the computer off when it's finished.'

'Are you sure?'

'Hey.'

I go out the way I came in, closing, and where necessary, locking all the doors behind me. When I get to the storage room on the top floor, I stand on the dining table chair I'd left under the skylight, grab the skylight frame with both hands and pull myself up onto the roof. The position of the chair will look suspicious if anyone pops in here, but what the hell.

Once I'm up there, I have a quick look and listen, then replace the skylight glass and all the clips. Everywhere is still pretty silent. About half a mile away I can see the ever-changing red, amber and green glow of a set of traffic lights. Always assuming I'm being watched and listened to, I silently traverse both roofs (the jump was better this time), make my way down the side of the building and in a couple of minutes I'm back on the Ducati, keeping to the speed limit and heading back to St John's Wood Road via Park Lane with The Dorchester on my right. When was it I had lunch with Paige there? Yesterday? The day before?

It's nearly a quarter to four by the time I let myself in to Paige's place. I take a quick look in her bedroom to make sure she hasn't died and then get comfortable on her couch. If I start thinking about all the stuff that was rearing its ugly head during my time in Yeoman's Row, I'll never get to sleep, so I put it all to one side, set the alarm on my watch for nine a.m., think about the sort of lingerie Daniella the cryptographic consultant would favour and pass out.

31

ELEEMOSYNARY

Paige is sitting next to me, holding a cup of coffee.

'What time were you back last night? Is this going to be a regular thing? I don't know why I got engaged to you. My mother was right.'

I look at my watch. 'Go away. I've got another ten minutes before my alarm goes off.'

'Don't change the subject!' She smiles. 'You didn't have to sleep *here*, you know. On the couch, I mean. You could have got in with me. I wouldn't have minded. I trust you.'

I sit up and stretch. 'Famous last words. I was back here about four o' clock or thereabouts.' I take the coffee from her and take a sip. It's good, with the sort of caffeine kick I need at the moment. Paige isn't wearing the pink silk pyjama top she wore yesterday or whenever it was. This morning she's wearing a cleavage-revealing black satin outfit. You'd probably call them lounging pyjamas if pushed for a description; they have that vintage look that makes me think that they're probably part of the Mademoiselle Véronique lingerie collection. Long, wide trousers and she's wearing black fluffy mules. Much too sexy for this time of day and I think she knows it. At least she's not wearing the black cherry and cardamom perfume she had on the other day. That would be a little too much.

'Did you find what you were looking for?'

I have to think. Yeoman's Row suddenly seems a long time ago. I must remember to pay Doug. 'Nothing specific, but maybe a few more pieces of the jigsaw.' I place a hand against my mouth to stifle a yawn. 'What does eleemosynary mean?'

'Eleemo-*what*?'

'Just a word I came across last night. I'd never seen it before.'

'Hold on.'

I sip my coffee and watch that wiggle once again as she leaves the room; it's starting to grow on me. I wonder how she'd respond to the wrong sort of stimuli. Pretty well, I think. She returns a few moments later with a battered old Oxford English Dictionary. I spell the word out for her and watch her face as she flicks through the pages. She frowns as she concentrates and a crease appears between her eyebrows.

'It's an adjective. It means relating to or dependent on charity. It's existed from the late sixteenth century and derives from the medieval Latin word eleemosynarious. Any use?'

I take a deep breath. I remember thinking last night about the freemasonry's longstanding associations with charity. Well perhaps there's nothing in it. Perhaps Footitt's lodge does charity work like many of the others and that's just their admin file.

Paige said she met Jamie Baldwin at some charity event. Charity Box Challenge, I think it was called. Is there a link there? Is that how Friendly Face discovered Jamie's address? Not to mention all Paige's woes starting from the first time she did a gig for Fly a Kite. Charities are involved in all of this a little too much for my liking. There was some charity stuff amongst Rikki's junk mail, but the significance of that was probably zero. I'm going to have to have a good, concentrated look at the files filched from that computer later on today.

'I don't know.' I reply. 'I was just curious. Listen – what are you doing for the rest of the day?'

'I'm having lunch with a friend, then we're going shopping in the West End, then we're going to The Tate. After that, I'm not sure. I might just have a quiet night in. Why?'

'I'm going to go back to my flat, then I'm going to pay a visit to Fly a Kite. I'll have my mobile on me at all times. If you see or hear anything suspicious, anything at all, call me immediately. You remember that dark green Audi Quattro with the tinted windows that was parked across the road last night? If you see that again, let me know straight away. Registration was 500 MPG. And don't worry. I don't think anyone's going to hurt you, but being extra vigilant can't do any harm. What about tomorrow?'

'Tomorrow? I promised to go and watch Creamy la Douce at The Pheasantry in Chelsea. A load of us are going. It's an afternoon thing. A promo for her photo book. Starts at one-thirty, finishes at six. After it's over I'm going home for a restful evening.'

'Don't make it too restful.'

She sticks her tongue out at me. 'Mind your own business.'

'Are you going to use Declan?'

'No. He knows about it, though. I'll be sharing a cab back with a couple of the girls.'

'OK. Watch yourself.'

'Are you related to my mother, by any chance?'

I get up and prepare to leave. Just as I'm going out of the door, Paige touches my arm. I turn around to face her and she stands on tiptoe and kisses me on the cheek.

'I know you're not working for me, but it feels as if you are. I just wanted to say thank you.'

I smile at her and brush a stray lock of hair away from her cheek. 'You're welcome.'

*

Back in Exeter Street, I take a long, hot shower, standing under the spray for ten whole minutes in an attempt to wake myself up. Once I'm dressed, I make myself a mega-coffee in a Pillivuyt French Coffee Bowl, switch on the computer and check that all the files I emailed to myself are actually there. Everything looks OK. I really owe Doug; I could never have sorted this out in ten minutes. I really want to start digging around in all this stuff, but won't have time this morning.

Fly a Kite is on the King's Road near The World's End pub. This area is a short walk from the Chelsea and Westminster Hospital. Maybe I can pop in on Annalise for lunch.

I can't be bothered with using the underground to get there, so go outside and hail a cab. The journey takes about fifteen minutes. I told Declan I'd be there at eleven o' clock and I'm a bit early, but if anyone has hopes of finding me hanging around this area, then they'll probably be early, too. I know I would be. Declan is an ex-cop. I'm hoping that will work in my favour and he'll be able to give Friendly Face and Co a pretty good description of me. I don't want to have to wave at them if I spot them.

I find a small café, sit outside, and order a large Americano and some scrambled eggs with smoked salmon on bloomer toast. I can see the Fly a Kite offices on the other side of the road. For some reason, I'd been visualising a charity shop with second-hand stuff for sale in the window, but this is an office, situated in an early twentieth century three-storey townhouse with the bright yellow Fly a Kite logo to the left of the letterbox.

The building is well-kept, freshly painted, and, from what I can see, the interior looks new and very smart. There's money here and I wonder where it comes from. I'd never heard of this charity before the other day, but they seem to be doing very well for themselves. Are charities OK with that, I wonder? Shouldn't they be doing very well for other people?

As I eat, I take a look around for a dark blue Mercedes S Class, but can't see one. Of course, I'm only working on a hunch here and this could be a waste of time. Declan may just be an ass and have nothing to do with any of this, but I'm guessing he was straight on the phone to Friendly Face or some other goon as soon as I told him that Paige and I were an item. The Audi Quattro outside Paige's flat last night would go some way to confirming that.

My main objective this morning is to find out who Friendly Face actually *is,* assuming that he turns up. Identifying him would be a huge leap forward. Finding out about Footitt was useful, but I think he's an auxiliary player, so not as important.

I just realised that Paige forgot to ask her agent about which company Declan came from. Or maybe she did and forgot to tell me. I'll call her about it later. On the spur of the moment, I decide to give Tom Nyström a call. Tom may well have been a darling, but his rapid departure from Paige's employ with its multiple explanations just didn't ring true. They were the sort of emotion-packed reasons that no one would question.

'Hello?'

He's Irish, which surprises me. With a surname like that I'd expected to hear a Swedish accent. I put mild aggression into my voice.

'Is that Tom Nyström?'

'Yes it is. Who's this?'

'You know who this is. Just checking up to see that everything's OK.'

'Of course it is. Why shouldn't it be?'

'It's just that some people have been nosing about, asking about why you stopped working for Miss McBride so abruptly.'

'What people?'

'They wanted to know why.'

'You know why.'

'Perhaps you could remind me, Tom.'

'Listen. Who are you?'

There's two seconds where I can almost hear his pain, doubt and fear, then he hangs up. Good. His tone of voice throughout that bullshit conversation told me everything I needed to know. Somehow he was manipulated out of that job. That puts Declan in the frame a little more and makes it likely I'll be given my initial warning sometime in the near future, even if it's not this morning. I can only hope that the worrying combination of Paige/New Boyfriend/Fly a Kite will make someone get their skates on.

I look at my watch. Five to eleven. I pay my bill, cross

the road and walk slowly past three or four houses before reaching the Fly a Kite building. I stop, check nothing on my mobile and look from left to right before continuing. I don't feel that I'm being observed, but I want to give them a fighting chance.

I don't actually know what I'm going to say when I go inside. Either I continue with the lie that Paige suggested I tell Declan: that I'm a freelance who connects charities to entertainment agencies for a commission, or I just come straight out with the truth: that I'm a private investigator working on a missing persons job. I don't have to tell them the whole story. I really can't make a decision; it must be fatigue. I just hope inspiration will strike when I get inside.

I trot up the eight steps to the front door and press the doorbell.

'Hello?'

'Oh, hi there. My name's Daniel Beckett. I don't have an appointment, but I was hoping I could have a quick word with Cordelia Chudwell.'

I was in two minds as to whether I should use 'The Honourable Cordelia Chudwell', but then 'The Honourable' isn't really a title, it's what's known as a 'style', so probably not. No one replies, but there's a loud buzzing noise, so I push the door open and go inside.

I'm in a high-ceilinged hallway with a wide, plushly carpeted staircase straight in front of me. The place is clean, air-conditioned and tastefully decorated. There's a table to my right with a display of white orchids and two Van Gogh prints on the wall to my left. I can see an open door about ten feet away and can hear typing noises and subdued voices coming from it. I walk up to the entrance and tap twice on the door to get someone's attention.

'Mr Beckett? Good morning. I'm Cordelia Chudwell.'

The tall, attractive woman who walks towards me with her hand outstretched is about thirty, with a classless, educated accent and an easy, friendly manner. I'm surprised. The Honourable Cordelia Chudwell suggested some sort of English Home Counties horse-riding aristocrat with a braying voice and a family history of enthusiastic inbreeding.

She's wearing a bright red short-sleeved pencil dress which cuts off a couple of inches above the knee. Wide hips, no bust and an expensively coiffured mane of jet black hair. To make things worse, she has enchantingly beautiful eyes with long black eyelashes and a yummy mouth. Talking of mouths, I notice mine has gone dry. I wonder if she's going to offer me a coffee?

I realise immediately that my charity worker backstory has to be dumped. She's too smart and she'll see through it straight away. I can see guarded amusement in those eyes and a pursing of the lips as she realises the effect her appearance is having on me.

'Hi there. I must apologise for dropping in without warning. I'm a private investigator and I'd be grateful if I could have a few minutes of your time.'

She flashes me an incredulous smile. 'A private investigator? Are you kidding?'

'No.'

'And is this to do with a case you're working on at present?'

She has a soft, smoky voice which is pleasant to listen to and not a little sexy. But she seems slightly uncomfortable talking to me. She seems slightly uncomfortable, period.

'Yes it is.'

Her eyes hold mine for a couple of seconds. It's unsettling.

'Let's go in the conference room. Would you like a coffee?'

Thank God. 'If it's not too much trouble.'

There are three young women working in the office. They all look up as I walk through. Cordelia turns to one of them, a dark, serious-looking girl with red-framed glasses. 'Gretchen – could we have a couple of coffees in the conference room, please?'

As I follow her, I watch the way she walks: arms hanging loosely at her sides and what's possibly an exaggerated sway of the hips. She has a big, well-shaped ass and I'd like to see her naked.

The conference room contains a big, erratically-shaped white plastic table surrounded by eight chrome and black leather chairs. There's a widescreen television screen down one end with a DVD player underneath. The windows are enormous and look out onto a well-tended garden. We sit opposite each other. She's wearing Black Opium, but I decide to keep that to myself.

'So how can I help you, Mr Beckett?'

'I'm working on a case that involves a woman being cyber-stalked. I'm sure you understand that there's a limit to what I can tell you.'

'Client confidentiality.'

'Exactly. And I may be asking you questions that you cannot or will not want to answer.'

She places an elbow on the table, rests her chin in her palm and smiles.

'So we're both entitled to be cagey.'

'That's about it.'

Gretchen comes in with the coffee things on a tray. I

thank her and wait until she leaves before continuing. I attempt to juggle all the facts of the Rikki Tuan case into some sort of chronological logic that can be comprehensively explained to a stranger without actually telling them anything. It's going to be difficult, particularly as I don't quite know what's going on myself. I look at her mouth as she pours two cups from a large burnt orange Le Creuset cafetière. Expensive stuff they have here. Business must be booming.

'Your charity organised four events at the Café Royal. They were burlesque evenings. Two of them were in March, one of them was in April and the last one was in May. I take it you know what I'm talking about.'

'Of course, I organised those events personally and they were a great success. We hope to do more like them in the future.'

I smile at her and make the tone of my voice casual. 'What made you decide to try that form of entertainment? It's pretty atypical for you, isn't it?'

'You're right. I'm always on the lookout for new things, though, and I like to try new things out. I was talking to Connie Kazprzak from Red Awareness just after Christmas. They're a humanitarian charity and they've always been a bit more showbizzy than we are. They've done benefits with comedians and bands and so on. She'd done a burlesque evening about a year ago and was telling me about it, so I decided to pinch the idea. Simple as that.'

'And it went down well.'

'Very well. Part of it was the venue. The Pompadour Ballroom is a great place to spend an evening and the luxurious surroundings meant we could charge a lot for the tickets. Also, burlesque is an up-and-coming thing now. It's been gradually moving into the mainstream of entertainment for years. It all kind of gelled. Are you a fan?'

'Of burlesque?'

'Yes.'

'I've seen a few shows.'

'And what did you think?'

'Fun. Sexy. Nice atmosphere. A good night out.'

'Do you like the women?'

'In what way do you mean?'

'Their bodies. Their sexuality. What they do on stage. The way they display themselves.'

'They're all different,' I say, noncommittally.

She nods her head and smiles. 'That's true. I have to say I admire them, though. I would be too shy to do something like that. I'm much too inhibited.'

'But you've thought about what it might be like?'

'Yes.'

'And you like the idea?'

'Yes.'

We stare at each other. I take a sip of my coffee. Things are going slightly off track here. I'm confused. Is she flirting with me?

'So the three subsequent burlesque evenings at the Café Royal. How did they come about?'

She clears her throat, drinks some coffee and appears to be composing herself. She's not making eye contact with me anymore. 'The first evening was a big success, so it was decided to do it again. We thought we'd do it as quickly as possible while people were still talking about it. It got a few reviews in the papers, which is always useful.'

'And you asked for the same three girls?'

'It was thought that there was a certain atmosphere on

that first date which made the whole thing work, which made the whole evening a success.'

'Did you attend the subsequent events?'

'I went to all of them apart from the one on the ninth of April. I was otherwise engaged.'

'So you asked for the same three girls, Kara la Fraise, Misty von Tassel and Véronique D'Erotique.'

'I love those names, don't you? Can you remember any of the names of the girls that you've seen?'

She's hedging. She was taking responsibility for things a few moments ago, but as soon as I asked her about the subsequent three shows and choosing the same three girls, she started using different language: *it was decided to do it again, it was thought that there was a certain atmosphere.* Then she changes the subject to burlesque stage names. It's as if everything was suddenly taken out of her hands after the first concert, and I wonder who by.

'I can think of a couple of them.' Both Anouk and one of Paige's support acts come to mind. 'One was called Suzette Rousseau and there was another called Strawberry Sapphire.'

She looks pleased with these names and claps her hands together. 'That's fab. What did they look like? Their figures, I mean.'

I smile. 'Both pretty busty, from what I can recall.'

She keeps touching her hair. 'And is that what you like?'

'In burlesque artistes or in real life?'

She becomes serious and looks straight into my eyes. She keeps touching and rubbing her left arm.

'Either.'

'I'm not fussy and I like variety. So have you organised any more burlesque evenings with the same line-up?'

'Why do you ask?'

'Just curious.' Now I have to improvise. 'The reason I'm asking these questions is that the woman who's being cyber-stalked was one of the performers at those charity events at the Café Royal. I'm sure you'll understand that I can't tell you which performer it was. She's been receiving sinister messages on her Facebook account from someone who seems to have been at all of those events. I was just wondering if it was at all possible to get a list of everyone who bought tickets.'

This is bullshit, of course, and I'm not that interested in her reply, but I have to keep up the façade: I've got what I want. She shakes her head slowly.

'No. No, that wouldn't be possible. The tickets go through agencies. They're mainly bought online but sometimes in person, as well. You could just go to a booking office and pay with cash if you wanted to. There are online agencies, but they would perceive the details they receive – names and card numbers and all the rest of it – as confidential. Quite rightly so, I think. We just hand the ticket rights out to these agencies and they do all the rest. We keep some tickets back for VIPs on occasion, but no – I don't think you could find out who's going night after night.'

This is just what Paige said. I'm going to curtail this meeting now, if at all possible. I start to stand up, but she raises a hand and points at my empty coffee cup. 'Would you like another coffee?'

'Yes, please.'

I sit back down and watch her. Her movements are even more self-conscious now. She runs a middle finger across her lower lip as she pours the coffee. She looks over her shoulder at me and smiles. She runs a hand through her hair.

'There are a lot of things one has to attend in a business like this,' she says. 'Sometimes they're interesting, other times not. Take tonight, for example. I have to go to a fundraising ball out in Croydon. Goes on until midnight. I went to one of these before, in the same venue. A little more boring than I'd have liked.'

As she places the coffee in front of me, I get a charming smile from her. She bends forwards so that her arm touches mine and her hair briefly brushes the side of my face. I can smell perspiration mixed in with the Black Opium. If, for whatever reason, she's trying to distract me, she's doing a pretty good job of it.

'Here we are,' she says. 'Hope it's OK.'

'I don't think I've ever been to a charity's offices before. It's not at all like I expected,' I say.

'Oh, you mean the house. Well, not all of it belongs to the charity.'

'Do people live upstairs? Do *you* live upstairs?'

She smiles to herself. 'Why do you ask?'

'Just curious. If you did, I was going to ask what it must be like living above your place of work.' I take a few quick sips of my coffee. I'm trying to finish it as fast as possible.

'No, I don't live upstairs.'

'Do you have a flat somewhere? A house?'

'Not at the moment. It's a little embarrassing, actually. I did have a flat in Islington, but it was on a short lease and I couldn't get it renewed. I'm staying with my sister this week. She was down with a really vicious bug that had wiped her out, but she's on the road to recovery now, so I'm moving out the day after tomorrow. Having to live with the parents until I get another flat sorted out. Pours cold water over one's social life a little. And my mother…'

She trails off. I smile sympathetically. 'I'm sure it does.' I finish my coffee and stand up. I have to get on and have had enough of her small talk. 'This has been very helpful, Miss Chudwell.'

'Cordelia. Is that it?'

'Yes it is. I just wanted to see if it was possible to trace who had gone to all those Café Royal evenings. Obviously it would be impossible to track down everyone, or if it was, it would take much too long and be ultimately inconclusive. I'd like to thank you for your time and for the coffee.'

She pushes her chair back and stands, but she's not finished with me yet. She walks over to a side table and picks up a business card from a small pile near a computer printer.

'Can I give you my business card?'

'Of course.'

'In case you need to speak to me again. My mobile number's on there; my personal email address, too.'

Our hands touch briefly as she hands me her card. 'Thank you.'

'Listen. I know we're strangers and this is a little embarrassing for me, but I don't usually come across people who are…who have seen and like burlesque concerts. I'd like to go to some more. I find them intriguing. Exciting, if I'm being honest. But they can't always be arranged through the charity and I don't want to go alone. Could you – I mean…'

I put her out of her misery. 'You'd like me to accompany you to one of these concerts, if you find one you'd like to go to.'

She blushes again. 'Yes. Just because – you know – you're interested and one doesn't often…'

I hand her my card. I'm not sure this is a very smart thing to do under the circumstances, but what the hell; I'm being hypnotised here and am not responsible for my actions. 'I'd be delighted. You can give me a call when you discover something of interest. If I come across anything suitable, I'll give you a call. OK?'

'Thank you. I'll understand if I don't hear back from you. I'll show you to the front door.'

'And don't worry. You don't have to be shy about this. Not with me.' I suddenly remember the burlesque guide I encountered in Rikki's flat. 'Oh, by the way – there's a thing called PictureRama's *Burlesque Map of London*. You can probably order it online. You may find it useful. Lots of venues, events and stuff.'

'I'll order one now.'

'You do that.'

'Good luck with your investigation, Mr Beckett. I hope you find what you're looking for.'

'You too, Cordelia.'

She fiddles with her fingers, her eyes downcast. 'I'm sure I will, Daniel.'

Good grief.

32

MR BECKETT, IS IT?

As I walk down the steps at the front of the house, I've almost forgotten what I'm doing here. Well, that was a pretty weird interlude. Was she trying to distract me? Once again, I get a feeling of some behind-the-scenes manipulation going on here. If she was involved in this in some way, I don't think there was any malice behind it, though I could be wrong. It could be that she's being played but doesn't realise it. She certainly knew there were areas where she couldn't go, though. Maybe she didn't like people like me snooping around and asking awkward questions. I can't wait to get back to Exeter Street and my A4 cartridge pad and start writing all of this down.

I turn left and head towards the junction with Beaufort Street. It doesn't look as if I'm going to get a warning from Friendly Face after all. I'm just about to give Annalise a call when I hear the sound of a car in low gear about a hundred yards behind me, travelling at around fifteen miles per hour. On a road like this, that just isn't right.

When it's about twenty feet away, I hear a gear shift, a sudden acceleration and a black Mercedes S Class sails smoothly by, pulling in behind a three-ton flat back lorry a few yards ahead. The front passenger door opens and out pops Friendly Face, looking very smart in a dark blue suit and an open-necked stripy shirt. He's putting something back into his left inside pocket, but I can't see what it is. He's right-handed.

Jamie Baldwin got his physical description exactly right. Two hundred and fifty pounds, six foot two, short salt and pepper hair, big shoulders and running to fat, particularly around the face and gut. I would put his age at sixty-five, possibly even older. He'd have been quite an opponent about twenty or thirty years ago and can probably still handle himself.

He walks towards me and he's grinning. It's the same MO as Jamie Baldwin experienced: that affable and avuncular demeanour would stop you being on your guard and give him time to get in his request for your cooperation.

I keep walking and don't make eye contact. After all, I'm not meant to know who he is. As he gets closer I can see the beaky nose, thin moustache and the crinkling around the eyes. A broad smile appears on his face. I'm seriously wondering if he's going to give me some money to buy an ice cream.

'Mr Beckett, is it?'

I look puzzled and glance behind me. Is he talking to me?

'That's me. Who are you?' My tone is cautious, fractious, uncooperative. He smiles at me. It's a friendly smile. A friendly smile from a friendly face. The car engine is still running. I can just about see his driver. He's looking straight ahead, but I'll bet he's got us both pinned in the rear view mirror. I can't tell if this is Big Bastard or not. I suspect not.

'I just need to have a quick word about a rather important matter, Mr Beckett.' He waves a hand casually towards the Mercedes. 'Would you mind getting in the car, sir?'

I like the 'sir'. Nice touch. Gives the impression that he might be police. Like Jamie Baldwin, I can tell that this might once have been the case, but not anymore. He really ought to let it go. Maybe therapy would help. I decide to needle him. I want this to escalate in a way he won't be expecting.

'My mother told me never to get into cars with strange men, and you look about as strange as they come.'

The smile falls away from his face. He didn't like that. He walks towards me so we're standing about two feet away from each other. He's almost invading my space, which would be a terrible error of judgement on his part. His eyes are locked on mine, as if he's trying to stare me out.

'This won't take long,' he says, recovering and giving me a cordial grin.

'I know it won't. 'Bye.'

I turn to walk away, but he grabs my arm. A policeman's grip: not too painful, not yet assault.

'It concerns Miss Paige McBride.'

I turn around to face him, surprised and suspicious. 'What did you say?'

'I understand that you've recently started a relationship with her.'

'You *understand* that, do you? Well understand *this* – fuck off.'

He smiles to himself. I'm sure people tell him to fuck off all the time.

'I'm just concerned about her. Concerned for her well-being,' he says.

'Who are you? Her grandfather? What are you talking

about? *Well-being*? What?'

'She's had a lot of bad relationships in the past. Made bad choices. Now she's found someone who can care for her properly.'

I keep having to assess how the person I'm pretending to be would react to this. Not very well, I suspect.

'What are you saying? She's seeing someone else behind my back? Is that it?'

He gives me a look that's so full of understanding and sympathy that I fear I might faint from it.

'You're treading on someone's toes, sir. That's the best way to put it. I think it would be better for everyone concerned if you backed off.'

My cover personality pauses for a few seconds, lets all of this sink in, tries to make sense of what he's saying. I want my expression to make him think things might be going his way. But this is only a brief respite for him. I have a plan. I narrow my eyes suspiciously.

'Who are you? How did you know I'd be here?'

He sighs with exasperation, ducking my questions. 'Are you sure you don't want to come in the car? We can just have a quick drive around and I can put you in the picture.'

'Listen, girlfriend. I don't know you. How can you possibly know I'm seeing Paige? And what business is it of yours anyway?'

He places a hand on my right shoulder. I swat it away and push him hard in the chest. I want to check what he put in his inside pocket. It's a mobile. He's starting to lose his cool now. I look in his eyes and I know he'd like to kill me.

'There's no need to be like that, sir.'

'And why do you keep calling me *sir*? Are you the

police or something? Is this what the police do nowadays? Turn up in chauffeured Mercedes and tell people to stop going out with girls?' I hold my hand out. 'Show me your warrant card.'

He's smiling again. He's giving me one more chance.

'Listen to me. You're a nice-looking chap…'

'Are you *hitting* on me now, sweetheart?'

He ignores this, but it's all grist to the mill.

'Let's face it,' he says. 'Miss McBride is nothing more than a common stripper. That's all she is. She's little better than a whore. Go off and find yourself someone a little more decent, there's a good boy.'

Now he's pushed my alter ego too far.

'Sorry. What did you just call her?'

'I think you heard me.'

'Yeah,' I say. 'I did.'

I flick out a hard, fast punch that connects with his lower lip, just enough to smash the flesh against his teeth and cause his mouth to bleed. He places a hand against his mouth and then pulls it away to look at the blood. Now the mask has dropped. His manner is malevolent and threatening.

'You just made one hell of a big mistake, Mr Beckett.'

'Oh really. Did I. I think you're the one that made the mistake, you creepy fuck.'

I take a step towards him and strike him in the solar plexus. He staggers backwards and almost loses his balance. His face is red. He bunches his right hand into a fist. The chauffeur gets out of the car and slams the door. He stands and waits for orders. He's a big bastard, but he's not Big Bastard. Stupid-looking. Bad teeth. Pained expression. No problem.

I can tell that Friendly Face didn't want it to come to

this – an altercation in the street in broad daylight – but I've given him no choice and he's losing his temper. He pulls his fist back and attempts a roundhouse swing to my face. I know his strength now and I know I'll be in trouble if that punch makes contact.

I block it with my right arm and sweep the palm of my left hand underneath his nose, breaking it and pushing him backwards at the same time. While he's considering that, I hook my right arm under his elbow, jerk it upwards and then bring him down. He lands flat on his back on the pavement with a heavy thump and I can hear the air wheeze from his lungs.

The chauffeur runs over to help, but Friendly Face, already getting up, waves him away. He's furious. Blood spurts from his nose and covers his mouth, chin and shirt. I can tell that he's in two minds whether to have another go at me, but good sense prevails and he returns to the Mercedes.

'You have no idea of the shit you're in, my friend,' is the best he can do as he's helped, sniffing, back to the car. 'You have no fucking idea. We'll meet again, Mr Beckett. You have my word on that.'

'Nasty nose-bleed you've got there, granddad.'

I smirk at him, as I know he'll like that. I wait until the car is in the distance and hail a black cab.

I think that went quite well.

I tell the driver to take me to Garrick Street so I can pick up a Vietnamese takeaway for lunch. I'll pop in on Annalise some other time.

Friendly Face's wallet is an expensive Mulberry billfold number. There's two hundred and fifty pounds in cash, which I take out and transfer to my own wallet. I'll save that for when I take Anastasija out to dinner.

There's a bunch of loyalty cards, several receipts for petrol and three credit cards, all in the name of Mr L. Tansil. So at least I've got a name. Stuffed behind the credit cards are three smart grey carbon fibre business cards for a company called Temple Security, and underneath the company name it says Larry Tansil, Director. There are three telephone numbers, an email address and a website.

I have a dig around for anything else interesting, but there's nothing. I put the wallet in my jacket pocket and give Paige a call. When she answers I can hear girls laughing in the background.

'Sorry, darling,' she says. 'No more nude pics. Your subscription's expired.'

More background laughter.

'You told me you got a major buzz out of sending them for nothing.'

'True. Are you OK?'

'I'm fine. Listen. Did you get on to your agent about where Declan came from afterwards?'

'Oh God. Didn't I text you? I'm sorry. She said he was from a company called Temple Security. Is that any use?'

'It might be. I'll speak to you later. Have fun.'

'I will.'

I sit back in my seat and look out of the window, watching the tourists mill about outside Buckingham Palace. Well, that's it: Declan's the official information centre concerning the love life of Véronique D'Erotique. So now there're four of them directly involved in all of this: Tansil, Footitt, Declan Sharpe and Big Bastard. This is so complex and perplexing I'm almost enjoying it. *Don't worry, Rikki; I'm almost there. We'll find out what happened to you yet.*

33

TEMPLE SECURITY

The cab journey took a little longer than I thought it would, so I don't bother with the Vietnamese, instead popping into Paul's patisserie in Bedford Street and picking up a tuna melt croque.

Once inside, I switch on the computer and make some coffee. With the information gleaned from Tansil's wallet I might, at last, be able to make some headway here. I search for 'Temple Security' and find the site straight away. I thought Doug Teng's site was pretty slick, but this is in another league altogether. Everything you click on fires up a well-produced promotional film accompanied by dramatic orchestral music.

Temple Security plc was founded in 2003, though it doesn't say who by. From the look of its scope and range of services, plus the length of its existence, I'd guess that it's basically a conglomerate of maybe half a dozen smaller security companies that were melded together by some bright spark in the City with a view to making it a public limited company.

It employs three thousand and ninety-four people, has a turnover of approximately £44 million and has accreditations, awards and quality approvals coming out of its ass. It's also SIA licensed, which would be extremely important for a big concern like this.

The SIA (Security Industry Authority) regulates the private security industry in the UK. It hasn't been in existence for long, but it's an essential licence to have whether you're a huge company like Temple or a lowly private investigator like me. I don't have an SIA licence.

Virtually anywhere you go and see security cameras, security guards, mobile patrols, dog patrols and all the rest, a company like Temple Security is behind it. Just scrolling down their client list is a mind-boggling experience in itself and you can hear the cash registers ringing: shopping malls, university campuses, rail networks, construction sites, supermarkets, office properties, fast food outlets, car parks, hotels, heavy industry, the National Health Service, theme parks – you name it. This is big, big business.

I take a look at the senior management page. The top guy is a wizened old geek called Nathaniel Fernsby. Used to work for a big chemical concern. Keen on country walks. One down from him is Judith Skelton, who's the Senior Commercial Manager. She has a string of academic abbreviations after her name and breeds Devon Rex cats. All these people are suits of one sort or another and flicking through their brief CVs tells me nothing. Then I find Larry Tansil. He's the Managing Director of City of London Operations when he's not busy ruining Paige McBride's personal life or being smacked in the mouth by me.

His brief résumé goes on about his long-term experience as a police officer, but it doesn't say what he did, where he served or why he left. But then why would it? For comparison, I take a look at one of the security managers, an aggressive-looking grey-haired gorilla named Robert Parry. He's also an ex-cop, but it says he was

Assistant Chief Constable in the Avon and Somerset Constabulary. Before that, he was a Detective Superintendent in charge of CID.

Just from a random search, I find two more ex-police and two ex-army. In each case it tells you what their rank was, where they served and what they did. But not Tansil. This may mean nothing, but I'll keep it in mind.

I flick through more staff until I finally find Big Bastard. He's Deputy Corporate Security Manager and his name is Mark Gable. He doesn't look like the sort of psychopath that Jamie Baldwin described to me and at least he was fully dressed and oil-free when this photograph was taken.

He seems like quite a cheery person, in fact, with a big, broad smile. But once again, all I can glean from his little paragraph is that he was ex-police with extensive experience of personnel management. Like Tansil, there are no further details. Well, at least Jamie's intuition about both of them being cops or ex-cops was on the beam.

I don't imagine that I'll find Declan Sharpe on here: with a couple of thousand employees, they're hardly going to put everyone's name and photograph up, but I have a look anyway. It's while I'm navigating around the site that my mobile goes off. It's Jamie Baldwin.

'Hi, Jamie. What can I do for you?'

He sounds edgy, as if he doesn't quite know why he called me.

'Oh, hi. Er – I was just – I thought I'd give you a call to see how things were going. With your investigation, I mean.'

'They're OK. I'm gradually getting there, I think.'

'Did you find out who Friendly Face and Big Bastard were afterwards?'

'Not yet. I'm still looking into that.'

'But you'll let me know if you find out, yeah?'

'Of course.'

'Have you seen Paige since you saw me? Or spoken to her?'

'No, I haven't. There was nothing more I needed to ask her.'

'Oh. OK. Listen…'

'What is it, Jamie?' I say. I can afford to sound a little terse and impatient when I'm several miles away from that seventy-four-inch reach. I take a sip of my coffee. It's cold.

'It's just that there's something I didn't tell you. I didn't think it was that important at the time. It was just weird. Creepy, really. And I just thought you might think *I* was weird if I told you about it. It's – it's just not the sort of thing you tell someone about, know what I mean? And it's probably – it's probably totally unimportant.'

'What was it, Jamie?'

'It was when, er, Friendly Face and Big Bastard came round to my flat. When they did my arm, yeah?'

'OK.'

'Well, you know I told you that Big Bastard stripped down to that thong thing he had on and he was covered in oil?'

'That image hasn't left my mind for a second.'

'Well it was when he was grabbing me round the chest. When he had me in that really strong grip and held my arm out so Friendly Face could use the iron bar on me. I could *feel* him against me, d'you know what I'm sayin'?'

I think I do, but my brain refuses to contemplate it.

'What do you mean, Jamie? What…'

I hear him take a deep breath and sigh. 'He was havin'

a stiffy, man. He was having an erection.'

For a moment, I can't think of anything to say. The strangeness of this, added to everything else, has given me temporary brain-freeze. I stare straight ahead of me, I look around the room, I glance at the computer screen, I push around some unopened junk mail on the desk.

'What are you saying? Was this caused by his proximity to you? Or was it to do with the violence that was about to happen?'

'God knows. Either would be pretty disturbing, eh?'

'Was this reacted to or commented on by him or Friendly Face?'

'Well, I wasn't in a good state at the time, but as far as I can remember they didn't seem to notice.'

'So Friendly Face wasn't fazed by Big Bastard's, er, *condition*?'

'If he was aware of it, he didn't seem bothered.'

I don't think I've ever asked anyone this question before, but here goes.

'Was he rubbing himself against you rhythmically?'

'You mean like dry humping? Like a dog or something? No, man. It was just there, you know? Like it was just a thing that happened that he took for granted or something. But I think he wanted me to *know*, you get me?'

Jesus Christ.

'You didn't imagine this at all, did you? From what I remember, Big Bastard gave you an uppercut that knocked you off your feet and Friendly Face kicked you in the head. I mean…'

'I didn't imagine this. I was fully conscious. Conscious enough to be frightened about what he was going to do with the iron bar.'

'OK, OK. I'll certainly take all of that on board. Thanks for calling.'

'And you'll let me know if you find out who they were, won't you?'

'Of course I will. Speak to you later.'

I click him off, place my mobile on the desk surface and press the balls of my hands into my eyes. Well, that's another slice of bewitching weirdness stirred into the mix. I can't imagine it has much bearing on anything, though. Once you've got a guy who gets out of his clothes and oils himself up when he's colluding in a spot of grievous bodily harm, then any additional quirks aren't really that shocking. Maybe the shocking thing was that Tansil was cool about it.

I return to the Temple site and take a closer look at their immense and impressive client list. I'm looking for Asset Properties, the insurance company who own Frampton House, where Rikki is or was domiciled, but they're not there. It would have been useful if they had been. That might have explained how that girl was smuggled into Rikki's flat and murdered.

I've no evidence that Day Manager Oliver Gallagher or Reception Supervisor Thomas Wade had anything to do with all of this, but I still get a strong feeling that someone working in Frampton House is connected to Tansil and Gable in some way and that the Terrible Two were probably responsible for killing that girl, aided and abetted by Footitt.

That whole thing with the girl is still nagging at me. I can't work out precisely how she fits in to all of this. It's as if her death was part of some plan, but I can't for the life of me work out what that plan would be. The overriding feeling I get is that she didn't have to die at all.

It's rather as if someone thought it would be a good idea to take her into Rikki's place and kill her. It's almost as if it was done on a whim; just for fun. A bit of a jolly jape. She was one of those people who just didn't matter. And to have the boldness to do something like that would indicate that you had no concerns about being caught, and even if you *were* caught, no concerns about any real consequences. Once again, I decide I'm going to have to be careful.

I make myself another coffee and start work on Tansil. I Google 'Larry Tansil police' and look at what turns up. Top of the list is, of course, the Temple Security website. There're a few junk sites that deal with security companies and he appears there, too, but only as one of Temple's senior staff. Come *on*: Tansil is an unusual surname. I rip through twenty-seven pages, but still there's nothing.

Eventually, I come across a sloppily-designed website called *Conspiracy Concepts*. The name Tansil is highlighted amongst a small block of maybe a dozen other surnames. I click on it. Nothing happens. The site seems to be defunct; the last post was made over four years ago. There's a small section that looks like it's a link to somewhere else, but, once again, it doesn't work. It says 'Tansil and Ricketts – those in the know spill the beans!!!'

Is this something, I wonder? I Google 'Tansil Ricketts' and see what comes up. Page after page of useless and irrelevant stuff is the answer to that. Then I find what seems to be the website of a Hertfordshire-based newspaper I've never heard of, *The Elstree Enquirer*. And there it is:

Chief Superintendent of Metropolitan Police Resigns after Corruption Charges Dropped.

It's him. Ch/Supt Laurence Tansil. And there's even a photograph of his friendly face, scowling at some hapless press photographer. I have to say, he looks very smart in his full dress uniform.

This all happened seven years ago. The article in *The Elstree Enquirer* reads like it was a cut and paste job from several different articles and is quite difficult to follow. The upshot seems to be this: Tansil took payment on two occasions from a known criminal called Martyn Ricketts. In return for these payments (they fail to give an amount), Tansil arranged to delay police response time to two armed robberies in the City of London. How he did this is not mentioned here.

He also took steps to impede the investigation. Once again, we're not told how he did this (are they keeping all the interesting stuff for a book or something?). The ordinary, non-corrupt police finally tracked down members of Ricketts's gang and a couple of them grassed Ricketts.

Ricketts didn't grass Tansil, but some smart detectives finally put two and two together (after nineteen months!) and Tansil was arrested. I'm guessing that this wasn't the first time he'd been involved in shady dealing, but I suspect it was the first time he'd been caught. I wonder why it took them nineteen months? Was their investigation being impeded in some way?

Even without the full details, this is very, very serious stuff, and it's nothing short of a miracle that Tansil was allowed to walk free. He must either have had one hell of a lawyer or been related to the judge.

It says that despite the charges being dropped, he resigned so as not to cause embarrassment to the police force and to take attention away from all the difficult work they had to do. He sounds like a real politician. And so, with that dark cloud hanging over his head, he's given a well-paid job in a private security company. Some guys have all the luck.

Mark Gable is not so easy to track down and it takes me fifteen minutes before I come across a small news item about him in the online version of *The Manchester Evening News*. Gable was a detective inspector in the Serious Crime Division of The Greater Manchester Police. This time, there was no dignified resignation. Gable was ignominiously booted out and was given a four-year suspended prison sentence. He was found guilty of a serious assault against a member of the public and that member of the public's girlfriend. This all happened three years ago to the day.

The incident had happened outside a nightclub in Manchester's town centre. Twenty-eight-year-old Matthew Bell and his girlfriend Julita Jaworska, twenty-two, were leaving Champagne Supernova at one-twenty a.m., when Gable, seemingly the worse for drink, approached Miss Jaworska, started calling her a slut and then tried to feel her breasts through her dress. He's quite the silver-tongued ladies' man.

Mr Bell attempted to intervene. Mr Gable punched him in the face, knocking him to the floor, then proceeded to repeatedly kick him in the chest, arm, neck and head. Miss Jaworska tried to stop Mr Gable. Gable punched her as well, breaking her jaw in three places and knocking her unconscious.

Mr Bell suffered multiple injuries plus a blood clot on the brain and it was touch and go whether he would survive. Miss Jaworska was in a coma for two weeks, but was expected to make a full recovery.

What the hell did Gable think he was doing? No sane serving police officer, particularly a DI in Serious Crimes, would do something like that unless they were completely crazy. It would be suicidal on a number of levels.

Unless, rather like I imagined in Tansil's case, you'd got away with it before and thought that you could get away with it again. If Jamie's guess about his age was accurate, I reckon Gable would have been in his late thirties or early forties when this incident occurred. Certainly old enough to know how much booze he could handle before launching himself at innocent civilians. And physically, he would have known that the averagely built guy (or girl) wouldn't have stood a chance against him.

A big, important police officer like that an insecure drunken bully? Well, it wouldn't be the first time. Did he not like seeing guys with their girlfriends? Was he jealous? Hey – now *there's* a thought. Could that behaviour be linked to what's going on with Paige? Are we looking at a cabal of violent, couple-hating ex-policemen? Unlikely, but there's an unpleasant streak of misogyny running through all of this that I don't like one tiny bit.

Also, it hasn't escaped my notice that Declan Sharpe was in the Serious Crime Division of the same police force and also left, I suspect, under a cloud. Sharpe is a fair bit younger than Gable. I wonder if they knew each other? Was Gable his boss? Did Gable get Sharpe his job at Temple Security?

I take a sip of my coffee and stare at the computer screen. Both Tansil's and Gable's stories seemed a little too big to be that difficult to find. Tansil's would have been the sort of thing you'd see in all the papers and perhaps on the television, and *The Elstree Enquirer's* scoop looked like it had been acquired from several other less obscure sources. So why didn't I come across any of those other sources?

Gable wasn't a cop in London and he wasn't as high-up as Tansil, but a brutal attack like that would have made the news even if he hadn't been in the police force. The article in *The Manchester Evening News* was relatively small, and Tansil's story didn't even make the front page of *The Elstree Enquirer.*

Were those two stories so small that they were missed? Did someone have a crack at killing all traces of those stories, but the two I found were somehow under the radar? And rather like Tansil, Gable lands on his feet with a well-paid, prestigious job at Temple Security. And Temple Security gloss over the background of those two scoundrels on their website.

Tansil and Ricketts – those in the know spill the beans!!!

So what have we got? Two senior staff in Temple Security are a pair of bent/psycho ex-cops who landed on their feet after doing stuff that would, under normal circumstances, almost certainly have got them both jail time.

Gable's attack on Ms Jaworska *alone* would have put a normal person away for anything up to twenty-five years, yet he gets a four-year suspended sentence. Perhaps some kind-hearted judge thought that being kicked out of the force would be punishment enough for the poor devil.

And as for Tansil, we have perverting the course of justice, accepting bribes, assisting the execution of armed robbery – I'd have to ask an expert, but I think he'd be looking at twenty years plus.

They were both directly involved in the assault on Jamie Baldwin, but that assault seemed to be planned by and executed on behalf of someone else, who I'm still calling Mr X. With Baldwin, Tansil mentioned these *very important people*, as if there was a committee of them, but when he tried to warn *me* off, it was down to treading on the toes of a single person. He probably just forgot his lines.

Both Tansil and Gable are, for want of a better word, *fearless*. Whatever they get up to, it looks as if they are confident that there will be no repercussions, or at least nothing like the repercussions that they *deserve*.

Temple Security (or someone working for them) seemed to have the clout to replace Tom Nyström with Declan Sharpe in a very short space of time, ostensibly to keep track of Paige McBride's love life. They were able to lean on Tom Nyström and effectively get him out of the way. Did they offer him a bribe or a better job? Declan Sharpe is also, perhaps not surprisingly, an ex-cop. An ex-cop who was not quite perceptive enough to see what the real relationship between Paige and Rikki was and who was easily taken in by me.

Someone places Declan in regular and close proximity to Paige. It's unlikely to be an official job by Temple Security itself, so I'm assuming that Declan receives his unsanctioned instructions directly from Tansil and reports back to him.

Declan's function must be to keep a close eye on Paige McBride and also those in her immediate orbit. The moment she appears to be on the cusp of having a relationship with any male, it has to be nipped in the bud, so he informs Tansil. Tansil, with or without Declan's help, then locates the male in question and firmly warns him off. If the male fails to heed the warning, something worse happens to him.

Of course, the only real example I have of this MO is Jamie Baldwin's unfortunate experience. I've had the skewed first warning myself, but I've no idea what happened to Rikki. The only hint came from Lee Ch'iu when he told me that Rikki had had hassle. Despite what I might think, or what Caroline Chow said, neither of us really have any idea how Rikki might have reacted to his first warning as neither of us witnessed it. We also don't know how many warnings he had; how many encounters.

I'm also keeping in mind something that Annalise told me about Footitt. The rumour about him selling off transfusion blood and getting away with it, plus that alleged assault on a nurse. That's another link between him, Tansil and Gable. All three did serious stuff and got away with it; relatively, at least. Are they somehow above the law? Is the law somehow on their side?

'You have no idea of the shit you're in, my friend. You have no fucking idea.'

I spend around fifteen minutes looking for stuff on Footitt. Apart from appearing on the Chelsea's website, there's little else: he gave a talk in Rhyl four years ago and attended a conference in Bradford a couple of weeks later. That's it. Declan, of course, is a complete dead end. Not a big enough fish to be mentioned on anything at all, unless *his* internet history has been whitewashed as well.

I'm just about to turn my attention to the Yeoman's Row files when I hear the barely noticeable noises outside my front door.

34

RÔLE PLAY

It's the cigarette smoke from that distinctive tobacco that gives her away. I think I'd sensed her silent footfalls coming up the stairs, but was too wrapped up looking at the computer. I can tell that she's right outside, maybe wondering if I'm in or not; wondering if she should start work on the cylinder locks again. I turn the latch and quickly jerk the door open.

'Shit!'

She almost loses her balance. She's squatting down in the hallway so that she's at eye level with the lower of the two locks.

'Are you the new cleaner?'

'You frightened me, baby.'

'I told you never to call me that.'

'Hah!'

As she walks by me into the flat, I take a quick look at what she's wearing. I can't believe she just walked down the street like this, though by now I should know better. I'll start with the unbelievably sexy, knee-length, tight-fitting, black pencil skirt with the five-inch slit up the back. If this didn't accentuate the impertinent jut of her bottom enough, the black five-inch heels with the red soles certainly finish the job. You'd almost miss the black seamed stockings from staring at that hot ass.

Above the waist is equally impressive and I'm beginning to get the picture. She's wearing a simple, white cotton short-sleeved blouse with the top four buttons undone so you get a tantalising glimpse of the curve of her small breasts which are dramatically pushed up by a black lace half-cup bra.

She has her hair tied up in a bun and, er, she's wearing black horn-rimmed glasses. I assume they have plain glass lenses. I follow her into the kitchen, inhaling the heady scent of Ombre Mercure Extrême. I visualise her spraying the perfume over her body while she was getting herself ready in her hotel room. I badly want to grab her.

'What are you trying to *do* to me, Caroline?' I say, laughing.

'You like it? I look pretty hot, uh? You remember I asked you if you thought I'd make a good secretary in an office?'

'I remember.'

'And I asked you if you'd take me out to dinner and then to have sex and you said probably? Well, I thought I'd become your secretary. We can do rôle play, yeah? You think I look the part? The glasses aren't too much? They cost forty pounds.'

'You look really secretarial. I see girls who look like you walking around London all the time. As soon as I opened the door I wanted to start dictating.'

'Good. I think I'm kinda shy and I had a crush on you for months and this is the first time we've been alone together in the office. I think about you just before I go to sleep each night, you know what I'm saying? So how's the case going?'

She drops her cigarette in the sink and turns a tap on to extinguish it.

I make us both a coffee. 'It's going OK. Those two guys who assaulted the boxer. I've found out who they are.'

Her eyes widen. 'Who? What are their names?'

'Larry Tansil and Mark Gable. They're both ex-police and they both work for a company called Temple Security.'

Her eyes narrow. 'Are either of them Mr X?'

'Very unlikely. And Rikki's friend. Paige McBride. The burlesque performer, yes? She has a bodyguard-cum-chauffeur who works for the same security company. His name is Declan Sharpe. He's certainly the leak in her entourage. I'm not sure of his motivation, other than sucking up to Tansil & Co.

'Every time Paige appears to form a relationship, whether it's a romantic one or, in Rikki's case, a drug one *mistaken* for a romantic one – he's the man that lets those two guys know about it. He was inserted into her retinue thirteen days after that first Café Royal gig. His predecessor resigned about five days before that with some bullshit story.'

'And then they get the iron bar treatment.'

'Well, that only happened once so far, and that was on the second warning. At least it was with Jamie Baldwin, the boxer boyfriend. I have that to look forward to, at least.'

'What d'you mean?'

'It was what we talked about yesterday. I made it clear to Sharpe that Paige and I were an item and he was dumb enough to swallow it. She played up to it last night at her fashion show at my request. This morning, I paid a visit to Fly a Kite, the charity who organised the burlesque shows at the Café Royal. It was after the first of those shows that all this started. I told Declan Sharpe that I'd be going there and I told him what time.

'There's something weird going on at that charity. Someone – and I can't help but think that it's Mr X – put pressure on them to book more shows that featured Paige McBride. It's suspicious. It always *was* suspicious: too many shows in too short a time and burlesque is a little out of character for them. I spoke to a woman there. The Honourable Cordelia Chudwell. When I came out, Larry Tansil was waiting for me.'

'So they got the wrong end of the stick with you, just like they did with Rikki. What happened?'

'I got into an altercation with him so I could lift his wallet. He told me we'd meet again. I don't think he was going to take me to the football.'

'So what was this Cordelia Chudwell like? Was she attractive? Would you have slept with her?'

'Yeah. I think I would. Very attractive. A provocative conversationalist. Fucked up. Tactile. Great hair. Pretty high maintenance, I would think. Rather like you, but with less expensive perfume and a bigger ass.'

'The sort of high maintenance you'd like to mess up?'

'I think so.'

'Huh. That's something I'd like to watch. So this warning happened with the boxer guy and it happened with you.'

'Which makes it pretty certain it happened with Rikki.'

'But we don't know whether Rikki got the second warning. The iron bar warning.'

'Well, that's the big question. Why isn't Rikki around nursing a broken arm or some other unsavoury injury?'

She frowns, lights another one of her cigarettes and drinks some coffee. I inhale the aroma of the tobacco.

I'm trying not to look at her, but it's difficult.

'I don't understand…' She looks down at her cigarette and blows on it. 'I don't understand what their motive could possibly be. Why stop a girl from having boyfriends? It's flaky.'

'Tansil mentioned that I was treading on someone's toes. He said it would be better for everyone if I backed off.'

'Better for Mr X.'

'Maybe.'

I don't tell her about Tansil's suggestion that Jamie and Paige be filmed having sex. I think that would just confuse the issue. Besides, I haven't really got my head around that one yet. It could have been just a bit of improvised weirdness by Tansil. Would it have pissed off Mr X if he'd found out? Impossible to tell at the moment.

'And what about the third guy?' asks Caroline. 'Who was that?'

For a moment, I don't know who she's talking about. Is it Declan? Of course it isn't. It's Footitt.

'There was a doctor who visited the boxer guy at the hospital. He was a psychiatrist. No professional business being there and a mildly intimidating bedside manner. It was as if he wanted to confirm that Jamie Baldwin was going to keep his mouth shut about what had really happened. He belongs to a masonic lodge. It's in Yeoman's Row near Harrods. Big house with too many security cameras outside.'

'Which didn't bother you in the slightest, eh?'

'Hm. I burgled it in the early hours of this morning and sent myself the contents of their computer.'

'Is this it? The contents?'

She points at the Yeoman's Row files waiting patiently

on the screen. I nod my head and sit down, waiting for her to drag a chair over and sit next to me. She's about six inches away. I wish she wouldn't wear that perfume. Her glasses are slipping down her nose. She pushes them up. I mustn't forget to call Anastasija today.

'This may be nothing, but they didn't seem to have any ordinary files that I could access without breaking locks. I didn't want to leave any evidence that I'd been there. Besides, I wasn't there to steal stuff, I was there to take a look around. I was just curious.'

'So I don't usually sit close to you like this, OK?' she purrs. 'You're aware of the warmth of my body. My perfume is driving you crazy. This is the first time you've really noticed me as a woman, rather than a secretary. You're beginning to wonder what I would look like naked. You're starting to be curious about how I'd make love. What my tastes are. What does that word mean on that file there, Mr Beckett?'

'Eleemosynary? It means relating to charity, Miss Chow,' I say casually, as if I've always been familiar with this word and its meaning. We turn and look at each other. We're both thinking the same thing.

'Open it up,' she says, stubbing her cigarette out in the ashtray. She takes her glasses off and places them on the desk.

'I've never seen you without your glasses, Miss Chow. You have the most beautiful eyes,' I say, without looking at her.

'Oh, Mr Beckett. You are embarrassing me.'

'Perhaps you like that, Miss Chow.'

'Perhaps I do, Mr Beckett.'

I click on the file. It contains three documents: 'Active', 'Dormant' and 'Possibles'. I click on 'Active' and the document opens up. It lists around a hundred charities, each one clickable for further details. AdoptAForest, AnimalAid, British Freedom for Hostages. Alphabetical. I scroll down and there it is: Fly a Kite.

I sit back in my seat and stare at the screen. Caroline pats her hair.

'You going to look at it? That's the one you went to see, isn't it?'

'Yeah. It's…'

I sigh. I'm trying to work out the logic and implications of what I've just discovered. It's difficult. Maybe it's just coincidence. Maybe I'm just tired. I click on the company name. The address in Chelsea I visited this morning is there, plus three telephone numbers. I take out my wallet and look at the card that The Honourable Cordelia Chudwell gave me. She had a hot figure, smouldering eyes and great hair. One of the numbers is hers. Well, that's no surprise; she seems to be in charge of the place, or at least that's what it looked like. I wonder if I should ask her out? I don't know why, but I like it when a woman wants to go and see strippers. It's fascinating and mysterious.

'Mr Beckett. It's rather warm in here. Would you mind if I let my hair down?'

'I think that would be rather inappropriate, Miss Chow.'

'But, Mr Beckett: I am so warm. I am starting to sweat. Perhaps *you* would like to do it. It is held up by a single pin at the back. It won't take a moment.'

'Well, if you insist.'

I remove the brass hair pin. It's in the shape of a dragonfly. Her hair loosens and falls down her back. She shakes her head to straighten it out, and I'm hit with the full bouquet of her perfume once more.

'Oh,' she sighs. 'That's much better. Thank you, Mr Beckett.'

'Shall we get on, Miss Chow?'

'Of course, sir.'

Beneath the telephone numbers are a record of monthly payments to the charity, presumably from masonic lodge funds, going back two and a bit years. I've no idea what would be normal for charity payments from a source like this, but they look pretty hefty; slightly different each month, but usually around three to four thousand pounds. No. That's an incredible amount of money. That's somewhere close to fifty thousand a year. Where does it all come from, I wonder?

I locate the main list of charities again and choose a random one for comparison. Football for Kids. They get a hundred and fifty pounds a month. I try another one: Lancashire Volunteers' Committee. They get two hundred a month, but the payments aren't regular; the last one was three months ago. And one for luck: The Katheryn J. Winner Children's Foundation. This gets regular monthly payments of sixty pounds, or has done for the last four months.

Then I see Charity Box Challenge. I'd almost forgotten about that. That's the charity that Jamie Baldwin did some work for. He and Paige met at one of their events. This lodge has been paying forty pounds a month to this charity for a little over two years. Was it through this contact that they managed to get hold of Jamie's home address? It wouldn't *necessarily* be through the boxing charity, of course. They managed to find Rikki's address easily enough. Or did someone torture it out of him? Did Mr X or someone else see Paige at the Charity Box event? It was just over a week after the third Café Royal gig and there would have been interest in Paige by then.

Caroline moves closer to me so that our thighs are pressed together. She's almost sitting on my seat.

'Some coincidence, huh?' she says. 'So what do you think?'

'Fly a Kite seems to be favoured, at least financially. There could be many reasons for that. The money could be coming from another source. There may be a finite time that each charity is supported; I don't know how it all works. But the fact that they get anything at all from this lodge connects Footitt with Fly a Kite and connects him with the Café Royal and connects him with Paige and connects him with Rikki. He's already connected to Jamie Baldwin, as we know.'

'Is Footitt Mr X?

'No. When Tansil and Gable assaulted Jamie, they did it in his flat and called an ambulance from there. He lives in Wandsworth. The Chelsea and Westminster would have been the nearest hospital with an A&E department. It occurred to me earlier that if Jamie had lived somewhere else, he would have more than likely been taken to a different hospital.'

'Where they'd have had another one of their guys waiting? Ready to put the squeeze on? Ready to make sure everything was going to plan?'

'Quite possible.'

'This is beginning to look like some pretty well organised shit, Mr Beckett, if you pardon my language. Would you mind if I unbuttoned my blouse? I'm still rather warm.'

'I'm not sure, Miss Chow. Do you not think your behaviour is getting a little reckless?'

'Now I feel ashamed.'

'Unbutton it then, if you must.'

'Thank you, Mr Beckett, for your understanding. But I must tell you; the shame I am feeling is making me feel a little…unsettled.'

There are only four buttons to undo. She takes it very slowly. It's starting to get to me now and she knows it; I can tell by her sly little glances in my direction.

'You like my posture?' she says, slipping out of the rôle play for a moment. 'I am very straight-backed, I think. Just like a real secretary. Is that it? Is that the only reason you think Footitt isn't Mr X?'

'No it isn't. It just doesn't feel right that it's him. I think we're looking for someone with an obsession with Paige. It's almost like a *romantic* obsession. Someone who sends her champagne and fur coats and works of art. Someone who moves heaven and earth to make sure that she's unsullied by relationships with other men. Someone who has trusted personnel at the ready to make sure it doesn't happen for her.'

'And someone who can't or won't approach her in real life.'

'Maybe. When I followed Footitt to Yeoman's Row the other night, he stopped off to pick up some rough trade. One male, one female. He drove them to Regent's Park. The guy went down on him while he repeatedly slapped and punched the girl.'

'Shit. That's some suave devil.'

'It's possible it *is* him, of course, but I can't quite square that type of behaviour with the Paige obsession. I could be mistaken, but I don't think I am.'

'That Footitt guy *hates* women, Mr X *loves* them. He puts them on a pedestal,' says Caroline, nodding her head affirmatively at her theory.

'Anything's possible here. Let's take a look at this other file.'

'I'm just going to take this blouse off. Just for a few minutes so I can cool down.'

She gets up. The blouse is removed and draped over the back of her seat. She pulls the bra straps off her shoulders and sits down again, straight-backed as before. I catch her grinning as she sees where my eyes are going.

Taking a deep breath, I click on 'Brethren 2068'. The 2068 is a little mystifying, but then I realise that it's presumably the number of the lodge as opposed to some notable masonic date in the future.

It's a list of names with dates of birth next to them. There are no headings, addresses or occupations. The names are bunched into groups. Sometimes the gaps in between these groups are wider than others. I take this to be indicative of some sort of categorisation or pecking order.

At the top of the first page is Viscount Ombersley. Is he the boss man of this lodge? The Sublime Commander of the Sun, or whatever they call themselves? I've never heard of him, though I may have to check him out in more detail later on. Caroline points at his name.

'Is that the Mr Big?'

'Hard to say. He might be a token peer. They like having someone connected to nobility or royalty at the top. Bestows gravity and social cred. He may not involve himself in their day-to-day affairs. They pride themselves on their egalitarianism, but you're unlikely to get an aristocrat making the tea, so to speak.'

As I scroll down the list I recognise the names of seven serving Members of Parliament who are actually in the current government and another three who are not. I also recognise six so-called captains of industry, two television presenters, a comedian, a high court judge, a former high-up MI5 officer, one minor royal, a couple of top cops and three senior churchmen, one of them an archbishop.

Most of the names, however, mean nothing to me. It's when I get to the fourth block of names that I find Lawrence Tansil, his forename spelt slightly differently from the report in *The Elstree Enquirer*. So he's a freemason, too. Ex-police. No surprise.

'Tansil's on here.'

Caroline snorts. 'They have them in HK, you know? British freemasonry lodges. Set up by the ex-pats a long, long time ago. All the cops join. It's how they get on. Of course, we've infiltrated them as well. People like Jiang are members, if you can imagine that. Huge waste of time. Ready-made mythology. All bullshit. Just add water. Real men wouldn't bother. If you want to give to charity that badly, write out a cheque, yeah?'

'They turned you down, did they?'

She laughs. 'Yeah.'

There are over two hundred and fifty names on this list. I try to visualise the lodge interior and wonder how they cram them all in whenever there's a full meeting. Maybe they do it in shifts. Maybe the late-night visit Footitt made was a typical thing that happened. Maybe you can pop in for a fix of Supreme Being Worship 24/7, as if it was an all-night grocery store where the customers wore aprons and rolled their trouser legs up instead of buying cigarette papers and bread.

It's not long before I find Mark Gable's name and also that of Martyn Ricketts, famed criminal and briber of senior policemen. That's quite a shock. Did Tansil and Ricketts arrange their crooked business at a masonic meeting? Is this where they met? I'd read about it, but it's still disquieting to see that it actually happens.

Barnaby Footitt is almost at the end of the list. In normal society, a hospital consultant might be seen as being a little bit superior to an armed robber, but this plainly isn't the real world we're dealing with here.

There's no sign of Declan Sharpe or Henry Parsons, the Olympic doping fixer, but there, three up from the bottom, is Thomas Wade, Reception Supervisor at Frampton House, Rikki's ritzy block in Ebury Street SW1.

That's it. That means it was almost certainly Tansil and associates who were responsible for getting that girl into Rikki's flat and murdering her. I wonder how Jiang Weisheng got on with disposing of her body. I wonder who she was.

'I think I'm gonna take this skirt off now. It really is so hot in here.'

I have to agree.

35

A FACE MADE FOR PUNCHING

By the time that Caroline was down to her black La Perla underwear, I couldn't stand it anymore and neither could she. I grabbed her arm and marched her into the bedroom, throwing her, giggling, onto the bed, while she voiced concerns about her fiancé, Malcolm, an optometrist, whom she was to be married to in the spring.

We both fell asleep briefly, and when I wake up, I'm amazed to find that it is still only twenty past one. I must get something to eat. Caroline leans across me, takes my hands and briefly places them against her breasts, before pulling her bra back down.

'I have to go and have a pee. It's your damn coffee. Don't go away.'

I watch her as she glides out of the room, still in her bra, suspenders, stockings and heels. I thought that I might be looking at Temple Security as the main culprit behind all of this, but now I'm not so sure. It could just be a convenient place for Mr X to get personnel; lots of former police officers, some of whom may have a shady past and will do what you tell them. I pull a sheet over myself and stare at the ceiling.

So is this some sort of masonic conspiracy with Paige

McBride unwittingly at the centre of it? It's pretty unlikely. The masonic angle might, however, explain how Tansil, Gable and Footitt got away with so much, if you happen to believe in all that sort of stuff. Perhaps there's a freemasonry connection with Temple Security that I haven't detected yet.

Declan Sharpe is the only one out of the loop as far as this lodge is concerned (or maybe they forgot to put him on the list). Even so, he's a former police officer too, and is connected to Gable. Is this an important lodge? Is Declan already a freemason, but in another lodge? Could the same be true of Henry Parsons? Anything's possible. Do they do transfers like football teams? Maybe Tansil or Gable said they'd put a good word in for Declan if he went along with everything, and might be in with a chance of joining the prestigious Yeoman's Row mob.

The finger is certainly pointing in this direction. Without doubt, there are four lodge members actively involved in this. Three of them definitely involved in Jamie Baldwin's assault and one of them almost certainly colluding with the smuggling of that girl into Rikki's flat.

I feel stupid that it's only just occurred to me that there's a big clue in the name: Temple Security. Whoever thought that one up must have been a freemason. Do freemasons own the company? There were a lot of senior and middle management on their website, but no owners or founders; at least none that I noticed.

I'm just wondering where Caroline's got to when she calls out to me from the kitchen. I can hear her tapping on the computer.

'What was the name of that girl again?'

'Which one?'

'The charity one. The high-maintenance one you said

you'd sleep with. The cheap perfume one with the bigger ass than me.'

'Oh, her. Cordelia Chudwell.'

'Come and look at this.'

I get up and join her. She flashes me a look of mock shock.

'Mr Beckett! You are naked!'

'Just keep thinking about that Christmas bonus, Miss Chow.'

'You said that last year. I got nothing.'

She taps the computer screen with one of her well-manicured fingernails. 'I thought I'd take a look at the top man at this place. The lodge, I mean. Just out of curiosity, you know? Viscount Ombersley?' I sit down next to her. She smells good. She smells of overpriced perfume and unthinkable sex. She places a hand over the centre of the screen, blocking something out. 'Now. Are you ready for a big surprise?'

'OK. Let's have it.'

She pulls her hand away from the screen with a dramatic flourish. It's a website called *MacJarrow's Peers and Baronets*. At the top is a heading: 5th Viscount Ombersley. There's a photograph of a smirking man with receding blond hair in his mid- to late fifties. He's pretty seriously overweight with the beginnings of a triple chin and a face made for punching. Underneath the photograph it says 'Hugo Walter Clement Jaspar Chudwell – 5th Viscount Ombersley'. Well, hello *daddy*.

He's the owner and chairman of Quadrivium Pharmaceuticals. His great-great-grandfather was the founder of the company and he was also the first viscount. He's married to Lady Ombersley (really?), formerly Nancy Deborah Cynthia Roberta Constance

Sillars. They have four children, The Hon. Reginald Tobias Fox Quentin Chudwell (heir apparent), The Hon. Jolyon Tancrede Murray Ralph Chudwell, The Hon. Cynthia Arabella Tabitha Othella Chudwell and The Hon. Cordelia Ellen Roberta Bryony Chudwell.

Well, well, well. So is this where the pressure and manipulation is coming from? Caroline looks almost manically excited, but I warn her not to count her chickens. We spend five minutes doing further research on the viscount. Silver spoon, useless in school, mega rich: it's a common enough pattern.

We find a four-year-old article about how he does most of his directorial work from home, thanks to the advances in computer conferencing. He like to boast about how he can attend three meetings at the same time from his living room while enjoying a double-malt whisky. It's more likely that the people who really run these companies would prefer not to have him in the office. I get a moment of doubt reading all of this stuff; it seems like I'm getting further and further away from Rikki, but at the same time I feel like this is the way in, possibly the only way in.

We find an interview with his wife, talking about how hard her life is managing their big estate in the country (or telling others how to manage it). She's a rather plain-looking woman with no hint of humour in a rather wan face. She's dark, like Cordelia, but without the looks.

With no obvious qualifications other than her husband's wealth and/or existence, she used to sit on the board of a couple of right-wing political think-tanks and was an advisor to the board of governors of Quadrivium. She also used to appear on television from time to time, being asked her opinion on various social and political matters. However, all that stopped about five years ago. No reason is given, at least not in this article. She speaks fluent French and Italian and studied Cordon Bleu cookery at the Tante Marie Culinary Academy. As I scan the interview, I notice that her conversation is clipped and fragmented, rather as if it was edited by a malfunctioning piece of computer software.

'What's wrong with her eyes?' asks Caroline.

'Looks like hyperthyroidism. Causes the tissues and muscle behind the eye to swell. Pushes the eyeballs forward. I don't think there's a lot you can do about it.'

'You're a bigtime smartass, aren't you.'

We find another article that features her name and that of Gail Mozelle, the actress, but when Caroline clicks on it, an error message appears, telling us it's a broken link. It makes me wonder how many pieces of useless, non-functioning internet debris are actually out there and how much cyberspace they use up. Does it even work like that?

There's a recent piece in *The Economist* about Quadrivium Pharmaceuticals, who are developing a new drug for anxiety and depression. There's a companion piece about Viscount Ombersley's (I'm just plain old Hugo Chudwell) other business interests, which are many and varied. Caroline spots it immediately and almost pokes her finger through the screen.

'Temple Security! He's a fucking director of it! It's him! He's Mr X!'

'Hold on. We don't know that for sure.'

'Are you kidding? He slings all that money to the charity so he can put the screws on his daughter to keep booking the burlesque lady, he's a director of Temple Security where all his goons work and he knows two of them from the lodge. It *has* to be him.'

She grabs my bicep tightly, her voice excited. 'OK. The two freaks who broke the guy's arm both work in Temple Security and they're both members of this lodge. It could stop there. It could just be those two. But you said yourself – they're working for someone, a *very important* someone. Chudwell is *kind* of their boss at Temple and he's *kind* of their boss at the lodge. And he's the only one with a direct family link to that charity.'

'OK. Maybe you're right. It *looks* like it is him, but it doesn't *have* to be him. He'd been slinging money to that charity before all of this started, remember, so it isn't all watertight.'

'Perhaps. But maybe the charity wasn't doing so good, you know? Who knows how these damn things work. Maybe he was trying to make his daughter look successful. But now it's payback time. His daughter is his bitch!'

'OK. Slow down.'

'That's not what you were saying half an hour ago.'

'Neither were you, Miss Chow. Let's just take this calmly and pick it apart slowly. Oh, I forgot to mention this. There's another member of this lodge who's probably involved. I rang up Frampton House, pretending to look for a non-existent reception job. One of the guys they said to contact was Thomas Wade, the Reception Supervisor. He's on that freemasonry list. I was curious as to how they could have got that girl into Rikki's flat without anyone noticing. I think this Wade guy arranged it in some way, or allowed it to happen. I'd be very surprised if he didn't.'

'I'm getting confused.'

'Me, too. Let's take a look at it all in black and white.'

I drag my A4 cartridge pad towards me and start writing down all the links I can think of, for Caroline's benefit as well as mine. I'm hoping something will leap off the page and solve the case. This never happens.

Chudwell: Masonic Lodge, Temple Security, Fly a Kite.

Tansil: Masonic Lodge, Temple Security. Ex-police.

Gable: Masonic Lodge, Temple Security. Ex-police.

Footitt: Masonic Lodge. Psychiatric Consultant.

Sharpe: Temple Security. Ex-police.

Wade: Masonic Lodge. Reception Supervisor\Frampton House.

Doesn't look too amazing at present, but it'll help me illustrate things to Caroline. She has to be in the loop where all this is concerned now. Plus, sometimes I get the feeling I'm working for her and not for Mr Sheng. I give her the lowdown on the principal scumbags.

'Tansil, Gable and Footitt have all fucked up in their careers in one way or another, but they've all fallen on their feet. Relatively, at least. That may be due to their membership of this lodge, which *could* mean that each of them is indebted to Chudwell in some way, or to the lodge as a whole. Tansil was charged with corruption, among other things, but the charges were dropped, he walked free then resigned from the police.

'Gable attacked two people when pissed out of his head, seriously injured them both, got thrown out of the police, but only got a four-year suspended sentence, which is nothing.

'Footitt was strongly suspected of selling off donated transfusion blood. It's thought he'd been doing it for years. This was just a rumour, but if it was true, it would have led to him being struck off the medical register and probably sent to prison. There was also a rumour about him assaulting a nurse. As it was, he flourished and is now a consultant, albeit one that no one seems to have any professional respect for.'

'None of them got their just deserts.'

'Possibly. We also have to assume that these incidents could be the tip of the iceberg. Then there's Declan Sharpe.' I point at his name on the list. 'He's also ex-police and was in the Serious Crime Division in Manchester, which means it's likely that he knew Gable who was in the same division in the same force. He's younger than Gable, but their paths could *just* have crossed. A surly individual. Bad attitude. Unprofessional and resentful. Didn't like Paige *at all*. He's somewhere in his early to mid-thirties I would guess, which means he left the police – or was *asked* to leave – well before his career would have normally ended. Let's just make an assumption for a moment. We can dump it later if it doesn't fit.'

Caroline nods her head. She's got it. 'Declan Sharpe was also booted out, which means Temple Security is a safe haven for former bent cops, yeah?' she says. 'Particularly if they're freemasons and particularly if they're aggressive woman-hating fucks maybe, yeah? They're probably grateful for their jobs. They have nowhere else to go. This will make them malleable and obedient. If someone at the top of that company asks them to do something, er…' She pauses for a moment, searching for the right word. '…*untoward*, they'll probably do it without question.'

'Sure. Now let's take the link with this masonry thing into account,' I say. 'If – and we still don't really know what's happening here – *if* Chudwell wanted to ask Tansil to do him a little favour, it would probably be through the lodge rather than from his position as a company director. That would just be too risky, too conspicuous, possibly difficult to arrange, not private enough and it looks as though he doesn't go into work much anyway. Probably a non-executive director of all of them apart from Quadrivium, and it seems like he does most of that from home.

'Tansil then delegates to people who work with him that he can trust. He probably chose Gable because he was an ex-cop, a fellow freemason, an effective heavy and he was known to Chudwell, but I don't know about Sharpe. His job was simpler, Tansil may be his boss in some way and he may not even be aware of the *existence* of Chudwell, let alone Tansil's connection with him outside the company. It's doubtful he knows the whole story. He didn't strike me as a trustworthy person or especially bright.'

Caroline picks up the two tickets for Emma Antonsen's show at Volupté next week and casually inspects them, turning them around with her slim fingers. 'Can we go to bed again now? I'm feeling romantic.'

'Sure. But let's get this all clear first.'

'Can we do that thing again?'

'Are you sure?'

'Yes.'

'OK.'

She lights another cigarette and looks at the list of names in front of her. 'You reckon it's likely that Chudwell got Tansil and Gable their jobs in Temple Security? Or at least pulled some strings?' she says.

'Yes I do. If I was looking to employ people for a big, prestigious security company like that and looked into their past, I sure as hell wouldn't hire those two and certainly not in high-up positions. No one in that line of business would. This would explain why their official CVs don't give any details of their police service. It might also explain why their history is so difficult to find on the internet. It makes sense that someone influential would have got them those jobs and then whitewashed their pasts.'

'OK. So can we agree that Chudwell probably has those two over a barrel?'

'I wouldn't say that, but if he got them their jobs at Temple, directly or indirectly, they'd unquestionably owe him. And as fellow freemasons, it would be a *duty* to assist him in whatever way they could.'

'What about the doctor?'

'He wouldn't have needed to know precisely what was going on and why Jamie Baldwin was injured. He just had a job to do when Jamie turned up. It's a probability that Tansil would have called him and let him know.

'I think it was just a belt and braces job. My instinct is that it wouldn't have mattered that much if they had no one at the Chelsea. Jamie Baldwin had been pretty much stitched up on a number of levels and wouldn't be squealing to anyone.'

'So maybe someone had the doctor over a barrel, too?'

'Or he may have been meeting his obligations and helping out a fellow mason. It wouldn't have done Footitt any harm, you know? I'm sure Chudwell, if he was behind all of this, would have been aware of Footitt's rôle and duly rewarded him in some way, if not now then sometime in the future.

'Perhaps Footitt's career had been helped by people in that lodge in the past. Maybe by Chudwell himself. He's a big man in pharmaceuticals whatever his actual involvement in the company is. Perhaps he has some clout in the medical world that we couldn't possibly know about.'

'So what now?'

'I still don't think we're seeing the big picture yet,' I say. 'We may have enough or we may not have enough.'

Then something clicks. It may be a wild goose chase, but I don't want any gaps. 'Hold on.'

I walk back into the bedroom and fetch my mobile. Doug Teng is costing me (or Mr Sheng) a fortune, but at least he got so drunk the other day that he paid for lunch, even though I said I would. I'll still charge it to Sheng, though.

'Mr Beckett! Are you still in that place? Was there a problem? Are you trapped?'

'It's all OK. This is something different. I need a high-speed hack. It's an NHS database.'

'Oh, man. Won't be easy nowadays. Five, ten years ago – piece of cake, but now…'

Yeah, yeah.

'You can name your price.'

'Three thousand?'

'Done. Have you got a pen? It's the Chelsea and Westminster Hospital. The guy we're after is a psychiatric consultant called Dr Barnaby Footitt. Let's go back five years. No. Let's make it ten years. I want to see if he's treated a patient called Hugo Chudwell aka Viscount Ombersley.' I spell all three proper names out for him.

'Got you. How soon d'you want this?'

'About three days ago.'

This gets a laugh. 'Red Buddha Temple Computer Hacking – Miracles are our business!'

'Call me the moment you find anything. See you, Doug.'

'What's that all about?' asks Caroline, suspiciously. 'Who was that?'

'Never you mind. Might be nothing. I want to see what the connection is between Chudwell and Footitt. I've got a strong feeling that Footitt supplied the girl that I found in Rikki's flat. I'm not saying that he killed her, but even supplying her is a pretty big high-risk thing. Without being overly dramatic, I think we're dealing with violent, corrupt people who think they can get away with serious assault, murder and who knows what else. This may not be the first time stuff like this has happened. I don't like walking into things blindfolded.'

'So what's the next step?'

'I'm going to have to speak to Chudwell.'

'You just going to knock on his door and ask for a chat?'

'What else can I do? Until we find out otherwise, he's simply another lead on the way to discovering what happened to Rikki, just as much as Jamie Baldwin or Paige McBride were. OK – he's linked to the lodge, to Temple Security and to Fly a Kite, and it looks pretty suspicious, but we still don't know exactly what's been going on; who's been talking to who. I want to meet him face to face. I want to look into his eyes.

'We know that Tansil, Gable and Footitt are complicit in the shitstorm that Jamie Baldwin pulled on himself, but we have no idea who told them to do it or why. We need explanations. That's the only way we can push this forward. It's the only way we can find out what's happened to Rikki.'

'And hey, Mr Detective. Don't forget you haven't had

your second warning yet. Be careful.'

'You're not concerned about my welfare are you, Caroline?'

'Very funny. How you going to find out where this guy lives? He's probably ex-directory and ex-everything.'

'No problem.'

I take Cordelia's business card out of my wallet and tap the number into my mobile. While I'm waiting for her to answer, I pick up one of the Volupté tickets that Emma gave me.

'Hi, this is Cordelia Chudwell. How can I help you?'

'Hi, Cordelia. It's Daniel Beckett. We met this morning.'

There's a couple of seconds' pause. Has she forgotten already?

'Hi. Um. It's funny. I was just thinking about you.'

I put a smile into my voice. 'In a good way?'

'Hmmm. I think so. Yes.'

'It's weird you should say that. I was thinking about you as well.'

Caroline rolls her eyes at this, then proceeds to take her bra off, very slowly, and lets it drop onto my lap.

'Were you? Really?'

'Listen. This is an amazing stroke of luck, but you know you were talking about going to see a burlesque concert sometime?'

'Of course. Have you changed your mind about taking me to one?'

Caroline removes her heels and places them next to each other, on the desk, then stands in front of me and starts to unclip her stockings from her suspender belt.

'Not at all. It's just that a friend of mine had tickets to a burlesque evening next week, but can't go, so he gave them to me. It's at a club called Volupté. It's near Chancery Lane. I was just wondering if you'd…'

'Oh wow. That would be great. Really? What sort of burlesque is it?'

Caroline starts work on the first of her stockings, her foot resting on my knee. She should be onstage at Bordello. Once it's off, she drapes it over her shoulder.

'Well, one of the girls performing is called LouLou DuBonnet. I've heard that her act verges on the pornographic. I hope you won't find it too offensive.'

'Oh no. I – I'm sure I won't. That's so kind of you. Thank you.'

'I think the entertainment starts at nine o' clock. If you like, I can pick you up at eight and we can go there together.'

'Are you sure?'

'It'll be no problem. It's next Wednesday, if that's convenient for you.'

'Yes. Yes, it is. I'm free on Wednesday. I'll be back at my parents' house by then.'

The second stocking is now draped over Caroline's shoulder. She points at her suspender belt, raising her eyebrows for permission to remove it. I shake my head.

'That's great. I'll look forward to seeing you, Cordelia.'

'What should I wear?'

'Something sexy. You have a great figure. Wear something that shows it off. The audiences are always very glam at burlesque shows.'

Slight pause. Her voice drops to a provocative whisper. 'I'm not exactly busty.'

'That won't matter,' I say gently. 'In fact, that's all the more reason to wear something tight-fitting.'

I hear her swallow. 'I'll have to go shopping.'

'Oh, just one thing.'

'What?'

I put a laugh into my voice. 'I just realised. I don't have the address. For when I pick you up.'

'It's Berkeley Square. Number one hundred and fifty-one. It's the only house on that side with a blue plaque on the wall. David Garrick once lived there.'

'Did he really? OK, Cordelia. I'll see you next week. Looking forward to it.'

'Me, too.'

I click off. Caroline laughs.

'You are such a slimeball, Mr Beckett.'

'She told me she lived with her parents. Now we've got Chudwell's address.'

'Detective work like that needs to be rewarded.'

'I'll leave the type of reward up to you.'

'Dangerous words, honey, dangerous words.'

She flicks her hair back and heads for the bedroom.

36

BERKELEY SQUARE

As I walk up Berkeley Street on my way to the square, I decide to give Anastasija from Zhodzina a call. I fish out the serviette with her number on.

'Anastasija? It's Daniel Beckett.'

'Oh, hi! I thought you weren't going to call me.' I can hear her customers ordering in the background.

'I've been a little busy. Look. I'll make it up to you. How would you like to come out for dinner next Monday?'

For a second I consider taking her to City of Willows, where I won't have to pay, but then decide that's a little ungracious. Besides, I want to spend Tansil's money on something worthwhile.

'Oh, wow! That would be fantastic.'

'There's a great Japanese place in Sackville Street, off Piccadilly, called Benihana. Have you ever been there? They do a fantastic Wagyu beef.'

'No. No, I haven't. It sounds cool. I love Japanese food. Wow.'

'OK. Let's meet in Graphic. It's a cocktail bar in Golden Square. You can find it on your mobile. Will seven-thirty be OK for you?'

'Oh, wow. Yes. I know Golden Square. I'll see you on Monday. I am *so* looking forward to this, Daniel.'

'Me, too. See you next week, Anastasija.'

I click off. It'll be an expensive night out, but I think she'll be worth it.

When I turn into Berkeley Square, I sit down outside an *itsu* and order a coconut water and some salmon sushi. Despite all the road works, noisy construction and traffic pollution, this is still considered a classy place to live, and to be fair, it's pretty central and close to a lot of interesting stuff. Most of the buildings are businesses of one sort or another and less than a quarter of the houses look residential.

I can see a big, six-storey townhouse across the square with a blue plaque outside. I can't read what's on the plaque. I wonder if that's number one hundred and fifty-one. If it is, I wonder if Chudwell is in.

Just as my food is being served, Doug Teng calls.

'Hey, Mr Beckett. I know what you're thinking. You're thinking *how could he be that fast*, right?'

'You never fail to amaze me. What did you find?'

'Well, you know, er, *nothing*, but at the same time, *something*.'

'Well that's great, Doug. Your cheque's in the post, with a hefty bonus. Thanks for calling.'

'Ha, ha. What I mean to say is that Dr Footitt hasn't been treating *Viscount* Ombersley, he's been treating *Lady* Ombersley. The real family name is Chudwell, yeah?'

'That's right.'

'Well, there's tons of stuff. Your girl has been a patient of Dr Barnaby Footitt for six years, six months and two weeks. Two appointments per week, more often than not, each one lasting for one hour. Sometimes there are gaps, anything up to a fortnight, which could mean that either she is on holiday or he is. Of course, it could not mean that at all. That's just my guess. Take it or leave it. A couple of spikes in the graph; a shitload of appointments in April, May and June, then it levelled off to the usual.

'She was referred to him by another doctor called, er, Donald A. Durham. There's no one of that name on the hospital database. I cast a wider net to cover all London hospitals and private practices, but still nothing. This would usually indicate that Durham is either dead, living abroad or retired.'

'What was she seeing Footitt for?'

'It's a bit difficult to understand. There are a lot of abbreviations and things that mean nothing to me. His typing is crap, as well, which doesn't help. All of this was in his private patient file, by the way. Maybe he can be a bit sloppier if it's not NHS.

'I keep seeing the name de Clérambault, which I guess is another doctor, and a reference to bipolar 1 disorder with a question mark in front of it and there's the word telepathy in brackets, whatever *that's* about. There are abbreviations like MSE, SQ and IOT. There are a lot of words with symbols in front of them or behind them. No idea what they mean. Some more medical-looking words: Seroquel XL, Invega, Risperdal and Latuda. Any use? I'm guessing they're drug trade names. There's a shitload of blood test results I've come across, but it's all gibberish to me. I can read some out if you like.'

'Don't worry. Go on.'

'Footitt rents rooms in Harley Street twice a week for a couple of hours and it looks like a lot of the consultations were done there, but that doesn't seem to indicate anything. There are invoices and payment details for each consultation and separate payments for the pathology. You wouldn't believe the prices. Don't ever go private, Mr Beckett. Big rip-off. It's only a guess, but I would think there are probably actual written notes somewhere. Proper doctor's notes. On paper, you know? Some people still do that. The stuff on here is too bitty. Maybe he keeps it all in his head. Who knows?'

'And there's nothing on Viscount Ombersley at all.'

'Nothing. If he's ever sick he certainly doesn't see Footitt and he's never been admitted to this hospital.'

'That's really useful, Doug. Thanks. I'll get the payment to you shortly.'

'Okeydoke. Hey – let's meet up for another drinking session soon. I was pissed as a pudding after that one the other day. I had to take the afternoon off work. Told them my brother had been in a car crash. Cool, yeah?'

'Sure, Doug. See you.'

I think I can class that as interesting but of no interest. I have to make sure I don't waste time thinking about connections that may have no relevancy whatsoever to this case. All I've got is that Chudwell's wife was a patient of Footitt. That connects Chudwell and Footitt outside the confines of the lodge. It may be that's why Footitt is in that lodge, but equally, it may not. I've got a lot of questions to ask Chudwell, and it's pretty likely he's not going to want to answer any of them.

When I worked in Italy as an insurance investigator, a cop called Prudenzio Boni told me that when you're investigating the wealthy and powerful, you just keep asking questions. You never stop asking questions. Eventually, you'll either crack the case or get yourself rubbed out. I keep this advice in mind as I press the ornate brass doorbell of number one hundred and fifty-one.

It's a well-kept, four-storey, early eighteenth century

townhouse with cute cast-iron boot scrapers on each side of the heavy wooden front door. All the windows, right up to the top, have big window boxes which are either filled with nasturtiums or petunias. Water drips off the plants and down the walls, suggesting they've been recently watered. More high quality detective work for Caroline to be impressed with.

There's a five-lever mortice lock and a Yale rim latch. Access to the basement is limited by nasty black spiked railings, but the matching gate has a two-lever mortice lock with an adorable rope effect handle that could be dealt with in two seconds if you were in possession of a hammer. The basement door only has a Yale. No security cameras and no brass plaques telling you who lives there. There is, however, a blue plaque which tells you who *used* to live here; David Garrick, Actor, 1717-1779.

When no one answers the door, I take a couple of steps back onto the pavement and look upwards for curtain-twitchers. Is anyone home? The houses either side are similar, but seem to be businesses of one sort or another. I look through one of the front ground floor windows. Gigantic fireplace, big mirror, grand piano, bookshelves filled with leather-bound hardbacks.

Then the door opens.

I recognise her straight away from her photograph. She's put on a few pounds since that article, but the bulging, inflamed eyes are still present. Mid-fifties. Her dark hair is dyed. She wears an inappropriate-looking embroidered rose prom dress. She looks at me as if I've just come to the door carrying a decomposing donkey carcass.

'Yes? What is it?'

Her expression is blank, supercilious and humourless.

Shop assistants must love her.

'Good afternoon. My name's Daniel Beckett. I wonder if I could have a word with Viscount Ombersley.'

'I'm Lady Ombersley.'

I can tell this isn't going to be easy. 'I'm pleased to meet you, Lady Ombersley. Is your husband at home?'

'Why?'

'Because I'd like to have a talk with him about something.'

She looks at my clothes. She glances across the road at something. She looks from left to right, then looks at me again. To her obvious surprise, I'm still here.

'What's it about?'

'It's a confidential matter. I'd prefer to discuss it with your husband.'

'Confidential.'

'Yes.'

'And you want to speak to my husband about it.'

Her voice manages to be both grating and characterless at the same time. I'm already getting sick of hearing it. I want to turn the sound off.

'That's correct.'

'Well you have to tell me what it's about, otherwise I can't know whether he'll want to see you or not. This is a private house. This isn't some company. Who are you? Are you selling something?'

I can't decide whether she's extremely rude, very poorly socialised or has the attention span and memory of the dumbest goldfish in the bowl. Probably all three. I'm going to have to come clean and see if that gets me anywhere.

'My name's Daniel Beckett. I'm a private investigator. I want to talk to your husband about Paige McBride.'

Her eyes narrow briefly, It's hard to tell whether this is with panic, fear or total incomprehension. Then she looks suddenly elated. 'Has she sent you with a gift for me? What is it?'

'A gift?'

She looks across the road once more, takes a step back and slams the door in my face. My mobile buzzes. It's a text from Daniella. Another naked selfie with 'call me' written underneath. Yeah. She's pretty hot. I'll give her a call when I've finished with whatever this is.

The door opens once again. This time it's him, though I still don't get the feeling my tenure of the doorstep has come to an end. He looks at me with suspicion. I suspect Lady O didn't put him in the picture.

'I'm Viscount Ombersley. What can I do for you?'

I take a deep breath. I learned a long time ago to control my temper, but sometimes I can still feel it energetically rattling the cage it's kept in. This is one of those times. Perhaps I should set it free.

'Hello, Viscount Ombersley. I'm Daniel Beckett. I'm a private investigator. I'd like to have a word with you if you have a moment. It won't take long.'

He stares at me for a few seconds. His voice is jolly, but his eyes are dead. 'Ah, yes! Mr Beckett. The *private investigator*. Of course. I was *wondering* when you'd turn up. Come in, come in.'

'Thank you.'

So he was expecting me. Tansil's work? Cordelia's? I walk up the steps and into the house. In real life, Hugo Chudwell's appearance is as unflattering as his photograph. The disdainful expression and triple chin are all present and correct, but he's a lot shorter than I'd expected, maybe dead on five foot or even a little under.

This guy is pretty seriously overweight and doesn't carry it well. I start thinking about beach balls.

He reeks of the sort of acrid aftershave that could easily double as paint stripper and I can feel it assaulting my sinuses. He's wearing a grey Givenchy polo shirt that shows off his gut and a pair of yellow Ralph Lauren chinos that his fat thighs are threatening to split open. He has the face and expression of an ugly, belligerent baby. Is Cordelia adopted?

He looks me up and down as he closes the front door behind me and accompanies me through the hallway into a large reception room. He doesn't walk, he waddles. Lady Ombersley is standing in front of the fireplace, staring at me, her expression flat and unemotional.

As I'd expected, it's a fabulous, lavish, tasteless place in mainly white, yellow and gold. Big sofas, big cushions, big mirrors, big everything. There are four matching yellow granite coffee tables pushed together in the centre of the room. Scattered across these are a backgammon board, a big bowl of pot pourri, two large glass candle holders and a stack of glossy magazines. On my left, there's a big pale rectangle on the wall where a painting used to be.

I get a jolt when I see Paige's photograph on the cover of a copy of *Burlesque Bible*. It's a big head and shoulders shot. She's wearing a royal blue wig, pink eye shadow, bright red lipstick and seems to be dressed in a tight black latex dress which pushes her breasts up and spectacularly accentuates her cleavage. Her facial expression is a combination of humour and surprise, as if she's been caught out doing something she shouldn't. Beneath the photograph, it says 'Véronique D'Erotique's Unique Mystique'. I'm suddenly reminded of how beautiful she is.

'Why are you looking at that magazine?' says Lady Ombersley, dully. I try to remember her name. It's Nancy. I'm not sure what I should call either of them.

'I…'

'Would you like to have a drink, Mr Beckett? Some tea? Coffee? Something stronger?' says the viscount. Or Chudwell. Or his lordship.

'Coffee will be fine, thank you. I'm not sure what I should call you.'

He laughs, but I can tell he's tense. I wonder why. 'Oh, Hugo will be fine. Lady Ombersley likes to be known as Deborah. It's not her first name, but she's never liked Nancy, have you, dear.'

Deborah looks at him, frowns slightly, then glances quickly at me, not caring if I notice. It's as if she's saying 'What are we going to do about this?' It's not just her facial expression which is odd, I realise; it's her posture, too. She stands with her hands behind her back, and slowly rocks backwards and forwards. There's a strange atmosphere here which is making me uneasy.

'So do you take milk and sugar, Mr Beckett?' says Hugo.

'No sugar and just a dash of milk.'

'Just like me! Would you mind, darling?' He looks over at Deborah, who looks baffled for a moment.

'Do you want me to make you one as well?' she asks me, looking me up and down again. These two do a lot of looking up and down. I just hope their heads don't fall off.

'Yes, darling. He would,' smiles Hugo. There's no emotional connection between them. It's as if they're strangers.

Her face still blank, she turns to her left and walks

433

slowly out of the room.

Hugo turns to me. 'We have a maid. Her name's Hana, but she's off with the 'flu' at the moment. Just one of those bugs that's going around. One of my daughters had it. Nasty thing. Would you excuse me for just five seconds, Mr Beckett? I have to make a telephone call.'

The pain is devastating and crippling. I have to use every iota of will not to drop to my knees. It feels as if someone has just crushed the back of my skull with the blunt end of an axe. I sincerely hope that hasn't actually happened. Chudwell's face is impossible to read. I'm seeing three of him; that's nine chins. I quickly turn to face my assailant. It's her, of course. She's holding a heavy black poker with a brass handle and she's coming in for the second blow. She looks simultaneously vacant and crazy. I can feel blood tricking down the back of my neck. There's blood on her face. It's mine.

I hear him cry out. 'Deborah! For God's sake!'

I haven't got long before I pass out; maybe seconds. She raises her right arm, and as she swings down, I block it with the side of my left hand and simultaneously strike her in the face with my right. While she's coping with that, I grab her right wrist, drive her elbow upwards and downwards and bounce her head off the floor. She's still, and her grip on the poker has gone. I stagger a few steps to my left, sink to my knees and fall flat on my face.

My last thought before everything goes black is, *I hope I haven't broken my nose.* Vain to the last.

37

SEEING STARS

When I regain consciousness, I'm careful not to take a deep inhalation or to move in any way. That'd be a sure sign to anyone observing me that I'd come round. I keep my breathing shallow and steady. I need time to think. I need time to remember.

After a few seconds, the pain from the back of my head kicks in and it's an eye-watering bastard. Under normal circumstances, I'd swear or at least write a letter of complaint, but these are not normal circumstances.

I feel nauseous, have a blinding headache and can't focus my thoughts. I don't think I could get up even if I wanted to. Am I concussed? More than likely. If she brought that poker down on the back of my head with the same force that she attempted the second blow, then it's a certainty. I wonder if my brains are leaking out.

I attempt to work out some sort of timeline. Chudwell was asking if I wanted a coffee. Something about his maid, then something about making a telephone call. Then the explosion of pain. I could feel the blood on my neck. I remember her face. It had been sprayed with my blood. So what does that mean? A severe laceration to the skull? A fracture? Worse? Anything's possible. He has his coffee the same way I do. No sugar and a dash of milk. I focus on my head. Does it feel bad? Can I feel blood trickling out of it now? Doesn't seem like it. Doesn't mean it's not serious, though.

I can't make sense of this. Did I say something to her that triggered the attack? I think about Kina from Jamie's gym. Did I ask her out afterwards? Was she meant to call me? I can't remember. She was Scottish. Great cleavage. Flowery perfume. Sexy mouth. Freckles. I try to shut my thoughts down as another wave of nausea suggests that I get up and vomit.

No. I didn't do or say anything that would have caused that attack. She asked me if I had a gift for her from Paige. What the hell was that about? Paige was on that magazine. The one on the table. Another great cleavage. *Why are you looking at that magazine?* Was that what triggered it? This is awful. I actually can't remember why I came here in the first place.

My face is against a cold, hard surface. The reception room had soft carpeting. Or was it a rug? I've been moved. Even with my eyes closed I can tell that there are lights on. I wonder what time it is. I start to feel an acute pain in my ribs. Are some of them broken? How did that happen? I took down Lady O pretty quickly. It can't have been her. Where was it that Caroline said she was going? To see Mr Sheng? I can't remember her real name. Was it Li-Fen? No. That was the girl. It began with an F, I think.

Then I remember the kicking. I was more unconscious than conscious when it happened and I'm not sure whether I imagined it or not. But my ribs hurt, I've got a dull ache in my left tricep and elbow and a terrible throbbing somewhere around the region of my left cheekbone.

I can taste blood in my mouth and have toothache somewhere in my lower jaw. I try to remember the poker attack once more. One robust strike to the back of the head and a second attempt which I stopped. Did she get up for more after I'd thrown her to the floor? Unlikely.

Then I can hear voices. They're coming from a different room. A man's voice that I don't recognise.

'I've given her a mild sedative. Cleaned her up. Made a little difference. Not much. Can't give her any more. You know why. She's mostly alright. Just shock. From what you said she was lucky she didn't receive a more serious injury.'

'I thought he'd broken her bloody arm or something. Or her neck!'

Now *that* voice I recognise. It's Chudwell. I can't bring myself to call him Hugo.

'Shoulder sprain, most probably,' continues the other voice. 'Can't tell for sure quite yet. From what you said, I'm astonished that chap could manage anything at *all* after a blow on the head like that. She has a bruise on her forehead from where she hit the floor. Lucky for her you have that thick rug there. Could have been worse.'

'How is she now?'

'Babbling. Crying. Keeps asking for the girl. She's convinced that this chap is the girl's new boyfriend, but she doesn't understand why he's not Chinese. She wants to come downstairs and kill him.'

'Oh, Jesus,' says Chudwell.

I'm in no fit state to work out what they're talking about. The other guy takes a deep breath. 'Don't worry. Pharmaceuticals'll keep her subdued for a while. I've never seen her this bad in all the time I've been treating her. It's not my fault, my lord. I've done everything that I could.'

This has to be Footitt. Chudwell must have called him

after my clash with his wife. I'm a little upset that he was called in to treat her and not me. I need more immediate attention than she does. What sort of doctor is he? I'll have him struck off for this.

There's silence again. I check my wrists and ankles. I'm not tied up. Do they think I'm dead or are they just cocky? Or are they just stupid? I feel warm. I still have my jacket on. I'm warm but shivering. I want to make sure that I'm alone in this room. I try to expand my consciousness to make sure I'm the only one in here, but I can't do it yet; it's impossible to focus. I'm just going to have to risk it and open my eyes.

It's a kitchen. I'm alone. I'm near some chairs lined up against a pine breakfast bar. I can see some red flowers in a vase. Fresh herbs in a wooden planter with 'The Kitchen Garden' stencilled across the side in black. There's a faint smell of cooking in here and I can detect tarragon. I can see a door that must lead to a garden, but can't see much through it.

The light outside is starting to fade and I wonder what time it is. I attempt to look at my watch. My arm feels as if it's made from lead as I lift it up. It's ten past eight. I can't remember what time I got here. Three-thirty, maybe?

I attempt to get up, but just stressing some relevant muscles is too much and brings with it an unpleasant spinning sensation, so I lie down flat again. I close my eyes. It feels like the room's expanding, so I open them once more.

I give myself a rapid physical. I touch the swelling on my left cheekbone. This is pretty tender and there's a cut there which is maybe two inches long. I'll almost certainly have a black eye. The cut feels wide, which means it'll have to be stitched. This is a real pain, particularly with the dates I have lined up next week.

I attempt a deep breath, then stop abruptly. I was right about the ribs; three of them have been fractured or severely bruised. Could be more; I can't tell without an X-ray. I move my jacket out of the way, lift my shirt up and take a look. Bad bruising and the skin is red and broken over quite a large area. This is a real pain in more ways than one. What's the recovery time for ribs? Three to six weeks? I rotate my left arm very slowly and bend it at the elbow. Painful, but I don't think there's any serious damage.

And now for the one I've been keeping until last as a special treat. I touch the back of my head as gently as I can. The hair is matted with a lot of sticky half-dried blood. My touch produces a twinge of discomfort, but nothing too bad. But now I'm going to have to explore the wound, and that's going to hurt a lot more.

I unknot the hair where the matted blood is thickest. Each miniscule tugging motion is agonising and my hand is shaking. I close my eyes tightly and grit my teeth so I don't cry out. It takes about five minutes of excruciating prodding and poking before I get the measure of what she's done. I'm starting to get soaked with sweat.

The laceration is five or six inches long and just less than an inch wide. It's diagonal and stretches from the top of the skull almost as far down as the occipital condyle. This explains all the blood. On the plus side, the wound isn't too deep, and I can't feel any bone or fragments of bone, but that doesn't mean I won't have a fractured skull. The other damage was fixable by me, but this is definitely going to need hospital treatment. I'll probably need a brain scan. Fuck it.

My thought processes seem to be working OK, or at least they are at the moment. I do a mental recitation of Mohs' scale of mineral hardness in reverse order. No hesitation and no mistakes. Good. More details of Lady O's attack are coming back to me. As far as I'm aware, I can recall every moment from ringing the front door bell to dropping to my knees after I'd decked her.

Now I have to decide what I'm going to do next. I stare at the ceiling. There's a wooden rack up there with a dozen bunches of drying lavender hanging from it. It's only now that I notice the smell. I want to focus on what just happened. It'll give me something to do while I start to recover.

Doug said that Lady Ombersley had been under Footitt's care for six and a half years. With that knowledge, her behaviour makes sense, or is at least a little more explainable.

Once again I try to guess what might have triggered her attack, but I'm at a loss. In useless hindsight, I can see that she must have been concealing the poker behind her back when she was standing in front of the fireplace. Her posture was strange, but so was her whole demeanour, which is probably why no alarm bells started ringing. That's no excuse, though; I was sloppy and paid the price.

Now I turn my fragmented attention to Chudwell. He knew who I was and he knew what I did. The telephone call he wanted to make must have been to Tansil. I can only assume that Tansil told him about our street meeting and got Chudwell to call Cordelia to find out the real reason I was visiting Fly a Kite.

Tansil's not stupid. Once he realised I'd lifted his wallet and identified him, he knew it would only be a matter of time before it led me to Chudwell. He must have told Chudwell to give him a bell when I inevitably showed up. If they've discovered that I'm a private investigator, they'll guess that I'm not really Paige's boyfriend and they'll have to assume that I'm on to them.

The kitchen door flies open. I turn my head to see Chudwell striding in, followed by Footitt, both of them trying hard to look serious and tough. Each one of them grabs a jacket sleeve and I'm hauled up to a standing position. I really don't want this. The shock of this sudden movement is overwhelming and I can feel my eyes rolling up into my head. I lean forwards and throw up over the floor and over Footitt's shoes. I can see the salmon sushi I'd eaten earlier. It makes me smile. It's like some old friend that I haven't seen for a while, if I was the sort of person who had friends. It's almost comforting to see it. A reminder of better times.

'Come on, you,' says Chudwell. I can see the fat on his face wobble as he speaks. I'm dragged over to the far side of the kitchen, spun around and plonked down on a brown Cheltenham chair that's up against the wall. There are two of these chairs. I wonder if they were bought at the same time. I don't like sitting up. I want to lie down on the floor again.

'Is he likely to try anything, do you think?' asks Chudwell.

'Not in this state, my lord,' replies Footitt. 'He'll barely know where he is after a bash on the head like that. Lady Ombersley is a star.'

Chudwell grabs the other chair and sits opposite me, about five safe feet away. He's puffing and panting from his exertions. Footitt leans against the breakfast bar and just stares. I watch his face. I remember him in Regent's Park. I remember the girl he punched. I remember the girl in Rikki's flat. No one's saying anything. I decide to break the ice.

'So what is it? Does your wife not like you having friends around?' My voice sounds a little thick. I'm panting but at least I'm not slurring. Speaking has made me feel slightly faint.

Chudwell clasps his hands together and repeatedly pushes both thumbs against his lower lip. It's as if the whole situation is a little too much for his brain to cope with.

'You've been a busy boy, haven't you,' he says, trying to sound suave and sinister. 'First my daughter, then Mr Tansil and now here. Sorry about the head, by the way. Wasn't on the agenda. If you hadn't mentioned that bloody woman's name to my wife it would never have happened.'

'I'll remember the next time.'

'Hm. Of course this seals your fate a little more decisively, eh? I can't have Debs getting into trouble with the police for grievous bodily harm or whatever. Though I suppose I could say she thought you were an intruder.'

'That sounds a bit thin to me. I think you'll have to do better than that.'

He smirks. He rubs the side of his nose. 'We still haven't decided what we're going to do with you, my lad. This is all so sudden and unexpected. This is such an inconvenience, *such* an inconvenience. What are you in all of this? What are you?'

'What about that coffee you were going to get me? The service here is appalling.'

'Some bloody snooper poking your nose into someone else's business. Business that is no concern of yours whatsoever. You really have no idea what you've got yourself into.'

I'm starting to remember why I'm here. I'm attempting to find out what happened to Rikki Tuan. Things aren't going well.

'So your wife hit me across the back of the head with a poker because I mentioned Paige McBride?'

'You're a private detective. My daughter said you were trying to get lists of everyone who obtained tickets to the charity evenings at the Café Royal, is that correct? Some cock and bull story about one of the performers being stalked, yes? My friend Mr Tansil said that you'd claimed to be the latest paramour of that bloody...' He looks over his shoulder as if he doesn't want to be overheard. '...of that bloody *stripper* tart. But that isn't true, is it.'

'What's it to *you*? Are you jealous?'

He leans forwards. His breath is bad. It reminds me of burning rubber. 'Listen here, my lad. I know people who can make you disappear off the face of the earth just like *that*!'

He snaps his fingers an inch away from my face. The doorbell rings. Chudwell turns to Footitt. 'Get that, Barnaby, would you?'

'Of course, my lord.'

'And get us some drinks while you're at it,' I say. This is ignored by everyone.

Footitt leaves the room to answer the door. I'm left alone with Chudwell and his exceedingly bad vibes and breath. If I was in better condition I could disable him and use him as a way of getting out of this madhouse, but I know I won't be capable of anything physical for a while without passing out, throwing up or both. I notice he has a slight squint in his right eye.

'You're not in my good graces, Mr Beckett, not in my

good graces at all,' he says. 'You appear on the scene from nowhere. All we know about you so far is that you are antagonistic towards us and possibly dangerous. Out of control. Violent. A con artist. A creep. A busybody. You're dabbling in affairs that are none of your business. And you're connected in some way to the McBride woman. Did she hire you? Is that what this is?'

He stands up and walks towards me. For a second I think he's going to attack, but he just leans forwards and hisses in my ear. 'You have interrogated my daughter as if she were a common criminal, you have sent a good friend of mine to the hospital with a broken nose, and you have assaulted my wife. What have you got to say for yourself?'

I turn my head slowly and look into his eyes. 'Where's that coffee?'

And talking of broken noses, Footitt returns to the kitchen with Tansil in tow. At last, a friendly face. That was almost funny. I'd laugh if I didn't know it would hurt so much. Chudwell takes him over to a corner of the kitchen and they have a little whisper.

Tansil is pretty smartly dressed. He's wearing an expensive-looking black wool suit, a white shirt and a dark green bow tie with grey spots. It looks like he was on his way to some formal occasion, perhaps a gala dinner for bent ex-cops. He doesn't seem annoyed, though. Perhaps the honour of having your evening disrupted by Viscount Ombersley is worth the hassle. Hassle. There's that word again.

There's one small feature that spoils Tansil's suave and sophisticated look. He has a hugely swollen discoloured nose from where I hit him, four or five stitches from the resultant laceration and two black eyes.

He walks over to me, smiles, and gives me one hell of

a punch on the jaw. This knocks me off the chair and onto the floor. All the various injuries I've been busy recovering from start their painful dance again. I'm seeing stars and wonder if I'm going to pass out. The nausea is back.

'That's for the nose, you piece of shit.'

I think of a few witty ripostes like 'It was my pleasure, fuckhead', but I can't be bothered to say them. Besides, I'm too busy throwing up again. I can hear Footitt say 'disgusting' as he stands and watches me. Some doctor he's turning out to be. Now I'm definitely reporting him to the GMC.

Tansil grabs both of the shoulders of my jacket and hoists me up, throwing me back into position on my chair. He drags the chair away from the wall by about four feet. I don't know why he's doing this, but I'm sure I'll find out soon.

Of the three, he's certainly the strongest. He grabs my wrists, takes my watch off and expertly slams a pair of rigid ASP police handcuffs onto them. The watch goes in his pocket. Damn. That watch was a cool-looking Bell & Ross Aviation that a girl called Giuliana gave to me four years ago.

He nods at Footitt. 'What's the damage here, Barnaby?'

'Big laceration to the back of the skull,' says Footitt, pleased to be able to help. 'Certainly concussed. Can't say how badly without a proper examination. All the vomiting is a sure sign. Mental faculties might be impaired, but once again, it'd need examination. He might have difficulty concentrating. Foggy thoughts. Memory loss.'

'Yeah, yeah. Bugger all that. Can he answer questions?

Accurately and quickly, I mean? We need to know what's what with this prick.'

Footitt looks crestfallen. 'More than likely in this case, Larry. Might be a bit slower than usual, but he was talking just now and sounded as right as rain. Sometimes you can get a delayed reaction, though. Different for everyone.'

'It's the memory loss I'm concerned about, doctor,' I say to him. He looks slightly alarmed that I'm addressing him directly. 'That boy the other night. I can't remember whether the snake tattoo was on his left forearm or his right one. Perhaps you can help me out.'

His smug expression instantly changes to a cocktail of bafflement, anger and embarrassment. Tansil taps my left cheek. I try not to flinch, but it's too painful not to.

'Who did all this damage to the face?'

'That was me, Larry,' says Chudwell, grinning. 'Had a little go at him while he was unconscious. Angry about what he did to Debs. Gave him a bit of a kicking.'

'He deserved it, my lord. Snooping round your business. Well done.'

I look at Chudwell. 'Perhaps we could have a rematch when I'm fully conscious. I'll find a chair for you to stand on.'

'How dare you speak to him like that!' says arselick Tansil, looking genuinely upset. He reaches into his pocket and produces a pair of black leather driving gloves, which he slowly puts on. He walks behind me and starts poking around the wound on the back of my head. The pain is so intense that I jerk forward. It feels as if someone has just hammered a chisel into my skull.

'That hurt, did it, sonny boy?' laughs Tansil. He walks around to face me and bends over so he's looking straight into my eyes. 'That was very, very sly of you this morning.

Getting me all riled up like that so you could lift my wallet. Very professionally done. Very clinical. You set me up, didn't you, old son. Told poor old Declan that you were that girl's new squeeze, so I'd come for you. Even told him where you'd be and what time you'd be there to make it easier. And we fell for it. And it's brought you here. But here is where it all stops. Now where's my wallet? Have you got it on you?'

'Left it at home. Sorry. How's the nose?'

He rifles through the pockets of my jacket. He pulls out my wallet, takes a look at the contents, sighs, and tosses it to one side. Looking for his money, no doubt, which is in my bedroom. From the inside pocket, he produces my tactical pen, doesn't recognise it for what it is and drops it on the floor. My keys get the same careless treatment. Then he pulls Anouk's mobile from another pocket and crushes it with his heel.

He scowls at me. 'We don't quite understand how you're involved in this,' he says. 'We don't quite understand who you could be working for, though we have a damn good idea. But don't fret. You'll tell us. We'll find out exactly what you know and who you're reporting to. And if you don't cooperate…' He walks behind me again. A second later, I get a terrific blast of pain as he slaps me hard on the poker wound. '…I'll hurt you in ways you hadn't thought possible and that's a promise. We know you're just the hired help. It's your employer that we're interested in. Don't take the fall for other people, sonny. It's not worth it.'

I hear Footitt and Chudwell having a chuckle. I'm bent double. I can see my vomit on Footitt's shoes. I think about Anouk losing control and lapsing into her native Dutch. Just as I'm starting to sit up and recover, I can hear a blood-curdling scream coming from somewhere upstairs. I hear Chudwell exclaim, 'My God!' and he and Footitt rush out of the room. Tansil looks at me and smiles. I think it's going to be a long night.

38

A BUNCH OF PUNKS

While Chudwell and Footitt sort out whatever the hell is going on upstairs, Tansil gives me a couple of friendly slaps on the cheek and goes over to make himself a coffee, while keeping a wary eye on me from time to time. He's obviously confident that I'm no threat to him at the moment and he's probably correct, especially considering the handcuff situation. I'll have to apply my mind to that little problem later.

I use this hiatus to take some deep breaths, channelling the ch'i around my body, trying to recover a little more. I feel a lot better now than I did when I was lying on the kitchen floor, despite Tansil's eager attention to the back of my head.

I have to tune out the physical pain and get my brain in gear. The nausea is fading, but it's fading very slowly. The headache ebbs and flows. I also have to prepare myself for aggressive questioning; maybe even torture. I know what they're capable of: all I have to do is think of Jamie Baldwin's X-rays.

It has occurred to me to try and make a break for it, but that would defeat the object of why I'm here in the first place. I have to remember that despite everything, I'm still working, and that the reason I'm here is to find out what happened to Rikki Tuan. I have to observe and analyse. Play for time and manipulate. Avoid and deflect. Antagonise and irritate. Disrupt and confuse. Divide and conquer. All the other clichés. Who knows – it might even work.

They have no idea exactly how I got this far or precisely what I know. What I'm going to attempt is a subtle, high-risk and potentially suicidal form of reverse interrogation. I make sure they think I know too much. I spill the beans. I mix truth and speculation. They decide that what I've discovered and/or am close to discovering is so damning that they'll have no choice but to dispose of me. With that in mind, they'll get relaxed and cocky and tell me everything I need to know. I escape. It brings a whole new meaning to the word 'optimistic'.

'Who knows you're here?' asks Tansil. 'Are you working alone? Who knows about all of this?'

His interrogation technique is all over the place. An ex-cop should be better than this. Perhaps he's panicking. The central puzzle they're struggling with is who's employing me. Could they even *begin* to guess?

Chudwell storms into the kitchen, walks up to Tansil and places a hand on his shoulder. His speech is a little above a whisper.

'She's in a terrible state, Larry. Can we get her here?'

'The girl?' murmurs Tansil.

'Yes.'

'That could be a mistake, my lord,' says Tansil gently. 'She doesn't know about us. She doesn't even know we exist. That's the very last thing you should…'

'Well, I don't see how it matters,' interrupts Chudwell, sounding jittery and sullen. 'It would just be a nice thing for her to do. We can tell her my wife's a big fan or something. We've got to do *something*.'

Chudwell is clueless. Tansil sighs patiently. 'It matters, my lord, because she's not stupid. Think about it. If you were her and you were coerced into comforting Lady Ombersley, a person who you didn't know from Adam, you might start to put two and two together; make connections. You, your daughter, the charity, the Café Royal, all the personal trouble she's been having; she'd be talking to the police before you knew it. It could get us in an awful lot of trouble. And your wife's behaviour is unpredictable. We have no idea what she might say to this woman. We have no idea who she might incriminate. She might tell her about the others.' He points at me. 'And we don't know how much *this* joker has told McBride. She helped him convince Declan they were an item, so she's a liability now. And we're going to have enough on our plate dealing with *him*.'

Chudwell looks as bewildered as I feel. It's as if he's never been besieged by so many sentences before. His face is red. His mouth opens and closes like a goldfish's.

'This is my *wife* we're talking about!' he barks. 'And I don't like it when she goes off the rails. This bloody idiot here has caused this. He made her attack him, then he assaulted her and now she's in crisis. And if a visit from the girl will make her feel better, then it *has* to be the right thing to do. We'll sort out the consequences later. There's nothing we can't handle. I'll take responsibility. I'm sure you can think of something. Can we just do it? Barnaby is with Debs now, but he can't hold her hand forever. If the worst comes to the worst, we'll just deal with the girl. One way or another. Money, threats, who knows what. You said yourself she was a liability. D'you understand? Is this penetrating your thick skull? Are you forgetting who we are? Are you forgetting who *I* am?'

Tansil nods his head. He acquiesces, but I can tell he's pissed. 'I'll give Sharpe a bell, my lord,' he says. 'He'll probably know what she's doing and where she'll be.'

Chudwell is pleased, but tight-lipped and quivering. 'Wherever she is, get Mark to go and fetch her and bring her over here. I don't trust Sharpe anymore. It's basically because of that gullible nitwit Sharpe that we've got *this* clown snooping around. And don't forget, Larry: *you're* partly responsible for this state of affairs as well. You're *too old* to have fallen for such a trick. *Much* too old.'

Tansil gets his mobile out and leaves the room, tail between his legs. What now? I have to admit I'm confused. Whatever's going on, I don't like the sound of this. What did Paige say she was doing today? Some book launch with another burlesque artiste? Started lunchtime and finished at six? She said she was going home by cab after it had finished. Mark must be Mark Gable. I don't like the idea of that guy manhandling Paige, particularly if she's spaced.

Chudwell sits across from me again. He looks angry. He's waiting for Tansil to return from making his telephone calls. I decide to needle him while we're waiting, as part of my excellent plan.

'Your daughter's a very attractive woman.'

'Never mind my bloody daughter.'

'She's a little messed up – no surprise there – but in a way that makes her interesting, vulnerable and sexy. I'd like your permission to call on her, sir.'

He gets up, walks over to me and slaps me across the face, right on the cut. It's a stinger.

'Or can I call you *Dad*?' I continue, my eyes watering.

He starts to tremble. Before he can think of a pertinent bon mot, Tansil reappears.

'Sharpe says she'll be at home,' says Tansil gently. 'I've given Mark a call. He'll be going round there post-haste.'

'Good. Now let's get this chap sorted out. Find out what he knows and who's employing him. Then we can take decisive action.'

So now Slim Jim is taking over. Tansil walks past me and pats me twice on my bad cheek. Ouch. He then stands right behind me, ready to whack my head wound if I don't cough up the right answers. He places both hands on my shoulders and squeezes. He's a friendly guy. I continue with my deep breathing.

Chudwell smiles at me as if he's some suave interrogator in a spy film. 'Make no mistake, Mr Beckett, you are out of your league here. I don't know what sort of work you usually occupy yourself with, probably divorce cases and the like, but this is something different. You've inadvertently got yourself involved with the big boys here, understand?'

'I understand fully, my liege.'

This morsel of flippancy has an unexpectedly devastating effect. His face goes purple. His eyes bulge. His chins vibrate. He stands up. He points a trembling finger at my face and shouts.

'I will have your *respect*! You will not insult me and you will *certainly* not disrespect my title.'

I can't help laughing. He tips Tansil the wink and he whacks me across the back of the head. It takes about thirty seconds for the pain to subside into something manageable. My eyeballs feel too big for my skull and my sinuses are on fire. Chudwell sits down again. He's trying to look composed, but he's still shaking. Even Tansil would be an improvement on this; Chudwell just doesn't have the temperament. They're faffing around so much that I'm getting annoyed and bored.

'Our guess is that you're working for Baldwin, the boxer,' he says. 'He'd have the money and he'd have the motivation, misguided and idiotic as it may be. What is he trying to do? Is he trying to get revenge on us? What is it?'

'Well, that's a pretty good guess as guesses go,' I say. 'Totally incorrect, but don't let that dampen your spirits. I'll tell you what I think. I think you're a little worried. I think you're worried about what might happen if all this gets out. You're pretty good at damage limitation; at least, you have been so far. But now you've got people like me sniffing around and you don't quite understand how it happened.'

Chudwell frowns. He glances at Tansil and raises an eyebrow.

'You're guessing I work for Paige McBride, you're guessing I work for Jamie Baldwin, but you're really pretty clueless and you're getting panicky. Your family's getting involved. Your gang of thugs are showing themselves to be careless and inept. You're considering making me disappear – and I'm sure you can do it – but you have no idea who I've spoken to about all of this; how many other people know what's been going on here.

'Jamie Baldwin doesn't know which stone you and your goons crawled out from under, but I do. I know exactly what you've been doing and how you've been doing it, and it's all going to come crashing down very soon; you just don't realise it yet. You're just a bunch of punks.'

Chudwell smiles and nods at Tansil, who whacks me across the back of the head once more. I get a moment of sudden dizziness that makes me wonder if I'm going to crap out, but it passes and I'm just left with the pain.

'Lovely little speech, Mr Beckett. Lots of words. Well done,' says Chudwell. 'All nonsense, of course. But you were right about one thing. The bit about us making you disappear. That was the only thing you said that rang true. What do *you* think, Larry?'

I hear Tansil sniggering like a schoolboy. Chudwell's expression changes from smarmy to grim.

'You seem to have it all worked out. What else have you come up with? Come on, old boy. Don't be shy. We could all do with a laugh.'

'Someone – and I think it's you – is obsessed with Paige McBride,' I say. 'It started when you saw her at the Café Royal on the eleventh of March. You wanted to see her again and again, but you didn't feel comfortable visiting her usual haunts. So you got your daughter's charity to organise more gigs at the Royal. I think you subsidise Fly a Kite financially, so your daughter maybe had no choice. Then you prevented Paige McBride from having any sort of love life. She's plainly out of your league and you couldn't stand it. It was a clear case of *if I can't have her, no one can.* You sent her gifts, champagne and…'

Suddenly the fog clears. It was staring me in the face as soon as I got here. We're both wrong. Chudwell thought I was working for Baldwin, I thought *he* was the one with the Véronique D'Erotique infatuation.

'It's your wife.'

All her odd behaviour. Asking if I'd brought a gift from Paige. Attacking me with a poker for no apparent reason. But the reason was the mention of Paige McBride. The screaming in the bedroom; the whispered plans. She's the one with the obsession. Lady Ombersley is Mr X. Charitably, I blame this atrocious lack of perception on my head injury and its side effects.

'Ah,' says Chudwell, nodding sagely. 'The penny drops. Perhaps you're not as stupid as we thought you were. Give him a little dose of medicine, Larry. I don't like him.'

Tansil slaps the back of my head once more. It's not as bad as last time, but I can think of more pleasant experiences. I think my nose is bleeding. I test this theory out with the back of one of my cuffed hands. The theory was correct. The cuffs hurt.

'My wife is a very sick woman, Mr Beckett. She has been for some time. But I adore her, you see. I worship her. I'd do absolutely anything to make her happy. Anything to stop her from being distressed. Anything to try and salvage what's left of the girl I married, and believe you me there isn't much. She's the mother of my heirs. She's an Ombersley, and that's more important than anything else. Of course, I couldn't expect someone like you to comprehend that.'

'Sorry – could you say all that again? I wasn't listening.'

Footitt strolls in, looking pleased with himself. 'I managed to calm her down, my lord. She's fallen asleep. Hopefully, the medication will keep her under for a short while. But when she wakes up…'

'Don't worry, Barnaby. The girl will be here fairly soon. Larry has kindly arranged it.' He snorts with amusement. 'Mr Beckett here has worked out that Debs is obsessed with Miss McBride!'

This gets a brusque bark of a laugh from Footitt, who looks at me contemptuously. 'What a buffoon. If only it were that simple, eh?' he says to Chudwell, with a sympathetic doctor's grin.

'Have you ever heard of de Clérambault's syndrome, Mr Beckett?' asks Chudwell, dying to let me know how stupid I am.

It sounds familiar, but I can't think from where. I shake my head. I feel my brain move. Why was my nose bleeding?

'It's a delusional disorder,' says Footitt, happy to have something to contribute. 'Also called erotomania. It's when a person believes that someone is in love with them. Sometimes it can be a celebrity, sometimes a complete stranger. The person suffering from this disorder often thinks that a secret admirer, in this case the estimable *Veronique D'Erotique*, is subtly declaring their affection by certain glances, signals or other means.'

'It's happened before,' says Chudwell. 'With Debs, I mean. But this time it was more intense. As far as my wife is concerned, this is a perverse, forbidden relationship. It is the reason that Miss McBride does not respond to any of the gifts that my wife has sent her, and there have been plenty, believe me. Champagne, chocolates, perfume and even a fur coat. It is an expensive business. It has been an expensive business for me for a long time.'

Champagne, chocolates, perfume and a genuine Weguelin that's probably worth a small fortune, but he's not mentioning that. The gap on the wall in the reception room here was the same size as the painting of Rodantha. As a gift that almost makes sense. The nymph who was turned into a rose to avoid unwanted attention from male suitors. Instead of supernatural metamorphosis, we have a sadistic blow on the arm with an iron bar from a bent ex-cop. Did they try to get it back? Was that what the scratch on Paige's front door was? Did they get inside? Did they not think to look behind the sofa? Come on, guys – keep spilling the beans. I haven't got all day.

'The fact that Miss McBride does not acknowledge the gifts is proof to Lady Ombersley that she wants to keep their forbidden love a secret; evidence that her obsession really exists,' says Footitt, as if he's giving a lecture to some medical students. 'That it is a real love. A deep, all-consuming love that Miss McBride wants to nurture and cherish despite her deep shame.'

Shouldn't it be Paige who's sending Lady O the gifts? God knows. I'm not really up to discussing complex and unusual psychiatric disorders at the moment, but I have to keep talking to play for time. 'But the real reason she doesn't respond is because she has absolutely no idea who the gifts are from,' I say. 'Is that right?'

I'm suddenly getting a slightly worse headache just from thinking about all of this. Handling divorce cases suddenly seems like a big fun option.

'You have to understand, Mr Beckett,' says Chudwell, smiling. 'There would have been no doubt in my wife's mind that Miss McBride knew that the gifts were from her. She would have known by dint of the telepathic communication that she believes they have.'

'Telepathy,' I say. 'The missing piece of the jigsaw.'

'It was that first night at the Café Royal. Miss McBride's act was erotically charged to say the least. She mimed to a French song while she stripped. My wife understands French. She speaks it fluently. It seemed as if the song was a direct message to her. After that it was hopeless. We were up until the early hours that night.'

Anouk told me that burlesque is the art of making you think you're the only one who's being seduced. That was certainly true of Paige's show. I felt it myself. Add to that the provocative lyrics of *Chaque Bouton Lâche*: all that *undress me, despoil me* stuff. What a mess.

'So she began to follow Paige on social media…' I say.

Chudwell pouts and nods. 'When she announced she was in a relationship with the boxer chappie, my wife attempted suicide. Barnaby here attempted to solve the problem with intensive therapy and pharmaceuticals, but – and this is no slight on his skills – it backfired and the drugs triggered a seizure. We have to be very careful what we give her now. We're monitoring her bloods all of the time. As I said, this had happened before and we had a tried and trusted method to deal with it.'

'Why don't you try getting her competent medical help? Footitt's a useless quack.'

He ignores this. 'Debs knows that Miss McBride is in pain from these relationships. Her heart belongs to my wife, but she's forced to torture herself, punish herself, by having unacceptable liaisons with unsuitable and uncouth men from the lower orders.'

The *lower orders*? What century is this again?

'Did she know you were discouraging Paige's boyfriends in such an aggressive manner?' I ask.

'Know?' Chudwell shakes his head and laughs. 'She *demanded* it, Mr Beckett. *Demanded* it. And what Debs wants she always gets. It's very simple, Mr Beckett. Paige McBride has a lover; my wife is unhappy. Paige McBride has no lover; my wife is happy. We keep an eye on things and make the necessary adjustments. Is that too difficult for you to understand?'

'She's been on milder pharmaceutical therapy for some months now,' explains Footitt, as if I give a fuck. 'It's getting results, I think.'

'Not only does the very thought of Miss McBride having a sexual relationship cause my wife to be physically sick, but she also has intense seizures and screaming fits,' says Chudwell. 'Once, she attempted to pull two of her molar teeth out with pliers. I was afraid we were going to have to have her sectioned. Drastic action had to be taken with the boxer. We gave him a chance, but he was too stupid to take it.'

'There's only one kind of language that his sort understand,' says Tansil. I'm shocked to hear his voice coming from behind me. I'd almost forgotten about him. 'He was a stupid boy and he made a stupid decision.'

'So where does filming him and Paige having sex come into all of this? I must admit you had me stumped there.'

I look straight into Chudwell's eyes for a reaction. Does he know about this? I'm getting close now. *Hang on, Rikki. Don't get impatient. Put the machete away.* Tansil kneads my shoulders again. I think this is his way of letting me know he's there, rather than *gratis* stress relief. Chudwell gives a bashful little shrug.

'It's something that had worked before. There was an actress. Same problem that we have now. Debs saw her in the theatre. Got the idea that this woman's lines were coded messages to her. Unlike Baldwin, this woman's boyfriend went along with it after Larry had paid him a visit.

'He was a property developer or some such. A worm of a man. We set up all the gear. Temple Security gave us access to all of that. They have everything. All the top-notch surveillance gizmos. We filmed them under the pretext of letting all the other threats fall away. It was good to watch. Very good. The woman was exciting, lusty and beautiful.'

He flashes me a cheesy pervert's grin, as if I'm an admiring accomplice.

'We told the boyfriend what to do,' he continues. 'What to do to the actress. It was good. He performed the precise acts that we demanded. That I demanded. I demanded acts that I personally found exciting.'

I can see that he's shaking slightly, just thinking about this.

'In this case we would have told Baldwin what to do. What to do to McBride. Anything we wanted to see, really. Anything that came to mind. You know what she looks like. McBride, I mean. She's an alluring little thing. A very pretty face. Good pair of charlies. And then when we had a copy of it, we'd show it to her. Tell her what her boyfriend had allowed us to do. Then that would be the end of them. Kills two birds with one stone. That's what we did with the actress.'

Chudwell looks pleased with himself. What was the name of that actress Caroline and I saw linked to Lady Ombersley? Gail Mozelle? Was it her he was referring to? Or were there others? I'd love to arrange it so that Jamie Baldwin could spend a couple of quality hours in a soundproofed basement with this fuck, even with his right arm screwed. Then when he'd finished, I'd take over.

'Gets us some free gentleman's entertainment,' chuckles Tansil. 'Something we can watch at our...'

'Lodge meetings?' I say.

There's a sharp intake of breath from Footitt. He looks in Tansil's direction then looks at Chudwell for a comment, reassurance, advice, plane tickets, anything.

'We *have* been doing our homework, haven't we, Mr Beckett.'

'It pays to be thorough, Hugo. I'm still waiting for that coffee, by the way.'

461

Chudwell holds on to his smug smile, but only just. Things are getting worse and worse. Tansil takes his hands off my shoulders. I'm waiting for another head blow, but it doesn't come.

'Are you really *that* intent upon digging your own grave, Mr Beckett?' says Chudwell. He's trying to conceal it, but his voice sounds brittle and unsure.

Oh well. Spade at the ready. 'The Yeoman's Row lodge is the key to the whole thing. I'd suspected that it might have been your links to Temple Security, but it isn't. Not really. That's just where you got a few of your trustworthy foot soldiers from. Your tame incompetent psychiatrist here is the chink in the armour. He was careless. Let himself be ID'd by Jamie Baldwin. I followed him to Knightsbridge the other night. Then I broke into the lodge and hacked your computer. You have an intriguing membership list.'

'Bullshit,' says Tansil. 'It would take a team of experts a month to hack into our system.'

'Oh, really?'

I must pass that on to Doug if I survive this evening. Chudwell gives me a patronising smirk, but I fear he's gone a little pale.

'There's a tangled web here involving Temple Security, Fly a Kite and your masonic lodge,' I say. 'Footitt's a member, it goes without saying. Tansil's a member, so is his old mate Martyn Ricketts.' I turn around to face Tansil. 'You remember Martyn Ricketts, don't you Larry? Is it OK if I call you Larry?' He's not hitting me, so I continue. 'The Martyn Ricketts who slung you all that money to slow down the investigations into his armed robberies? Dear me, people's worst suspicions about these little gentlemen's clubs are not unfounded after all.'

Tansil walks around to face me. He's trying his best to be sinister, but his cockiness is fading. For all he knows, I might have sent that membership list to the newspapers. If I get out of here alive, I'll do it anyway.

I give him a quick smile. The fact that my little speech might get me buried in an unmarked grave somewhere seems a fair price to pay. If it was good enough for Mozart, it's good enough for me.

'Then there's Mark Gable,' I continue. 'Another former shining example of our blessed constabulary. He's also a member. I'm guessing that he and Tansil owe you and your masonic brethren quite a lot, Hugo. I think their cushy jobs at Temple Security are just the tip of the iceberg. They'd probably do anything you asked them to for a number of reasons, all of them bent. Dr Footitt owes you quite a lot, too, I wouldn't wonder.

'But of all the great and good who belong to your lodge, there's another name that caught my eye. Thomas Wade. In case you'd forgotten, he's the Reception Supervisor at Frampton House. Does Frampton House ring any bells with any of you? Flat twenty-one? Fifth floor? Heating broken? Bad smell? You *are* in the shit, aren't you? I think you've overreached yourselves this time.'

'You're full of crap,' spits Tansil contemptuously, but I can tell he's feeling a little nauseous. I'll hit them with a little bluff. It might work.

'The police are harvesting DNA from that girl as we speak. I sincerely hope none of you touched her. Who procured her? Was it you, Barnaby? You're such a naughty doctor.'

Footitt exchanges a quick, nervous glance with Chudwell. Chudwell smiles back. That smile tells me all I need to know.

'And you *killed* her too, Barnaby, didn't you. Of course you did. Your chums needed a body in that flat and they knew *just* the person to get hold of a suitable victim and do the business. It had always been heading that way for you, hadn't it. It was your big thing, your big fantasy and now you had a chance to do it and get away with it, get some friendly help with it.' I smile at him. 'Well, I'm truly stuffed, aren't I. Are you going to slit my throat as well, Barnaby? Or am I the wrong sex? Or am I too conscious?'

They all stare at me. No one says anything. Footitt allows himself a timid little snigger.

'What was it like when you did it, Barnaby? Did it give you the hard-on you'd expected? Did she look into your eyes or was she drugged out of her head? Who was she? Just another one of your casual pickups? Someone who wouldn't be missed? Someone whose life wasn't worth a shit? How old was she, Barnaby? Seventeen? Twenty-two? Did you even *know*?'

'There's a point when some things just have to be done. She wouldn't have been around for long, anyway. Her type never is,' says Footitt, a disdainful sneer spreading across his features. He's not on the defensive at all. He's proud of what he did. He did the right thing. He has it all worked out in his head. I can feel it.

'You better hope I don't get out of here alive, Barnaby,' I say. 'Because if I do, I'm coming for you, my friend. It's going to be unpleasant, and it's going to take a long, long time.'

Footitt sneers at me, but I can see him swallow.

'You're trying oh-so-hard to provoke us, Mr Beckett,' says Chudwell, sighing. 'Keep it up if you must. Nothing you say will make any difference to anything now. We're not ashamed of anything we've done. We're certainly not going to be morally censured by the likes of *you*.'

Tansil looks at his watch. He's waiting for Gable to show. I'll keep pushing. I've already caused a bit of discord, useless as it may be, and I'm so close to finding out what happened to Rikki I can almost taste it. They all know I'm doomed now. I know much too much, but I need it to loosen their tongues a little more.

'So now we come to the sticky subject of Rikki Tuan,' I say. 'Barnaby murders the girl in Rikki's flat, the police think Rikki did it, and it explains his disappearance. Is that how it was meant to work? That girl's body was in a terrible state, Hugo. It ruined the whole ambience of the place. So what happened to him? I know you want to tell me. You're proud of it.'

Chudwell looks at me. He seems surprised more than anything else. He exchanges a quick glance with Tansil, who shrugs.

'So it wasn't Baldwin who hired you,' says Chudwell. 'It was someone to do with the little Chinaman. Is that right? Who was it? Was it the manager of the restaurant where he worked? Were they annoyed they couldn't squeeze more hours out of him?'

This gets a laugh from Tansil and Footitt. 'Very good, my lord,' says Tansil.

'Did he not turn up for one of his shifts, so they decided to hire a deadbeat private eye? Is that it?' says Chudwell, going for more chuckles from his pals. 'Are you being paid in Egg Foo Yung?'

'He was a cocky little bastard,' says Tansil, grinning. 'We gave him plenty of chances. Once, I caught him coming out of The Soho Theatre in Dean Street. Gave him a talking to. Pulled a fucking knife on me. Well, he'd cooked his goose doing that, hadn't he. The little slitty-eyed cunt.'

And then I get the whole story, which causes the three of them great merriment. They're telling it like they're three old pals describing some crazy party they'd all been to. Rikki was a non-person to them all as much as the girl in his flat was. He was Chinese so he simply didn't matter.

Chudwell and Tansil must have known that any investigation into his disappearance would be nothing compared to what might happen if they'd rubbed out Jamie Baldwin, an Olympic silver medallist and national hero, but they still had the sense to use the girl as a backup plan; to steer any possible half-arsed police investigation in the wrong direction. It was fool-proof. Dodgy Chinaman kills prostitute and does a runner.

Their confidence is chilling. It's the smug malevolence and fearlessness of people who've got away with it before and know they'll get away with it again. They fall over each other trying to get the details out, correcting each other, sniggering, getting high on the minutiae, tanked on the trivia.

All three are simply *dying* to tell someone how smart they've been and here I am, a captive audience. Tansil calls Rikki a few more derogatory names. Footitt giggles, Chudwell chortles. These guys are having fun.

'You don't get it, do you, Beckett,' says Chudwell, an imperious grin spreading across his fat features. 'I can see from your expression that you're magnificently perplexed. Why we do all these things. Why we *keep* doing them. Why we choose to do them the way we do. It's because we *can*, Mr Beckett. It's because we *want* to. It is our *right*.

Is this *so* difficult for someone like you to understand? We are the people who *matter*. You, the actress, the stripper, the boxer, the Chinaman, the whore in his flat and all the others, are some of the people who do *not*.'

'Well said, my lord,' says Tansil, starting to clap.

The resultant obsequious applause and laughter from Tansil and Footitt is only stopped by the ringing of the front doorbell and the screaming from upstairs. I must book myself a holiday if I ever get out of this.

39

NOT YOUR LUCKY DAY

From what I gathered from my garrulous new pals, this is what happened.

It was banal, stupid and ugly. If Rikki hadn't rented that flat in Ebury Street, they'd never have found him. The place that had been given to him in Great Titchfield Street would have been off the books, untraceable. That was probably one of the reasons that Mr Sheng disapproved of Rikki and his colleagues living in places that weren't sanctioned by him: it made them vulnerable in ways that they maybe couldn't imagine.

If Rikki hadn't rented that flat and held his dinner parties there, he may never have met Philip Hopwood, the costume designer. Hopwood would never have introduced him to Paige, and Rikki would still be alive now, chaining people to radiators by day and being witty by night.

He could never have suspected it, of course, but the moment Hopwood made that introduction, he was signing Rikki's death warrant.

After Rikki pulled a knife on Tansil, he and/or Gable made another couple of patient attempts to approach him in the street, but to no avail. He was a fractious and difficult customer.

On the third occasion, things got physical. Rikki

actually clipped Gable in the mouth and made him bleed before storming off and swearing at the terrible two as he left. Street meetings like these would have been the 'hassle' that he complained to Lee Ch'iu about. Why their MO with Rikki was different from that of Jamie Baldwin is anyone's guess. I get the impression that they did what they did as the mood took them. Perhaps they got a kick out of hassling Rikki. Perhaps it was fun.

Even after the knife incident and the Wing Chun, they still didn't suspect anything was amiss. They still didn't realise what they were dealing with, still didn't comprehend why he kept walking away. They assumed he was frightened and/or cowardly and the lightning-fast strike to Gable's mouth did nothing to change that opinion. Just a lucky punch. They all do a bit of the old kung fu, don't they?

Then they decided they were sick of being messed around by the little guy and made plans to teach him a lesson he'd never forget. After all, there was some urgency about this after his appearances on Paige's Facebook site, and they were getting more pressure from Chudwell, whom they had to please and who, in many ways, owned them both.

By this time, Lady O felt that Paige was beginning to lose her mind. She felt that she had forced Paige into consorting with a damned Chinaman, such was her almost pathological denial about their illicit relationship.

Her symptoms started to get more extreme. She could hear Paige's voice in her head, tormenting her with explicit descriptions of her sexual exploits. Footitt was being called to the house so much that he was starting to neglect his duties in the Chelsea. The damned Chinaman had to be dealt with and fast.

It was Tansil's idea to run Rikki down. Not to kill him, of course. Not at first, anyway. Just to get him totally incapacitated, maybe even crippled, and work him over until he finally got the message. Tansil and Gable would take him somewhere private and violate him until he agreed to get out of Paige's life forever. Chudwell picked those two well. They enjoyed their work. It probably reminded them of their days on the force.

It was easy for them to find his address. Tansil bragged that it took one quick telephone call. They extracted the details about his usual comings and goings from Thomas Wade, their tame Reception Supervisor at Frampton House. Chudwell crowed that they had people everywhere; that freemasonry is the best private intelligence service in the world.

Then one night they went out in Tansil's Range Rover and waited until they saw Rikki returning from one of his regular nights out. His habit, according to Wade, was to get a cab and get it to drop him off at Sloane Square. He'd walk along the north side of Ebury Street and then cross over a few yards before he got to Frampton House. I could have told him; never be a creature of habit.

As it was well past midnight, the roads were pretty deserted. Gable had scoped this out a few times and was confident that it could be done quickly and efficiently without attracting any undue attention. Besides, crazy stuff is always happening in London and the locals usually turn a blind eye. Rikki appeared as expected and Tansil put his foot down.

Rikki's reflexes were slow; he'd been drinking. His movements and reactions didn't quite match up to Tansil's expectations and after they'd clipped him, he fell back right under the wheels and was crushed. But he was still alive. Tansil made a snap decision to reverse over him and that was that. The two of them must have moved fast. They ascertained that Rikki was dead, got him in the back of the Range Rover and took him away somewhere.

This had to be covered up and fast. As if it was the most normal thing in the world, they reasoned that Footitt's unconcealed and longstanding ambition to actually kill one of his female pickups could be put to good use. Tansil thought this deranged plan up and Gable finessed it. They outlined their plan to Chudwell, who quickly persuaded Footitt that it was a good idea and one he could be assisted with. Footitt was over the moon and, of course, eager to assist his fellow freemasons. It's obvious now that he was crazier than any of his patients, with the possible exception of Lady O.

With the help of Yeoman's Row boy Thomas Wade, Gable and Footitt smuggled Footitt's choice of spaced-out pickup into Rikki's flat, doped her up a little more, and when Footitt had finished with her, he slit her throat.

I got the impression that this particular girl was a regular of Footitt's; that he'd had her before and had long harboured fantasies of killing her during or after the act. I suspect he'd confided this to Tansil who kept the information on the back burner until it became useful.

When the job was finished, all that was needed was for all involved to leave Frampton House as inconspicuously as they arrived. Presumably Wade let his usual staff go home early and/or killed the relevant security cameras for a while, at least while the girl was smuggled in.

After turning the heating up, it would only be a matter of time before the alarm was raised. The girl would be found and Rikki's disappearance would be explained. Game over. It never occurred to any of them that Rikki's disappearance *wouldn't* be reported to the police, but the end result would be the same: dead girl, no Rikki.

I can hear Tansil opening the front door. I'm expecting it to be Gable, and the freakishly deep voice confirms it; even from here I can feel it vibrating in my chest. They don't come in to see me, which I'm a bit hurt about, but talk in muted voices out in the entrance hall.

Footitt is upstairs, placating/drugging the ever-screaming Lady O. Chudwell stays with me, drinking sherry and smacking his rubbery lips. Despite everything else that's going on, I found the noise she was making quite chilling. It actually made the hairs on the back of my neck stand up, despite all the matted blood they're covered in. Ridiculously, I worry about what the neighbours might think, then remember that the houses on both sides of this one are businesses, so everyone's probably gone home.

While I'm waiting for whatever's going to happen next, I realise that I've completed the job. I've found out what happened to Rikki Tuan, even though I don't know what they've done with his mangled body. All I have to do now is report back to Mr Sheng and it'll be all over. Well, I can dream.

Gable appears briefly in the doorway. He's come to take a look at me. He's got a recent split in his lower lip. Well done, Rikki. He nods at Chudwell, who give him a weedy little salute in return. He's carrying Paige in his arms. She looks tiny. She's unconscious. She's wearing the cleavage-revealing black satin lounging pyjamas that she was wearing the other day. She isn't wearing shoes or perfume. There's a big bruise underneath her chin, as if she's been belted with a powerful uppercut.

Gable takes a long, disinterested glance at me, then

turns away and disappears. I can hear him going up the stairs. Tansil follows him, licking his lips and wiping the back of his hand across his wet mouth. He's carrying a small black shoulder bag, which I hadn't noticed before. I can hear Tansil and Gable talking, but can't make out what they're saying.

Jamie Baldwin's assessment of Gable's weight was spot on. Easily three hundred pounds and it's all muscle and it's all grotesque. It was hard to tell his height from a sitting position, but it's around six foot five. He was wearing black casual trousers held up by a black braided leather belt and a tight-fitting black t-shirt which looked as though it was a size too small to show off his massive pecs and biceps. I can see now how easy it would have been for him to restrain a light heavyweight boxer. There's a faint smell of cologne in the air. It's Black Gold by Ormonde Jayne.

I'm trying to contain my concern for Paige in case it gets her into more trouble than she's in already, but my curiosity gets the better of me.

'What are they going to do with her?'

Chudwell wrinkles his brow as if this was so obvious that there was no reason to ask and certainly no reason to reply.

'Shut up.'

I try to get a tone into my voice which is simultaneously mocking, sardonic, threatening and intimidating. It isn't easy.

'You do realise how laughable all of this is, don't you?' I say. 'Two dead, one crippled, a girl's life fucked around with all because of the selfish little ivory asylum you all live in. Murder, blackmail, GBH, kidnapping, amateur porn. God knows what else you and your crooked cronies have done in the past or what you'll do in the future. You don't see it. Perhaps you never will. But you're a total piece of shit. *My lord.*'

'You *will* not speak to me like that.'

'I'll speak to you how I like. You're a punk. Your masonic lodge needs a bomb dropped on it.'

'I'm warning you…'

Before I can experience the full terror of his warning, Tansil and Gable appear once more. Gable takes a look at me and flashes me a great big grin, just like in his corporate photograph. A definite trace of a Manchester accent, just like Jamie Baldwin guessed.

'Some private investigator you are, pal.'

'If I was *that* bad I wouldn't be here. Pal.'

He laughs. 'True.'

'I think you've put too much cologne on. We've had complaints from people in Norway.'

He ignores this and turns to Tansil. 'Did you search him?'

'No weapons or anything interesting. Wallet, keys, mobile phone and a pen.' He has a quick laugh. 'The mobile got accidentally crushed!'

Gable has a laugh, too. That deep voice is really ugly. I don't want to hear it. It makes me feel sick. I still have my own mobile in an inside pocket of my jacket, which had been overlooked by Tansil thanks to Anouk's Samsung Galaxy. He's getting slapdash in his old age. What good it'll do me I don't know, but I may need it. Let's hope nobody calls me in the next few minutes.

Chudwell steps up to Gable and shakes his hand. I look for some sort of unusual masonic handshake, but it looks like an ordinary one to me. Perhaps they save that sort of thing for people they don't know. Well, of course they do. That's the whole point.

'Goodbye, Mr Beckett. Not your lucky day,' says Chudwell. I'm disappointed. I was hoping for a dramatic speech.

Gable grips my arm and pulls me to my feet. Tansil hands him the keys to the cuffs and tells him to bring them back when he's finished. Tansil takes the lead. We follow him to the front door. He opens it, has a good look around, and then walks across the road to where a black Ford Transit van is parked. Lights flash as he unlocks it. He opens the back doors up, takes another look up and down the street and then returns to the house.

Gable is to my right, still grabbing my arm and Tansil walks next to me on the left as we cross the road. This tactic is presumably so that no casual observers can see that I've got handcuffs on. The fresh air is making me feel unsteady. There are a few people around, but it isn't too busy. I can hear an angry girl arguing with her boyfriend about a hundred yards away. Black cabs and ordinary vehicles appear now and then, but it's nothing like it was when I got here.

No one says anything. I'm quickly bundled into the back of the van and the doors are slammed shut and locked. It's dark. The van smells new. I can hear Tansil and Gable talking, but can't make out what they're saying. Then Gable laughs at something and says, 'You randy old sod!'

I lie on my back. I'm worried about Paige. I feel someone get in the driver's seat, and I can tell who it is from the effect of his weight on the suspension. There's something wrong with this van. Gable has to turn it over half a dozen times before it starts. Finally, it catches. The engine doesn't sound right. He gives it a couple of revs and we're off. So it's just me, Mark Gable, his oil and his thong. Now if *that's* not everyone's idea of a good night out, I don't know what is.

We're heading west, towards Regent Street. He's keeping to the speed limit, occasionally putting his foot down and hitting forty or fifty. If I wasn't feeling so damaged, I'd attempt to kick the back door open and roll out, but that's really only a good idea in films. In reality, hitting the floor after leaving a vehicle travelling at thirty miles an hour or more can be terrifically bad for your health, particularly when you're handcuffed. Apart from the high-speed impact when you hit the road, there's also the danger of getting run over by other vehicles who may not hit the brakes in time, if they see you in the first place.

Trying to kick at the doors when you stop at traffic lights or junctions is also a bad idea. Whoever's driving would just get out and give you a smack. I've had enough for one evening without being on the receiving end of a punch from someone built like Gable.

I'm trying hard to work out where we're going, but it's difficult. I know when we hit the Euston Road, and we're heading east, but then he takes a sudden right turn that rolls me over to the left side of the van. Are we going to Camden? Belsize Park? I really can't tell; I'm simply not switched on enough. On top of that, I'm starting to get motion sickness.

Of course, there's nothing I can do about these cuffs, which puts me at a huge disadvantage. There are no convenient paper clips or pins in here. If there were, I could be out of them in five seconds flat. I decide to lie on my back and wait; keep attempting to recover. At least my hands are not cuffed behind my back, which is something. I start wondering about what they're going to do with Paige. Are they just going to lay her on the bed next to Lady O and hope for the best? Will she be a living security blanket for a very disturbed woman?

Why did Paige answer the door to Gable? She has a security spy hole in her front door. Did she not recognise him from my sketch? Or did he flash a phony police warrant card at her and she just opened up? That bruise under her jaw. Perhaps she opened the door and he sucker-punched her, just like he did with Jamie Baldwin. I think of Julita Jaworska, the woman Gable beat into a coma.

We drive over a couple of bumps in the road. I can feel my brain moving around in my head. Apart from that disquieting sensation, I realise that I feel a bit more 'in the room', or perhaps 'in the van'. I hear a police siren a few hundred yards away, but the sound soon fades, so it's not about us.

I think about Paige again. When her presence has calmed Lady O down and stopped the screaming, what then? I don't think dimwit Chudwell has thought that far forward. They need someone smart directing all their nefarious activities and Chudwell isn't the man.

I didn't like the way Tansil was licking his lips as Paige was being carried up the stairs. The lip-licking was something Jamie Baldwin mentioned. I think the sooner she's got out of that place, the better, and at the moment, I'm the only one who can do it.

After about ten minutes, the traffic noise is dramatically reduced. It's not that late, so I can only assume that we're quite a way out of the centre of London and we're not near any towns or villages. I have a rough idea that we've been heading north, but no real clue as to our exact location.

The van slows down to ten miles an hour and then stops. Gable gets out, but keeps the engine running. I can hear the jangle of keys and then the sound of a metal gate being opened. He gets back in the van, drives forward about ten feet and then stops again. Now he's locking up behind him. I wonder where we are?

He drives slowly, maybe five miles an hour. After he'd locked the gate behind us, he turned the van lights off. I get the feeling this is a long driveway heading to some big house, but I could be wrong.

After maybe five hundred yards we come to a halt and he kills the engine. I hear him get out, close the door and walk around to the back. He opens the doors and immediately takes a step back. Just being cautious in case I've got out of the cuffs and have managed to get hold of a handgun during the journey. He has a brown leather messenger bag over his left shoulder.

'Right. Come on, pal. Out you come. I'm sure I don't have to tell you to watch what you do. I don't like sudden movements. I don't like funny comments. I just want everything to go smoothly.'

I don't reply. I just get out and look around. There's a quarter moon. It's a graveyard. It smells of the countryside. We're parked in front of what seems to be a mausoleum of some sort. Dirty grey concrete. One storey high. Fat Corinthian columns flank an ornate metal door with fake windows. Looks like the whole thing needs a lick of paint.

'You didn't have to go to all this trouble, darling,' I say. 'A pub car park would have done. I'm not fussy.'

'Very funny, pal. Just keep cracking the jokes. See what happens.'

'You'll laugh?'

'Perked up a little, haven't you.'

He grabs my bicep once more and guides me towards the door, which he then unlocks.

It's dark inside but not as cold as I'd imagined it would be. He closes the door behind us, locks it and flicks a light switch on. We're in a single chamber. High-ceilinged, twenty foot long and fifteen foot wide. The floors and walls are white marble. There's a brown marble altar in the centre with the masonic square and compasses displayed at the end in black. I hope I'm not going be sacrificed, but I'd put nothing past these people now.

The walls are decorated with memorial plaques. Each one has a name followed by an esoteric title: Prince of Mercy, Intimate Secretary, Knight of the East and West, Knight of the Brazen Serpent. There are no windows, but there's a door to the right of the altar. Gable releases his grip on my arm and pushes me towards it.

'Open it up and go down the stairs into the room. No funny business.'

I do as he says. The stairs and whatever's below are lit up, presumably by the same switch that illuminated the altar room. As I descend, I'm increasingly aware of a bad smell. I know immediately what it is. Gable's about six steps behind me.

'Stop.'

I stop just outside some sort of basement storage room. The door is partially open.

'Push the door open with your foot and go inside.'

I do as he says. The storage room is full of stacked chairs and green plastic packing cartons. It's cool down here but not that cool. From the look of things, I would say that Rikki's been dead for about nine days, which would be about right. I walk around him and take a good look in case I ever get the opportunity to tell anyone about this. I breathe deeply to get my brain used to the smell.

His face is bloated and green. His eyes are closed and the eyelids are purple, as are the dark shadows beneath his eyes. There's an immense wound on the right side of his face which is crimson and black and crawling with maggots. His stomach is extremely bloated. I think of the girl in his flat, with whom he now has a lot in common. I admire the flies for getting in here and laying their eggs on him. Flies are smart creatures; they'll always find a way.

His left shoulder is noticeably lower than his right and his arm is twisted out at an unnatural angle. He's wearing a black and white shirt with cowboys on horseback twirling lassoes. One of his shoes is missing. The area under his left armpit is dark with dried blood and it look as if most of his ribcage has been crushed.

I turn around to face Gable, but I'm in no state to anticipate or deflect the punch to my face. I lose my balance, and as I fall, I attempt to take the main part of the impact on my left shoulder. But thankfully I don't land on the floor. I land on Rikki's abdomen, forcing foul-smelling gas and a thick black viscous substance out of his mouth. I'm really beginning to dislike today.

40

DIM MAK

He lets me get up to my feet again. I have no idea what he intends to do. Is he going to beat me to death for fun? I make my breathing ragged and shallow. I allow my mouth to hang open. I defocus my eyes. It's important that he thinks I'm in worse shape than I am.

He takes out a small dark green towel and a bottle of something called Pro Tan Muscle Juice. I believe these products are known as Posing Oils by those in the bodybuilder competition world.

'Does it have to be the oil? Can't we try it *au naturel* for once?'

'Shut it.'

'Jamie Baldwin told me about your *condition* when you were cuddling him. What was all that about, Mark? What got you going? I'm baffled.'

He pauses, giving me a hard stare. 'It's going to be even worse for you now, pal.'

'Was it the violence? The iron bar treatment? Or have you got a thing for boxers?'

He smiles and nods his head. 'Just keep going, pal. Just keep going.'

He takes off his t-shirt and looks for somewhere to put it. He lifts a chair off one of the stacks and carefully drapes it over the back of that. He never stops watching me; not for a second. As he's taking his shoes off, I realise what I'm going to do. I cough. I fake a stagger.

'You're looking a bit fucked, son,' he says, undoing his belt and laughing. 'Even the little Chinkie looks in better shape than you!'

I put aside all the pain and discomfort I'm in and without looking directly at him, focus on his whole body, on every miniscule movement he makes. As I watch him undo his trousers and pull the zipper down, it's almost as if it's happening in slow motion. Then he does it. He raises his right knee up to get the first trouser leg off. He's standing on one leg. He's wobbling. His left trouser leg falls towards his ankle.

I quickly step forward and give the side of his knee one almighty kick. There's a bad-sounding crunch. Immediately, I kick again, dislocating the kneecap. He screams. He's on the floor. He takes the impact on his head and shoulder. He's hyperventilating. He's on his back. His hands scrabble for his knee to alleviate the pain. It won't work.

While he's down, I kick him in the temple with my heel. This puts him on his side for a moment. He's not unconscious or dead, which is what I was aiming for, but he looks angry.

I attempt another kick to finish him off, but he's too quick. He catches my ankle and gives it a painful twist. I come down hard, the side of my face hitting the stone floor. I can hear birds tweeting.

Pushing himself up with both hands and swearing profusely, he puts all his weight on his good leg and stands. He manages to grab my lapels and pulls me to an upright position. He's pale and sweating. The pain must be unbearable.

'You fucking cocksucker.'

He head-butts me and manhandles me towards one of the walls, his ruined leg dragging behind him, his mouth open and his teeth clenched in agony. In an alternative situation, I'd wait for him to pass out or go into shock because of that artery-tearing knee injury, but that may not happen quickly enough.

The force he uses to push me against the wall is staggering, and for a moment I think it's going to finish me off. Before I can recover from it his hands are around my throat and I can feel the results of all that gym time squeezing the life out of me. I can see the muscles in his forearms and biceps bulging. His face is red. He's perspiring from the pain. His neck muscles are straining. There's a murderous grin on his face. He's using all his strength to push me backwards while his hands put incredible pressure on the side of my neck and his thumbs start to trash my windpipe.

In a few moments, my peripheral vision is going and I can't breathe properly. My temples throb. He's standing side-on to me so there's no danger of me kneeing him in the balls. Smart boy. This feels like it's been going on for an hour, though it's more like ten seconds. With the handcuffs on, my options are limited, but not that limited.

I bring my cuffed hands up inside his arms and with my middle and ring fingers, strike him in the soft flesh beneath his jaw, a half centimetre each side of the thyroid cartilage. I push hard, upwards and inwards. I keep my fingers there for a count of two and then pull sharply away. He coughs, looks puzzled, laughs at me, keeps on throttling me. I was once told that this has a one in twenty chance of working. Let's hope the odds are on my side.

I know what it'll feel like. The pain will start at the sides of the neck, then it'll radiate down to the ribcage, a dull, awful pain like the worst kick in the balls you've ever had. Your jaw will clench and then your heart will stop. He's still looking at me, but his eyes are glazed over. *Give Rikki my regards, Mark.*

His hands are still around my throat. I peel them off, push him onto the floor, lean against the wall and have a coughing fit which lasts around two minutes. Once that's over, I find his trousers, search the pockets, collect all the keys I'll need and get the cuffs off. I get my mobile out, but there's no signal, which isn't too surprising.

I get outside, but when the fresh air hits me, I feel nauseous and have to sit down on the floor until it passes, my head between my knees. When I think I can manage it, I get up and get in the transit van. Whatever else is going to happen, I think my first task is to get back to Berkeley Square and get Paige McBride out of the clutches of those diseased fucks. I put the key in the ignition and turn the engine over. It runs for four seconds and then stops. I try it again and the same thing happens. Now I remember. Gable had a problem starting it when we were in Berkeley Square.

I look at the dashboard. No warning lights and almost a full tank of diesel. I turn it over again. For the few seconds that the engine comes on, it doesn't sound right. Is it the timing chain? I think about opening the bonnet and taking a look, but it's too dark and I don't have a torch. I try it one more time. I get my mobile out. Now it has a weak signal. I try to discover my location but the app isn't working. I give Doug Teng a call.

'Hey, Mr Beckett!'

I can hear the sound of machine gun fire and

screeching car tyres in the background.

'Hi, Doug. Listen. Where am I?'

'You sound fucked! You're pretty tanked up, huh?'

'No. I can't explain now. I just need you to tell me where I am.'

'Hold on.'

I listen to people screaming and police cars arriving. Is it always action/adventure films? Does he never watch arthouse?

'Sorry, Mr Beckett. Hold on. Can't find you. You're not on a road, yeah?'

'That's right. I'm in a graveyard.'

'Whoa! OK. Got it. Bad triangulation out there. Must be all the trees. You're in Saint Barbara's Masonic Church near Highgate, right next to something called the Noachite Mausoleum. It's Nowheresville. Hampstead Heath to the west, Highgate Cemetery to the east.'

'Give me the location details. Latitude and longitude. Whatever.'

'Okeydoke.'

With those memorised and a promise to go out for a drink with him, I call Caroline Chow. Her mobile rings for quite a while and for a moment I'm worried that my mobile battery will run out. When she answers I hear her say, 'Stop. Stop,' to someone, in a high, breathless voice.

'Caroline?'

'OK, baby. Just give me a moment.'

She's put her hand over the phone, but I can still hear her panting. Then I hear an ecstatic moan.

'OK. What's going on?' she says, her voice still cracking.

'Where are you?'

'I'm in your flat.'

'Who's there with you?'

'Oh, it's just this woman. It's OK. She's cool. High class girl, yeah? I just needed it and you weren't around. My hotel isn't cool about this type of visitor. Her name's Qawaya. You'd like her. She's hot.'

'Listen. I'm stranded somewhere near Highgate. You have to come and pick me up. My bike's parked around the corner in Burleigh Street, across the road from Daawat, the Indian restaurant. The keys are in the kitchen and there's a helmet in there somewhere. This has to be fast, Caroline, but don't get stopped by the police. Listen. I've found out what happened to Rikki.'

There's a moment of silence. 'Is he dead?'

'Yes.'

More silence. 'OK. Look. I can't ride a motorbike.'

Shit.

'Don't worry. Listen. The woman who's with you. Has she got a car? Ask her what type and if it's got Sat Nav. If not, a mobile with a GPS app will do.'

'Hold on.'

I can hear muffled talking. I can feel my heart beating in my chest. I'm shivering even though it's still warm.

'She's got a BMW X6 and it's got Sat Nav.'

'Tell her I'll give her two thousand to pick me up and drive us to Berkeley Square. It'll have to be quick.'

'Hold on.' More muffled talking. 'She said make it three thousand. That covers the risk of her getting a speeding fine or fines.'

'Done.'

I give Caroline all the location information that Doug Teng gave me.

'There's a big gate that leads into this place. I'll wait for you there. Let her know she'll have to wait in the car while I show you Rikki. Tell her I'm a detective if you like. And warn her that I'm not in good shape.'

'Why? What's happened?'

'I'll explain later. If she puts her foot down I should see you in about twenty-five/thirty minutes.'

'OK. We have to get dressed first, though.'

'Oh. And there's a hammer in my kitchen. It's in the cupboard under the sink to the left. Can you bring it with you?'

'Doing some DIY?'

'Putting some shelves up. Also, you need to find my spare key ring. It's somewhere in the bedroom. It's a black Maserati leather fob.'

I take a big gulp of night air and head back down into the mausoleum basement. I can't remember what I touched here, but I'm sure my fingerprints are all over the place. That problem can wait. I want to do a more thorough search of Gable's clothing. I look at him lying on the floor in his posing thong, one trouser leg still wrapped around his left ankle. His eyes are still open. I don't bother to close them.

I take his wallet and his mobile. His wallet contains a current police warrant card under the name of Detective Sergeant Samuel Conway, Fraud Squad. I take a careful look. It's an outstanding fake. God knows what he's been up to with that.

There's a driver's licence and credit cards in his real name, a gym membership card, a Paperchase loyalty card and a bunch of coffee bar loyalty cards. There's also forty pounds in cash which I slip into my pocket. His mobile is out of juice, but I keep it anyway.

I leave the mausoleum and lock the door behind me. I open the door of the transit van, turn the interior lights on and take a look inside. Nothing. I look at my face in the rear view mirror. It's much as I expected: big split on the cheekbone, incipient black eye, lots of small cuts, various swellings, bruising on the jaw and a lot of dried blood everywhere. My nose is bleeding, but at least that head-butt didn't break it.

My neck is red from Gable's throttling attempt and I can see the dark imprints of his thumbs on the front of my throat. My skin is so pale it's almost translucent and I look like I haven't slept for a few months. Apart from all of that, I'm looking pretty good. I may even go out on the pull later.

I shut the door, find the path that heads towards the main gate, sling my jacket over my shoulder and start walking. Apart from everything else in this phenomenally huge mess, that van will have to go. So this is it. It's coming to an end. I've done what Mr Sheng asked and found out what happened to Rikki. All I've got left is the fallout. I've got to get Paige McBride out of Chudwell's clutches, hand Sheng my invoice and tie up a couple of loose ends.

Gable's body and the van are a bit of a pain, and I'll probably have to sort it out myself. Perhaps someone else will deal with Gable when whoever it is goes to sort out Rikki's body. I can't imagine the police or any of the emergency services will be involved with that. Caroline will have to see both corpses. Perhaps she can help out. I'm tired of thinking about it all.

I'm going to have to get myself checked out in a hospital as soon as possible. Most of my injuries are superficial, but I certainly need a brain scan and someone to look at the back of my head. The first person I think of is Annalise, but then it's not her speciality. When that's sorted, I'll sleep for a few days, then book a holiday somewhere.

I sit on the floor with my back to the gate, staring into space. I start planning the logistics of rescheduling the dates I've got lined up next week with Anastasija and Cordelia. I've got to call Danielle, I'm still waiting on Kina and I may pop in on Brionna at the tattoo parlour at some point. And of course there's Anouk to consider. I'm sitting there for a little over ten minutes before I'm aware of the bright headlamps of a slow-moving vehicle lighting up the road.

I open the gates, stand in the road, let the lights illuminate me and watch as the BMW slows down. It looks new. It's dark red. I can't make out the driver, but recognise Caroline before she's got out of the passenger side. She's wearing tight black jeans, a tighter black t-shirt with a circular cutaway over the abdomen and a dark green quilted bomber jacket on top. There's a large yellow ostrich skin chain bag slung over her shoulder. I'm happy to see her.

'You look great.'

'You look like a walking piece of shit. What the fuck happened to you, baby?'

I allow her to run her fingertips gently over my face. I only flinch once, which is not bad going. As we walk towards the mausoleum, I give her a truncated version of what happened when I got to Chudwell's place in Berkeley Square.

'So it was the wife. Shit. You think she knew what was being done?'

'Well, I didn't get much of a chance to chat to her, but Chudwell told me that she demanded that any boyfriend she spotted on social media be aggressively dealt with.'

'So it wasn't all craziness. It wasn't like she didn't know what the results of her demands would be.'

'I don't think so. She wouldn't know exactly, but that's not the point. It sounds a little like schizophrenia mixed in with psychopathy, plus all the delusions. Add to that her background, wealth and power: she didn't live on the same planet as you and me. People like Jamie Baldwin and Rikki Tuan didn't really exist to someone like her. They were *other*. It was as if they were shadows. And it wasn't the first time this sort of thing had happened. It may have been going on for quite a few years, but in the past, they'd got away with it.'

'But this time they picked on the wrong guy.'

'Certainly looks that way, Caroline.'

'So the chain of command was this: Lady Ombersley can't stand the Paige woman having boyfriends. She requests that they be frightened off in whatever way. Viscount Ombersley executes this with the help of his two masonic thug bitches. They warn, threaten and hassle and if that doesn't work or it backfires in some way, then they kill and maim. So: Lady Ombersley at the top, then Viscount Ombersley, then Tansil, then Gable. Am I getting there?'

'Pretty much. You've got other players, too. Dr Barnaby Footitt helped out when Jamie Baldwin got admitted to hospital. Delivered a bit of mild threat into the mix. His function was to assure the others that Baldwin wouldn't be going to the police.

'Declan Sharpe, another ex-cop who worked under Tansil, was the intelligence source from within the Paige McBride camp. He knew her movements and could tell the others where she'd be.

'Then on a lower level, you've got Thomas Wade, the

Reception Supervisor at Frampton House. He made it possible for them to get that girl into Rikki's flat and kill her there. After they'd killed Rikki, his disappearance could be explained by that dead girl. I was wrong about it being Tansil or Gable who killed her, though. It was Footitt. He's a psycho. It's his thing, and the other two thought it could be used to their advantage.'

I unlock the mausoleum and indicate to Caroline where Rikki's remains are located. I wait outside. I don't really want to have a full-on dose of that smell again.

She's down there for a long time. My guess is that she's taking photographs for Mr Sheng. When she comes back up, her lips are pursed and even in the moonlight her complexion is pale. She looks down at her ostrich skin bag, opens it up and takes her cigarettes out.

'You want one?'

It's tempting. 'Normally I'd say yes, but I'm not feeling too good. I don't want to throw up in your friend's car.'

'Of course. You killed Gable with your bare hands, yeah?'

'It was him or me.'

She lights one of her cigarettes. The rich smell of the spicy tobacco fills the air: whisky, orange and vanilla.

'He deserved it,' she says. Then a flash of her usual humour returns. 'You must be some badass bastard to kill a huge guy like that. Like I said, I'm going to find out about you, baby. You see if I don't.'

'What were you doing down there?'

'Took a couple photographs. Mr Sheng would have wanted to see. I'm gonna text them to him in a minute.'

'All that time for a couple of photographs?'

'Then I defiled Gable's body.'

'OK.'

41

DÉNOUEMENT

The interior of the BMW is cool and comfortable and it smells new. I sit in the back. Caroline introduces me to Qawaya as if we're at some formal social gathering. She doesn't give her my surname. She starts texting Mr Sheng. Qawaya doesn't comment on my failed cage fighter look. We shake hands. From the name, I'd expected her to be Arabic, but she's Indian. Pretty, very petite, intelligent eyes, expensively manicured, pierced lower lip, much too much makeup and giving off an overpoweringly sexy smell of musk perfume.

She's wearing a black silk crêpe jacket with shoulder pads over a dark green corset. Stockings, suspenders, heels; I feel better already. If you saw these two women approaching you on a West End Saturday night, you'd think you were dreaming.

'You want to give me a quick route that the Sat Nav won't know, Daniel?' she says.

'This time of night? Head for Camden, then down Albany Street with Regent's Park on your right. You can put your foot down there. Fewer police. Aim for Regent Street. Cross over Oxford Circus then take a right into Conduit Street. You can drop us at Bruton Street. Is that alright?'

'OK. I've got you.' She has a lovely warm voice and tilts her head from side to side as she speaks. I'm pushed back into my seat as the car accelerates and we're soon travelling at forty, fifty, seventy, according to where we are, how much traffic there is and what she thinks she can get away with.

Caroline's mobile rings. She answers it. Her responses in Cantonese are subdued and terse. I can hear a calm voice on the other end and I think it's Sheng. I can see Qawaya checking me out in the rear view mirror from time to time. We swerve to avoid a drunken cyclist.

'Fan Mei said that you were a private detective. Is that right?'

For a moment I don't know who she's talking about, then remember that Fan Mei is Caroline's real name. Is this the result of some etiquette when you're hiring a professional dominatrix? No fake names? I must ask. I remember what Doug Teng said that name meant. Fan meant lethal, Mei meant gorgeous.

'That's right.'

We take a stomach-churning left turn. I notice with alarm that Qawaya is only operating the steering wheel with her right forefinger, her left hand flat on the gear knob.

'Are you Daniel *Beckett*, by any chance?' Those big beautiful eyes glance repeatedly in the rear view mirror, waiting for my response. How can she possibly know who I am?

'Yeah.'

'Ha!'

She raises her eyebrows. She's smiling to herself.

'Ha? What does that mean? Have we met?'

'No. But I heard about you.'

'Who from?'

'Well, that's something you'll have to put your mind to, isn't it? Use all your detecting skills.'

'That's very enigmatic.'

She laughs. 'Thank you.'

Caroline shuts down her mobile and stares out the window.

'Look,' says Qawaya, handing me her business card while keeping her eyes on the road. 'Here's my card. Give me a call when you're free.'

Her card is grey carbon fibre. All that's on there is her name and a mobile number. 'I don't think I'll be needing your services, Qawaya. Thanks, anyway.'

'Oh no. Not professional. Just for dinner. I don't like Italian or Hungarian and I don't fuck on the first date. After that, anything goes, and I mean *anything*. Just so you know.'

'Oh my,' says Caroline, putting her hand over her mouth to stop herself laughing. She shakes her head and looks out of the passenger window, apparently embarrassed.

'OK. I'll give you a call.'

'I'll look forward to it. We can settle up the money you owe me. Kill two birds with one stone. Three thousand. Don't forget.'

'I won't.'

Fifteen minutes later we're in Bruton Street. Qawaya pulls up outside the Osborne Samuel gallery and Caroline and I get out.

'Thank you for this,' I say to her. 'I'll be in touch soon with the money.'

She nods her head, then looks at Caroline. 'If you need me again, honey, you know what to do.'

'Sure, baby. I had a ball.'

'Me too.'

It's dark now. I wait until the BMW is out of sight, then turn to Caroline, holding her upper arm to get her full attention. Not for the first time since we left the mausoleum, she's looking distracted.

'As far as I know, there are four people in there apart from Paige: Chudwell and his wife, Tansil and Footitt. Paige and the wife could still be upstairs. They may be expecting Gable to return, they may not. We have to take into account that they've tried to call him on his mobile and he hasn't replied, so they may be suspicious and on their guard.

'The front door virtually opens into the reception room. There's a hallway, but it's not very long. The door's got a mortice lock and a Yale. Picking those would be easy but a little noisy. To go in that way would warn whoever was about and I don't want that. The basement door only has a Yale. I don't know what's down there or if it's used for anything, but it's the way we're going to have to go in.'

'OK. Are you alright? You look peaky.'

'I think I can last a bit longer. You?'

'I'm fine.'

'Did you bring the hammer and my keys?'

'Oh yeah.' She unzips her bag and produces a steel claw hammer. I take it from her and judge its weight in my hand. It should do. She hands me the key ring. Good.

'We're going to saunter along slowly. Link your arm around mine like we're some sort of romantic couple.'

'I want lots of babies.'

'Shut up.'

We stroll into Berkeley Square. As soon as I can see

Chudwell's house, I check for lights. There's a room on the second floor that's lit up with the curtains drawn, nothing on the first floor and lights on in the hallway and reception room on the ground. The basement is in darkness. For a brief moment, I think I see a flash of light from the second floor room, then decide it's my imagination.

We stay on the other side of the road from the house. As we get closer, it doesn't look as if there's anyone in the reception room. Perhaps they're in the kitchen, drinking sherry and cleaning up my blood. I realise that I didn't consciously check for motion sensor lights on my last visit, but I'm sure I'd have noticed if they were there. Besides, the house is equidistant from two street lamps and there's another across the road next to the square, so they'd probably be superfluous.

We cross the road. We're three houses away now. I turn to look at Caroline. 'Keep close behind me and don't speak. When we're down in the basement I want you to look up to the street. Watch and listen. Anything happens, touch me on the shoulder once.'

'Got it.'

I grip the hammer in my right hand as we approach the house. There's a group of three men heading in our direction about a hundred yards away. A smartly dressed woman in loudly clicking high heels walks past us. On the other side of the road, a small family are quickly approaching; two teenage kids, and the loud dad has had too much to drink.

From the engine noise, I can tell there's a black cab coming up behind us. The three men will look at the high-heeled woman whose walking speed will make her about ten seconds away from them. Then the lights from the cab will stop them seeing us clearly.

The moment the cab gets in between us and the family, I spin around and bring the hammer down hard on the metal rope effect handle of the railing gate. I catch it in my hand as it breaks off, push the gate open and trot down the stairs to the basement. Caroline's right behind me and closes the gate behind us. She takes the hammer from me and puts it back in her bag.

I get the key ring out of my pocket and go to work on the Yale with the burglar's tools. Caroline turns away from me and looks up at the street. There's a click as the Yale opens. Took two seconds. I push the door inwards. No audible alarms go off. I tap her on her shoulder and she follows me inside.

I close the door, stand still and listen. It takes a couple of seconds for my eyes to adjust to the darkness. It's another kitchen. Not as smart and hi-tech as the one upstairs. Probably a leftover from when these houses had servants' quarters. It doesn't smell like it's been used for a while. I realise now that I should have brought a torch. Maybe next time.

'What now?'

Caroline is so close it makes me jump. I realise that from the moment I broke the gate handle her movements were absolutely silent.

'We're going to go upstairs once I find the door that gets us out of here. Keep behind me and keep quiet.'

There's a wooden door right next to an old AGA. I turn the handle as slowly as I can, but it still creaks. When the handle is all the way down I have to pull it hard to make it open. This makes a quick, sharp report. I count to ten while waiting for a reaction to the noise, but nothing happens. I can see an old wooden staircase about ten feet away. I put my mouth right next to Caroline's ear and whisper.

'We're going to have to go up those stairs. We don't want any noise. Watch what I do and copy me. Walk on the edges of the steps, not in the centre. Don't tiptoe. Press your feet down slowly and firmly.'

'I like it when you whisper in my ear like that. Tell me you love me.'

'I prefer Qawaya to you.'

'Bastard.'

We get to the top of the stairs. There's a small corridor here with what looks like a toilet straight ahead. To my right is the end of the hallway and the entrance to the reception room where Lady O attempted to fracture my skull. It didn't look like this reception room was occupied from the street, but now I can hear voices from inside. It's Chudwell and his wife. Lady O sounds relatively calm and coherent. The door is open about a foot.

I walk down the hallway until I'm about three feet from the reception door. I can hear Caroline's soft breathing behind me.

'Why did he have to go home?' asks Lady O.

'He doesn't live here, Debs. He has his own life. He's done a lot for you this evening. Don't complain, for God's sake,' replies Chudwell.

'But what if she dies?'

'She's not going to die, Debs. Don't be silly. She'd been taking drugs before she came here. She's just passed out, that's all. And don't forget that Gable hit her in self-defence when she attacked him. Barnaby said it was opiates of some sort. Strong painkillers or diamorphine. Something or other. He didn't have the time or equipment to tell what sort.'

'She's taking drugs because she can't admit how she feels about me.'

'Very likely. I'm going to have a drink. D'you want one? Barnaby said you can have a small one.'

'But what are we going to do with her? She's going to hate me. She's going to wonder why I took her clothes off.'

'She was only in pyjamas. It's not a big thing.'

'But how are we going to explain things to her, Hugo?'

I can hear the sounds of drinks being prepared. So that's one down and three to go. I turn to Caroline and whisper, 'Footitt's gone home. We've just got the lord and lady in there.'

She nods. 'Where's the other guy?'

'I don't know.'

'You can say – you can *tell* her – that you took her pyjamas off because she seemed unwell. Just like loosening someone's clothes when they've fainted,' says Chudwell.

'A safety precaution,' says Lady O.

'Yes. A safety precaution. It's why Larry's keeping an eye on her now while you're down here. In case she becomes sick. Barnaby said to keep her lying on her side. And don't worry. When she comes round it's going to be overwhelming for her. She'll have to confront what she feels about you. If she makes any objections about anything, we can give her a little gift. A few thousand. I don't know. We'll tell her to pretend it all never happened. I know her type. Easily paid off.'

'She'll be grateful and embarrassed!' exclaims Lady O.

'Exactly. You know her so well.'

'She has such a delightful little body. And her hair feels so soft. I stroked her like she was a tiny pussy cat.'

God Almighty. This conversation brings a whole new dimension to the phrase 'messed up'.

'Tansil's upstairs,' I whisper to Caroline who nods. 'Probably the second floor.'

I hear her unclip her ostrich bag. 'Baby,' she says, kissing me on the cheek.

Before I realise what's happening, she's kicked the reception room door open and is striding straight towards Chudwell.

'Caroline!' I hiss. But it's too late. Chudwell almost drops his glass when he sees her.

'Who the *bloody hell* are y...'

I catch a tiny glint of metal in her hand. With a fast, wide sweep of her arm, she slashes his throat wide open, a spray of bright arterial blood splashing over the wall behind him and the floor beneath him. His hands instinctively reach up to cover the gaping wound in his neck, but the blood just squirts out between his fingers.

As he drops to his knees, his wife opens her mouth to scream, her hands in front of her face in a defensive position. Caroline quickly chops both hands down with her forearm and slashes to the right and then to the left, and now it's all over for Lady O, who, throat comprehensively slit, falls heavily onto her face, an ever-increasing pool of scarlet leaking out onto the pine flooring. She blows a few gory bubbles then expires.

Chudwell is still on his knees, gurgling and drowning in his own blood, but it won't be for long. The whole thing took about three seconds.

I can see it now she's stopped; it looks like a broad-bladed shredding knife with a razor-sharp cutting edge and a fancy ivory design on the handle. And now it needs a bit of a clean. She walks over and kicks Chudwell onto his side. I can hear the air rasping out of his lungs and then it stops.

There's someone coming down the stairs. It's Tansil. He's red-faced, panting and his flies are undone. He runs into the room and takes in the blood-soaked scene before him. He sees Caroline and her knife. His eyes widen. He's speechless. I can tell he's thinking of doing something positive, perhaps a citizen's arrest, but then I can see panic and fear in his expression and he turns to flee.

Caroline, quite naturally, has other ideas. The second he turns his back on us, she takes my claw hammer out of her bag, pulls her arm back in readiness and throws it straight at his head with everything she's got. I watch as it cartwheels through the air, just like in a film. When it makes contact, he manages a single 'uh' before dropping to the floor, senseless.

She walks over to him, grabs the collar of his suit and drags him into the kitchen. I follow her. She places a foot on his back, gets her mobile out and speaks in Cantonese to someone for about five minutes. While she does that, I'm wondering how all of this is going to affect my burlesque date with Cordelia. I take my watch out of Tansil's jacket pocket and put it back on my wrist.

When that call is over, she makes another one. This is less frantic than the first and I suspect it's to Mr Sheng. She has a different tone of voice when she's speaking to him, but it isn't deferent; just different. I still don't know who's in charge.

I've almost forgotten about Paige. I run up two flights of stairs and check out four rooms before I find the one I'm looking for. It seems to be the master bedroom. Paige is naked beneath a red silk sheet. I don't think she's unconscious, but she's not really in the room, either. Her eyes are closed and she's smiling; squirming around and arching her back, like she's luxuriating in the sensations of the bed and of the sheet against her body. I can see the outline of her hard nipples against the silk. Zoned out and turned on at the same time, I guess. Nasty bruise on her jaw, but I reckon Gable's had his comeuppance for that.

There's a Polaroid camera on a bedside table and a stack of Polaroids on the bed. I quickly flick through them. They're all of Paige, taken with the sheet pulled down, certainly by Tansil. They're pretty erotic. I put them in my inside pocket and sit down on the bed next to her. I notice there's semen on the floor a few feet from the bed. We must have caught Tansil on the hop.

'Hey, sexy.' I run the back of my hand against her cheek to bring her into the land of the living. After several seconds of this, she opens her eyes.

'What?'

'Do you recognise me?'

She stretches and smiles. 'What happened to your face? I didn't hear you come in.'

'This isn't the other night, princess, and we're not in your flat. You were kind of abducted, but you're safe now.'

If being in a house with a woman who's just slashed the throats of two people can be described as 'safe'.

She rubs her jaw. 'My face hurts.'

'You were punched. Look. I'll explain it all later.' I look around for her black satin lounging pyjamas. They're on the back of a chair. Avoiding stepping on Tansil's semen, I pick them up and throw them onto the bed. 'Get dressed. I'll be downstairs. Don't go into the reception room.'

'Why am I naked?'

Caroline is crouching down and tying Tansil to one of the Cheltenham chairs with a plastic clothes line that she's busy cutting up into suitable lengths with a big pair of steel kitchen scissors. He's still unconscious, his face slack and his fat tongue hanging out of his fat mouth. Her expression is serious, her movements quick and determined. She doesn't look up when I come in. It's as if we've had a row. I look at my watch. I'm amazed to see that it's only eleven-twenty.

'Do you want to tell me anything, Caroline?'

She sighs impatiently. 'I've made a few calls. There's a lot to do; here and in the mausoleum. It all has to be done tonight, before dawn. Speed is very important. Jiang Weisheng is on his way here. He will bring a girl who has special skills. He will also bring three assistants. I will keep the basement door open. Too conspicuous to have strangers using the front door here. They will come in separately so as not to attract attention. I will close all the curtains. Someone will do something on the other side of the square to take attention away. Maybe start a fire in one of the offices. Call the fire brigade. Make a big scene.'

'Anything else?'

'Different people will go to the mausoleum. A man called Lok Hsing and his apprentice will deal with the contents of the basement and the transit van. I will need you to give me the relevant keys.'

'OK. I guess you're not going to tell me what was going on tonight. With you, I mean. You've been preoccupied ever since we left the mausoleum.'

She stands up. Something's wrong. She's wound up tight. 'Of course I'll tell you. None of this could have been done without your help. We would never have known what had been going on. Not in a million years.

503

Your work on this was invaluable.'

'But this isn't a straight retribution job for you, is it? What's it all about, Caroline?'

She swallows. She purses her lips. Her eyes suddenly flood with tears. She opens her mouth to say something, then closes it again, as if the effort was too much. Then she tries again.

'My real name is Fan Mei Tuan. Rikki was my brother. Rikki was my baby brother.'

She starts sobbing, shaking. I hold her tightly. I can feel her tears against my face. She pulls away for a moment to look me in the eyes and then we're kissing. She grinds her body against mine. I can tell she's on fire, but we both know this has to stop.

'Oh Jesus. That was hot,' she says, sniffing and wiping the tears from her face.

'Why didn't you tell me?'

'I had to block it out. It would have been too distracting for me to think about it. When Rikki vanished, someone had to be sent here to deal with whatever it was. If it was discovered there had been foul play, someone had to track down and eliminate the perpetrators. I volunteered. I *insisted*. I told them I would be more motivated and therefore more successful. It would bring a lot of good luck for me to be the one. Listen. There's gonna be a lot of activity here soon. You've got to go. Take the girl with you. And get yourself to a hospital.'

I point to Tansil, still out for the count. 'What about him? Why didn't he get his throat cut? After all, he was the one that killed Rikki.'

'I've got something special lined up for him.'

She rummages around in her bag and produces a thirteen-inch combat hunting knife. She lightly touches the tip of one of her fingers with the blade. A cut appears immediately. Razor sharp.

'This is Rikki's knife,' she says. 'Call it poetic justice, if you like. Or a tribute to Rikki's techniques. You better go now. I've got work to do.'

I place a hand on her cheek, turn on my heel and go and fetch Paige.

I think Larry Tansil is about to lose face.

42

SOMETHING TO REMEMBER ME BY

At the hospital, they insisted that I stay in for three days. It was the head injury they were most concerned about. I had a CT scan to check for brain damage and the wound required nine stitches. When they put those stitches in it hurt like a bastard. I also had a couple of X-rays that revealed two cracked ribs. I told them I'd been mugged. I know they didn't believe me. The rest of the superficial stuff didn't concern them that much. The best bit was when a pretty Romanian nurse called Viorica cleaned me up.

I also had four stitches where Chudwell had kicked me in the face when I was unconscious and the doctor reckoned that the scar will have disappeared completely in four or five months, the resultant black eye and miscellaneous bruising in a couple of weeks. They also took a few blood samples, but I don't know what for. After I'd taken Paige home, I got a cab to St Mary's to avoid bumping into Annalise or, God forbid, Footitt.

I also had to visit the hospital dentist. One of my lower molars on the left was cracked and the gum around it was badly inflamed. From what I can remember, that was also the result of Chudwell's kicking.

While I was floating on painkillers for the first two days, I had a lot of time to think about Footitt. I kept on thinking about the girl in Rikki's flat. If I closed my eyes I could still see her face, and allowed my imagination to remove the maggots, slit throat and skin discolouration. Quite pretty, really; I remember thinking that at the time.

As I now know she was one of Footitt's pickups I wonder about the timeline that had taken her into Footitt's sphere. What went wrong? Was it drugs or desperation? I still can't work out her age. She could have been late teens or early twenties; maybe older, and quite possibly younger. Whoever she was, she's gone now.

I think of the tattoo on her forearm. A rose surrounded by musical notes. Hard to say what it indicated, but it must have been something that meant a lot to her at one point in her life. A musician boyfriend? Her own ambitions? Who knows.

But what's most upsetting about her fate is the fact that it was so unnecessary. A belt and braces ploy so Tansil could avoid a murder investigation while enabling Footitt to have a good time. So Footitt could strike 'fucking and killing a teenage girl' off his twisted bucket list.

And that fact that her death was just a logistical part of a cynical cover-up by people who had got so used to getting away with stuff that they saw nothing at all wrong with the whole thing. She was nothing. They didn't know her, they'd never met her, but she had their total contempt. She was just one of *those* people. And what were they? A sad bunch of flaccid middle-aged omega males scratching each other's balls at pathetic secret society meetings. Like Chudwell said: they can get away with it so they *do* it.

Now, on my third and final day here, I'm psyching myself up to go out into the real world again. I've rescheduled all the various dates I'd arranged over the last week and Anouk has agreed to take a quick break with me in the Caribbean.

There's a knock on the door of my room and a nurse pops her head around the door. She's a New Zealander. Her name's Hayley. I've already asked her out. 'Mr Beckett? You have a visitor. Shall I show them in?' She gives me a big grin. 'It's a woman. Are you feeling up to it?'

'I think I can cope.'

Caroline's hair is tied back in a ponytail and she's wearing no makeup. Her look is fashionable, kooky and touristy; a black silk bomber jacket over an outsize Donald Duck t-shirt, a nuclear-neon lime leather miniskirt, black tights, Converse Harley Quinn trainers and a green iguana print Dolce & Gabbana tote bag slung over her shoulder.

'I thought you'd be back in HK by now.'

'You want to get rid of me? I'm going back tonight. Eight o' clock flight. Non-stop from Heathrow. Airbus A380. Eleven and a half hours, baby. It's a bastard! I'm going to stock up on magazines.'

I smile at her. 'Will you be using the same passport that you came in on?'

'Ha. You think I'm stupid?'

She laughs and sits down next to my bed. She looks over her shoulder at the door. 'Is it OK to talk in here?'

'I think so.'

'OK. I just wanted to put your mind at rest. The house in Berkeley Square, the mausoleum, the transit van: absolutely clear of any fingerprints, cleaned from top to bottom and Jiang says hello. He also says you've got to look after me and care for me and he will be pleased to attend our wedding day. Here's these.'

She hands me a small freezer bag containing my wallet, keys, tactical pen and the remains of Anouk's mobile.

'Have you looked at the papers?' I ask.

'Yeah. Big mystery, huh? All these bigtime people disappearing without trace, police baffled. We cleaned out both their bank accounts and made it look as if it happened two days before our visit. Clever, huh? We took their passports and planted fifty thousand pounds' worth of cocaine and heroin around the house and in their safe. Jiang put some pretty evil shit on the hard drive of their computer. Gives the cops something to chew on. Nothing about Mr Tansil and Mr Gable yet.'

'It'll happen. And someone'll make the link eventually. The whole thing may even get blamed on them if someone's smart and digs around enough.'

'You worried about the girl? Chudwell's girl?'

'I called her to postpone our date. She told me about her parents' disappearance. She sounded subdued, concerned and strangely nonplussed. In shock, I suspect. I sounded stunned, sensitive and sympathetic. Of course, what I asked her about when I visited her didn't impact on any of this and she wouldn't know who Tansil and Gable were or what they'd been up to. Or my – *our* – connection with them. Maybe she thought her parents had fallen foul of bad people and done a runner.'

'You gonna sleep with her?'

'Probably.'

'She needs a bit of stress relief, her parents vanishing like that. Tell me what it was like. I'm not kidding. I'm into stuff like that. I'll text you one of my fake email addresses.'

'It's a deal.'

'She had a bigger ass than me.'

'But not as striped.'

She blushes. 'Oh, and Mr Sheng said thank you. I don't think he believes that you sorted this. It seemed impossible to him. You can go into The Blue Lantern any Saturday morning and he'll be there, waiting to give you your money. And you're getting a really big bonus for this. At first, it was just a big bonus, but I gave him one of my sinister looks and it became a *really* big bonus. Wily old guys like him, they always try to get away with stuff.' She laughs. 'Him and his fucking *jazz*.'

'And the restaurant thing still stands, yes?'

'Oh yeah. Of course.'

She leans over, kisses me on the mouth, then heads for the door. 'Bye, baby.'

'Bye, Fan Mei.'

She turns and smiles sweetly, then she's gone.

*

A few days later, I'm sitting in The One Anchor in Shepherd's Bush with Jamie Baldwin. It's eight-fifteen. The place is crowded and has a lot more atmosphere than it does in the daytime. I sit opposite him, facing the entrance. He rang me a couple of times when I was in hospital. He's not the sort of person who can let things go and he's strongly motivated where the people who damaged his arm are concerned. His anger had started to outweigh the possibility of his reputation being destroyed. He was even talking about hiring a private investigator, hinting that if I wouldn't do it, he'd find someone who would.

It's all extremely tedious, but if he ever decided to look

into all of this, he could find himself in very deep water indeed and, worse still, the trail could lead back to me. So I called him for a casual meeting in the pub. I told him it was important that I speak to him about all of this.

He waves at some old black guy who walks past our table, takes a couple of large gulps from his pint of bitter and narrows his eyes suspiciously. 'So what's this all about? What's going on? Have you found out anything about those two bastards? What happened to you? What happened to your face?'

'Look at me.'

He can't make eye contact at first, but after a few seconds of staring I break him down and he cracks, looking into my eyes, blinking rapidly.

'What happened to you was part of an enormous, complex conspiracy, which ultimately involved people you really don't want to get involved with. I know you're angry about what happened to you and one day you may decide to hire someone like me to get to the bottom of it. Don't.'

'But it's not just my arm. It's what they've got on me. It's always going to be hanging over me. I can't...'

I hold his gaze. 'Listen carefully to what I'm telling you and don't ask me to elaborate. Those two guys that visited your flat will never blackmail you. They will never blackmail anyone ever again. They will never harm Paige McBride in any way whatsoever. Believe me, their days of harming people are over.'

He looks a little puzzled, then the realisation slowly hits him and he looks spooked. 'That's what you said, wasn't it? When we were here last time? You said that if I came clean with you, you might be able to make what was hanging over me disappear. Is that what's happened?'

He's got the wrong end of the stick, but I don't let him know. I just look at him.

'OK, man. I'll trust you,' he says. 'I'll leave it. I think you're telling the truth.'

'Good.'

I look at my watch, then look over at the door, which has just opened. My good deed for the day has just walked in and is looking around.

'I'm going to leave you, Jamie. I have to visit a friend. Nice to see you again. Don't get up.'

'Thanks, man.'

I shake his hand and pat him on the shoulder as I head for the exit.

Just like when I met her in The Dorchester a million years ago, she has her hair tied back and twisted into a bun at the nape of her neck. She's wearing a grey pinstripe jersey dress which stops just above her knees. She's wearing her blue-tinted glasses, too. She smiles when she sees me.

'He's over there,' I say. 'I've got something for you. Forgot about it in all the excitement. One of Chudwell's boys took them when you were not yourself.'

I hand her an envelope with the Polaroids that Tansil took of her while she was out of it in Chudwell's house. I don't mention the semen on the bedroom floor as I don't want to make her vomit. She has a quick flick through them.

'My God. Talk about explicit. What must have been going through my mind?'

'I'd love to know. That's all of them. I had thought of destroying them and not telling you, but they look really sexy, so I thought you might want them. Maybe do a book.'

She grins and nods her head. 'They are, aren't they. Sexy, I mean. Pretty pervy when you consider the circumstances. Jesus. Look at this one. I can use that pose onstage.'

She holds it up so I can see. Her hands are clasped behind her neck. Her head is turned to the side. Her eyes look pained. She's biting her lower lip. Her back is arched and one thigh is crossed tightly over the other.

'Here,' she says, handing it to me. 'You have this one. Something to remember me by.'

'Are you sure?'

'Of course. It's the least I can do. I owe you quite a lot, don't I.'

'You owe me nothing. Oh, and that painting. Take it to Sotheby's in New Bond Street, get it valued and get it auctioned. Do it tomorrow.'

'Really?'

'Really. They won't charge you for valuing it.'

'Come and see me. You'll always be welcome. And look after Anouk.'

She kisses the tip of her right forefinger and places it on my lips. 'Another time, another place, eh?'

'You said it. 'Bye, Paige.'

I push open the door and walk out into the warm night.

*

It's a spacious, smartly decorated three-bedroom flat in Belsize Avenue. This is a quiet, leafy, residential area and it's a quick walk to a villagey little shopping area and the local tube station. It probably takes around fifteen minutes or less to get into the West End. There's no doubt that the occupant lives alone.

Only one of the bedrooms has a bed in it. The others have been turned into an office and a mini-library. Someone from fifty years ago would be amazed to find that so many people now have offices in their homes. The mini-library is impressive and well-stocked. I've never seen so many books in one room before. I flash my torch across some of the spines. They're all hardbacks. *Rural Rides* by William Cobbett, *History of the Plague in London* by Daniel Defoe, *Belinda* by Maria Edgeworth and *Tropic of Cancer* by Henry Miller.

The kitchen has all the usual hi-tech stuff, but it doesn't give the impression that much cooking is done here. All of the cupboards are fairly empty (apart from one containing many packets of dried pasta) and the refrigerator only contains long-life milk, butter, half a loaf of bread and a solitary bottle of Yattarna Chardonnay 2011, probably worth about a hundred quid. There's a cupboard with tea, coffee and sugar, but only one mug. I get the impression that no one ever comes here.

The dining room has a circular dining table that seats eight. There are two prints on the wall, The Fall of Phaeton by Rubens and one I don't recognise of a woman standing in a stone hallway talking to a guy in a red coat and a tall hat. Probably Flemish.

What might be called the living room has two big sofas and a wall-mounted television with a seventy-five-inch screen. Beneath the television is a black Bose stereo system that looks old. There are no DVDs that I can see, but there is a small shelf with a bunch of CDs: Janácek, Borodin, Prokofiev, Dvorák, Whitney Houston, The Eagles and Céline Dion.

There's a small dining table in here that seats four, so I

turn off my torch, slip it in my pocket and sit down, facing the door. My hands are beginning to sweat under the latex gloves.

I think about Daniella, the cryptographic consultant selfie queen. When I called her she couldn't stop apologising for her outrageous texts. I told her not to worry. She looked great in all of them. Then she fretted about being overweight, like she needed reassurance that she had a sexy figure. But she knew she did, so I didn't get drawn in.

I'm meeting her for dinner in three days. I'm going to take her to Amaya in Knightsbridge. She's never been there. She won't believe it. I booked a private dining room. They do a fantastic lobster dish that my mouth is watering just thinking about. I stop fantasising about her and clear my mind, thinking of nothing at all.

Then I hear the mortice lock being turned and the front door opening. A light comes on in the hallway and I can hear the mail that was on the floor being picked up and shuffled. I took a quick look after I came in, before dropping it all on the floor again. Nine letters: three junk mail, one electricity bill and five birthday cards.

There are a few more sounds, then the front door is closed. I can hear footsteps heading straight towards the door that I'm staring at, and then it opens and the light is turned on. Footitt just stares, his mouth hanging open like an idiot. His grip on his briefcase loosens and it falls to the floor. I can see a dark stain spreading down his left trouser leg. He's pissing himself.

There are a lot of smart, witty phrases that come to mind at times like these; stuff like 'welcome home, punk' or 'what time d'you call this?' or 'happy birthday, scumbag', but looking at the expression of abject terror on his stupid, chinless face, I think I can boil it down to just one word.

'Hi.'

THE END

Books by Dominic Piper

Kiss Me When I'm Dead

Death is the New Black

Femme Fatale

Bitter Almonds & Jasmine

Printed in Great Britain
by Amazon